BROOKE J LOSEE

Published by Golden Camel Press

Content Warning:

This book contains mild romance (kissing only), reference to suicide, and
mild violence.

ISBN: 978-1-954136-26-7

DEDICATION

To my husband who has supported me through thick and thin and always encourages me to follow my dreams. I am grateful for the experience of true love and devotion and for the best muse a romance author could ever ask for.

Los Angeles, 2022

R ule number one—never wear the pearls.

Maggie stared down at the string of iridescent beads, considering her decision one last time. The tiny orbs had rested inside the intricately carved wooden box since Dad gave them to her five years ago on her eighteenth birthday. A note, written on a thin sheet of lined paper in less than legible handwriting, had accompanied the pearls, and Dad had refused to hand either item over until she agreed to the *rules*.

Because apparently antique heirlooms came with restrictions.

Muffled, frustrated voices on the other side of her bedroom door drew her attention. Even though Mom loved parties, they always stressed her out, and since this particular event happened to be one of the largest of the year, her irritation levels were off the chart. Everything had to be perfect, and the staff knew following the woman's directions, no matter how over the top, would save everyone from a headache.

Maggie turned her focus back to the box. Rule number two stated the importance of secrecy. No one could know she owned the pearls. Dad had made this point particularly clear, going as far as to suggest even Mom wasn't allowed to know.

Which seemed ridiculous unless she considered her parents' messy divorce and lackluster approach to getting along with any sort of civility.

So far, Maggie had managed to keep knowledge of the stringed beads' existence from the world, although she had nearly let it slip to her best friend, Diana, a time or two. That would have thrown a catastrophic wrench into Dad's rules given Diana's difficulty with keeping secrets. Diana had a penchant for trouble—had even snuck off to Maggie's house as a teenager and climbed the trellis to her bedroom a few times.

Maggie glanced toward the open window across the room and smiled at the memories filling her thoughts. A warm breeze tousled the curtains, and Maggie inhaled. The air smelled like smog and an impending storm, not abnormal for an LA summer night.

She ran her thumb over the final rule—keep them safe.

That one made her feel like the beads were part of a witness protection program or something. Keep them safe from what? Being stolen? Sure, the necklace was valuable, but that didn't mean it should be locked away in a box to collect dust.

Well, maybe not *too* much dust. It was a really nice box.

When Dad gifted her the heirloom, the rules had sparked a billion questions, all of which he refused to answer. "Stick to the rules," he'd said in that way that meant any further discussion wasn't happening. After a lot of begging, she'd only gotten a ridiculous story about the pearls, kind of like the one about the monster in the closet who ate socks and cereal.

Footsteps preceded a knock on the door. Maggie placed the note inside the box and snapped it closed before crossing the bedroom. She opened the door and found Mom with her hands planted on her curvy hips, the sequined cocktail dress she wore sparkling like a disco ball under the overhead lights and the faux color in her cheeks matching the fire in her glare.

Maggie leaned against the doorframe and studied her mother's features. The woman's eyes were puffy and, despite the thick concealer she wore, shadowed with dark circles. "You look stressed, Mom."

"Everyone is incompetent. You'd think this was the first party we've ever held."

It wasn't. Not even close. Mom insisted on her soirees with irritating regularity and expected her daughter to attend. Always. With perfect presentability.

Maggie twisted her fingers together. "I'm sure they know what they're doing. Relax. That's what you do at parties, isn't it? Relax?"

Shame she couldn't seem to follow her own advice. While her mother enjoyed these sorts of high-end events, Maggie hated them. Being around so many people made her anxious.

Her mother's gaze shifted from frustrated to worried when she looked her over. "You're going to get ready soon, aren't you?"

Maggie retreated deeper into the bedroom and Mom followed. This was the reason Maggie had moved out months ago. Mom liked to hover and had a difficult time accepting her twenty-three-year-old daughter had no need to be micromanaged. Maggie had thought spending one night in her old room would be manageable, but...

"I can't get ready with you in here," said Maggie, doing her best to keep the irritation from her tone.

"I'll be quick. I expect—would *like* for you to be on time. It's rude to keep our guests waiting."

"Your guests," Maggie retorted.

"*Our* guests. Many of them work for the company."

Her mother was the owner of *Giobane Tex Industries*, a billion-dollar-per-year textile company that Maggie's three times great-grandfather had started. Maggie was expected to take over soon, which meant she spent most of her time at the corporate office learning the ins and outs of the business. But after a four-year degree and nine months of playing Mom's shadow to meetings, Maggie wasn't so sure becoming a business mogul reflected what she wanted out of life.

That bothersome feeling to confess her concerns rose to the surface. She hadn't told Mom about her declining interest in becoming CEO. She needed to voice her intentions sooner rather than later. Mom had announced her impending retirement, an event that would take place at the start of the new year, at which time Maggie would take charge. While Mom gushed over the trips she intended to take the moment her daughter took over, Maggie's insides knotted like a ball of yarn thrown into the washing machine. If ownership fell into her hands, she would never escape a life of board meetings and endless hours at the office.

Time was running out.

Mom would need time to find a suitable replacement, and disappointment would follow the confession, but she needed to do it. Drop the dream bomb, rip off the Band-Aid, and hope for the best.

But the words always stuck in her throat like they'd been super glued there, and the opportunity to breach the subject faded as it always did. She could say the timing wasn't right—Mom was stressed enough about the party—but the timing was *never* right.

Or maybe she simply lacked the courage to face the criticism and disappointment her decision would bring.

Maggie bit her lip and nodded an illusion of agreement. "Right. Our guests. I'll be on time."

"I'll leave you to get ready then," said Mom. "Consider wearing something nice to go with your dress. How about that gold broach from your grandfather? Did you bring it with you?"

"*Mom.*" The word came out through gritted teeth. "I'll wear something nice."

"Okay, okay." Mom retreated with her palms positioned for defense. "I'll see you soon."

The door closed with a soft thud. Maggie heaved a sigh as she trudged over to her wardrobe as if she had bricks tied to her feet. Mom's parties always made her feel like a guppy in a fish tank. Everyone was watching—waiting for her to prove herself as the next head honcho.

Or worse, fail completely.

The responsibilities of running a business Maggie could handle, but the idea of being in charge was a leap beyond miserable. Success was much easier to achieve when a person *wanted* to find it, and she couldn't imagine ever experiencing the same happiness Mom did with the company. Maggie smiled more while milking cows on Dad's farm than she ever did in a boardroom.

At ten minutes to eight, Maggie stepped in front of the floor to ceiling mirror leaning against the wall. She turned from side to side, analyzing the way her champagne-colored dress fell over her body and covered her toes. Not that it was difficult with her five and a half feet of height.

Alright, she was five-four, but that didn't sound nearly as appealing.

The fabric hugged her curves but not in an overly dramatic way, and the gown actually left her feeling comfortable. Many might call it plain and old-fashioned, a far cry from the trendy glamor of 2022, but unlike Diana, simple had always been Maggie's style.

Speaking of Diana, she was supposed to meet Maggie at the party. Attending Mom's events was easier with her around, mostly because her friend enjoyed socializing and that provided Maggie with an excuse not to. Diana talked enough for the both of them.

Maggie picked up her phone and sent her friend a quick text.

MAGGIE: What time will you be here?

Maggie tugged at one of the brown curls resting against her shoulder. The strands hung just below her collarbone in layers of tight spirals, the deep color a sharp contrast to the paleness of her dress. She hadn't bothered to put on any make-up, something she rarely indulged in anyway, but for a moment she considered it.

Would she be expected to wear a fake face as a CEO? Mom certainly preferred it when she wore a bit of foundation and some eye-liner, but that had little to do with looking the part of an heiress and everything to do with attracting a suitable...well, suitor.

Mom said husbands could be *assets*. Could be, as in Dad hadn't been and Maggie had better make good choices in regards to whom she chose to tie the knot with. Obviously, the man would need to have a gorgeous face and be supportive of the family business—a home-runner with gobs of money and high social standing if Mom had any say in the matter. But how did one decipher the difference between genuine interest and fortune hunters? She might never know since every guy she met had knowledge of her monetary worth. Her last name gave it away if her mother didn't.

Her phone buzzed in her hand.

DIANA: Sorry, can't make it. Got a date with some Sparks tickets. Don't die.

Maggie groaned, her fingers flying over the touchscreen and completing a text before she could even blink.

MAGGIE: Who is it this time? Dan or Emilio?

Diana responded with an emoji sticking its tongue out, and Maggie rolled her eyes.

MAGGIE: Your fault if I die. Traitor. You don't even like basketball.

She heaved a sigh, settling the phone back on the nightstand, and ambled over to the vanity on the opposite side of her room. Gently, Maggie scooped the pearls from their resting place inside the wooden box. Twenty round spheres, divided into two strands and each separated by a silver bead, glistened under the overhead light. On the right side, the strands were joined to a pendant in the shape of a chrysanthemum, its intricate petals inlaid with their own tiny beads.

The piece had been passed down for generations, and even though its value would have brought a nice penny to her father's family, they'd held onto it.

Going against her parents' wishes had never been something Maggie was inclined to do. Even as a teenager she'd been well behaved. Rule breaking wasn't in her nature, but tonight she wanted things to be different. Telling Mom she didn't want to be CEO, which she planned to do first thing tomorrow morning, was a big step, one she needed to work up to before she lost the chance completely. Defying Dad was easier with his lax nature. He wouldn't be too upset that she'd broken his rules.

Right?

Right. Maggie secured the pearls around her neck. Their cool surface settled against her skin and made her shudder. She glanced in the mirror, and her heart sped up like it was part of a NASCAR race as she looked at her reflection—at the intentional defiance.

It was a necklace. Nothing *bad* would happen because she wore it. Dad had said the heirloom was cursed, but her father made up ridiculous stories all the time.

The self reassurance did nothing to ease her anxiety. She turned away from the mirror and sucked in a deep breath. "I can do this."

With the glossy spheres resting against her neck, Maggie left the room and followed the long ornate rug toward the stairs. As she descended with her hand gliding over the dark cherry banister, her gaze flitted to the music room where she glimpsed the edge of the baby grand piano through the open door. Her fingers twitched with a familiar itch, one that often accompanied a wave of nerves. Music always set her soul at ease.

But now wasn't the time for that.

Now was the time for doing what was expected of her, like plastering on a smile for a room full of guests. She reached the bottom of the stairs and touched the pearls as she drew in another fortifying breath. A high-pitched chuckle filled the foyer, one that made chills slither up her spine like when she entered a haunted house on Halloween.

Maggie glanced around. The space was empty, though plenty of noise came from the room to her left where all the guests had gathered. She tapped her finger against her necklace and shook her head. She'd definitely imagined it.

Because curses weren't real.

Chapter 2

Los Angeles, 2022

Maggie resisted the urge to shift on her feet. Remaining engaged in the conversation proved more difficult with every passing second. Mom prattled on about the upcoming deal with another company—one that would likely secure a lot more deals and increase the company's cash flow—with so much pride it practically oozed from her.

Why could Maggie not find the same joy? Sometimes she wished things were different—that she shared Mom's enthusiasm—but her mother's life was loud and busy, the exact opposite of what Maggie wanted.

It had been nearly two years since she'd caught a flight to the Midwest to visit Dad, and she missed the peace she felt on his farm. The closest she came was her little side business teaching piano, which had given her more sense of accomplishment than any bargain made in a stuffy boardroom ever could.

"Magdalena?"

Maggie blinked, her full name bringing her back to reality. Back to the party where she was supposed to be happily socializing with every guest. She met her mother's gaze, and the woman tilted her head, her brows tightening with an expression meant for scolding without saying a word. "Gerard asked you a question."

"Who?"

The young man standing across from her chuckled—not the mocking sort, but more the kind that gave away his amusement despite him trying to hide it. Maggie's cheeks burned all the same, though. Perhaps it was his devil-may-care part in his golden brown hair or the perfectly fitted black suit, but Mr. Gorgeous made her look like a gaping ninny.

Mom shifted from Maggie's side to stand beside him and placed her dainty fingers on his arm with that *look*. The one that meant she'd labeled him as a good asset, and Maggie ought to explore the option.

"As I told you already, Magdalena, this is Gerard Burke. He's the architect designing our new corporate headquarters."

"Oh." Maggie stepped forward, offering him her hand. "I'm sorry I missed the introduction. My thoughts were elsewhere."

He accepted the gesture with a grin. "You're forgiven, but only if you tell me what had you so distracted." His eyes twinkled with mischief, and Maggie narrowed her own. She'd met her share of flirtatious men. The problem wasn't that she disliked it; she just couldn't tell whether they wanted to get to know her or her family's bank account.

Mom had thrown at least a dozen men into her life the last few years, many of whom seemed to have promising boyfriend potential. But it always ended the same. She cared and they didn't—at least not about her. Experience had taught her to proceed with caution, and she couldn't help but wonder how much flattery she would receive if her intention to walk away from the family business were made known.

Regardless, she wasn't about to confess she'd been daydreaming about Dad's farm. That was sure to make Mom livid. "My thoughts weren't occupied with anything too adventurous. I was wondering about the dessert bar and how much sugar I could get away with eating."

Mom rolled her eyes, but Gerard's smile ticked upward another notch. "I've been wondering the same thing. Maybe we should investigate together. You know, to keep each other from overindulging."

"And what do you intend to do if I start devouring every ounce of chocolate in sight? Drag me away?"

"Absolutely not. I'll match your pace and join your sugar overdose."

Okay, so maybe Mr. Gorgeous wasn't so bad if he was willing to fall into a junk food-induced coma with her. That proved his dedication if nothing else.

The smile that overtook her face must have assured him she was open to his accompaniment, because Gerard turned his attention to her mother. "Would you excuse us, Mrs. McCarthy? It seems Magdalena and I have a date with the refreshments."

Mom swatted at the air, her expression revealing how happy she was to be rid of them—together. "Don't let me stand in your way. I hope you find something that suits your taste."

"I have no doubt we will."

Gerard nodded toward the back of the room, and they weaved through the throng of fine suits and sumptuous gowns. A long table with a lacey cloth lined the wall, every inch of it covered with finger foods and treats that made her stomach grumble with appreciation of the staff's hard work.

"Where should we start?" she asked, eyeing the selection and the small plates that would never hold even a sampling of everything she wanted.

"With a question," said Gerard. "Well, perhaps a compliment first. I wanted to say you look lovely this evening."

"Thanks."

"I must also compliment your necklace. It's quite the piece."

Her hands instinctively jumped to the pearls, and guilt pricked at her stomach. She reminded herself that she hadn't *shown* anyone specifically. It wasn't her fault if Gerard noticed. At least Mom hadn't thought anything of it, likely presuming it was another trinket from Grandpa or too busy matchmaking.

"A necklace like that," Gerard continued, "must have a story."

Removing her attention from something that smelled like cinnamon, Maggie met his gaze. "It does actually. They're cursed."

Gerard lifted his beautiful, thick brows with the exact mixture of confusion and uneasiness she'd hoped her statement would achieve. "Cursed?"

"They have mystical powers," said Maggie. "These pearls have been in my family for generations, and rumor has it they belonged to a witch before that. She enchanted them." At least that's what Dad had told her.

Gerard looked pleasantly entertained. She gave the man credit. When the corners of his mouth lifted like that, he looked like he could put in a run for *sexiest man alive*, especially in that fine getup of his.

"What sort of spells did the witch place on them?" he asked, his green eyes dancing with mirth.

Maggie shrugged. "Well, she was no Harry Potter, but the stories typically end with the disappearance of the person wearing them. Sometimes they would come back, and sometimes...they wouldn't."

This was the reason Dad had given for leaving the pearls in the box, but the silly superstition had kept the heirloom from the light of day for long enough. What was the point of giving them to her if she couldn't wear them? Why even keep them if they were destined to stay in the box?

Gerard's brows lifted again. "And you thought wearing them tonight was a good idea?"

"A brilliant idea, in fact. What I would like more than anything right now would be to disappear."

"Magdalena." Mom appeared out of nowhere like she was Houdini's assistant, her voice low and full of warning despite her smile. "Would you mind assisting me with something in the foyer?" She turned to Gerard, forcing her lips even higher. "Please excuse us for a moment."

Gerard nodded. "Of course."

Maggie glanced at him over her shoulder as they walked away, expecting to find him repulsed by the entire display, but instead, he offered her a look filled with sympathy. His company hadn't been appalling. Perhaps she would give him a chance.

She and her mother entered the foyer. Light from the chandelier reflected off the sequins on Mom's dress, casting a multicolored sprinkle of dancing lights on the wall. The two of them came to a stop in front of a large potted fern under a painting of the Golden Gate Bridge, and Mom spun around with a glare ready to shoot through her like a laser beam.

"Magdalena, I know you hate parties, but that's no excuse for telling that man you want to disappear."

"I've asked you to stop calling me Magdalena; you know I hate it. And I'm sorry I'm such an embarrassment to you, but it shouldn't be surprising at this point."

"You're not an embarrassment." Mom massaged her temples. "You know that's not how I feel. I'm proud of your hard work, but if you would put a little effort into keeping up appearances, people would respect you more."

"This is exactly what I mean. *This* is why I don't—" she snapped her mouth closed.

"Don't what?" asked Mom.

The opportunity lay before her, freedom within grasp. She could confess the truth now and step away from the company for good. But Mom would never see her the same way. She would look at her with utter disappointment. Her mother wasn't easy to live with, but she meant well, and Maggie had never felt a lack of love. How could she shatter everything they'd worked for the last few years?

"Nothing," said Maggie. "I have a headache. I'm going to bed."

"Magdalena—"

"*Mom*, I can't do this. Not tonight. Please try to understand."

Her mother shook her head. "You can't simply run away every time you feel overwhelmed. How do you expect to head a company if you don't face things?"

Maggie didn't respond, instead turning around and shuffling to the staircase. She darted up the steps as fast as her dress would allow, ducked into her old bedroom, and closed the door. She didn't want to head a company. She didn't want to face things, especially telling her mother the truth.

She plopped down on the bed and heaved a sigh before bending over to grab a book from the duffle bag at her feet. At least she could spend the evening getting lost in a novel.

She ran her fingers over the embossed title. *Saving Lord Hawthorne.*

What was it about historical romances that drew her in? In some ways, she envied the characters' more simplistic life without the noise of modern civilization.

She tightened her grip on the book. "I want to experience life outside of LA. I want to live somewhere quiet, like an estate in the English countryside with a gorgeous garden. That isn't asking too much, is it? Bonus points if there's a handsome gentleman who doesn't care about the millions backing my name."

The skin at her neck prickled, and she lifted her hand to rub the smooth surface of the pearl necklace. Light flashed through the lace curtains draping her window and was followed by a thunderous *boom.* The earthy scent of rain hung in the air, and a light patter on the rooftop created a symphony of sound. Thunder she could handle, but Zeus's wrath had never been her favorite thing. It scared the bejeebies out of her, perhaps for the simple fact that it could stop her heart in an instant.

Tossing her book aside, she jumped up from the bed to close the curtains, but the room spun, throwing off her balance and tipping her backwards. She collapsed onto the bed, her vision blurring into a kaleidoscope of color. Warmth encompassed her body as if the soft blankets had enfolded her.

What was happening? She hadn't felt ill before, but now her stomach curled. She couldn't even blame the food since she'd left the party before trying anything.

Another clap of house-shaking thunder jolted her heart. What remained of her sight narrowed into pinpricks of dark shadows. An eerie voice flooded her mind, whispering something she couldn't understand. The words muffled until darkness completely filled her view.

Then, all grew quiet.

Chapter 3

London, 1815

A deep inhale failed to temper Luke Halford's frustration as Miss Norburt's enthusiasm fueled their one-sided conversation. When he mentioned how fine the weather had been today, he hadn't expected her to prattle on about her ride through Hyde with Mr. Jenkins or the walk she had shared with...

Well, he could not say with whom she'd walked as he had ceased listening then, but her high-pitched voice remained enough to make his head ache. He contemplated taking leave of her with the excuse of dancing, but that would require him to actually stand up with a woman. Given the way Miss Norburt had remained at his side through the last two sets, he imagined she hoped to be on the receiving end of any dancing requests he made, but the woman would be severely disappointed.

He would not take a partner tonight, and his resolve could withstand the young lady's diligent efforts given how practiced he had become over the years.

Such practice, however, had not prevented his grave error in attending.

Regret had found him the moment he stepped through the mahogany entry of Viscount Sutherby's home. The hungry gazes made him feel a great deal like a fox about to be run down by hounds. Young ladies hopeful for a title and matrons eager to help their daughters obtain one—the very base desires of the marriage mart—ensured he would suffer pursuit after pursuit.

One expected to see young ladies dancing about in fine gowns during a ball, but the sheer number in attendance, all with eyes instantly trained on him the moment he entered the room, incited the urge to turn tail and run.

But dukes did not run. He would stand his ground, and if ignoring every batted eye and flirtatious remark caused offense, so be it.

The music began again, and Miss Norburt turned a demure smile on him. Luke kept his gaze firmly on the couples taking the floor, but the woman at his side was unrelenting. Out of the corner of his eye, he could see her watching him with what he might call seductive glee.

She shifted closer, and her shoulder brushed against his. "A fine night for dancing, is it not, Your Grace?"

"As we are indoors, I cannot imagine why tonight would not be."

"Then why have you yet to take the floor? There are a number of ladies without partners." Her dainty fingers fell on his arm, and he tensed. Keeping the discomfort from his expression required all of his focus.

"I will not be participating tonight." The words fell out in a tone harsher than he'd intended, but perhaps that was for the best given Miss Norburt's determination. Unfortunately, she did not seem to take notice.

"Surely you could be convinced otherwise. The music is lovely. The company ideal. Those must be taken into consideration."

Ideal. Luke shook his head. There was nothing ideal about being hunted. He may put on a display of stoicism, but internally he wriggled with unease. How many times had he been approached by misses and matrons alike who lacked graceful subtlety in their intentions? How many times had he narrowly avoided being ensnared?

He had lost count, and each experience only furthered his distaste for ventures into the social scene of London.

Movement in his peripheral caught his attention. Mr. Jenkins approached them, and hope filled Luke's chest. The man stopped in front of Miss Norburt, and his chestnut hair fell over his eyes as he bowed. "Good evening, Your Grace. Miss Norburt." Luke returned a slight nod, and to his great relief, the gentleman focused his attention on the lady. "Pardon my intrusion, but if you are not presently engaged, I would like to request this set."

Miss Norburt had the decency to feign a smile. "I am not. It is such a wonderful night for *dancing.*" She shot Luke a look that was meant to chide, and he shifted on his feet. He would not give in to her hints no matter how she persisted in giving them.

Mr. Jenkins offered Miss Norburt his arm and guided her to the line for a reel. Luke's shoulders fell, the most relaxed they had been all night. Miss Norburt was well known for how she spent her time among gentlemen, and he'd panicked the moment she came to his side. Last Season, he'd attended a ball during which she had offered him a diversion in a private parlor. He had no desire to be associated with those sorts of *diversions*, especially when being caught would coax him into marriage out of honor.

"I expect your deepest gratitude," said a familiar voice from behind him.

Luke closed his eyes, willing his frustration to dissipate. Could he not be given a single moment of peace? "For what do I owe you gratitude, Branbury?"

Nicholas Betham, Earl of Branbury, stepped into view carrying a glass of ratafia, his grin so wide Luke wondered how the man fit through the front door while wearing it. Although Luke had been friends with the earl since childhood, they did not share the same love for social outings.

Nicholas jutted his chin toward the dancers. "For rescuing you from Miss Norburt, of course."

"If it was you whom I owed gratitude, would you not be the one making circles around her at present?"

"Not when I am responsible for convincing Jenkins to dance with her. It took little, really. One mention of her golden hair and endearing smile had the man's feet in motion before I could even list compliments to her personality."

"That would have been a short list, indeed. If Jenkins were wise, he would not associate with her at all."

"Come now, Avendesh, she is not so bad." Nicholas drank from his cup and winced. "Very well, I confess she does have a reputation, but perhaps Jenkins does not mind. He seems happy enough in her company. Miss Norburt is as deserving of attention as anyone else."

"Then she cannot be offended at my lack thereof as I have not given anyone else a speck of attention, nor do I have plans to do so."

"Quite the sour tart tonight, aren't you? Tell me, why did you bother to come if you only intended to stand here scowling at the other guests?"

Luke grimaced. He had not intended to come at all, but the opportunity to speak to a few men about his political ambitions had coaxed him into attending. His regret was only amplified by the fact that those with whom he had wished to have a discussion were not here.

"The reason for the poor decision is of no consequence," said Luke. "But my patience has run dry for the evening."

"I was not aware you possessed *any* patience for Society given how much time you spend in Lords avoiding it."

Luke crossed his arms. "Some of us do not take our duties so lightly. With the war, you ought to spend more time there rather than in such frivolity. Regardless, I have certainly made a mistake in coming tonight, and there is no one in this room whose company could convince me otherwise."

"Not even me?" One of Nicholas's brows lifted, and his face contorted in that way that made it difficult to determine whether he was jesting or entirely serious. "Your self-proclaimed closest friend?"

Luke pondered his answer for a moment. If he could not speak with his political allies here, then he would simply seek them out on his own. His time would be much better spent in that endeavor.

When he took too long to respond, Nicholas tapped his finger against his glass, his features sobering with veiled offense. Bother. It had been a serious expression this time. "You know I enjoy your company in other settings. You may join me in my exodus if you would like."

The earl's lips ticked upward, a relief for the guilt building in Luke's chest. He'd meant what he said. Spending time with Nicholas outside of social gatherings was one of the few things Luke found pleasure in.

"I think a little frivolity sounds more appealing tonight." Nicholas turned to face him, his wide grin fully in place once again. "So, you plan to make a run for it, do you?"

"I am not running." Luke tugged at the cuff of his shirtsleeve. "I have business to attend to this evening. If you do not wish to come along, then perhaps you could accompany me to the door and offer to dance with any eager misses that cross our path."

"You always have business. There are other joys in life besides politics and managing estates. You know, if you were to give the young ladies in this room a chance, you may find yourself enjoying the Season."

There had been too many instances of young misses hoping to help him *enjoy* the Season already. "Are you going to help me escape or continue your badgering?"

"Escaping is quite similar to running, is it not?"

Luke released an irritable growl, and Nicholas chuckled. "You know I shall assist you, but I cannot understand why you have stood here the last hour with such a miserable countenance. Do you know how many broken hearts you will leave for us of less desirable titles to mend once you have gone?"

"Unlike you, I care about Society's opinion enough to not offend the host. If I stay for at least an hour, they cannot accuse me of poor manners. And I have not broken anyone's heart."

"Miss Norburt might disagree." Nicholas cocked his head and smirked. "She will be completely put out to find you've gone."

"No more so than the last time I turned her down. I am certain she will recover. Perhaps you might offer yourself in my stead?"

Luke's lips curled, and he lifted an accusatory brow. "Rumor has it the two of you have already become acquainted."

Which Luke knew to be untrue, as most rumors about his friend were.

"I find myself surprised by the tales of my own actions, especially given I cannot seem to recall actually participating in them." Nicholas's fingers drummed against his glass, and when the man spoke again, frustration laced his tone. "Not caring what Society thinks would be convenient if it were true, but what difference does my concern make? I cannot change the opinion of the *ton* when they have so thoroughly made up their minds about me."

Luke could not argue that point. Nicholas had been the subject of gossip for years, and the rumors about him spread so fast they were nigh on inextinguishable. Sympathy for his friend swelled within him, and Luke placed a hand on the man's shoulder. "One day they will all come to their senses."

Nicholas shrugged off the comment with feigned indifference. "Shall I offer you my arm? You are clearly in need of my protection and escort to the door."

Luke scoffed, and Nicholas took another drink, this time more deeply, which created an equal grimace of disgust.

"Why are you intent on making yourself miserable?" Luke nodded toward the glass when Nicholas gave him a confused look. "I know you hate the ratafia."

"It is this, brandy, or remain parched all night."

Ah. Nicholas Betham rarely drank brandy, mostly to avoid having any similitude with his father or being reminded of the man. Not that he could avoid it much given how closely he resembled the marquess.

"Shall we make a mad dash of it, then?" asked Luke, glancing toward the open double doors and noting the clear path to freedom.

"I am in no mood to do any dashing, but a fast paced stroll will suit me fine." Nicholas patted Luke's shoulder, his wretched smirk returning. "You needn't look as though you are about to cross a battlefield, my friend."

"A battlefield is precisely what I am crossing. Miss Norburt is but one young lady I need to avoid."

The earl's brows hiked up his forehead, nearly disappearing beneath strands of his sandy brown hair. "I shall never understand you. Would it mean your death if you gave a woman a chance?"

"Quite possibly, yes."

Luke did not need him to understand. He could handle his own endeavors. He needn't rely upon anyone, most certainly not a wife who would see no more in him than the number of pounds he was worth and the title he could offer. Certainly he would not avoid marriage forever, but at eight and twenty, he had time to fulfill that particular expectation that his title demanded.

"Ready?" asked Luke.

"Yes, yes. Let us get on with it. I suppose you want me to take the lead." Nicholas did not wait for Luke to answer, He straightened his coat and strutted to the door with his head held high. Luke followed a pace behind, his gaze firm on their destination.

They entered the foyer, and Luke exhaled with relief. The footman required only a moment to fetch Luke's hat and gloves and call for the carriage.

"Your Grace!" A moment, apparently, was more than enough time for someone to take notice of his departure.

A woman with a tall coiffure and a lavish burgundy gown approached them from behind. Luke turned around, but Nicholas's entire frame went stiff as a board. It seemed he needed time to work up the courage to face Lady Garrick, not that Luke could blame him. By all accounts, the woman hated his friend.

Lady Garrick dropped into a curtsy, and the young woman who had trailed behind her did the same. Luke bowed, doing his best to retain the smile he forced onto his face. "Lady Garrick. Miss Garrick. I hope you are well?"

"So kind of you to ask." Lady Garrick gave the air a dismissive wave. "We are very well, of course. It is a pleasure to see you in attendance tonight. It has been far too long."

Her gaze flicked to Nicholas for the briefest of moments. The poor man had been completely slighted, but it was not Lady Garrick on whom Nicholas focused his attention. His eyes remained firmly on the matron's daughter, and Luke noted the familiar longing his friend often displayed when in Miss Garrick's presence.

The music began once more inside the ballroom, and Lady Garrick's eyes sparkled with delight. "What perfect timing that we should catch you, Your Grace. My daughter has yet to acquire a partner for this set."

Luke swallowed, struggling to keep his smile from falling off completely at the presumptuous remark. "My feet are halfway out the door, I am afraid. An urgent matter has come to my attention. I will have to forgo the opportunity for another time." Luke gestured to Nicholas, who looked rather like an enamored schoolboy. "Perhaps Lord Branbury could assume the honor."

Judging by the matron's frown, she was not in agreement, but Luke bowed once more and spun around. He grabbed his things from the footman and exited the townhouse without a look over his shoulder. Perhaps he should entertain an ounce of guilt for leaving his friend in Lady Garrick's clutches, but Nicholas would manage well enough.

And Luke? He would finish his business in Town and leave. Although Parliament remained in session, they could live with his absence. He'd certainly devoted more than his share of time the last few months. Returning to his country estate was the reprieve he needed from the busy social life of London.

First thing tomorrow morning, he would leave for home.

Suffolk, 1815

C old drops rolled across Maggie's cheeks, and a wave of chills spread over her body with a violent shudder. She opened her eyes. Dark clouds hovered above her, and the smell of dirt filled her nose. The material of her dress stuck to her skin like glue. Everything was sopping wet, and a few sprinkles dripped from the sky. Slowly, she sat up, lifting her hands to vigorously rub her arms, but the movement provided little relief from the cool air and smudged mud onto her sleeves.

A low rumble rattled through the sky. Rolling green hills stretched as far as she could see, their only disruption the muddy dirt road she sat on. She couldn't make out a single building in the misty haze, and beyond the occasional growl from the clouds, a deafening silence surrounded her.

Where on earth was she? The last thing she remembered was sitting on her bed after leaving the party.

Maggie dug her fingers into layers of mud, hoping it might wake her up, but it appeared the dreary world before her wasn't a dream-induced illusion. A tight knot formed in her stomach. How had she gotten so far from home? Had someone abducted her?

Her hand shot to her neck. The pearls still rested against her cold skin. Kidnappers wouldn't have left those.

She held out her hands and grimaced. She didn't mind getting dirty, but her current state made her want to do nothing more than take a shower and drink hot chocolate. Rain had drenched her from head to foot, and if she stayed out in this weather much longer, she'd undoubtedly catch a cold.

She stood and gave her hands a few flicks to dispel some of the brown muck. Which way should she go? Without the slightest idea of where *here* even was, how could she decide which direction would take her home?

Another rumble from above made the decision a quick one. It didn't matter which way she went so long as she got out of the storm. Wrapping her arms around her midsection, Maggie started walking. The mud-laden road grasped her black flats, making each step require extra effort, and soon, brown grit covered her feet past her ankles, filling the space between each of her toes.

A chilly breeze blew past, swishing the leaves in the oak trees to her right. Tall grasses covered the hills to her left, and the road in front twisted into the shadows. She kept as fast a pace as the conditions would allow, and after a few minutes, sunlight peeked through the clouds.

Was it morning? Afternoon? It had been late when she left the party, but it wasn't nighttime now. Though the storm covered everything with a dingy gray tint, she could still see clearly. How long had she been lying in the road like some dead animal? Her cell phone would have given her the answer, but she'd left it on the nightstand during the party.

Because for some reason, evening gowns with pockets weren't a thing.

The road wound into a clearing, and Maggie scanned the horizon. Not a single sign of civilization, which made no sense. She couldn't possibly be that far from home, could she? Was Mom looking for her yet?

As she rounded a turn, a soft whinny halted her feet. Ahead, three brown horses nibbled on the lush grass next to the road, and an equal number of men conversed under the branches of a tree.

Finally, she'd found people.

"Help! Please!" She raced toward them lifting her dress, and the mens' expressions shifted to surprise upon spotting her approach.

One of them pushed away from the tree and sauntered forward until she stopped in front of him. "Please, I need your help. I'm lost, and I have no idea how I ended up here or where here even is."

The man's eyes wandered up and down her body before landing on her neckline. "You look as though you have been out in this storm all night, miss. We would be glad to help."

"Awesome. I need to get back to LA. Can I borrow your cell phone?"

The man's bushy brows furrowed. "My what?"

It was only then that she noted his heavy accent—his *British* accent. Her gaze swept over him. In her rush to ask for help, she hadn't realized he was dressed like he'd walked out of one of her novels. Leaning sideways, she studied the other two men, who were staring at her with smirks. They were dressed less cleanly, their clothes a little ragged and splotched with mud. By contrast, the man in front of her wore a dark-colored tailcoat, brown pantaloons, and a starched white cravat, though he looked a little rough around the edges as well.

Weird. Maybe there was some sort of reenactment happening and these guys were way too into their characters. She'd heard crazy stories about the CONS that went on in the city. People got really into the costumes and acting sometimes.

"Your cell phone," she mumbled.

The man closest to her stole a glance at his companions and then stepped forward. "Not to worry, miss. We will take you someplace safe."

His lips curled into a sinister grin, and his gaze wandered over her again, slowly, as if he were taking in every inch. Something in his eyes glistened with...desire? He licked his lips, and her instincts screamed for her to run. Nothing in that smile suggested his *help* was something she wanted.

She bolted. Mud clung to her feet, and the sticky substance stole her balance. She staggered forward, but an arm wrapped around her waist, keeping her from toppling onto the road. The man lifted her from the ground with ease. She kicked and screamed, but it did no good.

"Where ye off to, darlin'?" asked one of the other two men as he stopped in front of her.

Maggie caught the faint scent of liquor on his breath, and her nose wrinkled. What had she been thinking? In her desperation, she'd trusted complete strangers. And intoxicated ones, at that.

The closest guy caressed her cheek, and Maggie jerked away from him.

He chuckled, grabbing her chin between his thumb and forefinger. "I thought ye needed help? With a necklace like this, maybe ye think yerself too good for us? That it?"

She tried to wiggle free, but the arms holding her were thick and strong. A warm breath tickled her neck, sending shivers down her spine that had nothing to do with the cool air.

"Easy, Brimmer," said the whispered voice next to her ear. "She's lost and needs our assistance. Perhaps we should take her somewhere warm? She's trembling."

"Let go of me," Maggie demanded, the words too soft to be convincing but all she could manage.

Brimmer slid his fingers around her neck and removed the pearls. He started to tuck them into the pocket of his coat, but the man holding her ordered him to stop. "My pocket, Brimmer."

Brimmer scowled but dropped her heirloom into the other man's coat. "Fine, but I 'spect to be compensated in other ways. I think taking her elsewhere is a perfect idea, Doxly. Think yer old man would mind if we holed up at his estate? Assumin' he ain't sold it off already."

Doxly, the one who had a better fashion sense and held her arms, growled. "Not yet. I'm sure we could spend a comfortable few days before he noticed."

She put all the strength she had left into squirming as Doxly's hold around her tightened and he dragged her toward the horses. Panic seized her, and some dormant instinct took over. Images of a brief stint of self-defense classes floated through her mind. She'd never understood why Dad had insisted on them, but she'd be thanking him for it later.

Assuming she survived this.

She tucked her hand behind her back. With the layers of clothing this guy had on, her last grasp at hope seemed dreary, but she had to try. She shoved her fingers between the buttons holding his waistcoat and found what felt like a belly button. She grabbed fabric and skin and pinched hard.

Doxly's feet came to a stop with his yelp. His hold loosened long enough for her to thrust an elbow into his abdomen. She sank to her butt, falling between his legs, and leaned back until her head met the ground behind him. Kicking upwards, her foot landed in the *other* most accessible weak spot.

He wailed, and Maggie rolled out of the way before he could fall on top of her. She clawed at the ground to find her footing, a difficult feat in a soiled dress, but something large tackled her back to the ground the moment she stood. Brimmer pinned her wrists; his body settled next to her in the mud, and his face hovered inches above her own. She attempted to move out from under him, but he placed his weight on her waist.

"Impressive, darlin'. Now I'm even more excited to get ye out of here."

A loud *bang* rippled through the air. Maggie jumped, and her attacker's eyes widened, fixated on something farther down the road. His movements became a blur as he swiftly stood and dashed away, all while the clop of hooves against the muddy road filled her ears.

Freezing, covered in mud, and completely exhausted, shadows threatened her vision. She fought to remain conscious, but it was a losing battle. A shape appeared above her, one with a full head of black hair carefully swept to the left side. A man—likely in his late twenties—crouched next to her, and his warm brown eyes looked over her with concern. He wore a neatly tied cravat and a navy tailcoat, which did nothing to calm her nerves. Was he with those men?

She attempted to roll away, but firm hands gripped her shoulders. "Do not fret. I only wish to help. Have those men harmed you?"

Several horses whinnied somewhere behind him, and muffled voices rang in her ears. The clouds beyond the man tilted and spun as if she'd been on a merry-go-round.

Minus the merry part.

"Are you hurt?" he asked, his voice soft—gentle like a whisper of wind through the trees. He didn't give her a creepy smirk like those other men. He didn't have that frenzied look in his eyes. Perhaps she could trust him.

"No, they didn't hurt me. B-but they stole my necklace."

"I am sorry to hear that," he said, his tone consoling. "We should get you out of this weather. Do you think you can stand?"

She nodded, but the attempt had her nearly in mud again before he caught her, his hand holding the back of her neck.

"She's going to faint," the man said to someone over his shoulder. "I will have to carry her. Please open the coach, Thomas."

The last thing she wanted was some strangers' hands around her, but she had little choice. Lightheadedness muddled her thoughts. She couldn't fight it. Exhaustion pressed on her more thoroughly than she'd ever experienced.

"I need to go home." The words came with the last of her consciousness.

LUKE SCOOPED THE YOUNG WOMAN'S LITHE BODY INTO his arms as another roar of thunder sounded overhead. Her clothes held so much water and mud he could scarcely make out the actual color of the fabric. What had she been doing out here all alone?

From what he could tell, her attire suggested she came from money, and she lacked the accent of a commoner.

In fact, her accent was rather peculiar, though certainly not lower class.

His coachman, Thomas, stood next to the carriage, his gray brows furrowing as Luke approached. "Is she injured, Your Grace?"

"I do not believe so, but I think it best we get her back to Windgate and call for Dr. Thistlewaite."

Thomas nodded his agreement and assisted Luke in positioning the lady on the seat inside the carriage. Mud coated everything by the time they had secured her safely and were on their way. Luke grimaced at the state of his clothing. His valet would give him an earful, no doubt, but he could not regret it when the reason had possibly saved the young woman's life. He'd fired one shot from his pistol, and that had been enough to scare off the scoundrels, but he dared not think what would have happened to her had he not been journeying to his country estate at this precise moment.

The silent ride allowed him to study her unabashed. She had brown hair, though he suspected the mud made it a darker shade than its true hue, and a rounded chin. A handful of tiny freckles dotted her cheeks, drawn out by time spent in the sun. Even in such a disastrous state, Luke could see the loveliness of her features.

He shifted his gaze to the window. Admiring the woman after such an ordeal while she rode in his carriage unconscious was far from gentlemanly behavior. He ought to focus on what precisely he was going to do with her. An unchaperoned young lady had no business staying at a bachelor's house if she wished to preserve her reputation.

But he refused to pawn her off on someone else, especially in her condition. Luke had the resources to locate her family, wherever they may be, and ensure she received adequate care. Surely it was his duty to see to her needs until he could assess the situation? Once she woke, the lady could tell him what had happened. After that, he would find a more suitable place for her to stay.

The coach came to a rest, and Thomas assisted Luke in getting the woman out of the carriage. Luke ordered the coachman to alert the staff, and the man ran ahead of him. Raindrops fell from the leaky clouds onto Luke's head and the lady's face as he carried her to the house. She whimpered, her expression growing tight, and Luke wondered if she were reliving the trauma of the last hour. Her fearful brown eyes filled his thoughts. She'd been completely terrified when he'd crouched next to her on the road.

A feeling of protectiveness swelled unbidden within him. For all he knew, those men could still be after her.

The butler, Mr. Tolley, opened the door for him, and he entered the familiar foyer, relief settling over him. London had taken a toll, as it always did, but the added excitement of the ride home had only increased the need to feel the security these old walls offered.

Luke started for the stairs, but a gasp from the upper landing halted him. A woman with silver hair pinned in a bun gathered her skirts and descended at a rate far too fast for someone of her age.

A smile came to his lips despite the circumstances, and he momentarily forgot about the woman in his arms. "Good evening, Mrs. Bielle. I hope you are—"

"Do not waste your breath with pleasantries," she chided. "We must get her out of those clothes before the poor dear freezes solid."

"I believe that is improbable." The lady was unlikely to freeze given the warm June temperatures, nor was *he* a part of the *we* that would be assisting in the removal of clothing in any way.

"What happened, Your Grace?" asked Mrs. Bielle over her shoulder as they climbed to the first floor.

"Ambushed by highwaymen," answered Luke. "I fired a shot and spooked them but not before they laid hands on her. She fainted not long after."

Mrs. Bielle shook her head, entering one of the guest chambers. "Terrible. She is fortunate you came along. I dread to think what could have happened."

"As do I." Luke laid her on the bed and backed away with a sigh. "I'll send for Dr. Thistlewaite, but she'll need tending. If you would call for a maid—"

"I will take charge of her."

He bit his lip. As head housekeeper, watching over the young woman was far below Mrs. Bielle's station. She seemed to sense his hesitation and swatted at the air. "Do not worry yourself over it. I wish to look after her. She will not be a burden."

"Thank you, Mrs. Bielle. I trust you to see to her needs."

Not that the rest of his staff was untrustworthy. Those serving at Windgate were competent enough, but the head housekeeper had experience. Not only had she raised him, but Mrs. Bielle had served as his mother's lady's maid before that.

"I will take care of her, Your Grace, but I cannot say we have the proper necessities lying about. Perhaps one of the maids can spare a gown and—"

"No." Luke shook his head. If this young woman were, in fact, a daughter of the peerage or gentry as he suspected, he would not have her donning his servants' clothes. "Find her something suitable for tonight and tomorrow you may visit town to purchase whatever you feel is essential."

"Very well. I shall see to some of the mud while you call for the doctor." Mrs. Bielle sighed, tilting her head to the side, the skin near her eyes wrinkling with her sympathetic expression. "The poor thing. This was not how I expected tonight to go."

"That makes two of us."

"How long do you believe she will stay?"

He glanced at the young woman. She seemed peaceful enough, her facial features smooth and her chest rising and falling in steady breaths, yet he was loath to leave her. "I cannot say until I have the opportunity to speak with her and make an informed decision. Hopefully, locating her family will not take long."

But regardless of the amount of effort and time, he would make certain of her safety. His honor would allow nothing less.

Suffolk, 1815

Quiet. Too quiet. Why did the absence of noise make Maggie's ears hurt? Her body felt numb, almost heavy, like she'd spent the entire day running around the track at Eldridge Preparatory School—which was silly since Maggie had graduated five years ago.

She lifted a hand to her face, every muscle protesting the fight against gravity, and rubbed her forehead before following the contours of her face down her cheeks and over her mouth. Blankets hugged her sides, and the soft cushion below meant she still lay in her bed.

What an odd dream.

No. What a *nightmare*.

She blinked, but the bright light from the nearby window blinded her and sent a sharp pain through her head. Lying there a few more minutes wouldn't hurt. Then she could take something for the headache.

Even with her eyes pinched closed, the light still pestered her. She needed to draw the curtains, but that would require her to get up, and—

Her heart lurched. This was all wrong. The light shouldn't have been coming from her left side. The window in her old bedroom was on the right.

Maggie shot upright, frantically scanning the room. She ignored the throbbing in her head, or perhaps the realization that the room *wasn't* hers took priority. A dying fire smoldered in the hearth opposite the four poster bed. Paintings she'd never seen before decorated the walls, and the furniture had an antiquity about it, both in style and build, that made the entire room feel...

Well, she didn't feel like she was in Kansas anymore. Even the unfamiliar scent of the place, a mixture of something floral and citrusy, made her heart race. Where on earth was she?

An image infiltrated her thoughts—a man with black hair and a warm gaze. His clothes had looked exactly like the man's who'd taken her necklace.

Her hands leaped to her bare neck. She'd lost her family heirloom.

Or had she? The rain, the muggers, the stranger—hadn't it all been a dream?

Maggie ran her fingers through her brown curls. She'd straightened her hair yesterday, but it was naturally wavy when wet, and the presence of the soft ringlets suggested it had recently been soaked. The strands were free of mud, and the long nightgown that draped her body appeared clean, too. Glancing down, she noted that the sleepwear definitely didn't represent something she'd normally wear to bed. A nice set of fleece pajamas paired with a good book suited her much better.

She tossed the covers to the middle of the bed and slid off the mattress. The cool wooden planks sent a wave of shivers through her shoulders as she tiptoed toward the window. She needed to figure out where she'd woken up before she alerted...whoever lived here.

The unfamiliar view outside did nothing to calm her rapid pulse. Her room appeared to be situated on the second floor, judging by the distance from the ground. A circular driveway curled around in front of the home and wove through lines of well-tended shrubbery cut into perfectly-formed spheres. The road—little more than a lane of dirt— continued as far as she could see into a grove of trees.

Secluded.

Wherever the stranger had brought her was certainly off the beaten path. What did that say about him? Why hadn't he taken her to a hospital or to a police station? Her stomach twisted. Her dream hadn't been the result of an overactive imagination, and the reality left her skin prickling. Nineteenth century clothing, no cities, British accents, and antique furniture all suggested one thing. Dad had said the pearls were cursed, made people disappear, but...

No. There had to be a logical explanation, one that didn't involve crazy stories about witches and enchanted necklaces.

A loud knock made her jump. She turned in time to watch the door gently swing open and reveal a woman—probably in her late fifties like Mom. She had salt and pepper hair which made Maggie wonder what shade her mother's would be if she didn't dye it every few weeks.

The woman smiled brightly and entered the room before closing the door with a soft thud. "Good morning, miss. It's good to see you up and about. You gave us quite a fright."

Her accent was *not* British. Maggie opened her mouth, but words eluded her. How could she even begin when every question demanded priority?

The woman approached slowly with her hands clasped in front of her. Maggie avoided her gaze, instead studying the way she'd styled her hair in a tight bun and the simple cream gown she wore. Her wrinkled face conveyed a softness, an air that she could be trusted, but that didn't alleviate Maggie's anxiety.

"My name is Mrs. Bielle," she said. French...that sounded decidedly French. Which equaled more questions, but the woman continued before Maggie could get any out. "I'm the housekeeper here at Windgate. What is your name?"

Windgate? Had she ever heard of it? She couldn't place any sort of familiarity in the name, and the mixture of British and French accents confused the poo out of her.

"My name is Maggie—Magdalena McCarthy. Where am I?"

The sweet smile never left the woman's face. "Windgate Estate, Miss McCarthy. What can you remember? You have been unconscious for almost two days."

Two days? Fudge. Mom had probably had a heart attack by now.

"I remember walking...and there were three men. I asked them to help me, but..."

The coy grin of the man who'd grabbed her appeared in her thoughts. Brimmer, one of them had been called. Beyond that, she knew nothing about them...nothing except what she suspected they'd planned to do to her.

Maggie groped for something solid, but her fingers found only air. Her knees buckled, and she hit the floor. Mrs. Bielle crouched beside her, tucking her feet under her skirts. She brushed Maggie's hair over her shoulder and placed an arm around her. The warmth and comfort felt good. Weird that it came from a complete stranger.

"Those men were going to...to..."

Maggie swallowed against the burning in her throat. She wouldn't cry. She refused to let *what ifs* take control of her emotions right now. Those men had intended to do horrible things, no doubt, but they weren't given the chance, and she wouldn't dwell on their thwarted plans.

Mrs. Bielle's hand rubbed over Maggie's back, and the pressure magically eased some of her panic. "Not to worry, dear. You are safe now. They cannot hurt you."

Maggie sensed the sincerity in her words. She was safe, at least for the time being. "I heard a gunshot, and then a man helped me. I don't remember anything after that. Who was he? Did he bring me here?"

"Yes, he brought you here. 'Twas luck he happened to be on his way home from London. Fired off a shot when he saw the squabble. Those men wasted no time disappearing."

London? She'd suspected she wasn't in the dry desert outside LA anymore, but...*London?* Had there been anything in her stomach, she might have lost it.

"We called for a doctor," Mrs. Bielle continued. "He said you would recover with some rest. You did not have any injuries of concern, but he is due to visit again this afternoon. He and His Grace will be glad to see you awake."

"His Grace?"

Mrs. Bielle nodded. "The Duke of Avendesh."

The horrible suspicion she'd shoved to the back of her mind took hold, swelling with more certainty as she analyzed every detail of the last few days. The accents, the strange clothes...even the dirt roads. She'd seen nothing of modern civilization. It was like she'd fallen into one of her books.

More questions bubbled inside her, and she needed answers to them all, but one seemed to take precedence. Her lungs constricted, the words stuck on her tongue, caught in the clutches of fear. But she had to know.

"Mrs. Bielle, what year is it?"

The woman blinked, her thick grey brows furrowing. "It is the year of our Lord eighteen hundred fifteen."

1815.

The pearls weren't simply cursed; they didn't just make people disappear. Maggie swallowed. Her family heirloom was a time machine, and without it, she was stuck in the past.

LUKE NARROWLY EVADED NICHOLAS'S JAB, TWISTING OUT OF reach. They had been fencing for nigh on thirty minutes, and his distracted mind was finding it difficult to keep up. What if the young lady staying at his estate woke while he was gone?

"Losing focus again," said Nicholas.

Luke lunged, partly to prove his friend wrong and partly to give himself a reprieve from defending. But the earl, smaller than him in stature, surpassed him in agility. Nicholas dodged the attack, and with one quick spin, poked the point of his foil into Luke's back.

"That is what? Five now?" Nicholas chuckled, and Luke crossed the room to sit down in one of the chairs against the wall. Losing to the earl was not abnormal for him, but generally he did not fail so profoundly. Or quickly.

Nicholas took the chair next to him and crossed a leg over his knee. "Are you going to tell me why you are more terrible than usual or must I guess at the problem?"

"Are you going to tell me why you left London the same morning I did?"

His friend shifted in the chair. "I saw no reason to stay."

Luke hummed, fighting back a grin. "I suppose the fact that the Garricks also left Town had nothing to do with it."

Nicholas stiffened, and Luke nearly lost himself to a laugh. The man had developed a *tendre* for Miss Garrick but refused to admit it, though anyone paying attention could see. Were it not for Lady Garrick's utter contempt for the earl, Luke suspected the banns would have been read by now.

"How do you know the Garricks have returned?" asked Nicholas.

"I was privileged with an invitation to dinner tonight."

Nicholas scowled and shook his head. "The woman is determined to marry you to her daughter."

"You needn't be jealous, Branbury. I have no intention of going or even entertaining the idea of marrying Miss Garrick." Or anyone at the moment.

"I am not jealous."

Luke lifted his brows in disbelief, and Nicholas's scowl deepened. "It hardly matters either way. You know her mother despises me."

That much Luke could agree with. "True, though I cannot say why. One would think a future marquess would be nearly as appealing as a duke."

"Said duke does not possess the reputation of said future marquess."

Another point beyond argument. Nicholas had earned the reputation of a rake, bestowed upon him by the *ton*. But rumors and truth were not the same, and the man next to him was as undeserving of that title as Luke. Nicholas enjoyed flirting, but he never spent time in unscrupulous activities despite what the gossips said.

What would the wagging tongues say about Luke if they knew of the woman staying unchaperoned at his estate? He shuddered to think what such knowledge would do to *her* reputation.

"I have lost you again," said Nicholas with an irksome grin. "What weighs on you so heavily?"

"Nothing." Luke would not be informing his friend of the situation. That would guarantee an endless round of teasing, and he hadn't the time or patience for it. "I must be going."

Luke rose, depositing his foil on the chair and marching to the door. Nicholas followed. "Those thoughts must be dire indeed to have you scurrying off to avoid answering me."

"I have a commitment. I am not scurrying off for the sake of avoidance." Not really. Doctor Thistlewaite would be arriving soon. Luke should be present in case there was any change in the young woman's condition.

"Very well, I shall drop it for now."

Luke almost scoffed as he left the room and continued toward the stairs. Nicholas would not drop the interrogation for long—he could read Luke too easily—but that could be dealt with after he had seen his new charge on her way.

Perhaps then he would stop thinking about the woman and the way her terrified eyes had bore into his. Perhaps then the sense of unease he felt while away from her would dissipate.

Suffolk, 1815

Time travel. Dad could have been a little more specific when he said people disappeared. Better yet, he could have kept the cursed family heirloom to himself. Her mind had played repeatedly over her last moments in the twenty-first century. She'd wished to escape the party and the expectations, to experience life outside of LA. The pearls had granted the request in the worst possible way.

She gripped the railing at the top of the staircase, peeking over to see the level below. Mrs. Bielle had helped her dress, and even pinned her hair into something presentable. The ensemble was followed by a light breakfast in Maggie's bedroom that had restored her energy and staved off exhaustion, but now she feared she might vomit.

She'd analyzed her options throughout the morning, going as far as to wish herself home, but apparently time travel didn't work without the pearls. She couldn't even be sure it would work *with* the heirloom, but that didn't matter at the moment. She'd been out for two days, and the thief was likely long gone by now. With her luck, he probably wasn't even in this era anymore.

Her mind conjured a picture of him being hit by a cab in some populated modern city, but she pushed the thought away. The cab driver didn't deserve to be traumatized over such a wicked man.

Maggie shook her head. She needed to focus on what she was going to do about this mess.

Mrs. Bielle had informed the duke that Maggie was well enough to venture down when the doctor arrived. She'd looked forward to leaving her room, if for no other reason than to gain final confirmation that this whole thing didn't exist solely inside her head. But as she continued to take in every detail of the large house, each observation only proved her sanity.

Her room was near the end of a long hallway on the second floor, and she'd peeked into a few others on her way to the stairs. All of them displayed a certain finesse that screamed money, but the interior design pleaded guilty to old-fashioned by the standards of her time. From the color schemes to the wacky-patterned wallpaper—each chamber seemed to have its own theme. Hers, for example, had been outfitted in reds and creams while the room next door featured pale yellows with hints of lavender.

"Are you finished exploring?" Mrs. Bielle spoke in her subtle French accent. "The doctor has arrived. I should take you downstairs, now." The woman had watched Maggie patiently for the last twenty minutes as she looked into each room like some tourist at

Buckingham Palace. She probably thought the guest was nosy, but Maggie couldn't bring herself to care. The place was beautiful.

"Yes. I'm sorry for making you wait."

"Not to worry, dear. This must be overwhelming for you."

Maggie nodded. "That's an understatement."

Mrs. Bielle chuckled, muttering as she moved down the stairs. "I can only imagine."

They passed several servants on their way to the drawing room; a tall man by the door gave her a friendly nod. With her worst fear reaffirmed, she now faced a different problem. She would need to act like a nineteenth century lady if she had any hope of blending in.

And she needed to blend in. Like a full-fledged chameleon.

If the duke thought she was anything less than a lady, he might throw her out. And where would she go? To an early grave, that's where. Her only chance of getting out of the situation had disappeared with that crook. She had no way of getting back to when—and where—she belonged. Accepting the fact that she'd time hopped was one thing, but coming to terms with being stranded in 1815 was another. She had no idea what she was going to do.

She had no money and no experience living without modern conveniences and technology. Her arsenal of information and understanding came only from the many novels she'd read, and something told her stories of fictional characters would be nothing like life in the real nineteenth century.

Still, she at least had something to go on.

She needed to act like a lady, a daughter of a gentleman who was in need of a gentleman's assistance.

She could do that, couldn't she?

Her stomach seemed to disagree as Mrs. Bielle guided her down a corridor. Maggie rubbed her sweaty palms along her pale yellow gown, which did no good since she wore gloves. Mrs. Bielle had mentioned the duke had given her permission to purchase the dress on Maggie's behalf along with the many other things a lady supposedly needed. The gown wasn't a perfect fit since most things in this era were tailor-made, but it was comfortable. *And* it had pockets.

The petite woman stopped in front of what Maggie assumed was the drawing room where low, muffled voices echoed from inside. Maggie leaned against the wall and drew a breath. Mrs. Bielle patted Maggie's shoulder. "Don't worry, dear. You have nothing to be nervous about."

If the woman only knew.

Mrs. Bielle pushed open the door. Both men faced away from them, neither noticing their entry.

"Are you certain of her character, Your Grace?

"Though our interaction was brief, she spoke as a lady would, and her clothes spoke of wealth. I cannot be certain, but my instincts are generally accurate. We shall know soon enough."

That one was her rescuer. She recognized his soft voice, as soothing now as it had been that day. The tightness in her chest eased a little.

"Curious, the whole thing," said the other man. "Why would a lady be alone in the country?"

"Curious, indeed."

Mrs. Bielle cleared her throat, and both men turned around.

"Good afternoon, Your Grace. Dr. Thistlewaite." Mrs. Bielle dropped into a curtsy, and Maggie was glad the woman had accompanied her because she certainly would have forgotten to give one on her own. Not a word said, and she'd almost made a mistake. Propriety and respect meant a great deal to the people of this era. She couldn't afford to forget.

Her curtsy made her legs wobble, and she nearly toppled over. If either of the men noticed, they didn't say anything, but embarrassment kept her staring at the floor.

"This is Miss Magdalena McCarthy," said the housekeeper. "Please let me know if you require anything else, Your Grace."

"Some tea would be greatly appreciated, Mrs. Bielle."

"Of course." Mrs. Bielle left the room, and Maggie wanted nothing more than to follow her. The housekeeper might have noticed the peculiarities about her and said nothing, but a gentleman of high station wasn't likely to overlook them.

The sound of footsteps lifted her gaze. The duke stopped a few feet shy of her, his black hair neatly parted to one side and his expression almost hesitant as if he were unsure how to proceed. That made two of them.

He dipped into a shallow bow. "Miss McCarthy, my name is Luke Halford, Duke of Avendesh, and this"—he gestured to the man behind him, who wore thinly framed glasses and must have been twenty years his senior—"is Dr. Pierce Thistlewaite. He saw to you after the incident. May I ask how you are feeling today?"

Maggie wrung her fingers together. "I'm feeling better...Your Grace. Definitely exhausted, but better. Thank you for asking." She turned to the doctor. "And thank you, too, Dr. Thistlewaite."

The two men exchanged glances. Had she said something wrong?

"I'm glad to hear you are well, Miss McCarthy," said the doctor, "but if you wouldn't mind taking a seat, I would like to give you a small examination to be sure?"

Maggie nodded and followed his lead to the dark green sofa across the room. She sat down, watching Dr. Thistlewaite intently as he opened his leather bag and removed a notebook and pencil.

"If I may ask you a few questions first, Miss McCarthy?"

"Okay."

He blinked at her a moment before continuing. "Are you experiencing any pain?"

"A headache, but it's improved since I ate something."

He nodded, scribbling away at his notepad. "And you found that you, indeed, had an appetite when you woke?"

"Hungry enough to eat a horse." Her hand shot up to cover her mouth. She should not have said that.

The doctor's brows lifted. When had people started using that expression? Her nerves were getting the best of her. "It's a figure of speech. Not that I would actually eat a horse. What I meant is that I was terribly famished."

"I know what the expression means, Miss McCarthy," said Dr. Thistlewaite. "I do not often hear it from young women, however."

Maggie shifted on the sofa. "Right."

"Clearly you remember your name," he continued. "Mrs. Bielle said you didn't know where you were, which of course is understandable being that you fainted, but she also mentioned you asked her the year. Do you find you are struggling with your memories?"

The honest answer would have been *no*, but Maggie saw the opportunity for what it was. If they were to ask her questions that led closer to the truth—questions that would make her sound insane—then she needed a reasonable way to avoid answering them. The doctor had handed her a golden ticket.

"I do seem to have difficulty recalling some things."

Dr. Thistlewaite hummed, his brows tight as he scribbled, and Maggie noted that the duke mirrored the expression.

"Do you presume this amnesia is only temporary?" the duke asked.

"Most likely, Your Grace. A traumatizing event can often cause these sorts of issues. I suspect they will clear up in time. Miss McCarthy should make a full recovery, but I do advise that she receive ample rest."

He spent the next few minutes checking her pulse and listening to her heartbeat, which required him to press an ear to her back. The entire thing unnerved her.

"I believe you will be fine, Miss McCarthy." Dr. Thistlewaite stood, replacing his things into his bag. "Should you require anything or have questions, do not hesitate to call for me, Your Grace. If her memory condition worsens, we can always try bleeding."

Maggie stiffened. "What? No. I don't need to bleed. I'm good."

"That will not be necessary," said the duke. "Thank you for your time, doctor."

Thistlewaite bowed and left the drawing room. Mrs. Bielle returned with tea, and Maggie hoped her expression conveyed that she wished for the woman to stay.

The message failed to send.

Mrs. Bielle left her alone with the man who'd saved her life. What should she say? She wanted to thank him, but the more she spoke, the odder she sounded.

The duke sat down in the armchair next to the sofa, and his gaze darted between her and the tea. Was she to pour it? Ladies usually poured the tea, didn't they? But this wasn't her house. She couldn't claim the role of hostess. Then again, Maggie had never heard of a duke pouring tea. The uncertainty made her squirm, as unspoken expectations always did. This very thing had prompted her desire to move out of her mother's house.

"May I offer you some tea, Miss McCarthy?" he asked, pouring himself a cup.

"Yes, please." Hopefully she hadn't offended the man beyond repair.

"How do you take it?"

Her stomach lurched. How did she take tea? Had she ever actually *had* a real cup of English tea? "I'm not sure."

He gave her a sympathetic nod and began pouring her drink. Maggie studied him while his attention remained on the task. He was dressed in a fine waistcoat, and his cravat had been tied with perfect precision. He had a firm jaw and cleft chin, both of which were clean shaven. The duke may not have been the most handsome man she'd ever met, at least compared to Mr. Gorgeous Burke, but the more she observed him, the more she found to like in his features.

Which she should most definitely *not* be doing.

He passed the cup, and her fingers brushed over his when she accepted the china, releasing a horde of butterflies in her stomach. Who knew butterflies liked tea so much?

She took a sip, and a pleased groan escaped with the warmth that spread through her.

The duke chuckled. "I take it you enjoy your tea *that* way?"

"This is fabulous. I can't believe I've never had the real stuff before now."

"Never...you've never had *real* tea? What sort of tea do you normally drink?"

The cold, bought-at-the-gas station kind. Non-caffeinated. With a hint of lemon.

Maggie shrugged. "The not-this-delicious sort."

He pursed his lips as if to restrain a laugh, but it still showed in his eyes. "Then I'm happy to have provided you with the real experience."

"Thank you," she whispered before taking another sip. "And for saving me. I can't think about what could have happened if you hadn't come when you did."

"I am glad to have happened upon you. Are you certain those men did not harm you in any way?"

"Yes, but they didn't bother to hide their intentions. Scumbags."

"I beg your pardon?"

Communication error. What sort of derogatory nouns did these people use? She thought for a moment. "Hoodlums?"

His brows knitted even closer.

"Not that one either, huh. Dirty scoundrels?"

The duke leaned forward, resting an elbow on his knee and placing his hand over his mouth. Was he smiling behind it?

"I see," he said, finally dropping it to reveal a stoic expression. "Indeed, they were. It is not safe for a lady to travel without escort, especially in the countryside. May I ask what you were doing out there all alone?"

"I can't remember what happened. I woke up by myself on the road. Figured if I started walking, I'd eventually find someone who could help me. Approaching those men wasn't the best idea, but I wasn't thinking clearly."

The duke nodded and tapped his finger against his cup before gingerly placing it on the small side table next to his chair. "Miss McCarthy, I know you must be exhausted after everything that has happened, but what I want more than anything is to help you. I'm afraid the only way for me to do so, however, is to ask you some questions. The more I understand, the better the odds of providing you assistance."

Maggie set her teacup and saucer on her lap. "Of course. I appreciate that."

"May I ask where you currently reside?"

Her body tensed. She hadn't expected that to be the first question. What was she to say? She couldn't tell him she lived in LA. The city was little more than a Spanish colony during this time, and she was certainly no Spaniard.

"Philadelphia."

"Philadelphia? So you are from the American continent?"

"I would call myself an American, yes."

He chuckled. "I suspected you were far from home. Your accent is certainly unique."

No wonder he and the doctor had passed each other perplexed looks when she first spoke. The duke didn't seem bothered by it, though.

"Tell me, Miss McCarthy. How did you come to be in England?"

That qualified as a question she didn't want to answer. Maggie feigned deep thought for several long moments and shook her head. "I believe I traveled here with my father, but I can't remember why."

"That is quite all right. What is your father's name? If I can track him down, we can at least return you to your family."

"Weston McCarthy. He...he owns..."

Another long pause seemed to have the desired effect. The duke's forehead furrowed. "Do not strain yourself on my account. A name provides me with a good place to start. With my connections, I am certain to locate him. He is likely looking for you as well."

The duke wasn't exactly wrong. Her mother and father probably *were* looking, but they wouldn't find her. And the kind man before her would never find them, either. She hated withholding information from him, but what choice did she have? A single mention of time travel would land her in an asylum. They had those now, didn't they? Regardless, she had no desire to find out.

"You also mentioned a necklace before you fainted," said the duke. "Was that something of great importance?"

Maggie nodded. "A family heirloom." And her only chance at going home. "One of them named Brimmer took it."

"Brimmer?" He tapped his finger against his leg. "I saw three men. Did you catch any other names?"

She thought for a moment. The whole event had happened so quickly. "A Doxly, I think? He ended up with the necklace. Made Brimmer hand it over."

The duke's expression darkened. "Lord Doxly. I should have known. His family faces financial ruin, and he is the most disreputable of men. I believe he is staying at his father's estate not far from here. I'll call on him. Perhaps we can still recover the heirloom."

Her gut twisted. This might be her only chance to get the pearls, but the thought of the duke handling them, of what could happen...

"I'll go with you," she blurted.

"Absolutely not. I do not want you anywhere near him. I ask that you trust me in this, Miss McCarthy."

"With all due respect, I am perfectly capable...of..." Her words slowed with the raise of his brows. "Oh, fine. I haven't exactly proven myself capable as of late, but I'll have you know, I gave this Lord Doxly an injury he won't soon forget."

She couldn't read his expression; there was too much to see there. Amusement, confusion, and what looked like admiration all played across his handsome features.

She cleared her throat. "I'm going with you."

The duke lifted his teacup leisurely and took a few sips before returning it back to the side table. "I will consider it, Miss McCarthy, once you have rested."

In all honesty, she would prefer to never see Lord Doxly again. *Nobody* in this era would likely see him again. But she had to try. "I hope you give it real consideration; otherwise, I will have to stowaway in your"—Maggie paused to lean forward and whisper—"are you taking your carriage?"

A smile slipped onto his lips. "Yes, I will take my carriage."

Maggie straightened and squared her shoulders. "I'll have to stowaway in your carriage."

"Where do you intend to *stowaway* in the carriage? There is not exactly anywhere to hide."

She bit her lip. "Then I'll follow on foot."

"And if the journey is long?"

"I'll complain about my aching feet nonstop the entire way back. It will be torturous for you. I'm an expert at obnoxious complaining."

The duke lost composure to a deep chuckle. "I shall keep that in mind while making my decision."

Maggie gave him a curt, satisfied nod before slumping a little in her chair. "I can't thank you enough. You've been so kind. I'm sorry to be such a pain in the neck."

"A pain in the neck?"

"Burden. Inconvenience. Perhaps those would be better."

"You are none of the above, but I admit your unusual phrasing is entertaining."

"If providing you with entertainment is my only means of offering gratitude, then I'm happy to oblige. I don't blame you for finding me strange."

He was grinning again. "Perhaps a little, but not in a bad way. Know that you are welcome to stay here, and I will do what I can to locate your family." He rose and bent into a bow. "I will leave you now, but I think it best you follow Dr. Thistlewaite's advice and rest. Let either myself or Mrs. Bielle know should you need anything."

Maggie stood and curtsied, this time a bit more confidently. "Thank you again, Your Grace."

Her gaze followed him to the door where he paused to look at her over his shoulder, another hint of a smile appearing before he disappeared completely into the hall.

He thought her strange but at least amusing enough to offer his help. She'd allow him to look for her father though the endeavor would prove pointless. Maybe his search would give her enough time to figure out what to do. The pearls were long gone. That *scoundrel* had likely wished himself somewhere else by now. Her best option would be to win the duke's favor. Perhaps she could take on a position as a maid.

Maggie winced. Until then, she needed to keep her weirdness to a minimum. How hard could it be?

Chapter 7

Suffolk, 1815

M aggie stared at the very *un*fancy, non-painted ceiling of her room. She'd tried to rest, but her mind refused. How could she sleep when she'd been thrown two hundred years into the past and robbed? Normally, she wouldn't question a doctor's orders, but after the whole *bleeding* suggestion, Maggie had lost faith in the man's capabilities.

She sat up, and her feet found the floor. She needed to get out of this room before she died of boredom.

The hallway was quiet and empty. She shuffled onto the long rug that lined the length of it and tiptoed to a room containing a mural ceiling. She'd wanted another peek at it since Mrs. Bielle escorted her to the drawing room earlier that morning.

Cracking the door open a smidge, she peered inside. It seemed devoid of people except for the busts that rested on rows of wooden pedestals. They wouldn't mind if she ventured into the room. The stone faces were probably the best secret keepers in the whole house.

She pushed the door open farther, and her eyes immediately shot toward the painted ceiling. Every intricate detail blended in with the next in a continuous expanse until it met the walls. Clouds and cherubs and instruments...who'd painted this thing—da Vinci?

It might have been the most exquisite piece of art she'd ever seen, and she gawked at it from the doorframe like some uncultured—

"Miss McCarthy?"

Maggie screamed and jerked on the knob, swinging the door into herself. The collision threw off her balance, sending her slippers sliding across the wood planks and her arms flailing. She landed flat on her back with an *oof.* The duke was at her side in an instant, hovering over her with the same concerned expression he'd displayed after she'd been robbed.

At least she wasn't covered in mud this time.

"My apologies, Miss McCarthy. Startling you had not been my intention."

Maggie covered her face with both hands. That very ungraceful trip to the floor must have looked like something from an episode of Looney Toons. She couldn't even blame a banana peel.

"Are you injured?" the duke prompted when she didn't respond.

"No, but I'm extremely embarrassed and may prefer to die right here on the floor, thank you." Her words came out muffled, but she didn't dare lift her hands. She couldn't face him.

There was a pause before he said, "Would you prefer I left and pretended I saw nothing? You can resume your position, and I'll try again, this time making sure to announce my presence with a bit more subtlety."

The amusement in his tone made her smile despite her embarrassment. "That sounds like a fantastic idea."

"Shall I help you up first?"

"That would ruin the whole you pretending not to have seen part."

"So it would. I will be in the hallway then."

She clenched her eyes closed and lifted one hand to give him a thumbs up. More silence.

"I thought we agreed to try again rather than let you die on the floor?" he asked.

"What?"

"Your thumb. You imitate the fate of a roman gladiator, do you not?"

"No, I was giving you the okay."

"I beg your pardon?"

Good fudge. "Please go to the hallway before my face burns to ashes."

He chuckled, and she kept her eyes closed as she listened to him shuffle to his feet. His boots tapped against the wooden floor, the echoes bouncing off the walls outside the room. Maggie heaved a sigh and, with a great deal of effort, got to her feet. She backed into the doorframe...and waited.

This time she heard his approach, and although it was completely unnecessary, he cleared his throat. "Miss McCarthy."

Maggie spun around and dipped into a shallow curtsy. "Your Grace." She met the duke's gaze. His lips were pressed firmly together, clearly holding in amusement.

The most unladylike snort escaped her nose. She buried her mouth into her arm, and they both descended into a bout of belly-aching laughter.

Maggie squared her shoulders and took a deep breath. "Trying again didn't make me any less embarrassed. In fact, I'm pretty sure it made everything worse. I changed my mind; your idea was *not* fantastic."

"Forgive me. I should not laugh when you've had a rough few days."

She placed her hands on her hips to complement the faux irritation in her tone. "No, you shouldn't, and if you hadn't rescued me, I might be appalled. But alas, I cannot be mad at my knight in shining armor, now can I?"

The duke grinned, and she decided it was far more handsome than Mr. Gorgeous Burke's grin. He clasped his hands behind his back. "Thank the heavens. I would not wish you to be angry with me." His expression relaxed, and his gaze shifted past her. "What were you doing in here? You should be resting."

"Resting is boring. I thought snooping through your house sounded more fun."

"Snooping?"

"I was being nosy."

Now the poor man simply looked confused. "I do not see anything wrong with your nose."

Maggie groaned and touched her steepled fingers to her mouth for a moment. "I only meant I was curious to see your house. At this rate, we may need to hire a translator."

"Perhaps so. I did not realize Americans spoke a different sort of English."

"We're kind of an odd lot."

The duke stepped closer, offering his elbow...like the gentlemen did in her novels. Maggie's heart fluttered. The butterflies wanted tea again.

The duke smiled down at her. "Since you are so interested in seeing the house and resting is far too boring, would you allow me to give you a tour?"

Maggie wrapped her hand around his arm. "I'd like that."

He reached past her for the knob and pulled the door closed. "I suppose we can skip this room as you have already become well acquainted with it."

She looked up at him, wrinkling her nose. "You need to up your pretend-I-didn't-see game. I find it pretty lacking."

"My apologies. I am afraid I cannot unsee your fall from grace."

Nothing in his tone or smirk suggested he was sorry *at all*.

"I may have to rethink the not being mad at you thing," she said as he guided her toward the stairs.

"I promise to be more cordial during your tour. So long as you remain upright, I believe I can manage. If you feel the need to fall over, do warn me though, and I shall do my best to catch you."

He was teasing, but the idea of having his arms around her sent a wave of unexpected heat over her skin. The man was handsome, but it was more than that. She'd only known him a few hours, yet an unexplainable ease existed between them, as if they'd been friends for a long time. The idea both comforted and confused her.

"I have no intention of falling again today, Your Grace. Once is more than enough."

He peered down at her, taking the stairs at a slow pace. "Then I shall wait for tomorrow."

MAGGIE COLLAPSED ONTO HER BED AND STARED UP AT THE ceiling, heaving a sigh of contentment. Spending the afternoon touring the inside of Windgate estate had been nothing short of glorious. She had explored the house some on her own or had at least attempted to before the duke completely startled her out of her skin. The man skulked about the halls like Casper the Friendly Ghost.

Or perhaps she'd been too mesmerized by the exquisite ceiling mural.

Regardless of her embarrassing display, she was glad he'd offered her a tour. Each room impressed her more than the next, and she wondered why such beauty had been lost to modern architecture. Something about the extravagant wallpapers and furnishings, though different from what she was accustomed to, felt warm and inviting. Quaint.

Of course, having a man as kind and handsome as the duke give her the tour certainly helped. He'd seemed genuinely happy to escort her around the house, and his amusement with her odd words hadn't stopped after her fiasco in the mural room. Or when she'd inadvertently brought up hot dogs. And baseball.

Someone knocked on the door, and Maggie voiced her permission for them to enter. Mrs. Bielle closed the door with a smile. "Are you ready to change for dinner?"

"I guess." Why couldn't her morning attire be worn at dinner? Did it honestly matter if she looked a little fancier for the evening meal? The rules of this era might make for charming tours with her arm interlocked with a handsome duke, but others seemed silly. And annoying. She'd never given some of them much thought while reading, but experiencing it was completely different.

Maggie wriggled out of her dress, and Mrs. Bielle helped her into a different gown since wearing the same one to dinner was inconceivable. Under the duke's orders, the housekeeper had purchased two for day wear and one for evening. His generosity did nothing but add to her guilt, but what was she supposed to do? She couldn't tell him the truth.

"Did you have a lovely afternoon, miss?" asked Mrs. Bielle. "Enjoyed your tour of the house?"

"The house is beautiful. Every room is so unique and interesting. I don't know how you manage to keep track of all the dusting."

Mrs. Bielle chuckled, guiding Maggie toward the vanity. Maggie sat down, and the woman went to work fixing her hair. Between resting on the bed and her earlier fumble to the floor, the pins had all fallen out.

The housekeeper put a new one in place. "How do I manage the dusting? Certainly not on my own. Delegation is key, but it helps that I have decades of experience."

"How long have you worked for the duke?

"Since before he became the duke. I worked for his father, first as a lady's maid to his mother. Over time, I took on other duties. But before all that, I lived in France."

A long list of impertinent questions raged in Maggie's head. Mrs. Bielle didn't fit the mold of a housekeeper, at least not the ones Maggie had always imagined from reading books. She spoke like a sophisticated lady, not one born to the lower class. That she was a lady's maid at one time explained a little, but what about the rest of what she'd said?

"What other duties do you mean?" asked Maggie.

"A great deal of my time was spent looking after His Grace when his mother passed. Unconventional, certainly, but I had been with the family a long time. With my service as lady's maid no longer needed, my position shifted to more of a nurse. Mourning is difficult, especially for children."

"That makes sense."

Mrs. Bielle secured a stray curl. "You and the duke get on quite well."

Maggie met the woman's gaze in the mirror, the abrupt shift in topic catching her off guard. "What?"

"You and His Grace get along well. I could hear you laughing in the halls earlier. It has been some time since I heard him laugh like that."

"He finds my strange ways and words amusing," said Maggie. "Falling on the floor didn't help."

"Handsome men can have that effect. Weak at the knees, as they say."

"No, that's not—he startled me. It had nothing to do with his good looks."

"So you do think him handsome?"

Maggie's face caught fire. "I..."

"This is going to take less time than I expected."

"What's going to take less time?"

Mrs. Bielle smiled, a twinkle of mischief in her eyes. "Your hair, of course. See, it is already done. Now, let's get you down to dinner."

Right. Dinner. She could do dinner. A simple meal with one of the most influential men in England. What could possibly go wrong?

ALWAYS PORTRAY AN APPEARANCE OF STRENGTH. THE LATE duke's words rang through Luke's mind as he leaned against the mantel in the drawing room, staring down at the empty hearth. There were few people Luke allowed to see past the façade—Nicholas and Luke's brother, Edwin, namely. Even then, he kept to himself, never revealing anything that might make him appear weak.

A duke did not have that privilege. Too many people looked to him for guidance or watched his every move. Too many people wanted things from him, and he had learned that a steely expression and unwillingness to open up to others provided the best means of deterrence. Intimidation alone kept most people at arm's length.

But not Miss McCarthy.

She had spoken to him this morning as though he was not at all intimidating. And he hadn't been, his concern for her well-being creating a hole in his façade. Perhaps the trauma of the last few days and his saving her life had eroded the natural gap between the two of them as strangers, and shockingly enough, the ease they established after one conversation had not bothered him.

He could then conclude that their interaction in the corridor had followed the established pattern created in the drawing room. There would be no changing their relationship with what had occurred to bring about their acquaintance unless whatever repose Miss McCarthy felt faded. Surely she would soon take into account his station and withdraw into something more subdued—into what he expected?

Luke tapped a finger against the mahogany mantel. He was uncertain he wanted the young lady to transform into someone more representative of the *ton*. Everything he'd noted about Miss McCarthy thus far intrigued him—her accent and odd turn of phrase. Even her easy smile. She had taken great delight in the tour of the house, her warm eyes wide with absolute awe. Luke had certainly preferred them that way over the terror shining there before and had found himself giving her far more details about his estate—and by default, his past—than he would ever offer a normal guest.

An image of her sliding across the floor and landing on her backside entered his thoughts, bringing a smile to his lips without permission. When had he last laughed so hard? He could not remember.

The sound of footsteps and muffled voices drew his attention. Mrs. Bielle stood at the door, gesturing for Miss McCarthy to enter. The young woman did so with an expression of hesitation. Perhaps her ease around him had already faded. The notion twisted Luke's stomach far more than it ought to have.

Luke suppressed a grin when Mrs. Bielle's departure increased the young lady's anxious grimace. She opened her mouth as if to protest but quickly snapped it closed and turned to face him.

"Miss McCarthy." Luke offered a slight bow. "You look lovely, this evening."

"I changed," she blurted.

Her face took on a light red hue, and his blasted grin escaped. "Yes, that is generally what one does before dinner."

"Right. You changed, too. Not that I pay attention to what you wear."

Her deepening hue suggested otherwise, as did her shifting feet. Why the hidden confession satisfied him so greatly, he could not say.

He crossed the room to stand in front of her and words tumbled out of him before he could think them through. "And do you approve of my change in attire?"

Why had he asked her that? His ears grew warm, but if Miss McCarthy noticed, she did not show it in her expression. She looked him up and down as if truly pondering the question, and he felt rather...well, intimidated by the scrutiny.

Ridiculous. He was a duke. He abstained from flirting for numerous good reasons, but somehow Miss McCarthy pulled it out of him. He would need to be more mindful. Such interactions were better left to someone like Nicholas.

When he could no longer stand her thorough study, Luke cleared his throat. "Miss McCarthy?"

She met his gaze, and her wide eyes had his lips lifting again. Why could he not control it?

"You look...nice." Miss McCarthy turned away, her eyes roaming the room—over anything but him.

Luke hid his disappointment. What had he expected her to say? He had made the woman uncomfortable and himself in the process. Yet as he watched her expression soften while taking in the room, his regret faded. That awe had returned to her eyes.

"You look as though you've entered this room for the first time, Miss McCarthy, despite having been here twice."

"It feels like I have. Everything looks different now that you've given me a tour."

Luke tilted his head. "How so?"

"Rooms are like people, I guess. We can observe them from afar, make presumptions about them, but it's not until we get to know them that we truly see. When you showed me around, you gave me details I wouldn't have had otherwise. The history, the stories and memories—those things speak to the house's character more than I could deduce by my own observations. Rooms hold secrets, and like people, you can't see their full potential or worth until they're revealed."

Her words dug under his skin and bore into him. His entire life was nothing but secrets. Not bad ones, of course; he merely did not allow anyone to know him fully. Did that mean others could not see his full potential or worth?

When the silence had gone on too long, Miss McCarthy lifted her gaze. Her lips pinched together, a bit of worry furrowing her brow. Perhaps she wondered if she had overspoken. Luke would not allow her to believe that even if her words had left him perplexed.

"I have never given it much thought, but rooms are a great deal like people," he said. "Thank you for acquainting me with the notion."

She opened her mouth, but Mr. Tolley entered the room, stealing her attention. The butler announced dinner, and Luke offered Miss McCarthy his arm. She accepted it with a gentle smile, one that portrayed a slight shyness that he found endearing. Intriguing, he decided, was not an adequate description of the woman on his arm.

Suffolk, 1815

Maggie released a wistful sigh as she stared out her bedroom window. The rain had finally given way to sunny skies, and the air had warmed enough that an adventure outside called to her.

A light knock sounded from the door, and Maggie turned to see Mrs. Bielle enter with her tight bun, apron, and wide smile. "Are you ready for a walk out of doors, miss?"

"Yes," said Maggie, drawing out the word with heavy exasperation. Mrs. Bielle had promised to escort her around the gardens this afternoon. Dr. Thistlewaite had sent a note stating that the fresh air might do Maggie's memory some good. It wouldn't, given that there was nothing *actually* wrong with her memory, but she'd been excited about the order all the same. Wandering the grounds would be nothing like seeing a glimpse of the estate from her window.

Mrs. Bielle chuckled. "Very well, dear. Grab your bonnet and gloves, and let us be on our way. I cannot stay out long. I have much work to do inside the house."

"Bonnet? Right." It was unacceptable for a young lady to be out in the sun without her bonnet because freckles were not in fashion...or so said the chiding matrons in her novels. Who would have thought all that time spent reading romance novels would come in handy?

Maggie yanked the baby blue covering over her head and tied the ribbon under her chin before tugging on a pair of white gloves. By the time she and the housekeeper reached the top of the staircase, the ribbon already irritated her skin.

Mrs. Bielle came to a halt, and Maggie nearly ran into her. "Oh, my. I have forgotten one last thing I must take care of first. Would you mind waiting a few moments, dear?"

"No, go ahead. I'll wait here."

Mrs. Bielle spun around but not before Maggie caught the mischievous glint in her eyes. The housekeeper always seemed up to something, but rather than causing unease, it only made Maggie like her more. The woman was like a spark of lightning, ready to strike when least expected.

"Good afternoon, Miss McCarthy." The duke's voice echoed from the staircase behind her, making her jump. And squeal.

Maggie spun around and glared at him. "Why are you always in stealth mode? How does a man your size move around so quietly?"

His brows lifted. "My size?"

"Yes, your height and your...your..." She flourished her hand, gesturing to his body. "Muscles."

"Muscles?" Now he sounded thoroughly amused.

"Your broad-*ness* and general masculinity." Not that she should be noticing, but the man clearly worked out. She could tell despite all those layers. Did he fence? Box, perhaps?

He took the remaining steps to the landing and placed his hand on the rail, a lopsided grin pulling at his lips. "It has taken great practice to move about this house with graceful masculinity. Thank you for the compliment."

"I didn't mean it as a compliment. You scared the bejeebies out of me again. Like full on heart attack."

"I scared the *what* out of you?"

Maggie drew her brows, thinking. She didn't even know how to begin explaining that word. "Never mind. Just stop startling me."

"I shall do my best, but thus far, it has not been intentional."

"I suppose I have been jumpy lately."

His expression softened. "I cannot blame you for that after what happened. I should better announce my presence. Having a young lady about is...well, I do not normally entertain houseguests."

"Never?"

"No."

"Not even family?"

The duke cleared his throat. "My family lives nearby, therefore there is no need for them to stay here. Besides, I spend a great deal of time in London."

"*Oh.*" Maggie held the word, her mouth rounded.

"Oh?"

"Oh, you prefer the social life of the city."

He scoffed, shaking his head. "Certainly not. I prefer the countryside, but I do have duties, Miss McCarthy."

"Why do you prefer the countryside?"

The duke tossed her an incredulous look. "Must I have a reason?"

"I was just curious. No need to get so defensive, *Your Grace.*" Maggie shifted past him and took the stairs to the ground floor. He followed her to the door, and Maggie wished Mrs. Bielle would hurry up and finish...whatever she had gone to do. The man was in a mood today.

"Where are you going, Miss McCarthy?" the duke asked.

"Out." Maggie whirled around, and he nearly toppled into her in his attempt to stop. The duke looked almost anxious with his brows furrowed the way they were.

"Out where? You should not go anywhere without a chaperone. It is dangerous, as you well know."

She did know, but messing with the duke was harmless fun she couldn't pass up. It took some effort, but she managed to keep her smile from showing. "*Outside.*"

He dropped his gaze and practically growled, as though it would temper his irritation. "Outside *where?*"

Behind him, the butler ducked his head. He seemed to find the exchange as entertaining as Maggie did, judging by his half concealed smile. Her grin broke free. "To the countryside, of course."

"Why do you enjoy vexing me?" asked the duke.

"Must I have a reason?"

The duke narrowed his eyes, but amusement had sneaked back into his expression. He was right; she did enjoy it, and she had a hard time believing he didn't enjoy her teasing, too.

"Oh, there you are, Miss McCarthy," said Mrs. Bielle, holding her skirts as she glided down the stairs. "I thought you might have gone on to the gardens without me."

The duke's lips twisted. "A walk through the gardens."

He looked so triumphant, as if he'd deduced some secret. Maggie turned away, holding in her laughter. She'd let him think he'd won some victory.

Mrs. Bielle stopped in front of them, tugging on her gloves. "Indeed, Your Grace. Dr. Thistlewaite advised that Miss McCarthy receive ample fresh air to help with her memory. Today is such a lovely day for a walk, wouldn't you agree?"

"I would agree, and I should like to join you."

"I thought as much." Mrs. Bielle shuffled past them, and Maggie barely caught her muttered words.

The three of them took the cobblestone path around the side of the house and entered the gardens through a wrought iron archway, the duke at Maggie's side and Mrs. Bielle following close behind. The vast display of colorful flowers and dark green shrubbery immediately stole Maggie's breath. The walkway split into three paths, each disappearing into a maze of hedges lined with specks of color.

Maggie heaved a contented sigh. She'd wanted to escape to the English countryside to a place with a garden. The pearls had taken her desires quite seriously, it seemed. "This place is amazing. Even the Queen would be impressed."

"Am I allowed to take that as a compliment?" asked the duke.

"This time I meant to compliment you—er—your gardens, yes."

He clasped his hands behind his back. "Do you have a garden at your home in Philadelphia?"

"More like a well-manicured lawn. I might be a tad jealous. A place like this would make a nice retreat from life."

"Do you find yourself in need of retreat? What about life makes you wish to hide?"

"Not hide," said Maggie, bending over near the edge of the path to stick her nose into the petals of a dark red rose. She breathed the scent in deeply, and a smile emerged without permission. "We all need a break sometimes. A moment to recharge."

"Recharge?"

Right. That likely made no sense to him. She was quickly realizing how much she took words for granted. "Renew our spirits and minds?"

"I see. A garden does provide a place for respite. I often come here when I wish to think."

"And what do you think about?"

The duke averted his gaze. "Many things."

"*Like?*"

The muscles in his jaw clenched. The duke didn't like personal questions; that much she'd gathered in the short time she'd known him. Her mother would tell her to drop it, to leave the man to his business, but she found herself wanting him to open up. Perhaps he didn't feel as comfortable with her as she did with him. The thought bothered her more than it should have.

Maggie glanced over her shoulder. The farther they walked, the farther Mrs. Bielle fell behind...which was impressive considering how slowly they were moving.

"I'm sorry," she said, unable to contend with the silence. "I don't mean to be so nosy all the time, but I haven't figured out how to restrain myself."

That brought out his deep chuckle. "I still do not understand your phrasing, Miss McCarthy, but you are forgiven."

"That's good. I wouldn't want you to kick me out for being too inquisitive."

She'd meant to tease him, but the way his lips turned down suggested the duke hadn't found her comment funny. "I would not do that. I promised to help you, and I intend to do so. This morning I sent letters to at least a dozen of my contacts. We should hear from them within a few days. Until then, you are welcome here."

"I can't thank you enough." How long would the man search for her father before giving up? Fear crept into her mind, and the uncertainty made her skin prickle. At least in 2022 she'd had a path to follow even if it wasn't the one she necessarily wanted. She had security and safety if not contentment. Here she had nothing.

The duke had been hospitable, more so than she could have hoped, but everyone's generosity ran out at some point, and Maggie wondered how long the duke's would last.

THE LOOK UPON MISS MCCARTHY'S FACE AS SHE STARED down at the flowers constricted Luke's chest. Worry creased her brow, and he searched for something to say that would smooth it away.

Reaching to the bush at his side, Luke broke the stem of a large red rose and held it out to her. Miss McCarthy glanced up, her brows drawing closer together to display her confusion. Luke offered her a soft smile. "You needn't worry. I will find your father."

There. His reassurance would comfort her, would it not?

She accepted the flower and twirled it between her fingers. "Your kindness means more to me than you know, Your Grace."

Her dejected tone weighed on him. The words had not had the effect he hoped. No matter. He would simply try again. "It is my pleasure and honor."

Miss McCarthy's expression shifted, the hopeless look in her eyes exchanged for one that suggested she did not believe him. At least not entirely.

Luke's stomach twisted rather uncomfortably. Was his lack of willingness to answer her impertinent badgering the cause of her incredulity? Did she truly believe he would cast her out for asking questions? There was nothing for it but to reassure her further. It had nothing to do with earning her good opinion, either. This was a matter of his pride.

Yes, that was it. He simply could not allow his honor to be questioned.

He opened his mouth, but Miss McCarthy spoke before him as if intentionally cutting him off. "We've lost Mrs. Bielle."

Very well, the woman did not wish to continue on the topic. He would let it rest for now. "She does not seem keen on joining us, does she?"

"I guess she's tired. It does take a lot of work to keep your ginormous house clean."

Miss McCarthy drew out his laughter...again. How did she manage to keep doing that? "I'm certain it does, but I do not believe exhaustion is why she is keeping her distance."

"Then why?"

Luke studied her. The confusion in her eyes seemed genuine, but surely she had not missed the housekeeper's insinuations? He certainly hadn't, and were it not for how deeply he respected Mrs. Bielle, he would have reprimanded her. What was more, he had yet to establish whether he could fully trust Miss McCarthy. Ladies often went to extreme measures to keep his company, their hopes and dreams latching on to his title and bachelorhood with no intention of letting go.

But the woman in front of him appeared oblivious to his suspicions. She teased him, yes, but it lacked the coyness he had experienced with others. Miss McCarthy did not lay her accomplishments before him as though she were applying for the position of duchess. She often forgot to curtsy and spoke to him with a level of familiarity she should not have. Society would demand he be repulsed by it.

He was not, however, and that confused him.

Luke offered her his arm, deciding to forgo answering yet another one of her questions. "Perhaps we ought to make our way back to her."

Miss McCarthy took his arm, and Luke ignored the jolt it sent to his heart. She matched his slow steps, keeping her gaze forward as the moments passed in silence. He wished he could hear her thoughts, for the woman at his side was every bit as perplexing as she was lovely. His mind could not seem to make sense of her, and each time he presumed to have done so she would surprise him with her unusual remarks and disregard for everything Society had taught her to be.

A rustle in the hedge preceded the emergence of wings. The bird crossed their path, taking flight into the cloudless sky with a twitter. Miss McCarthy squealed, tightening her hold on his arm and jumping against him with such force he nearly toppled over. Her free hand joined the other, clutching his sleeve like a vice, the rose he'd given her pinched between her fingers.

"It is only a bird," said Luke, holding in a chuckle.

"Yeah, well, that bird startled me out of my thoughts." Her gaze dropped to where she clenched his arm. A rosy color tinted her cheeks, and she immediately released, stepping away from him completely. "Sorry."

Luke felt the loss of her touch keenly. *Too* keenly. He should not have taken such satisfaction in her reaction—the way she had nearly jumped into his arms out of fright. What would it have felt like to wrap her in them, to hold her petite body against him? She would fit there perfectly, he knew from experience. He'd held Miss McCarthy after rescuing her, but this would not be the same. This would be better.

He scolded that line of thought and swept it away before it could fester into something more. Luke stepped forward, scooped up her gloved hand, and returned it to his elbow. Because he was a gentleman. And there might be more birds.

Luke guided Miss McCarthy to a bench still within view of their chaperone and took a seat on the rough stone beside her. She twirled the rose, her gaze on the petals but her thoughts clearly elsewhere.

"You are troubled," said Luke, keeping his voice low so as to not startle her.

Miss McCarthy turned to face him. "Not troubled. Worried, and maybe even a little scared." She heaved a long sigh. "Alright, more than a little. I'm ashamed to admit I'm terrified. I can't stop thinking about what will happen to me—"

"Nothing will happen to you."

"We both know I can't stay here indefinitely. Even if you do have the most exquisite gardens."

"I would like to think the company is not so bad, either." Luke lifted his brows and grinned, hoping his teasing would pull a smile from her. He possessed an inexplicable desire to rid her of that worry and fear if only for a short time.

With an expression as stoic as stone, she responded, "Mrs. Bielle is *excellent* company."

Luke blew out a stream of air as if extinguishing a candle. "You do me great injury with your words. My pride shall be cracked the remainder of my days."

She smiled then, a twinkle returning to her brown eyes. "I doubt my opinion could affect a duke so much."

"Quite the contrary, Miss McCarthy. I find your opinion means a great deal to me."

Surprise flickered over her expression, and he averted his gaze. What had possessed him to say that? Upon further analysis, the words were true. He did care what she thought of him, though heaven only knew why. Regardless, expressing such things made him feel vulnerable. Dukes were not meant to show weakness, and Miss McCarthy often broke through his mask of stone and aloofness.

He found that did not bother him so greatly. Until recently, he had never hoped for someone to see beyond the mask. It was as though everyone else threw stones at him with the intention of breaking through his walls by force, while Miss McCarthy slithered her way in through the cracks that already existed—cracks he himself created, if only subconsciously.

Luke cleared his throat. "I have some news for you."

"News?"

He nodded. This would not help her depressed mood at all, but he needed to tell her about visiting the man who had stolen her necklace...or his attempt to do so. "I called on Lord Doxly this morning."

Her scowl was not the reaction he had expected, and the irritation she displayed almost made him laugh.

She folded her arms. "You went without me?"

"I never agreed to take you. I said I would consider it."

"You didn't consider it well enough, then," she muttered.

Ignoring her pout, Luke continued, "Unfortunately, the man has left the area. None of the servants have seen him in days even though they had been expecting him. I am sorry about your heirloom. I had hoped to find it and, perhaps, provide you with a bit of justice. With the state of his family's affairs, the odds of retrieving it are rather slim. He has likely sold the piece by now."

After a deep breath, she whispered, "Thank you for trying."

Silence settled between them, the fiery spark he'd seen in her doused. The desire to take her hand threatened to overwhelm him into action. Despite the ease between them, they were strangers, and offering a gesture so familiar would be improper. A few days did not make them close friends. He could not act on unwarranted feelings.

And yet the glisten in her eyes broke his resolve. Luke reached for her, but the sound of light footsteps halted his progress. He snapped his hand back to his side as Mrs. Bielle stopped before them, saving him from the mistake.

The housekeeper clasped her hands in front of her. "I believe it is time to dress for dinner, Miss McCarthy."

The young lady grimaced and gestured to her current attire. "And I can't wear this gown?"

Mrs. Bielle's cheeks wrinkled with obvious mirth. "No, miss."

Miss McCarthy scoffed. "Changing is such a chore."

Luke suppressed a laugh. Why such an expectation would irritate her so, he didn't know. American customs must differ greatly from those in England.

Miss McCarthy rose from the bench and walked several yards, the housekeeper on her heels, before she stopped to face him again. Her brows drew together, and she tilted her head at an endearing angle that highlighted the smattering of freckles on her cheeks. "Aren't you coming?"

"Of course." Luke joined them, his steps always a pace behind. Hiding his satisfied grin from the two ladies proved difficult. It seemed Miss McCarthy enjoyed his company after all.

Chapter 9

Suffolk, 1815

U
nable to convince her mind to sleep any longer, Maggie wiggled out of bed mere minutes before light taps echoed from the hallway. The housekeeper greeted her with a smile and helped her into the same gown she'd worn the previous day. Maggie had read about the layers of clothing women wore during the era, but now that she'd experienced the process of dressing, she swore to never complain about pants ever again.

A pair of comfy denim jeans and a tee shirt would have felt like heaven compared to this. Would she ever grow used to it?

Mrs. Bielle guided her to the chair in front of the vanity and set to work on her hair. "You must forgive me, dear. I'm out of practice with styling a lady's hair, but it is slowly coming back to me."

"I'm perfectly capable of doing my own—"

She swatted Maggie's hand away. "You do have such lovely hair. The late duchess—His Grace's mother—did as well." She sighed wistfully, her gaze distant as if recalling some long-lost memory.

"What was the duchess like?" asked Maggie.

"Oh, she was the kindest of people. Mild tempered and always eloquent. She treated everyone with respect."

"Would you say the duke is more like his mother or father?" If he wouldn't open up to her, perhaps his housekeeper would spill the beans.

"His mother, for certain. The late duke was not a terrible man, but he...well, he lacked attentiveness. Neither His Grace nor his brother turned out much like their father."

So, the duke had a brother...who must live nearby since there were never houseguests. At least the duke had someone to keep him from getting lonely, assuming they were on good terms.

"Are you sure you have time for this, Mrs. Bielle? You must have so much to do as it is. I don't want to take you away from your other obligations."

"His Grace wanted someone to tend to you whilst you are here, and I volunteered without a second thought. You have been through a great deal the last few days, and besides, we must protect your reputation."

Maggie reined in the desire to turn around and face the woman as she slid another pin into her hair. "What do you mean? The duke and I haven't been *alone* alone. There are servants everywhere, and the doors are always open."

The woman chuckled and moved to Maggie's other side to pull up more of her brown curls. "You are staying as a guest in an unmarried man's home without a proper chaperone. His Grace would not pawn you off on someone else; he is too kind for that. But rumors catch as easily as kindling. You know how it is, especially amongst the wealthy and titled in this era."

Maggie met her eyes in the mirror. In this era? What did Mrs. Bielle know of other eras? Maybe she was overthinking the statement.

"I know what you mean," she said. "My...*father* is wealthy enough to provide me with that understanding." Her stomach curled. She hated lying, but what choice did she have? Her father worked as a middle class farmer while her mother lived a life of luxury. But she couldn't tell Mrs. Bielle that. She couldn't tell the duke. A woman in charge of so much money and property in this century was vastly unheard of. Add that to her parents being divorced...

Best to stick with the story that her father owned a successful business. It wouldn't matter once the duke gave up his search, anyway. No one would care what her parents were if she became a maid.

"Mrs. Bielle, can I ask you a favor?"

The housekeeper's fingers stilled. "Of course. What may I do for you, Miss McCarthy?"

Maggie drew a breath. "If, by chance, the duke is unsuccessful in locating my family, would you help me find a place to work? I have nothing and no one here in England. I won't pretend that doesn't scare me."

Mrs. Bielle studied her for a moment, and when she spoke, this time with a tone cradling deep emotion, her accent became a little heavier. "I will always do what I can to help you, but you worry too much. The duke will see to your care until you are safe at home."

"But if not—"

"Then I will see to your needs myself. I will help you find your place. But rest assured your concerns are unwarranted. All will be well."

Maggie's shoulders slumped. "Thank you, Mrs. Bielle."

The woman placed several more pins in Maggie's hair before taking a step back, a satisfied look on her face. "Ah! There we are. It is certainly not perfect, but I think it will do."

Maggie turned her head from side to side, watching the way several strands of hair bounced against her face. The rest had been pinned neatly at the back of her head. Mrs. Bielle didn't seem out of practice at all.

"It looks wonderful, Mrs. Bielle. Thank you."

She patted Maggie's shoulder. "Now, I shall escort you down to breakfast, but there are things I must attend to while you eat. Other obligations, as you so rightfully said."

"Would you eat with me?" asked Maggie, rising from the padded chair.

Mrs. Bielle laughed but quickly replaced her reaction with a more composed one. "Oh, you were in earnest. I could not possibly dine with you, dear. A housekeeper dining with a duke and a lady? Goodness, that would be rather out of sorts."

Maggie turned away to hide her disappointment. "How silly of me to suggest it."

Stupid rules.

She thought of Mrs. Bielle as a friend, perhaps her only one at present. The duke had been kind, of course, but she wasn't certain she could call him a friend. She'd like to, but friends didn't keep each other at arm's length, and the man seemed in no hurry to share the details of his life with her.

"I appreciate that you think so highly of me, Miss McCarthy, but I'm afraid it is the way of things. Come. Let's get you downstairs. His Grace is likely already there."

Maggie's heart lurched into her throat. Dining with the duke always made her nervous. She never failed to say things she shouldn't when around him. She botched speaking like a lady most of the time, but at least Mom's insistence on etiquette training had come in handy. Knowing which piece of flatware to use gave her one less thing to worry about.

She followed Mrs. Bielle into the hallway and down the stairs, twisting her fingers together as they went. The duke already thought her weird and seemed to accept her modern words and phrasing as the result of her being from America, but she still needed to be cautious.

"I will see you after," said Mrs. Bielle, gesturing toward the breakfast room.

Maggie nodded, and with a deep breath, entered the room. The duke sat at the end of a long table, his face hidden behind a newspaper. Whatever news the piece contained, it held his focus.

She cleared her throat. "Good morning, Your Grace."

The duke dropped his paper and jumped up from his chair so quickly he had to stabilize it before offering her a bow. "Forgive me, Miss McCarthy. I did not hear you come in."

"You mean *I* snuck up on *you* for once?" He hadn't squealed like she did, but she still found satisfaction in the achievement.

A very handsome, lopsided grin filled his face.

She dropped her gaze. Why were her insides suddenly in such a knot? "I'm sorry to disturb your reading. I wasn't sure whether I should announce myself. But you are a duke, and I thought it would be impolite of me not to say something. The last thing I want is to offend you. I guess interrupting you was also rude, though. Maybe I should have—"

His black Hessian boots appeared in her field of view. Her chin lifted without permission, and her eyes roamed up his body. He wore brown pantaloons and a forest green waistcoat today, fitted perfectly to his body as any fine-tailored outfit would. The colors made the deep browns of his eyes even warmer, accentuating the bits of gold hidden in them. His neatly-parted hair looked darker in the dim lighting of the breakfast room, and the ends had a slight curl to them, especially around his ears. He hadn't shaved yet today, a few dark shadows hiding along his firm jaw. How she hadn't thought him the most handsome man to walk the planet when they first met, she'd never know. If Mr. Darcy was a ten, the duke scored a solid five billion.

The duke's smile widened, and he cocked an eyebrow.

Fudge. How long had she been ogling him?

MISS MCCARTHY DIPPED INTO A CURTSY, HER FACE RED AS THE rose he had given her yesterday. She had studied him thoroughly when he crossed the room to join her. Luke had never appreciated being admired by a lady before now, and Miss McCarthy's reaction to him catching her in the act was exceptionally entertaining.

Her hasty attempt to cover the embarrassment, however, left her curtsy rather off balance Luke grabbed her shoulders to steady her. "Are you well, Miss McCarthy?"

"Just peachy."

"Peachy?" What did fruit have to do with it?

Her eyes widened. "I'm fine. I think."

"That is not exactly convincing."

She lifted her shoulders, his hands rising with them. "I need to eat, that's all."

He released her with reluctance. Perhaps the lady had not fully recovered from the event on the road. "Very well, but if you still feel at odds after breakfast, I believe we should call for Dr. Thistlewaite."

"No!"

He lifted his brows.

"I have no desire to be bled," she added. "I promise I'm completely fine."

Luke held up his hands in surrender, suppressing the smile threatening to emerge. Apparently Miss McCarthy did not fare well with blood. "We shan't call him then. Did our outing yesterday help with your memories?"

"Nope. Still fuzzy."

The conversation should not have amused him. Miss McCarthy's lapse in memory was a serious matter, but her turn of phrase simply caught him so off guard it became a struggle to keep a stoic expression. "Things will return to you in time, I am sure."

Miss McCarthy nodded and brushed past him to the sideboard. Luke followed, his hand hovering at her back. He still worried after her despite her claims. Perhaps he ought to ask Thistlewaite to visit. She needn't know he summoned him.

"Peachy?" she muttered, scooping things half-hazardly onto her plate. "Why did I say that?"

Luke grinned. "I would not mind knowing the answer to that myself."

She jumped and nearly dropped her food to the floor. He should be more cautious about startling her, but he found he enjoyed the way her nose scrunched to accompany the playful glares that followed too much to give it up.

And glare at him she did. "Why must you do that?"

"Forgive me." His expression likely displayed no plea for forgiveness, which was why her eyes narrowed. "Peaches?"

"Just another weird phrase, I guess," said Miss McCarthy. "Peachy generally means wonderful or well but is often used with a nice helping of sarcasm."

"Ah, I see. So, are you truly well or were you merely being sarcastic?"

"I'm well. It's been a long few days, but I'll manage. And for the record, I've never been so self-conscious about what I say. You're making me nervous this morning."

"*I* make *you* nervous?" He pointed to himself as if it were the most ridiculous thing he'd ever heard. "What have I done to leave you so unsettled?"

Miss McCarthy added a honey cake to her plate, watching him out of the corner of her eye. "You haven't *done* anything. Your title, on the other hand, is enough to make my thoughts incoherent sometimes. I've never met a duke before, you know."

So, she had finally taken his position into account. The ease between them would surely disappear. For the best, of course. He would soon need to find her a place to stay that did not threaten her reputation.

Luke's stomach twisted at the notion. He was not quite ready for her to take leave of him. "I do not wish to make you uncomfortable. Sometimes it is nice to forgo one's title, or at least the idea of doing so sounds like a pleasant experience. I cannot say I've ever been given that opportunity."

"Are you asking me to ignore your title?"

"No." That would be preposterous. He was a duke. One did not simply *ignore* that. "It is only that...well, you seem less concerned about it than most of Society. I would ask that our relationship remain that way. It is refreshing."

"Our relationship?"

"Yes. Our time alone together—not alone. What I mean to say is our interactions while you are here. When we are not in the company of other members of Society." Luke ran a hand through his hair, leaving it in complete disarray. "I have failed to explain myself properly, haven't I?"

"Yeah, you've butchered it, but no worries. I'll keep acting like my typical weird self. Sounds easy enough."

"I find your typical self both intriguing and att—" Luke snapped his mouth closed, his ears catching fire. What the devil was wrong with him? "I find you intriguing."

Her brows drew together. "Thanks, I think."

"I meant it as a compliment." He needed to dash away from this topic. The woman had muddled his mind and pulled him onto dangerous ground. He did *not* flirt with young ladies because he had no need for the pastime. Marriage remained a distant notion, one he would avoid to preserve his independence as long as possible.

"Are there other fruits that have odd meanings that I should know about?" asked Luke.

Miss McCarthy thought for a moment. "Bananas sometimes means crazy."

Luke laughed and gestured to the table. He assisted her into the chair next to his place at the end and took a seat. She began eating, and Luke resumed his perusal of the newspaper.

Or he attempted as much.

Having Miss McCarthy next to him proved quite distracting. He wanted to continue their conversation, but he also needed to allow her to eat. She had claimed an empty stomach as the reason for her off-kilter balance.

He glanced at her, and she seemed to sense his gaze, meeting it briefly with a smile. Luke turned his attention back to the paper. There had been a riot in London, and another column presented details about the war. He chose to read the latter first. Staying informed of the efforts against Napoleon was important.

Miss McCarthy's subtle movement drew his attention. She had picked up her honey cake and was analyzing it with a curious expression. Perhaps she had never had one. She took a bite, and her features softened with pure delight. Luke smiled. Her unmasked emotion only added to her beauty.

He shook his head and forced his attention back to the newspaper, grimacing when he realized he hadn't any idea where he'd left off in his reading. No matter. He'd simply start from the beginning.

Miss McCarthy leaned forward, her eyes on the paper, squinting as though trying to read the smaller print.

"Are you looking for something in particular?" asked Luke.

"I'm sorry. I was curious what day it is."

"The fifth of June."

"Thank you."

She leaned back, sweeping a stray curl behind her ear, but the piece dislodged immediately when she took another bit of cake. For a moment, he contemplated assisting her with the pesky strand.

Napoleon. Bother, where had he left off? He chose a random paragraph near the beginning, but none of it sounded familiar. Surely he had read this part once already?

"Is there anything exciting happening in the world?" asked Miss McCarthy.

He dropped the paper to the table, resigned to read about the Frenchman later. "Besides the ongoing issues with the French? Not particularly. Bonaparte remains elusive as ever and a complete"—he smirked, recalling her unusual phrasing—"pain in the neck."

"He hasn't surrendered yet, then?"

Luke scoffed. "I do not believe he has any intention of doing that."

"No one ever *intends* to surrender in any aspect of life until the situation becomes dire—whether it's war or a simple game. We humans are stubborn that way."

"I cannot argue with that point, and I certainly wish the man would concede. Enough lives have been lost."

She seemed to ponder for a moment. "Well, I think the war with Napoleon will soon end. I firmly believe he'll surrender."

Luke folded his arms, appraising her. "What makes you so certain?"

She shrugged. "Call it female intuition."

"Female intuition?" He chuckled and pushed the newspaper farther away so he could lean an elbow onto the table. "Do women have good instincts when it comes to war?"

"We have good instincts about everything, Your Grace. Women can be very formidable opponents." She tilted her head, her brows raised in challenge.

Luke leaned closer to her, his lips curling as he prepared to disarm his new opponent. "Of you, Miss McCarthy, I cannot deny that is true. *You* are formidable, indeed."

His words had the desired effect. She lowered her gaze, and her cheeks turned that delightful hue he so enjoyed. When she looked up again, those deep brown eyes considering him from beneath her dark lashes, his heart stumbled into an erratic pace.

Neither of them spoke—a blessing given how much his mind raced—but entranced as he was, he could not turn away, either. Something about Miss McCarthy captivated him in a way no other lady had. He felt drawn to her. Intrigued by her. And the walls around his heart crumbled more with every moment he spent in her company.

"Good morning, Your Grace."

Mrs. Bielle's voice broke his trance. The housekeeper's eyes darted between him and Miss McCarthy, a half-hidden smile on her lips. She dipped a curtsy before continuing. "I came to retrieve Miss McCarthy, but it seems she has not yet finished her breakfast. I thought we might take another turn about the garden if she feels rested enough."

"That sounds nice," said Miss McCarthy.

The idea of losing her company suddenly held no appeal. He had something to attend to that would not allow him to join them in the garden this time, but perhaps...

"Actually." Luke shifted in his chair when both women set their eyes upon him. He tapped his finger against the table as if that would dispel the burst of nerves knotting his stomach. "Would you like to take a ride with me, Miss McCarthy? I need to visit with one of my tenants, and your company would make the journey more pleasant."

She smiled, and his stomach ceased knotting and proceeded into a series of flops rather like a stranded fish out of water.

"I would love that, Your Grace."

Love. Luke had not allowed himself to consider it before, but the notion settled in his heart, prepared to make a home there. And he was not so certain he wanted to evict it.

Chapter 10

Suffolk, 1815

After retrieving her bonnet and gloves, Maggie made her way toward the stairs. The duke had surprised her by requesting she accompany him on a ride to see one of his tenants, and those butterflies in her stomach had wanted tea again.

She halted on the landing at the top of the stairs, her gloved hand resting on the smooth banister. From where she stood, she couldn't see the duke and Mrs. Bielle, but their tense voices met her ears. They were arguing.

"I received enough looks with everything I purchased for her before," said Mrs. Bielle. "People do not drop gossip like they would a kettle. The hotter it is, the longer they hold on to it. She will be the talk of everyone in attendance, and you understand how cruel some of them can be."

"So tell them the purchase is for Juliana. It would not be the first time I have doted upon her, therefore they cannot take suspicion with something that should not be their concern anyway."

Maggie adjusted the bonnet covering her head. Juliana? Who was she? Someone the duke doted upon, apparently. Perhaps the man was courting someone. That shouldn't have surprised her. A man in possession of a fortune needed a wife, after all. How else was he to have an heir?

Her stomach twisted.

Irritation laced Mrs. Bielle's words. "Do you honestly believe Mrs. Fletcher would not discern the difference between an order for Juliana and Miss McCarthy?"

Maggie's heart lurched at the mention of her name. They were arguing about *her*.

"And that aside, what about a chaperone?" Mrs. Bielle continued. "You cannot think her going without one is acceptable?"

"Of course not. I had intended to ask you to accompany her."

Mrs. Bielle's laugh provided evidence of her feelings about *that*. What exactly did the duke want her to attend?

"You have played the role thus far," said the duke. "Why should this be any different?"

"If you cannot see the difference between pretending to be an appropriate chaperone while within the walls of your home and within the walls of someone else's where all of Society can see, then you have ostracized yourself far more than I thought. I presume you did not bother to attend any balls during your time in London this Season?"

The duke's voice raised. "That is no business of yours. I had more important things to concern myself with besides standing on display for all of the *ton* to gawk at. The war—"

"We can blame Napoleon for many things. Your lack of enthusiasm to settle down is not one of them."

Maggie could hear the man's low growl even from her place on the stairs. The duke didn't want to settle down? Surely a gentleman of his wealth and...well, he had a pleasant face. A generous heart, too. Someone like him wouldn't need to search *that* hard to find a wife.

When the duke spoke again, his voice held a hardness and finality she'd never heard from him before. "I intend to go to Lady Garrick's ball at the end of the week, and I expect the purchase to be made, regardless of your opinion on the matter—an opinion I did not ask for. Do not forget your station. You are not my mother, and I shall not allow you to chide and nag me as though you are."

The silence that settled in the foyer created an ache in Maggie's chest. She felt sympathy for Mrs. Bielle, but she also understood the duke. Her mother had a habit of nagging, and if Maggie didn't make time to vent her frustrations, she exploded too. The duke definitely didn't seem the type to vent to anyone when he wouldn't even answer personal questions.

Mrs. Bielle's resigned whisper barely reached Maggie's ears. "Forgive me, Your Grace. I am out of line. I will wait in the carriage."

Maggie tapped the banister with her finger, waiting until well after the door thudded closed before completing the descent to where the duke stood, his shoulders slumped and both hands messaging his forehead. He straightened when he noticed her approach and gave her a tentative smile.

"Thank you for joining me, Miss McCarthy. The ride is not far, but perhaps it will provide you with enough fresh air to satisfy Dr. Thistlewaite's orders."

"Hopefully, you're right." Because she didn't like the doctor's alternatives.

He offered her his arm, and Maggie's lips lifted for no reason. She wanted to know more about his argument with Mrs. Bielle—to know exactly what they were referring to—but she didn't dare ask. Not yet. The duke needed a little time to calm down, as she knew from experience with battling her mother.

The duke led her outside, and a thrill of excitement shot through her at the sight of the black carriage. What would it be like to take a ride in such an old mode of transportation? Sitting next to the duke, with his fancy tailcoat, black hat, and gloves while riding along a dirt road through a quiet countryside would be like living in a period drama.

Come to think of it, she *was* living in one. There was certainly plenty of drama, at least from her point of view. What could possibly be more dramatic than a strange girl from the future upending the life of a gentleman?

The duke handed her into the carriage and took the spot next to her. Mrs. Bielle sat on a bench behind them, facing the opposite direction. Glancing over her shoulder, Maggie could see the dejection evident in the slight pinch of the housekeeper's brows. Again, sympathy washed over Maggie. The woman cared about the duke—Maggie had no doubt of that—but she also couldn't help but admire how he so readily expressed his frustration with the woman's meddling.

The narrow bench forced enough proximity between her and the duke that she could feel the heat radiating from him. Chills crawled across her skin, kindling the desire to scoot closer. What was the matter with her? Now that the rainstorms had finally passed, the air had grown hot and humid. It wasn't as if she were cold.

The carriage jerked forward and made its way down the long, dirt driveway. Maggie took in the lush foliage and manicured shrubs as they passed. The estate captured the beauty she'd always imagined in her novels and then some.

"You have a lovely estate, Your Grace."

"Thank you, but I'm afraid I cannot claim responsibility. My groundskeepers take great pride in their work. Tell me about your home. Do you live within Philadelphia or outside of town?"

Maggie swallowed against the lump in her throat. Lying to the duke left her stomach in an awful state. "In town. My mother would never consider the idea of living in the country." That, at least, wasn't a lie. Before her father had completely given up on her parents' marriage, he'd begged her mother to move away, convinced the distance from the expectations and monetary influence would somehow bring back the woman he'd fallen in love with. Her mother had refused and filed the paperwork for divorce a month later. Maggie had been fourteen at the time.

"And your father?" asked the duke. "Does he enjoy town? You said he owned a business. I imagine living in town helps with his profession."

Quite the opposite, actually. Her father was a farmer and by modern standards, a businessman. But Maggie couldn't tell the duke that.

"If I could remember what type of business my father had, I might be able to answer that." The lie left a bad taste in her mouth, but she continued, "However, I do know he doesn't like town. He's told me numerous times that he feels more at ease away from busy streets and crowds."

And sirens, crime, and smog.

She sighed. "My parents' difference of opinion has led to a lot of arguments over the years. Now my father spends most of his days away from it all."

"And your mother does not mind?"

Maggie scoffed and shook her head. "Not in the slightest."

"I understand what that is like."

The duke stared ahead, his face twisted with an internal pain she longed to understand. Questions burned through her mind, ones she shouldn't want to ask of the man she'd known for only a few days. Yet she couldn't ignore them.

"Did your parents not get along?" she asked.

He stiffened, and Maggie's heart raced. The man beside her held the title of *duke*, one he could only claim if his father were no longer alive, and Mrs. Bielle had confirmed his mother's passing. Pestering him on a topic so sensitive was a bad idea. "Don't feel obligated to answer. I shouldn't have asked you that."

She wiggled on the bench, and the movement caused her leg to brush against his. The irrational desire to shift closer to him struck her again, but she pushed it down, hopefully hard enough that it fell off the cart and became trampled under the wheels.

For several moments, he didn't say anything, leaving her to focus on the rattle of the phaeton rolling over the uneven road and clop of horse hooves.

"My parents were always at odds with one another," said the duke. "An arranged marriage can have that effect. My mother passed when I was ten, and my father's reaction was that of a man who'd acquired freedom."

"And your father? When did he pass?"

"Three years ago."

"I'm sorry. I shouldn't have brought it—"

"Do not apologize." The duke's hand left the reins and fell over her clasped ones, where they rested in her lap. Though they both wore gloves, the warmth that spread over her skin burned like a blowtorch. She glanced up at the duke, and he quickly withdrew, turning his attention back to the road with a deep furrow in his forehead. Had he felt the same thing? What did it mean if he had?

Minutes of awkward silence ensued until the thoughts blundering around in her brain threatened her into madness. She needed to distract them with something. "Why do you not enjoy going to balls?"

Fudge. That probably hadn't been the best choice.

The duke's head snapped in her direction, his eyes dark. "You were listening? That was a private conversation."

"It's not private if you shout about it in an entryway."

Mrs. Bielle chuckled, and the duke shot her a glare over his shoulder, not that the housekeeper could see it facing the opposite direction.

His grip tightened on the reins. "Regardless, it is none of your concern."

Maggie lifted her brows. "Not my concern? Pretty sure I heard my name, so.. But I totally understand why you lashed out. You need—"

"You presume to tell me what *I* need? You barely know me, Miss McCarthy."

"But I'd like to know you. The problem is you won't let me. Every time I ask you something personal you shut me out. Do you let *anyone* get to know you?"

The duke pulled on the reins and brought the phaeton to a stop. He fixed her with a hard glare that made her squirm. "Why do you wish to know me?"

She looked down, afraid her composure would wane under his scrutiny. She'd only meant to suggest he talk to someone—vent whatever pent-up frustration he had. Talking to Diana was the only way Maggie had dealt with her mother that prevented an explosion. In fact, having a friend to confide in helped her get through life in general without becoming an emotional wreck. Perhaps that was why she felt so out of sorts now. She had no one to confide in.

She swallowed back her emotions, but they laced her tone despite the effort. "I don't have much in the way of friends at the moment. I guess I was hoping..."

Everything caught up to her. She had nothing here in 1815—no family or friends. No money or even experience to recommend her for a job. Her future was more uncertain than it had ever been. She'd offended the man who'd so willingly offered to help her with prying questions she shouldn't have asked.

"Perhaps it would be best if I returned to Windgate," she managed to whisper.

Without looking at him, she scooted to the edge of the seat and jumped to the ground. She would have to face her uncertain future alone.

Suffolk, 1815

The carriage squeaked when Luke tossed the reins and shuffled over the seat with anything but grace. Mrs. Bielle met his gaze, a chiding look in her eyes that he chose to ignore when he passed her the reins. He did not need to be told how grave an error he'd made.

He sprinted after Miss McCarthy, his pulse pounding in his ears. He'd hurt her, the pain clearly visible in her glossy brown eyes and soft tone ripping at his heart like claws over a tapestry. Part of him still seethed with frustration from his earlier quarrel with Mrs. Bielle, but it was panic that coaxed him to build up his walls, to keep Miss McCarthy at a distance. What if she turned out to be like every other lady of his acquaintance?

No. Miss McCarthy was different, and that surety alone encouraged his pursuit of her along the road.

"Miss McCarthy, please wait!"

His fingers caught her arm and gently tugged her to a stop. She turned around but refused to meet his gaze.

Luke dropped his hand to rest against his side. "Forgive me. I—"

"It isn't your fault." She glanced up, and the regret shining in her eyes stabbed at his chest. He had not meant to upset her, but fear invoked his defensiveness. His concern and distrust.

When he said nothing, she continued, "I shouldn't have eavesdropped on your conversation, and I definitely shouldn't have asked you such personal questions. I'm sorry."

"And I have spoken harshly for no reason. I beg you allow me to correct my ungentlemanly behavior."

"Ungentlemanly?" She looked some mixture of amused and annoyed by his words. "You are by far the most kind gentleman I've ever met."

Pride swelled within him at the compliment. "Then will you accept my request for you to join me on the grass?" He gestured to a spot beneath the oak tree next to the road, and Miss McCarthy bit her lip. Fearing she might turn him down, he added, "Please."

"Okay."

Luke was not completely certain, but he believed that meant she conceded to his request. He considered taking her hand as he had in the carriage. The elation he'd felt in that moment had scared him, yet curiosity begged him to test whether the sensation would return.

He glanced over his shoulder and found Mrs. Bielle watching them with a smug grin. Perhaps now was not the time for conducting an experiment. He offered Miss McCarthy his arm instead.

He led her to the tree, and she sat down on the grass, tucking her feet beneath her sky blue skirts and shoving her bonnet from her head so that it dangled between her shoulders. He took the space next to her, stretching his legs out in front of him. "You were correct in your statement. I do not allow many people to become close to me."

"Why not?" she asked without pause.

"It is not easy to determine the person's motives, especially in regards to young ladies. People always want something from me, whether it be my money, influence, or a title through matrimony."

She gaped, horrorstruck. "I'm not a fortune hunter. Is that why you get so moody? You're suspicious of me?"

"I am not moody." The incredulous look she gave him put off his denial. He cleared his throat. "I suppose that is a blunt way to put it. I cannot help but have suspicions. Surely you can understand my reasoning."

"I can, but I already have an inheritance so I've no need for your money. And a title? No thank you."

He chose to ignore the second half of her response and the way the words gutted him in such a ridiculous manner, instead focusing his question on the more important part. "You have an inheritance?"

The grin that crept onto her lips, coupled by the mischievous glint in her eyes, did nothing to ease his pounding heart. She tilted her head, allowing the dappled sunbeams to illuminate her freckles. "It's not fair for you to ask me questions and refuse to answer mine, you know. I didn't mean to be presumptuous before. It's only that I've found telling someone else about my frustrations helps."

"I am to confess everything to you, then?" asked Luke. "Give all my secrets to a stranger who knows little about me?"

"I'm the perfect person. As you said, I don't know you. I have no reason to pass judgment, and once you've located my father, you'll likely never see me again. You won't have to worry about someone who knows your secrets embarrassing you in public—not that I ever would."

Luke plucked the grass. He had no doubt Miss McCarthy would keep his secrets. He wanted her to see his full potential and worth, that much he had decided after she compared rooms to people. But it was the statement about never seeing her again that bothered him the most.

"And after I have confessed my struggles, what then?" he asked. "You offer me advice?"

"Only if you want it. As your friend and confidant, my job, first and foremost, is to listen. We don't always need advice. Sometimes, all we want is someone to hear us. I don't believe you're incapable of figuring out your problems on your own, but you can't do that unless you confront them. Admitting our struggles out loud won't make them go away, but it does help us accept they are real."

"A wise notion I cannot argue against. Tell me, though, do you take your own advice? Do you have a confidant to whom you confess?"

Luke hoped she did not, for he would very much like to be that person for her.

"I do have a confidant," said Miss McCarthy. "Anytime I'm feeling particularly down or blue, I call Diana. She's—"

"Call? You mean you visit her?"

Her eyes widened. "Yes. That's what I meant. Diana always listens to me complain, even if she disagrees. Venting to her is much better than facing my mother. That has repercussions I'd prefer not to incur, although I admit I haven't successfully avoided it lately."

"And what did you do to earn these repercussions?"

She shook her head, and the movement made the ribbons holding her bonnet dig into her throat. Miss McCarthy tugged on them, a look of irritation sweeping over her face. "Uh-uh. We didn't sit down here to talk about my bad behavior, Your Grace."

He chuckled, picking another blade of grass. "You do realize that only makes me more curious?"

"Now you know how I feel."

She had him there. "How about a trade? I will confide in you, and then I wish to know your reprehensible deeds."

She considered him with narrowed eyes. "Alright, you have a deal."

His excitement for victory did not last long. His pulse quickened, the thought of revealing his deepest turmoil already haunting him. But he trusted the woman at his side not to judge his confession or think less of him.

Luke ran his hands down his thighs with a slow exhale. "Where should I begin?"

She did not answer, and he appreciated that she gave him time to sort his thoughts. To begin when he felt ready.

"As I mentioned, my parents' marriage was arranged, an agreement made by my grandparents. They had only met once before their wedding. I am not sure two more different people have ever been forced together. After my mother gave birth to my brother and me, the two of them rarely spoke. Even as a young boy I could sense how unhappy my mother was, though she did her best to hide it. The discontent ate away at her and my father for years.

"After my mother died, my father spent more time away. It was as if her death had freed him, and I hated that he responded with such eagerness. Such lightness. I may as well have lost them both when she passed. He never spared much time for me, at least not until I reached an age where it became imperative for me to learn how to run the duchy. By then, our connection had grown stale, cold, and indifferent. Mrs. Bielle raised me, which is why I have such a soft spot for her despite her station."

Luke turned his attention past the carriage where the road rounded a bend and disappeared within a grove of trees. "I do not attend balls or invest time in Society because I am afraid that, should I wed, my marriage will be no different than the one I spent my entire life watching fall apart. I am expected to marry, to have an heir, but how can I put a child through the same experience? The same pain."

The wind tousled strands of his hair, and he closed his eyes. Images of his mother in tears often plagued his thoughts. She had never felt secure or loved by her husband, and Society had taught her such a thing was acceptable, expected even. Luke wanted his marriage to be different, but a love match for him was nigh on impossible. His title did not give way for genuine interaction with ladies.

At least it hadn't until recently.

When Miss McCarthy finally spoke, he kept his eyes closed. The warmth in her voice soothed him, and her words acted as a balm on his heart. "I can't tell you what to do. But what I do know is that your situation is different from your parents'. You have a choice where they did not. You can choose to marry whomever you wish, to find someone that brings you happiness, or you can choose not to marry at all. There will always be expectations. You don't have to conform to them."

She chuckled, and the sound made him smile.

"I'm a hypocrite for saying that," she said. "Conforming to expectations is easy. Defying them is far more difficult."

"Here, not fulfilling one's duties is highly frowned upon," said Luke. "But you are correct; I have a choice in whom I marry. My title, unfortunately, makes finding genuine affection difficult. I am not certain I trust myself to judge the attention I receive. What if I marry only to discover my choice of a bride had no real love for me? You must think me foolish for being afraid of such a thing. For even dreaming of a love match in my position."

Soft fingers settled over his hand, and a prickle of chills raced up his arm. Luke's eyes flew open, and he turned to face her.

"I don't think you're foolish at all," she mumbled. "Based on your life experience, your concern sounds legitimate. Determining the motives of others isn't easy, and I understand what it's like to fear something that logic says to embrace."

Her gaze fell to their hands, and a faint blush crept into her cheeks. Miss McCarthy withdrew, but Luke was not ready to lose her comforting touch. He snatched her hand back mid air, and she gasped as he settled it back on the grass, secure within his hold.

"Miss McCarthy, I..." Luke brushed his thumb over her knuckles, unsure what he had even meant to say. She had asked for friendship, but he was not certain he could give it to her.

Not when his heart wanted more.

THE FEAR MAGGIE HAD HEARD IN THE DUKE'S VOICE DURING his confession spread into the man's expression. Did he regret trusting her? They were practically strangers.

Maggie patted his hand with her free one. "Don't worry, Your Grace. I promise your secrets are safe with me. I won't tell anyone."

He offered her a smile, one that appeared somewhat forced, and nodded. The duke released his hold, and Maggie immediately missed the warmth that had encompassed her.

Which was ridiculous.

He'd only grabbed her to emphasize his plea, to beg her to keep his reluctance to marry to herself. She shouldn't be lingering on the way he'd gently squeezed her hand or on how his thumb had skidded across her knuckles, tenderly massaging them through her white gloves. The duke likely hadn't even realized he was doing it.

His shaky exhale stole her focus from the discontenting thoughts.

"Feel better?" asked Maggie.

"Surprisingly...I do feel better."

Maggie clasped her hands, fighting the smirk that attempted to form on her lips. She failed miserably, and the duke noticed.

"You needn't look so smug about it," he said, amusement filling his tone. "Besides, now it is your turn."

Right. She'd agreed to tell him about her *reprehensible deeds*. "Well, lately my mother has insisted on me meeting eligible bachelors. My reluctance to entertain her attempts frustrates her."

"And why are you so reluctant to your mother's efforts? Do you not wish to be courted?"

"I'm an only child, Your Grace. That makes me an heiress. As you can imagine, that common knowledge brings a plethora of fortune hunters the same way your title does." She yanked at her bonnet ribbons, pulling them away from her neck only for them to slide back against her skin. "I'm not against marriage or date— *courting* someone. My mother just chooses to introduce me to men who have no qualms about taking over the family business one day. I'm not even certain I want to inherit it at all."

"Why not? Without it—"

"I would have nothing. Yes, I know. Sometimes the monotony suffocates me, as do the expectations." And her annoying bonnet.

She tugged at the ribbons again. How did women wear these things? She wanted to take it off, but the ribbons had somehow worked their way into an unrelenting knot.

"Allow me." The duke chuckled as he took her wrists and pulled them away from her neck. He leaned close, giving her an opportunity to bask in his spicy scent, which she pretended not to enjoy. The warmth of his hands heated her skin, each brush of his fingers leaving her mind more discombobulated. He pinched the ribbons, and she held her breath as he slowly pulled until the bow came loose. He removed the bonnet from her head and placed it in her lap. "Better?"

"Huh?"

He grinned. "Is it better without the bonnet?"

"Oh. Yeah, much better."

He leaned away. "Having nothing is not an easy life to live. You know this, do you not?"

The inheritance. Right. "Of course I do. But is it wrong that I want to forge my own path? Sometimes I wonder if I even know who I am. I'd like the opportunity to find myself. Maybe one day I'll meet someone who sees me for more than the money attached to my name." She turned to face the duke. "Maybe one day you will, too."

She expected him to smile, but he didn't. He said nothing in response to her wistful words. The way his dark brown eyes stared at her made her feel exceptionally self-conscious. She turned away and shifted on the grass.

"Have you considered discussing these matters with your father?" asked the duke. "Perhaps there is a better solution to be had."

Maggie huffed a laugh. "I've considered it like a bajillion times. Actually doing it, though..." She shook her head. "I don't have the courage. My mo—father would be really disappointed. I don't know if I can live with that."

"But you can live with being miserable the rest of your life?"

The question struck her, and Maggie had no good answer. "It's easier than facing the alternative."

The duke hummed, nodding his head slowly. "It is, but perhaps one day you will discover the courage to find out which of the two is more valuable."

"Maybe." She plucked several blades of grass and tossed them in front of her. "We were supposed to air out your problems, not mine."

"Do *you* feel better, Miss McCarthy?"

Now the duke wore a smug smile. Maggie wrinkled her nose and shook her head. She deserved his teasing, but she couldn't deny it *did* feel better to talk to someone, and since Diana wasn't here and Maggie had volunteered to be the duke's secret keeper, logic stood that he should be hers.

Completely logical.

"It seems we have become each other's confidants, Your Grace."

"Luke."

Maggie blinked. "What?"

"If we are to be one another's confidants, then we should call each other by our given names, should we not? At least when we are out of the public eye."

He wanted her to call him by his Christian name? But that was always a big deal in her novels. Usually that only happened when the characters were close family or friends or...

"If that makes you uncomfortable, Miss McCarthy—"

"Maggie. I prefer Maggie. I've always hated Magdalena. It just sounds so...graceful? Like the exact opposite of me."

"I would disagree, but I've yet to banish your fall from a few days ago from my mind."

She tilted her head back and groaned. "I wish we could both forget that particular moment of inelegance."

"I'm quite content to remember," he said quietly. "I would not wish to lose a single memory of you."

An unbearable heat flooded her cheeks. What was she supposed to say to that? And why was he looking at her that way, with that teasing smile and those eyes full of...something else. No. She was being ridiculous. "You only say that because I'm so entertaining."

His expression softened, which only highlighted whatever emotion lay hidden in his eyes. "You are, but that is not the only reason. The world is brighter with you around. I can see the effect your visit has had on my staff. Mrs. Bielle has certainly been livelier, and I find myself enjoying the company. I do not believe I've been this happy in a long time. I am fortunate to have you."

She made him happy. He was fortunate to *have her*. She shouldn't read too much into the statement, but her heart and mind insisted on it. The man may as well have wrapped her in a fleece blanket straight from the dryer with those words. "Thank you, Luke."

He shifted on the grass and in seconds stood before her with his hand outstretched and a bright smile. Sunlight glistened off the flakes of gold hidden in his dark irises the way treasure glittered in movies when a chest was first opened.

Fudge. Comparing the duke's eyes to lost treasure was ridiculous and completely inappropriate. She took his hand, and he pulled her from the ground with what she considered far more force than necessary. She smacked against him, her hand landing flat-palmed on his chest.

His free hand steadied her at the waist. "My apologies."

He didn't look apologetic, but he did smell nice. Like cinnamon and...

She took a step back, but Luke kept hold of her hand. She liked the way it felt wrapped around hers. "I guess we should go see your tenant now."

"Indeed. Thank you for listening and for encouraging me to confide in you."

"Encouraging is a nice way to put it. I can be a little stubborn."

He barely restrained a chuckle. "Regardless, I am grateful for your determination."

No one had ever thanked her for that before, and quite frankly, she didn't know how to respond. He squeezed her hand. "Come, we should make sure Mrs. Bielle is well."

Maggie nodded and followed him to the carriage. He helped her up and then rounded to the other side. Her pulse quickened when he sat down on the bench beside her and took the reins. On second thought, it hadn't slowed since he'd pulled her against him.

Something had changed between them during that conversation. She had already lost her heirloom in 1815, and if she wasn't careful, her heart might soon join it.

Chapter 12

Suffolk, 1815

Maggie pressed her body against the fence. She hadn't thought playing with the children while Luke talked to Mr. Townsend would have her pulse throbbing. Perhaps if she kept very still, Theo might wander in a different direction. She could run, but there were too many twigs scattered on the ground that would snap beneath her feet and give her away.

And she had no desire to be the blind man.

Theo inched closer, his hands searching in the open air, and she dared a small inhale. Her face was probably growing purple, and staying quiet didn't seem to deter the young boy at all. Maybe making a run for it wasn't a bad idea. At least she'd have a chance. Peter, Theo's younger brother, stood several yards away. He hadn't spoken a word since their game began. Maggie, on the other hand, had burst into laughter every time Theo bumped into something. It was no wonder he'd been able to follow her.

Now or never.

Maggie darted forward, but Theo's fingers grazed her arm. "I caught you, Miss McCarthy!"

She groaned as he pulled down his blindfold. The nine-year-old looked nothing short of triumphant, and his expression was contagious.

"You caught me," agreed Maggie. "I guess it's my turn now?"

Theo nodded and grabbed her hand. He led her back to the center of the lawn. Near the cottage, Luke conversed with Mr. Townsend about his roof. The little home seemed in need of repairs before winter. She had overheard the duke promise that the work would be completed long before the cold set in, and he'd also made several suggestions for other repairs. Mr. Townsend had tried to brush off the concerns, but Luke wouldn't hear of it, insisting he would make sure their needs were met.

"Crouch so I can tie the blindfold," said Theo, his voice firm with command. "I don't trust you to do it. You might cheat."

She feigned a gasp. "A lady would never cheat."

Both Theo and Peter giggled. Maggie squatted and allowed him to tie the double-layered cloth around her head. At least the game had given her an excuse to dispose of her wretched bonnet. She'd left it with Mrs. Bielle, who'd gone inside to visit with Mrs. Townsend out of the sun.

"Stand up, Miss McCarthy. Now you have to spin around five times!"

"Five whole times? What if I get dizzy and fall over?" Both boys giggled again. "We'll see who's laughing in a minute. Peter, I've got my sights set on you."

As Maggie began to spin, she heard them dash off in opposite directions. She counted to five, and sure enough, nearly fell over once she came to a stop. The dark cloth didn't allow even a sliver of light to slip through, and that did nothing to aid her balance.

She staggered around until she bumped into something, a metal pail by the sound of the clank. She gave the bucket a kick, and the action brought out Theo's laughter. She could track him down, but she hoped to catch Peter. He'd evaded them both this entire time. *He* was the challenge.

Movement behind stole her attention. Peter had run past her. She followed as best she could until the sound of swishing grass stopped. Maybe if she acted foolish enough he would laugh.

"Where have you gone, Peter? You can't escape me." She clawed at the air like some crazed animal.

No luck. The kid was a master at quiet. Perhaps he'd grow up to be a spy. Or a ninja.

Maggie lunged forward, hoping the movement would do something, and the grass swished again. "Ah, hah! You are here!"

She followed the sound, waving her arms dramatically in hopes of eliciting Peter's giggle. The chase led her farther from Theo's laughter, but she wouldn't give up, not when she was *so* close.

A flapping sound from above startled her to a halt. Peter had led her to the trees. Her attention fell from the pursuit of the boy, and she looked up despite the blindfold ensuring she couldn't anything. Something flew past her, and the flutter of wings made her gasp. She stumbled backwards, and her heel snagged on what she assumed was a thick root. Her flailing arms probably made her look like she intended to take to the sky herself.

Spoiler alert: she was a flight bird.

She never met the ground. Instead, a sturdy hold wrapped around her waist and settled her against a tree. Her hair snagged on the bark, and her hand gripped an arm. A muscular arm.

Peter didn't have arms like that.

The smell of cinnamon and citrus wafted over her. She couldn't see, but the warmth radiating from the duke told her he was close. *Very* close.

Heat spread through her cheeks. "You saved me, Your Grace."

"It seems I have been caught." His muscles tightened as he leaned closer, and his breath tickled her ear. "I thought we agreed for you to call me Luke."

"Not in public."

"Everyone else has gone inside, Theo and Peter included."

"I'm blindfolded. How was I supposed to know that?"

He chuckled. "*Touché.* May I?"

Before she could work out what he meant, Luke's fingers weaved through her hair and fumbled over the knotted fabric. She shuddered. The blindfold fell away, and she became aware of just how close he was. His exhales rustled her hair. Mere inches separated her chest from his. Luke looked down at her, his warm eyes glinting with dappled sunlight.

The air between them felt charged, the moment almost intimate. She'd never experienced anything like it. Her heart pounded, yet she didn't want whatever was happening between them to end.

But it did. Luke pulled away, his expression tight. He took a few steps back, and the distance eased her racing heart.

"Would you care to take a walk with me?" he asked.

"And where are we walking to?"

"Mrs. Townsend informed me that some of the bilberries have begun to ripen." He pointed past the carriage to a hedge. "I thought we might walk there and back. Perhaps sample the fruit. Do you like bilberries, Maggie?"

"Possibly? I don't actually know what a bilberry is?"

He laughed and moved closer to her again, offering his arm. "Then we should fix that."

"How did your talk with Mr. Townsend go?" asked Maggie as they began walking. "Did you get everything squared away for his roof?"

His expression took on a light Maggie had never seen, one filled with pure excitement. "We did. The work will begin in a month or so, leaving plenty of time before winter comes. I'll need to visit my other tenants as well. We had several harsh storms last winter. There are likely more in need of repair. But that is a matter for another day. Mrs. Bielle will wish to return to her work."

"Is she enjoying her visit with Mrs. Townsend?"

They stopped in front of the bilberry bush, and Luke plucked a few dark berries for her. "I believe so. I thought I'd give her as much time as she wanted. It's not often she gets to visit with others."

"You really do have a soft spot for her. She's nothing like I imagined for a housekeeper." She tossed one of the berries into her mouth and grimaced. "These are more tart than I expected."

Luke smiled and began searching for more. "She is an interesting woman. Mrs. Bielle grew up in France, the daughter of a wealthy gentleman. I do not know the specifics, but at some point the family fortune was lost. She moved to England and eventually found a place as my mother's lady's maid. She's been with our family ever since."

"That definitely makes more sense. She was raised as a lady and still acts like one." She elbowed his arm. "Especially when she chides you."

"She certainly takes no issue with doing that."

Maggie shrugged. "You probably deserve it most of the time."

Luke chucked a bilberry at her, and Maggie gaped. "Don't be wasteful, Your Grace."

"Indeed." Mrs. Bielle's voice rang over the hedge. "Mrs. Townsend intends to make a pie with those. Come along, the two of you. I have work to do."

The duke threw another berry at Maggie as she walked past him to follow the housekeeper. She wrinkled her nose. "You're proving my point."

He responded with a cheeky grin. Every time he smiled like that, a bubble of happiness exploded in her chest. Luke made her forget about her problems, about being stuck in a time that wasn't her own. He made her forget about the pearls and her fears about finding a new place.

Instead, a new fear had taken hold of her—one that involved the gradual loss of her heart and what would happen should Luke learn the truth.

Chapter 13

Suffolk, 1815

L uke stared down at the ledgers on his desk. He had made little progress in checking over his steward's notes, his mind decidedly elsewhere. The duchy needed a duchess; he needed an heir. There was no avoiding those things, and duty demanded he see to the matters.

Until recently, he would have protested—argued his accumulated reasons why marriage could wait. Maggie had changed that, and he doubted she even realized how much her falling into his life had affected him. Confessing his deepest fears to her had been both a relief and a burden. She had not judged but instead offered comfort, guidance, and understanding.

He firmly believed she would keep her word and not reveal his fears to anyone. Their discussion had provided him clarity—he wanted a companion in whom he could confide when the rest of

Society only wished to steal his time, money, and influence. Luke wanted a wife who would share the burden of his title and position.

Days ago, he would have thought finding such a woman impossible, but Maggie seemed to understand him in a way no one else could, and his growing attraction to her only steered his course. He wished to court her.

But that presented a problem at present. Luke had not found her family, and he wanted to do things properly. How would her father feel if he discovered Luke had begun courting his daughter without first granting his permission?

Especially when Luke was currently playing the role of her guardian. Society would certainly frown upon it.

A knock at the door drew him away from his troublesome thoughts. "Enter!"

The door opened, and Mrs. Bielle entered the study, her demeanor still somewhat reserved after yesterday's argument. Guilt constricted his chest for having bruised her feelings, but he would only tolerate so much nagging, even if he did care for the woman a great deal.

"Mrs. Bielle," said Luke. "Did you need something?"

"I went into town, and you will not believe the rumors drifting about."

Luke's stomach flopped. "What sort of rumors?"

The housekeeper gestured to the hallway as though that would explain everything. When he only titled his head, she continued, lowering her voice to a whisper. "About Miss McCarthy...and *you*. I told you people would notice your purchases. Hats, gloves, gowns—the entire community is in an uproar over it."

"How do they know for whom the purchases were made?"

"You know as well as I do that staff between houses talk. This should come as no surprise. Not everyone is loyal enough to keep their tongues under lock and key."

Luke heaved a sigh. Yes, he had known word would escape eventually, but he had also hoped to locate Maggie's family before then. Did this mean he ought to arrange for her to stay somewhere else? It had been the plan all along, but...

"What do you intend to do?" Mrs. Bielle took a step further into the room and closed the door, leaving only the barest of cracks. "I am not blind to your attentions toward her, Your Grace, and seeing you happy brings me no greater joy, but I do fear for how such rumors may harm Miss McCarthy. I only ask that you keep that in mind while you attend the ball."

Mrs. Bielle's points were valid, of course, but he did not want to attend a ball unless Maggie went with him. There was no reason to go without her when she remained the only lady whose company he desired. He wanted to dance with her, to see the awe that would surely light her eyes under the grandeur of hundreds of candles.

"I will speak with her on the matter," said Luke. "The decision of whether to attend will be left to Miss McCarthy." But he certainly hoped she chose to do so.

Mrs. Bielle nodded. "Then I suppose I had better work on altering her dress."

She started to leave, and Luke stood, his chair screeching against the floorboard in his haste. "Mrs. Bielle?"

The housekeeper halted and turned to face him. Luke swallowed. The two of them did not always agree, and perhaps their differences in station should not compel him to feel sentimental toward her, but he did. He owed her a great deal, and he had never discovered how to properly thank her. He felt the gratitude deep in his soul and yet could not express it as he wished to. Whether it was out of fear or an ingrained expectation to keep his emotions guarded, he could not say. Regardless, the words refused to come.

Luke sighed. "Please bring the dress to me. I would like to give it to Miss McCarthy myself before you make any alterations."

"Very well, Your Grace."

"And...I apologize for yesterday."

Mrs. Bielle's lips lifted into a knowing smile, and Luke suspected that the housekeeper sensed his unspoken gratitude even if he could not vocalize it.

She left without another word. He sat down and slumped in the chair, his head resting against the back. He should wait for word from his contacts before considering a courtship with Maggie, but what if he found her father and they returned to the American continent before he had the chance?

Luke tapped a finger against his desk. He needn't make any decisions now. Once he had studied all options, clarity would present itself. Until then, he could do with some breakfast and the pleasant company of his unexpected houseguest.

MRS. BIELLE DARTED AROUND THE ROOM WITH THE KIND OF energy that only a toddler could possess. It made Maggie tired just to watch. The woman had seemed lighter in her step since last night, which Maggie was grateful to see. She still didn't entirely know what the housekeeper and Luke had argued about the day before except that it somehow involved her.

And she didn't want to be responsible for anything that came between them.

Mrs. Bielle guided her to the vanity and scooped up some pins and a brush.

"You must have a ton of work to do," said Maggie, her tone pleading. "I can take care of my hair."

"Nonsense."

Maggie swallowed against the lump in her throat. "I don't want to be a burden, nor do I want to come between you and Lu—the duke."

There was no hoping Mrs. Bielle hadn't noticed the mistake with the way her mouth lifted ever so slightly. "You have not come between us. I am but a servant, Miss McCarthy."

"That isn't true. The two of you are close. Anyone could see how fond he is of you. I don't want to ruin it."

Mrs. Bielle proceeded to run the brush through Maggie's hair, and she sighed at the way the bristles massaged her head. The woman chuckled. "You will not *ruin* anything. In fact, I believe your presence here is most beneficial."

"How?"

The woman pursed her lips, but a smile hid behind them. "As you said, His Grace and I are fond of each other. Sometimes I forget he is not my own, perhaps taking my motherly instincts too far. I merely wish to see him happy, and you help achieve that end."

She said no more, moving from one side of Maggie's head to the other as she pinned her curls into a simple coiffure. The silence left Maggie to her thoughts, specifically focused on Mrs. Bielle's statement about her making the duke happy. It shouldn't have made her heart beat the way it currently insisted on beating.

She rubbed a hand over her chest, as if that would fix the problem. "I've done nothing but add to your work, and the duke has wasted precious time searching for my father."

"You are not a waste of time, dear. And believe me, if that man didn't want to help you, he would find someone else to take on the task. I know how stubborn he can be when his mind is made up on something."

The mirror reflected Mrs. Bielle's frustration, and Maggie chuckled. She spoke of Luke as if he were her own child, and even in her irritated state, her tone exuded tenderness and revealed how much she cared for him.

Mrs. Bielle pulled Maggie from the padded chair and looked her over, beaming. "You look lovely, though I cannot claim any responsibility for it."

"You're too kind, Mrs. Bielle."

She swatted the comment away. "Come, dear. Time for breakfast."

They followed the hallway to the stairs, and for the first time, Maggie didn't hesitate to descend to the first floor. She'd spent too much time worrying about appearing odd or using the wrong words, and weighing herself with those concerns hadn't stopped her from sounding foolish. Luke seemed to find her peculiarities intriguing and, often, amusing.

Luke stood outside the breakfast room, leaning against the wall in a navy waistcoat with his arms folded. The gold buttons drew her gaze up to his neck where his cravat had been tied. He straightened when he saw her, and a smile tugged his lips up on one side. Her stomach fluttered. Was he waiting for her?

"Good morning, Miss McCarthy," he said, bowing. "Mrs. Bielle."

She and the housekeeper both dipped into curtsies.

"Have a pleasant morning, Your Grace." Mrs. Bielle's eyes darted between him and Maggie, a mischievous look filling her expression. "Though I am certain you do not need my encouragement to do so."

With that, she continued down the hall, and Luke waited until the housekeeper had disappeared before turning to face Maggie. "It seems I owe you another debt."

"For what?"

"Mrs. Bielle's improved spirits." He stepped closer. "I must know your secret. What did you do to make her more amiable?"

Maggie shook her head. "Telling you would betray her trust. A friend would never do that." Not that she had done anything. At least not that she could figure out.

Luke leaned forward until his lips hovered next to her ear, making her pulse erratic. "I do not believe it counts if you tell your confidant, Maggie."

Shivers crawled across her skin, and she looked around before whispering her response. "It definitely counts when my confidant intends to use my answer for nefarious purposes, *Luke*."

"Nefarious?" He pulled away in laughter. "You wound me with your accusations."

"You don't appear to be bleeding. I think you'll survive."

"That would depend on your definition of survival."

She started to question what he'd meant by that, but a knock at the front door drew their attention. Down the hall, the butler welcomed a gentleman inside, who immediately removed his black beaver hat and passed both it and his walking cane to the servant.

"Much appreciated, Mr. Tolley," the man said to the butler. "Now, might I ask—" He stopped short as he turned and spotted the two of them standing in the hallway. "Ah! It seems I have no need to ask. He is conveniently standing right in front of me."

"Perhaps I should take that as my warning to hide in my study," said Luke. "A visit from you at this hour is troublesome indeed, Branbury."

"Your Grace, you offend me. I am never trouble."

Luke scoffed. "I can think of countless moments that prove otherwise."

The man chuckled and shifted his attention to her. "Well now, who do we have here? I heard rumors of you holding a young woman hostage."

Hostage? Well, that didn't bode well.

Luke's brows furrowed. "Tell me that is not what you actually heard."

The man shrugged. "I exaggerate, but do not withhold an introduction because of my mischievousness."

"Very well. May I introduce Miss Magdalena McCarthy," said Luke, gesturing to her. "Ma—Miss McCarthy, this is Nicholas Betham, Earl of Branbury."

Curiosity flickered in the earl's green eyes. An *accusatory* curiosity. Had he noticed Luke's almost mistake? Perhaps they shouldn't have given each other permission to use their first names.

"A pleasure to meet you, Lord Branbury," said Maggie, dipping into the formality she was quickly growing accustomed to. At least her knees didn't wobble anymore.

Lord Branbury took her hand and brought it to his lips. "The pleasure is mine. Do feel free to call me Nicholas, though."

Fudge. He'd noticed.

Luke gripped the earl by his collar and pushed him away. "Enough. You needn't flirt with every woman you meet, and I will not allow you to badger my guest."

"You mean your hostage," said Lord Branbury, still holding her hand. He lowered his voice, but still spoke loud enough for anyone in the vicinity to hear. "Tell me, are you in need of rescue from the most boring duke in England's history? I am happy to volunteer."

She yanked her hand away. Judging by the way the earl's eyes kept flicking to Luke, the man merely meant to get a rise out of him, and she wanted no part in it.

Maggie folded her arms. "The only person I need rescuing from at the moment is you, and His Grace is far from boring. I've enjoyed his company. Whether I could say the same of you is debatable."

Lord Branbury placed his hand over his heart, feigning shock. "My *sincerest* apologies, Miss McCarthy. My friend had not made me aware he possessed such skill in woo—"

"Shall we excuse ourselves to the drawing room?" asked Luke, pinning the earl with a death glare. "I presume that you are in need of my assistance to get you out of trouble again. I can think of no other reason for you to call this early when you rarely rise before noon."

Lord Branbury heaved a sigh. "I am in need of advice but admit you were not my first choice to ask." His gaze settled briefly on Maggie, and then he smirked. "However, it seems you may not be such a bad option after all."

Luke glanced heavenward. "Have you made a mess with Miss Garrick again?"

"*Lady* Garrick, unfortunately. She has banned me from the estate."

"Were you not already banned?"

Lord Branbury scratched the back of his neck. "Yes, but she seems rather serious this time."

"Pray tell, what did you do?"

Lord Branbury started for the drawing room. "I have insulted her. She kept prattling about the necklace Lord Garrick reaped at some gaming hell on King Street. Something about winning a game of whist against a drunkard if the woman is to be believed. I may have questioned the legitimacy of the claim in front of a few people. We all know Lord Garrick isn't the brightest of sorts, nor does he often win at anything."

"What sort of necklace would make Lady Garrick insistent on bragging?" asked Luke as they reached the entry.

"Apparently, one made of lovely pearls."

Suffolk, 1815

Maggie sucked in enough air to fill the Hindenburg. The paintings that hung on the walls appeared to tilt, making the one of the shore and waves look as though it were about to fill the hallway with water.

Pearls. Drunkard. Coincidences happened, but this...*this* couldn't possibly be purely happenstance. Could it?

She'd assumed Lord Doxly had taken a trip through time to who even knew where...or when. The whole thing made her head hurt.

She gripped the door frame as Lord Branbury and Luke filed into the drawing room. The duke made it halfway to the sofa before turning to look over his shoulder. He rushed back to her the moment he noticed she hadn't followed.

His hands settled on her shoulders, their weight strangely comforting rather than a burden. "Maggie, are you unwell?"

"Just a little dizzy, that's all."

"I will have someone call for Doctor—"

"No." She couldn't have them calling the doctor now. She needed to find out more about the pearls. This might be her only chance of getting home. "I'm fine. I just need to eat something, I think." She glanced up at him and lowered her voice. "My heirloom is a pearl necklace."

Luke's eyes widened with understanding. "I see. Mr. Tolley." Luke gestured to the butler, who stood next to the front door. "Please have someone bring a breakfast tray to the drawing room."

The butler bowed and disappeared down the hallway. Luke dropped his hands. "Come sit down."

She nodded and made her way over to the floral-patterned sofa, intensely aware of Luke's soft touch on the small of her back as he walked a pace behind her. Lord Branbury watched her sink into the cushions. She half-expected the man to tease her, but his expression mirrored the duke's concern.

"Are you sure you are well, Miss McCarthy?" asked the earl. "You do look rather pale."

"Miss McCarthy has been through quite the ordeal." Luke took the place beside her. His leg pressed against hers, and he remained close despite the extra room on his other side. Where once the proximity would have left her anxious, she now welcomed it. Something about his presence calmed her. While Luke gave Lord Branbury all the details of her rescue and how she'd come to be a guest in his home, Maggie gathered her composure.

"It's been a very long week," she said. "And His Grace has been so kind to let me stay here until he's located my father."

"Miss McCarthy is from the American continent," said Luke. "Philadelphia, to be exact."

"Ah! So that's where the adorable accent hails from, then? You must be careful. Something so unique and endearing will attract all sorts of suitors."

Maggie shook her head. "Adorable is not how I would describe my accent or my turn of phrase. More like ridiculous and totally weird."

Lord Branbury cocked his head to one side. "Well, I disagree. I've known you but a few minutes, and already I'm intrigued."

He wriggled his brows, and she laughed. Luke slide his arm along the back of the sofa, spreading warmth down her neck and over her shoulders. "Must you constantly act a cad? Maggie nearly faints, and you continue to flirt."

Twice now he'd called her by her first name in front of the earl. She didn't think Luke even realized he was doing it, but the smirk on Lord Branbury's face suggested he'd noticed.

The earl scooted to the edge of the dark green armchair he sat in and leaned forward with his elbows on his knees. "You see what I mean, Miss McCarthy. His Grace is positively no fun. You could not have been in earnest in saying you enjoy his company."

"Did my nose grow?" asked Maggie. "Why would I lie about that?"

"No, your nose does not appear to have grown," he responded with slow, confused hesitation, each word drawn out with the pinching of his brows and a bemused smile. "What *exactly* do you like about His Grace?"

The grin he'd maintained this entire conversation fell slightly. The subtle shift in his expression held a seriousness to it that made her pulse quicken. Did he suspect something more than friendship existed between her and the duke? Should he?

To her relief, a maid entered the drawing room. She placed a tray of bread, cakes, and a steamy beverage on the table between them and then curtsied without a word before striding off. Maggie grabbed a cake and fought the urge to stuff the entire thing in her mouth.

On second thought, she might avoid answering the earl's question if she had her mouth full.

Lord Branbury waited patiently while she scarfed it down but stole the second cake from her hand when she reached for it. "I realize you need to eat, Miss McCarthy, but I would still like an answer."

What was she supposed to say? She liked Luke, perhaps more than she should, and admitting that would only fuel the earl's taunts. Refusing to answer might offend the duke. She groaned inwardly. Why had she allowed Lord Branbury to pull her into this pit of demise?

"His Grace is kind and generous." He'd saved her after all. Lord Branbury couldn't possibly make more of that.

The man's wicked grin returned. "Anything else?"

Luke stiffened next to her. Did he anticipate an answer that he wouldn't like? Surely he didn't believe the earl's words? That he was boring? Maggie lifted her chin. If Luke needed reassurance, she'd give it to him.

As his confidant, it was her duty.

"His Grace is also thoughtful, intelligent, and easy to talk to. He makes me smile and laugh. I can think of very few people I've connected with in such a short time. He's a wonderful listener and knows how to prioritize the things that matter most. After paying a visit to one of his tenants with him yesterday, I can honestly say he cares for his fellow man and does everything in his power to help those under his charge."

She took a deep breath. If she wanted this conversation over and to move on to more important matters, she needed to put the earl in his place. A man like him would only back down if his pride took a blow. "His Grace is also the most attractive man I've met since coming to England."

LUKE'S STOMACH LURCHED. MAGGIE THOUGHT HIM ATTRACTIVE. Her bold statement should not have surprised him given how many times he had watched her appreciative observance of his form, yet the words thrilled him all the same.

"My word, Avendesh. She leaves no one to guess at her opinion, does she?" Nicholas slouched in his chair. "Miss McCarthy, you stabbed me deeply with that last comment." He grimaced in mock pain and gripped a handful of fabric over his heart. The man had a thing for theatrics, but his subtle smile gave him away. Nicholas enjoyed sparring with her, and Luke could hardly blame him. He did, too.

Maggie turned toward him, and he wondered if his face was as red as it felt. "You flatter me too much, Miss McCarthy, but I do appreciate your compliments."

She shrugged. "You're welcome, but don't go getting an ego like your friend, Lord Branbury."

"Miss McCarthy, you are completely savage!" said the earl. "Avendesh, you must keep this one. She is surprisingly tolerable. Of course, there is the added benefit that she actually likes you."

Luke glared at him. "Yes, it is *so* shocking that someone besides you might enjoy spending time with me."

"That is no one's fault but your own. Perhaps if you did not sulk about in ballrooms with such a fearsome scowl and refuse to be even a little personable, I would not have to be surprised by this lovely woman's admission."

Maggie glanced at Luke, grinning. Her shoulders lifted with her innocent *he-is-not-wrong* look. Which happened to be too adorable to cause any offense, but he made a show of it with a feigned scoff anyway. "It is a miracle I manage to keep either of you around."

Nicholas scooted to the edge of his seat, his expression promising more mischief. "Would you like to know how? Do you want to know what *I* like about you?"

"Do tell."

"I like..." The earl took a deep breath, and his mouth hung open in a dramatic pause. "Nevermind, that is someone else. I'm afraid I have no answer."

The three of them laughed. At least his friend had put Maggie more at ease. She shifted, and the movement caused her shoulder to first brush against his arm, which rested on the back of the settee, and then his fingers. The resulting chill that raced through his body nearly made him shudder.

"I believe you were going to tell us about Lady Garrick and a pearl necklace, my lord," said Maggie.

"Ah, yes. As I said, Lady Garrick mentioned that her husband won it in a game of whist. I had happened upon the family in town and stopped to offer my greetings to Miss Garrick—"

"Of course you did," said Luke with a smug smile.

Nicholas narrowed his eyes. "Anyway, I told the woman the story sounded unbelievable. Even if it were true, only someone of poor taste would brag about winning from a drunkard."

"And I suppose you offered your opinion on the matter aloud."

The earl leaned back and rested his ankle on the opposite knee. "I may have said that word for word. Lady Garrick rescinded my invitation to her ball on Friday. I need you to fix it."

"Fix it? What makes you think I have the ability to do so?"

"Your title, for one. And the fact that Lady Garrick likes you." His eyes shifted to Maggie, who seemed to be deep in her own thoughts. Nicholas lifted his brows and pinned Luke with a look. "That may change soon enough, though."

There was an accusation in those words, one mere weeks ago he would have fought to deny, but Nicholas knew him too well—knew Luke had started to lose his heart to the woman at his side. Every minute she consumed a little more of it.

"Perhaps," said Luke, careful to avoid a full confession. "But regardless, the best I could do is ask her to reissue the invitation. That does not solve your problem in perpetuity. You need to fix things with the viscountess yourself."

"Do you hear this, Miss McCarthy?" asked the earl, gaining her attention. "He insists that I solve my own problems. What sort of person leaves his friend in dire need?"

"I am not speaking to Lady Garrick on your behalf." Luke dipped his chin and muttered. "I would rather not speak to her at all."

"Why are you so adamant about attending the ball, Lord Branbury?" asked Maggie.

"You mean besides all the handsome women?"

Luke shook his head and folded his arms. "He will never admit to it, but there is one woman in particular he wishes to see. She also happens to be the only one who refuses to flirt with him...or at least she was." He winked at Maggie, and she grinned.

Nicholas ran his hand through his sandy blonde locks and stood. "I have no idea what you are on about. They all flirt with me. Just because you are jealous—"

"I am certainly not jealous," Luke defended.

"You would be if Miss McCa—"

"Enough, Branbury. This is hardly an appropriate discussion to have with a lady present."

Nicholas darted around the table and dropped to his knees in front of Maggie. Luke stiffened when the earl grabbed her hand and she gasped. Why did the man insist on provoking him?

"Miss McCarthy," said Nicholas, "should I find myself permitted to attend Lady Garrick's ball, would you do me the honor of a dance...or perhaps two?"

Luke resisted the urge to clench his fists. That Nicholas had his gaze firmly set on him instead of her confirmed he wished to rankle him, and he would not give in to the man's antics.

Maggie leaned closer to the earl. "I think you'd better focus on winning Lady Garrick's favor. How do you expect to win Miss Garrick's heart if you don't?" She ripped her hand from his grasp, and his stunned expression nearly made Luke laugh. She tucked her hand deep into her lap. "As it stands, neither of us have an invitation, making this discussion pointless, but even so, my answer is no.

"Now, if you want to attend the ball, then I'd suggest you apologize to Lady Garrick. Take her some flowers and tell her you were a fool. And if you really want to earn her forgiveness, tell her you become flustered around her daughter and say things you normally wouldn't...even if it's not true."

Nicholas grimaced. "It would not be entirely inaccurate. Your advice does seem rather sound."

"Would you like another piece of advice?"

"I am not certain, but tell me, regardless."

"Ask Miss Garrick for the first dance."

He scowled, and she gave him a cheeky grin. Luke found himself resenting his lack of participation in this playful conversation. Perhaps he was a bit jealous.

"The two of you deserve each other," said the earl. "Presumptuous co-conspirators." He stood, restoring his passive expression as he faced Luke. "If I am to get no help from you, then I suppose I must be on my way."

"And where are you going, exactly?" asked Luke, watching his friend march for the door.

Nicholas stopped and grinned. "To see the florist, of course. Good day, Your Grace." He dipped into a bow, flourishing his hand dramatically. "Miss McCarthy, it was a great pleasure to meet you. The two of you stay out of trouble."

Once he'd disappeared, Luke heaved a sigh. "I apologize for him. He is a bit..."

"Ostentatious?" Maggie offered when he couldn't seem to decide on a word.

"That may be putting it lightly. It sounds as though we have found your heirloom, though."

"Possibly. I won't know for sure without seeing it."

"If you would like, I can secure you an invitation to the ball."

He held his breath as he waited for her response. In a way, learning of the heirloom worked to his benefit. It gave Maggie more reason to attend.

And he very much wanted her to accompany him.

Her eyes widened for a moment, as though whatever thoughts stirred in her mind were frightening, but when she met his gaze, her expression softened. "That's probably a good idea."

He smothered his excitement. Barely. "I will send word to the Garricks straight away. I have no doubt they will humor the request."

"How can I ever thank you? You've done so much for me."

"You are most welcome. I hope Lord Branbury has not exhausted you too terribly. He is not the only person calling today."

"Oh?" said Maggie. "Who else are you expecting?"

"Dinner guests, and I'm looking forward to introducing you to them."

His stomach flopped when she smiled.

"Then I look forward to meeting them, Luke."

Suffolk, 1815

fter dressing for dinner, Maggie sat in one of the armchairs near the empty stone hearth in the drawing room, her eyes glued to the pages of a book. Luke had given her permission to take advantage of his library, perhaps one of the most glorious things she'd ever seen. Though she'd had one growing up, it paled in comparison to the duke's collection. Something about the antique bindings held a beauty that modern publishing had lost. She could spend a lifetime in that room and never get bored.

Despite the extensive array of options, most of which she'd never heard of, she'd chosen an old favorite. Besides, reading *Pride and Prejudice* would prove more than entertaining. The reminder of how she needed to speak and act in this era was a necessity.

"Are you enjoying your book, Maggie?"

She jumped, and her eyes flicked to the man in front of her. Luke's smile immediately sent her heart into a robust rhythm. Apparently, he need only enter the room for her to get a workout.

"I am." She set the novel on the side table next to her. "Thank you for giving me permission to explore the shelves in the library, Your Grace." His brows knitted, and she chuckled. "Sorry, *Luke.*"

"Much better. For a moment I thought I'd lost your favor. I would have blamed Lord Branbury, of course."

"It will take far more than Lord Branbury for you to lose my favor."

"A comfort to know, especially when I have a bit of unfortunate news. I received word from several of my contacts this morning. Not one of them has heard of your father, I'm afraid."

Maggie feigned disappointment. She'd known he wouldn't have any luck, and the guilt of wasting his time twisted her stomach. She hated lying to him.

Luke sat down on the sofa next to her armchair. "I have not given up. I promise to find him."

He promised. The sincerity in his eyes might eat away at her until nothing remained. Luke leaned forward and took her hand. Her fingers curled around his in a natural response that required no thought, and the light squeeze he gave them sent a ripple of shivers through her.

"Maggie," he said softly. "The gossip created by you staying here...I will not stop searching for your family, but having Mrs. Bielle as a chaperone may not be enough to keep your reputation intact."

Her heart thudded so loudly she was certain he could hear it. Where would she go? He couldn't look for her family forever, nor could she, in good conscience, allow him knowing he would never find them. And what about the pearls?

"What do you want?" she whispered. "Do you want me to go? I understand if you—"

"No." His hand tightened around hers. "That is not what I want, but I also do not wish to ruin you, especially out of selfishness. I enjoy your company, but that is not worth so great a risk to you. Perhaps I should have arranged for you to stay elsewhere sooner. That would have been the proper thing to do, but I cannot...it is not a decision I regret."

Conflict warred in his expression. He truly didn't want her to leave, and warmth blossomed in her chest, a kind she'd never experienced before. Lord Branbury's visit had given her hope of returning home. Days ago she'd have traded anything to get her old life back, but now...

Luke's free hand moved to her shoulder, and his thumb caressed the fabric of her dress. "Please do not cry. I only wish to protect you."

"I know. It's just that..." She wanted to tell him everything. But how could she? He would never believe her. "I don't care about my reputation. When I return home, it won't matter what society here thinks of me. I don't know anyone beyond the people in this house and Lord Branbury. I feel safe here. What I'm asking...I know it isn't proper—"

"Consider it done." His throat bobbed with a hard swallow, and he squeezed her hand again. "If staying makes you feel safe, then stay. I already said you were welcome here as long as you needed. The devil with what society thinks." His eyes widened. "Pardon my language."

She laughed and shook her head, the sting of her sorrow melting away. "Don't worry; I've heard much worse."

"Your father may not be fond of this decision," said Luke. "I do not wish to—"

"My father will be more concerned for my safety than my reputation, I assure you. He'll not place any blame on you."

His fingers slid from her shoulder all the way down her arm until it found her hand. He searched her face, and she found it difficult to breathe. How was she supposed to keep her distance when he looked at her like that—held her like *this*, as if she were a treasure he couldn't lose?

Luke turned away, wetting his lips. Were his hands trembling?

"Maggie, I realize we have only known each other a few days," he said, keeping his gaze on the floor. "But what if...what if you didn't go—"

Someone cleared their throat from the entry of the drawing room, and Luke pulled his hands away. Mr. Tolley stood inside the doorframe with his hands clasped behind his back. He bowed, and his gray hair fell into his eyes. "Forgive the intrusion, Your Grace, but Miss—"

His words were cut off as a small figure pushed past him, nearly knocking the man into the wooden frame. A little girl in a pale pink dress dashed forward with a wide grin.

"Luke!"

The duke chuckled, jumping to his feet and darting to the center of the room to meet her halfway. He scooped her against his chest, and she wrapped her arms around his neck.

"Miss Halford and Lord Edwin are here," said the butler, a façade of annoyance in his tone. His twitching lips gave him away, though.

"Juliana," said the man entering the drawing room after her. "That is hardly a proper way to greet someone."

His voice was stern, but he also seemed to be suppressing a smile. Maggie took him in. At first glance, she might have missed the similarities between the two men. Luke was taller, and his hair was several shades darker than Lord Edwin's rusty brown. They shared the same eyes, though—deep brown with hints of golden flakes.

Luke set Juliana on the floor and crouched to her height. She couldn't be more than five or six years old. Her flaxen hair had been braided and wrapped into a bun at the back of her head, and when she grinned, Maggie could see a hole where she was missing a bottom tooth.

"Your father is right. That greeting was not nearly proper enough." Luke outstretched his arms, and Juliana dove back against him. He squeezed her so tightly she squealed. "Come with me," he said, taking her by the hand as he stood. "There's someone I wish you to meet."

He led the little girl toward her, and she rose from the armchair. Lord Edwin joined them as well. "This is my niece, Miss Juliana Halford," said Luke. "And my brother, Lord Edwin Halford. May I introduce Miss Magdalena McCarthy?"

Edwin bowed. The little girl smiled bashfully up at her as Maggie curtsied. "Hello, Lord Edwin. Miss Halford. It's a pleasure to meet you."

Juliana shuffled behind Luke's leg, and he chuckled. "She's a tad shy at times."

And adorable. No wonder he doted upon her.

"Luke?" Juliana whispered, tugging at his coat.

The duke leaned sideways, and Juliana mounted on her tiptoes to mumble in his ear. Maggie didn't catch her soft words, but they lit up Luke's expression, and he nodded. Juliana sped across the room and plopped onto the bench at the piano. Her fingers plucked the keys loudly in an aggressive cacophony of chaos that made the three of them laugh.

"I am sorry, Miss McCarthy," said Lord Edwin. "She is absolutely entranced with the instrument. I intend to have her start lessons soon, if not for her sake, then for the sake of my sanity."

Maggie watched Juliana for a few moments. The sounds she created were anything but pleasing to the ear, but her wide grin countered any displeasure that may have come from it. "There's no need to apologize. I'd be a hypocrite to criticize her enthusiasm when ten years ago I acted the same way."

"Do you play the pianoforte, Miss McCarthy?" asked Luke, curiosity burning in his eyes.

She shrugged. "I suppose you could say that. I'm no Mozart, but I thoroughly enjoy playing, much to my mother's dismay."

Edwin's brows furrowed, and Maggie nearly laughed at how similar the two men looked with matching expressions.

"Your mother does not approve of the pianoforte?" asked Edwin. "I thought most ladies were encouraged to pursue an instrument?"

"I don't think it's the instrument she despises, but my choice of arrangements."

This she knew for a fact. Had she stuck to Chopin or Beethoven, her mother might not have minded her playing, but she'd fallen in love with music created for film. She'd spent hours listening to compositions meant to accompany animated scenes or garner more emotion from live-action scripts. She took no issue with pop covers either, but songs meant for the cinema had found a special place in her heart.

"Does your mother have selective tastes?" asked Edwin.

The man had no idea.

"You could say that. Please excuse me." She shuffled past them and ambled over to the piano. Juliana stopped plucking the keys and looked up at her, color filling her cheeks.

"Can I join you?" asked Maggie.

The little girl nodded, and Maggie took a seat next to her. "Do you like to play, Juliana?"

"I do," she answered, her brows furrowing as she pressed on the keys. "But I'm not very good at it."

"You just need someone to teach you and lots of practice."

Luke and Edwin joined them a minute or so later. The duke leaned over the top of the piano, resting his elbows on the lid. His sleeves pulled tight against his arms, exposing the outline of the muscles beneath his coat. Her breath went stale in her lungs.

"Do you want to play?"

Juliana's quiet voice startled her out of her ogling—thankfully.

"I'd love to." Maggie nibbled her lip, her fingers throbbing with the familiar itch to reach for the keys. What should she play? Hundreds of options flashed through her mind, but many of them would be too much for the people in this room.

"Have you forgotten how to play?" asked Luke, his voice filled with concern.

She smiled, hoping it would reassure him. Avoiding Dr. Thistlewaite and his bleeding practices were a top priority and would remain so...forever. "No, I was trying to decide what I wanted to perform. I do have a duke watching me, after all. I need something impressive."

He shook his head. "You do not need a song on the pianoforte to impress me."

Fudge. Why must he say things like that? Her cheeks burned, and for once, she wished she had a bonnet to hide behind. Edwin passed Luke a curious look.

"What was the last song you played?" asked Juliana. "Maybe you should do that one."

"That's a brilliant suggestion," said Maggie, and the little girl beamed. Maggie racked her brain. Her last student, Ann Ixby, had requested to learn the main theme to *How to Train Your Dragon* for a recital. She'd spent hours helping her with the more intricate parts of the piece.

Well, that would have to do. She'd have to adjust a few parts since modern pianos had more range, but that was easily managed.

She dropped her hands to the keys. "Alright. This one is about a boy who trains a dragon."

Juliana grinned, her eyes sparkling with excitement. "A dragon?"

Maggie nodded. "The first thing you need to know about playing the piano...forte is that music is meant to tell a story. Touching the right keys isn't enough. You must use your fingers to express something deeper, something that words alone may not convey. Listen to the sounds; feel what emotion each note invokes like a painting or a poem might make you happy or sad."

Juliana seemed to hang on her every word. She would make a wonderful student.

Drawing a deep breath, Maggie began. Her fingers danced across the keys, slow and quiet before building with fervor. She poured her heart into the melody, allowing the story she knew to guide her. Freedom, happiness, acceptance...love—all the notions the film expressed were reflected in the sounds she created. She used the notes like a vessel for her own emotion—a raw display that left her vulnerable to the spectators who watched her in silence.

Her heart hammered by the time she'd finished, and it took a moment to convince herself to look up from the ivory keys. Juliana clapped, and Edwin joined his daughter with a grin of approval. Luke simply stared at her with an almost trance-like expression.

"That was pretty," said Juliana. "I want to play like that someday."

"I must disagree with your earlier statement," said Edwin. "I think you could give Mozart a run for it. You have great talent, Miss McCarthy."

"Mesmerizing," said Luke, finally finding his voice. "Your performance. I...I have never heard someone play like that."

Edwin gripped Luke's shoulder, his lips pulled into a smirk. "I do not believe it is her playing you are so mesmerized with."

Flames seared Maggie's cheeks. No matter how she tried to deny it, her heart leaped at Edwin's words.

Luke cleared his throat, rubbing his hand along the back of his neck. Before he could respond, a footman appeared in the entry and announced dinner. The duke offered her his arm with a sheepish expression that accurately reflected her own feelings.

She needed to find out if those pearls were her family heirloom, and she needed to do it before losing any more of her heart.

Suffolk, 1815

Dinner with Lord Edwin and Juliana the night before was probably one of Maggie's favorite evenings in 1815 so far. Not only was Juliana absolutely adorable, but Luke seemed far more at ease with his brother and niece around. The duke's interactions with the little girl had only increased her admiration for him.

Maggie ran her sweaty palms along her pale yellow dress as she paced across the drawing room. The tarts she'd eaten for breakfast churned inside her stomach. Perhaps she should have skipped the meal entirely, but she'd hoped eating would distract her for a moment.

It hadn't.

Her mind raced with too many thoughts and scenarios that didn't end well. She'd spent all last night contriving a plan about the pearls. First, the duke would secure her invitation to Lady Garrick's ball. Before she could do anything else, she had to know whether the pearls Lord Garrick had won were hers, although the circumstances seemed too convenient for them not to be.

What she would do if they were her family heirloom was another thing entirely. Assuming they worked like she hoped they did, the pearls could take her home. She could leave all of this behind—trade chamber pots for indoor plumbing and walk outside without a bonnet.

But, she'd be leaving behind Luke, too.

Staying in 1815 was a big risk. She could end up a poor servant or worse. Unless...

Unless she never left Windgate. Her heart gave a happy flutter. The signs were there, each one more unmistakable than the last. The way Luke looked at her, held her, said more than words. How had this happened so fast? The idea petrified and elated her in some chaotic mixture that made her brain fuzzy. The man, who only days ago had confessed his fear of marriage, had grown attached to *her*. Whether he'd fallen completely, she couldn't say, but a yearning deep within her hoped his feelings were headed in that direction.

What did that say about her? Perhaps she was falling. Perhaps...

Trying to sort this out might drive her to madness. Each pass across the room took her closer to one conclusion, one crazy confession—she wanted to stay in 1815 with Luke. She had fallen in love with a duke, and despite her lack of grace and sophistication, he might care for her the same way. She suspected he had wanted to ask her to stay in England before Edwin and Juliana arrived. It would make him happy if she didn't return to the future.

A smile settled on her lips. As scary as the notion was, she felt at peace with the decision. She would stay in this era. She would put her trust in the man she'd come to know and maybe, just maybe, this time travel disaster would turn out to be the best thing to ever happen to her.

That decided, she heaved a sigh.

Regardless of her decision, she still had to find those pearls. She couldn't leave the dangerous beads with anyone else.

And that led to part two of her plan—the part she had little control over and feared the most. How would she find the pearls once she arrived at the ball? Escaping the crowd to pilfer through someone else's things didn't sit well with her. She'd never been particularly good at being stealthy, unlike a certain gentleman who had startled her more times than she could count.

She held her stomach as her insides writhed. This was a horrible idea.

The simplest solution would be to have Luke ask about the pearls on her behalf, but that invoked a whole other set of concerns. What if he touched them? What if the heirloom took him away?

"It will be fine," she muttered. "Luke will ask about them, and I'll make sure he doesn't handle them. I just need a valid reason so he'll actually listen to me."

She glanced at the boxwood wall clock. Luke had taken breakfast in his study but had sent her a note saying he'd come find her once he finished looking over his ledgers. She had attempted to read, but that had proven pointless. Who needed fictional drama when her own life looked like an exploded bag of flour? The only thing missing was a proper villain.

She groaned and made for the piano in the corner of the room. Playing had always calmed her in ways nothing else could. Maggie hadn't meant to impress anyone with her performance yesterday—in fact, she probably shouldn't have revealed the talent at all—but she missed the instrument. She missed modern music.

Sound poured through the room with each key she pressed. She allowed the music to take hold, transcending her into a space of security that freed her from all concern and sorrow. Masterpieces her heart and fingers had long since memorized resounded off the walls, each one calling to memory the images and stories they'd been created for. *Star Wars*, *The Avengers*, *Avatar*—she became lost to melodies that played both in her mind and from the keys.

Her movements quieted as she slowed into the *Jurassic Park Main Theme*, the soothing chords calming her. Staying in 1815 would not be easy, but she couldn't help but wonder if part of her reasoning was based on the opportunity to escape the life planned out for her. Perhaps by choosing to stay in the past, she was avoiding the decisions she needed to make in the future.

LUKE LISTENED TO THE SOFT MELODY COMING FROM THE drawing room with his eyes closed. Many women of his acquaintance could play the pianoforte with precision and skill, but there were few who could infuse so much emotion into their music. Maggie conveyed much with each finger she pressed to the key, and it only furthered his admiration of her.

He entered the room, his arm clutching a large piece of linen against him. He had secured an invitation for Maggie to attend Lady

Garrick's ball, and it was time to present her with the gown Mrs. Bielle had purchased on his behalf.

He stopped in front of the instrument, but she did not look up from the keys, and for several moments he watched her fingers dance across the ivory.

"What is this one called?" he asked once she had finished.

She jumped, and her fingers responded by banging multiple blocks, creating a dissonance that hurt his ears.

Luke winced. "Forgive me for startling you. Is this one about dragons as well?"

"No," she answered, lifting her chin. "It's about a park."

"A park?"

"A park with..." Her brows furrowed with contemplation. "A park with interesting animals."

"What sort of animals?"

"The interesting sort." She leaped from the piano bench, and the new angle allowed her to see what he held. "What's that?"

"A gift for you, actually."

Luke rounded the instrument and offered her the bundle without meeting her gaze. Why did he suddenly feel so nervous? It was only a dress. Of course, gifting a lady a dress certainly went beyond propriety, especially with the lack of understanding between them. Was this a mistake? No, she needed a gown. She simply could not attend a ball and retrieve her necklace without one. But would Maggie think more into the gesture than he'd initially intended? He could not help hoping that she would.

She set the wrappings on the lid of the pianoforte and peeled away the linen to reveal the cream-colored dress. She held it up in front of her with eyes roaming over the ruffled bottom and puffy shoulders while her mouth hung open.

Luke cleared his throat. "I know it is not the most fancy of gowns, nor will the fit be precise. Given the lack of time to have it—"

Her hand fell to his arm and halted the explanation. She tilted her head, the smile she wore making his stomach fill with flutters.

"It's beautiful," said Maggie.

Relief settled over him. She liked it.

"I requested an invitation for you to attend Lady Garrick's ball," said Luke. "I know we decided it was the best way to check on your family heirloom, but even before Lord Branbury mentioned the necklace, I had hoped you would agree to attend with me—er—accompany me. What I mean is that you would go to the ball...with a chaperone, of course. One that isn't me." He tilted his head back and groaned. "I am struggling to express myself clearly again."

She chuckled. "Don't worry. I understood what you meant. And thank you for the dress, but you'll probably regret this. I despise parties, so you have my apologies now if I become moody by the end of the night."

"You dislike parties as well? I daresay we have that in common."

"All the more reason I should thank you. If not for me, you could stay home and enjoy a quiet evening."

"The necklace is important to you. I can sacrifice one evening of solitude." He raked a hand through his hair and stared at the floor. "Also, it provides me the opportunity to ask you to dance. I hope you will forgive me for requesting a set before we've even arrived at Rusgrove Hall."

"Of course, I accept," said Maggie, "but you don't need to feel obligated—"

"Obligated is the last thing I feel." He met her gaze. There was a question in her eyes, one he longed to answer. He stepped forward and leaned close to her ear, whispering, "If I haven't scared you off after the first, I may steal a second, Maggie."

"Fudge," she muttered, the word barely audible.

"Fudge?" Luke reared back. "Do you believe me dishonest?"

Her eyes widened. "What? No. I...in America fudge is a very sweet dessert."

He grinned. He would never tire of her unusual words and phrases. "Am I to understand that dancing with me is comparable to a sweet dessert?"

Her cheeks tinted. "I've no doubt dancing with you will be a pleasant experience."

"Like fudge?"

"Like *chocolate* fudge. Or maybe peanut butter. Both are good."

Luke chuckled. "I shall take your word for it. I cannot say I have ever tasted peanut *butter.*"

"Well, someday you should. Unless...nevermind." She looked at the gown draped over her arm. "Thank you for this, Luke."

The way she said his name, with such reverence and care, sent shivers down his spine. He wanted to offer her his gratitude. How drastically he felt his life had changed since she stumbled into it. His days seemed more complete—more full of purpose and joy.

"Your Grace?" Mr. Tolley's voice sounded from the door, stealing the opportunity. "Lady Garrick and Miss Garrick are here. Are you at home for visitors?"

Luke groaned. He had suspected the woman might impose on him after the request he sent last night. The missive regarding Maggie's invitation had likely shocked the viscountess and stirred her curiosity.

Luke clenched his jaw. He may as well get it over with. "Yes, please show them in. Thank you, Mr. Tolley."

The butler disappeared, and Luke turned to Maggie, prepared to warn her, but the way she stared up at his hair gave him pause. "What is it?"

A hint of a smile appeared before she grabbed his coat lapels and pulled him down. He bent, his eyes round with surprise as she flattened his hair, running her gloved fingers through it until he could only assume it had resumed a more satisfactory state. With his face only inches from hers, his lungs seemed to have forgotten how to breathe.

When she released him, he remained bent in front of her. His gaze fell to her lips, and her breath hitched. He had thought about kissing her before—that afternoon at the Townsends'—but this time the desire threatened to push him into action.

"Your Grace!"

Luke straightened and turned to face the woman charging toward them. His ears burned, but he put on a stoic expression. The woman stopped in front of them, joined moments later by Miss Garrick, and they both dipped into a curtsy.

"Good afternoon, Your Grace," said Lady Garrick. "It is lovely to see you today."

Luke gave her a courteous nod. "A pleasure as always. It is wonderful to see you both."

Miss Garrick clasped her hands at her waist, a shy smile filling her face. Her blonde curls fell over her cheeks when she tucked her chin. Despite the viscountess pushing her daughter into his company on a regular basis, Luke did like the girl. She had a sweet nature about her and the proper poise expected of a young miss of the *ton.*

But he had never connected with her in a more meaningful way. The two of them had even discussed as much on an outing in the spring.

That had not deterred Lady Garrick from insisting they spend time together, however.

"Allow me to introduce Miss Magdalena McCarthy," said Luke. "Miss McCarthy, this is Lady Garrick and her daughter, Miss Katherine Garrick."

Maggie curtsied, and Lady Garrick watched her with the eye of a predator. He swallowed down the desire to sweep Maggie away and hide her from the matron's glare of death.

"So this is the young lady who is to attend my ball?" asked Lady Garrick. "How nice to meet you. I have heard so many rumors about your predicament. I do wonder how many of them are true." She chuckled, but there was little humor in the sound.

"I guess that would depend on what exactly you've heard," said Maggie with perfect politeness.

The matron swatted the air. "You know how the gossip is. Often ridiculous and unfounded. I simply cannot abide it."

Miss Garrick made a face that suggested she did not believe her mother's words. Luke had to agree with her, but perhaps the woman's taste for tittle-tattle could be helpful. "Speaking of gossip, Lord Branbury told me an interesting story about Lord Garrick winning an *exquisite* piece of jewelry not long ago." He flashed her a charming smile. "Is that rumor true?"

The viscountess batted her lashes at him, all too pleased with the question. "Indeed, Your Grace. It is quite an exquisite piece."

"Then I hope you'll grant me permission to see it at the ball." Luke stole a glance at Maggie and gave her a subtle wink.

"I would be delighted to do so!" Lady Garrick gestured to the sitting area. "Might we sit down? I would love to hear more about

Miss McCarthy. Her situation has been the talk of everyone, you know."

"Of course, my lady. I would be happy to set the record straight." He met Maggie's eyes long enough to see if she was looking at him and then sent his gaze heavenward with a sigh. She bit her lip as if to hold in her laughter while Lady Garrick ushered her daughter to the settee. The matron took the armchair across from Miss Garrick, leaving the space beside her daughter vacant. Luke suppressed his annoyance.

Fortunately, Maggie claimed the seat beside Miss Garrick, which gave him leave to claim the armchair next to her. Lady Garrick appeared murderous with her tight brows and pinched expression. Luke nearly guffawed at the display.

The viscountess quickly washed herself of the expression. "Your Grace, I must admit that we expected for you to call on us by now. It has been a sennight since we have seen you."

Only a sennight? It seemed like longer since he attended Viscount Sutherby's ball in London. "I hope you will forgive me. Things have been rather busy, I'm afraid."

Lady Garrick glanced at Maggie. "So I can see. My daughter and I were just discussing how wonderful it would be if the two of you took a ride. She had such a lovely time last spring. Is that not so, Katherine?"

Miss Garrick lifted her gaze from where her hands rested in her lap. "I did have a wonderful time, Your Grace."

Luke returned her sympathetic smile. "I am glad to hear that."

Silence filled the room as Lady Garrick undoubtedly waited for him to offer his company, but he did not feel inclined, and he suspected Miss Garrick had no desire for another carriage ride.

Lady Garrick pinned Maggie with a calculated look. "How long will you be staying with His Grace?"

"I'm not sure," answered Maggie. "I hope not to burden him for long."

"Miss McCarthy is not a burden," Luke interjected. "She will stay until I have located her father. I cannot, in good conscience, do anything less." He shifted in his chair. "And once I have found Mr. McCarthy, I will ask him to stay until he has finished his business here in England."

All three women appeared surprised by his declaration, but the matron took on an especially perturbed expression. "How kind of you, Your Grace. It seems Miss McCarthy is rather fortunate, indeed. I do worry over her reputation, though. A young woman alone in this house with you makes the gossipers' tongues waggle."

"Actually, Mrs. Bielle has been a wonderful chaperone while I've stayed here," said Maggie. "My reputation will survive. I have been very fortunate, all things considered."

Lady Garrick's irritation became replaced with confusion, but Luke had no desire to offer her clarity by explaining Mrs. Bielle was his housekeeper. Let the woman muse it out on her own.

"I would hardly call being attacked by highwaymen and losing some of her memory to be fortunate," said Luke. "But as Miss McCarthy has stated, she has been properly chaperoned."

"Her memories?" asked Lady Garrick. "Whatever do you mean?"

"The situation has left some details about her past a bit unclear. For example, Miss McCarthy can remember that her father is a businessman on errand from Philadelphia but not what sort of business he owns."

Maggie dropped her attention to her clasped hands, her expression riddled with guilt. He wished to comfort and reassure her, but he could not do so with the viscountess in the room.

"And you have found no success in locating her family?" asked Lady Garrick.

Luke shook his head. "Not as of yet, but I have not lost hope in the matter."

The matron's lips curled slightly. "I see. Well, with your connections, I am certain it is only a matter of time. After all, any *real* man of wealth and esteem cannot roam about England undetected."

Maggie shifted on the cushion with obvious discomfort. He needed the Garricks to leave before he ended up doing something brash...like taking her hand. He stood, and all three women followed suit.

"Thank you for visiting," said Luke with a hint of finality that would ensure the Garrick women departed.

Lady Garrick curtsied. "We shall see you in a few days, Your Grace." Her gaze darted to Maggie. "I look forward to seeing you both at the ball."

As they walked away, Luke exhaled. The matron's determination to match him with her daughter had not been something he'd considered when requesting Maggie's invitation. He hoped the viscountess would treat her with civility.

He turned to Maggie, and she offered him a tenuous smile. Regardless, he would do everything in his power to protect her.

Chapter 17

Suffolk, 1815

Mrs. Bielle's foot tapped against the hardwood floor, her slippers creating light thuds that echoed through the hallway. The woman seemed far from pleased about the situation.

"A ball," Mrs. Bielle muttered. "What kind of a housekeeper attends a ball?"

"I'm sorry he coerced you into this," said Maggie. "But I'm also glad. I feel better having you go with me."

The housekeeper patted Maggie's arm. "I'm happy to chaperone you, dear. I merely find there are very few people in this world I like. Lady Garrick isn't one of them."

Maggie couldn't blame her for that.

The day had passed by at an agonizingly slow pace, her nerves on edge not only because of the daunting task of finding her pearls, but also because she'd never been to a ball. Sure, her mother held soirees, but this was different. And Luke had already requested to dance with her—which she had no idea how to do.

Footfalls on the staircase drew her attention. Luke stopped in front of them. His emerald tailcoat hugged every curve of his arms, and she flushed at the thought of him holding her close. Mr. Tolley handed him a pair of black gloves, and he tugged them on before meeting her gaze with a smile. "You look lovely, Miss McCarthy."

He adjusted his coat, and Maggie stared. The man could have been a nineteenth century version of a certain double-o secret service officer. "You look ho—handsome. You look handsome." Her face ignited. Why did she never have a bonnet when she needed one? "And thank you for the compliment, Your Grace."

The corners of his eyes crinkled, but he was kind enough to not tease her in front of Mrs. Bielle and Mr. Tolley. He leaned sideways to catch a glimpse of the housekeeper, who stood directly behind her. "You look lovely as well, Mrs. Bie—"

"Do not waste your flattery on me, Your Grace. I am determined to be angry with you for no less than three days." She turned toward the door, swiping her shawl from Mr. Tolley, whose wrinkles had deepened with his grin. Mrs. Bielle stormed outside, muttering.

"I think you'll be lucky if it's only three days," said Maggie. "She's really irritated."

Luke chuckled, accepting his beaver hat from Mr. Tolley and placing it on his head. Strands of his dark hair stuck out from beneath the edges, and Maggie wondered if it would be completely disheveled by the time they arrived at the ball.

Not that it would do anything to make him less attractive.

"It may take her a few days, but she will forgive me," said Luke. He leaned down next to her ear, rustling the curl that Mrs. Bielle had left unpinned. "She is the only one I trust as your chaperone since I cannot do it myself."

Maggie picked at the invisible lint on her gloves. Moments like this gave evidence to the man's growing feelings. Or at least she thought they did. Perhaps she should test him with a response. "A blessing, I believe. How are you supposed to find a wife if you're following me around the ballroom? That would be counterproductive."

"I'm inclined to disagree. I think it might prove *very* productive."

She stared up at him, noting his playful smile. It didn't reach his eyes, however. Something more lay hidden in their depths, something that flooded her chest with unbridled heat.

She needed a fire extinguisher—their entire relationship needed one—but those hadn't been invented yet. Honestly, she didn't want to put out the flames, anyway. Letting something burn had never been so appealing. Perhaps she was turning into an arsonist.

"You know," she said, "if you keep saying things like that, I'm going to think your intentions go beyond dancing with me."

Luke said nothing, but that smile crept into his eyes. He offered her his arm. "Shall we?"

She accepted, and together they stepped outside. Luke handed her into the carriage. She sat down beside Mrs. Bielle, and with a few taps on the roof of the coach, they were underway.

Rusgrove lay nestled deep in a grove of birch and alder fifteen minutes from Windgate. The grounds were ornamented with an array of white and pink flowers, the garden beds tucked between several small ponds and narrow stone walkways. The sun had set behind the vine-covered mansion, leaving layers of clouds to bask in warm glows of orange. Though not as extensive as the duke's estate, Rusgrove certainly didn't lack in its own grandeur.

Luke exited the coach first before assisting her and Mrs. Bielle. The carriage rolled away behind Maggie as she stared up at the building. Somewhere in those walls might be the one thing that could allow her to go home, yet she no longer had the desire. She would miss her friends, her family, but Luke gave her a sense of belonging she couldn't ignore.

Her gut writhed. Accepting she had fallen for the duke was one thing, but a problem still remained. She'd lied to him, and continuing to do so would rip her apart. He deserved to know the truth.

A warm touch to her arm shook her from her musing. "Maggie, are you well?" asked Luke. "You look pale."

Her mouth went dry, and uncertainty gripped her like a monster bent on dragging her into the shadows. "I...I need to speak with you before we go inside."

Luke's brows pinched, and he glanced at Mrs. Bielle, who swatted at the air. "Do not concern yourself with me. I shall wait here for you. A good chaperone knows when to give her ward space."

The smirk on her face did nothing to ease Maggie's nerves. The woman was far too intuitive for her own good.

Maggie clung to Luke's arm as he guided her around the side of the estate, still within view but out of earshot of the guests that continued to arrive. Her heart pounded.

"Is something amiss?" Luke asked, releasing her arm to take her hand instead.

His warm eyes roamed over her, and the genuine concern she saw in them tugged at her heart. She knew what she wanted, but the situation wasn't simple. He needed to know the truth—the *whole* truth. She refused to take his heart based on a lie.

She swallowed. "There is something I need to tell you."

"There's something I need to tell you as well." With a few steps backwards, he pulled her into the shadows of the trimmed hedges and out of sight of Mrs. Bielle, not that the woman had once looked in their direction. What a terrible chaperone.

Holding both of her hands, Luke tugged her closer, and her heart seemed to think it was time to perform a samba.

She didn't even know how to samba.

He curled his finger under her chin, lifting her gaze to his. She had to tell him. He needed to know before—

The thought evaporated when his lips descended on hers. His mouth moved tentatively, at least it did until she lost control and returned the gesture. One of his hands cupped her neck, while the other glided over her shoulder and down her back until it found her waist. Heat exploded through her body at a level even the sun at high noon in Death Valley couldn't compete with. He brought her closer, his deepening kisses stoking the flames.

Forget the fire extinguisher. It would take a Noah-size flood to put this out, anyway.

When she'd wished to escape her life of expectation, she hadn't expected this. She hadn't known the universe would place her in Luke's path. It felt unreal, like a dream too far out of reach to be reality, but each brush of his lips over hers confirmed the impossible.

And she wasn't sure she could risk losing him to the truth.

LUKE HAD NOT INTENDED TO KISS MAGGIE WHEN HE GUIDED her around the side of the estate, but once set upon the idea, his mind had refused to relinquish hold. Then she had returned the kiss and, well, he certainly held no regrets. Kissing her was everything he'd thought it would be and so much more.

Her hand roamed up his chest and found its way to his head. She knocked his beaver hat off backwards, and it fell to the ground as she wove her fingers through his hair. Luke groaned and started to follow her lead, lifting his hand to the curls at the base of her neck, but Maggie grabbed his wrist and yanked it away, whispering between kisses. "Mrs. Bielle will be angry for ten days if you mess up my hair."

"I had best behave then."

And he would...eventually.

His lips sank against hers again, eager to fill the unsatiated desire. Her kisses ignited a fire within him that he was certain nothing could douse.

Nor did he want anything to temper the flames.

When he finally stopped for lack of air, he rested his forehead against hers, his smile wide. "Forgive me. I should have allowed you to go first. What did you wish to tell me?"

Something flickered in her eyes. Not regret, but a hint of that same fear he'd seen there when he found her on the road. Before he could question the reaction, she tightened her hold around his neck. "I realized on the way here that I don't remember how to dance."

He chuckled, enfolding her in his arms. "I suppose no cotillions for you, but a waltz is not out of the question. You do not need to know the steps if you have the right partner to lead you."

"What if someone else asks me?"

"Then we tell them your memory is compromised. All will be well, Maggie. You shall have me and Mrs. Bielle at your defense should the need arise."

Her nose wrinkled slightly. "And where can I find a partner who can lead me in a waltz with such proficiency that knowledge of the steps is not required?"

Perhaps taking the floor with a deficient memory would prove difficult, but he had no intention of losing his opportunity to dance with her. Luke feigned contemplation, humming. "I may know a gentleman willing to take on the task."

She tilted her head and her playful eyes caught a glimmer of moonlight. "Is it Lord Branbury?"

"Oh, certainly not. I think you will find this man much more charming. We should return before Mrs. Bielle grows suspicious, and you can determine this man's level of charm for yourself."

Maggie scoffed, bending down to pick up his hat. Mounting on her tiptoes, she plopped it onto his head and adjusted it until it sat straight. He resisted the urge to pull her against him, and he was likely to struggle with the desire the rest of the night.

Luke offered his arm, and she looped hers around it. "If you don't think she's already suspicious, then you are very naïve, Your Grace."

"Quite the contrary. I was counting on her to be. I think she has a wager going with the other servants."

Maggie halted and stared up at him with wide eyes.

He shook his head, laughing. "I jest, but I do believe she is hopeful for one outcome in particular."

Mrs. Bielle hadn't kept her opinion about them a secret, and for the first time, his own desires mirrored the housekeeper's hopes completely. Any doubt he might have possessed had been washed away with Maggie's kisses, with her touch. He would spend a lifetime showing her how much she had come to mean to him. Starting right now, he would court Magdalena McCarthy, and he did not care if all of Society knew of his intentions.

Chapter 18

Suffolk, 1815

Maggie had never seen so many candles in her life. From the three crystal chandeliers dangling from the ceiling to the dozens of tables covered in them—there had to be hundreds. The wall to her right was lined with tall mirrors, each reflecting the small flickering flames around the room, while the full moon provided slivers of silver light that passed through the large windows on her left. Her eyes wandered over the guests mingling on the intricate chalk arabesque floor. The room had an air about it, nothing like one of her mother's soirees.

Luke guided her through the crowd, her hand nestled against his elbow. He stiffened beneath her hold when Lady Garrick bustled toward them. Several peacock feathers danced atop her head with each step she took. The woman held up her intricately beaded skirts with a firm grip, as if that somehow assisted in maintaining her balance.

"Good evening, Your Grace," said the woman, bobbing a deep curtsy. "A pleasure to see you and Miss McCarthy. Thank you for attending." Lady Garrick's brows knitted together as she leaned sideways to catch a better view of who stood behind them. "And who might this be?"

The woman definitely wouldn't like this.

"My housekeeper," said Luke.

Lady Garrick's face paled. "Your...housekeeper? I am afraid I do not understand, Your Grace."

"Forgive me. You see, Miss McCarthy was in need of a chaperone, so I asked Mrs. Bielle to fill the role for this evening. I hope you do not mind, but if it is a terrible bother, we can return to Windgate."

Lady Garrick unfolded a floral-patterned fan and wafted air to her face. "Oh, no! 'Tis no bother at all. How wonderful that you have such trust in your servants."

"I thank you for allowing the accommodation," said Luke.

The calculated expression on Lady Garrick's face twisted Maggie's insides. "Well, you could thank me by asking my daughter for her first set. I am sure she would be delighted, as would I."

Maggie restrained her eyes from rolling into the back of her head. This woman needed a lesson in subtlety. Luke squared his shoulders. "Very well, I would be honored to dance with Miss Garrick."

"Wonderful! I will let her know. The musicians shall be starting any moment."

Luke plastered on a fake smile and nodded. Maggie held in her giggle until Lady Garrick ambled off to speak to more guests.

"Do you find my discomfort amusing, Miss McCarthy?" asked Luke.

"I'm afraid I do. Will you forgive me?"

He rubbed his chin, and the movement drew her attention to his lips. The memories that resurfaced made her face catch fire. Luke smirked, as if he knew the cause of her flushed cheeks. "I can think of one way for you to earn my forgiveness."

An elbow to his side made him grunt. Mrs. Bielle glowered at him. "Such conversation should not be conducted in a public ballroom, Your Grace. I suggest you wipe that grin off your face before the other guests take notice. It is my duty to keep Miss McCarthy's reputation intact during this ball, and I will not allow you to sabotage my efforts."

"You seemed to have no quarrel about me stealing her away a few minutes ago."

"A few minutes ago, the ball had not yet begun."

Maggie and Luke laughed.

"Do tell me what is so entertaining." Lord Branbury sauntered toward them, already a twinkle of mischief in his eyes. "I feel as though I have missed out on something."

"Indeed you have," said Luke, "and you shall never know what it is."

"I could fancy a guess."

That knowing look in his eyes told Maggie he'd likely guess correctly. Luke seemed to agree because his face tinted, and he tugged at his cravat. "I see you managed to secure a new invitation. What did you do to persuade Lady Garrick?"

"I did as Miss McCarthy suggested," the earl said with a shrug.

Luke cocked an eyebrow. "And she forgave your impertinence so easily?"

Lord Branbury drummed his fingers against his tan pantaloons, and his grip tightened around the glass in his other hand. "It may have required some begging on my part."

"Begging?" Luke's expression shifted into a façade of horror. "An earl—a future marquess—*never* begs. You have shamed us all. Unless, of course, you did so in the name of something noble? Or perhaps for a lady—"

"What the devil are you on about now?" Lord Branbury took a long gulp of the amber-colored drink he was holding, but it didn't conceal the sudden rosiness in his cheeks. Maggie suppressed a laugh. The man was completely enamored. She couldn't help but wonder how Miss Garrick would feel if she knew the man had fallen head-over-heels for her. She found it difficult to picture the shy young woman with someone as flamboyant as the earl, but stranger things had happened.

A few low notes signaled the start of a dance, and Luke heaved a sigh. "I hope you will all excuse me. I have promised myself to Miss Garrick for the next half hour." He leaned closer to her. "I shall be back for our waltz."

Our waltz; not *the* waltz. Her stomach seemed to think it was skydiving.

Mrs. Bielle gave him a gentle shove. "Heavens above, go on before Lady Garrick comes back to abduct you."

Luke weaved through the crowd to the other side of the room where Miss Garrick stood with her mother. The matron looked nothing short of ecstatic. Maggie glanced at Lord Branbury, who had his gaze fixed on the duke and young lady. Jealousy flickered in his eyes as he downed the last of his drink.

"You could always ask her for the next dance," said Maggie.

Lord Branbury turned to her, immediately falling into his theatrics. "Who? Mrs. Bielle? Come now, Miss McCarthy, a woman of such beauty would never accept my offer to dance."

"How right you are, Lord Branbury," said Mrs. Bielle.

Maggie may not have found the earl's flirtatious comments charming, but she could see he was a kind man, and her heart went out to him. "Regret is a chain of lost opportunities. You shouldn't bind yourself because you fear failure. I bet Miss Garrick would love to dance with you."

He lifted his glass to take a drink, only to bring it back down and glare at its lack of contents. "I cannot fail if I do not try, and I can assure you, there is no reason to give any effort to"—his eyes followed Miss Garrick as she bounced to the music—"*that* tonight. Not with Lady Garrick watching."

"Why not?"

"History, Miss McCarthy. A long one. Please excuse me; I believe I need another drink."

His dejected expression as he walked away pierced her heart. What sort of history did Lord Branbury have with Miss Garrick that left him so irrevocably convinced he couldn't even ask her to dance?

The music finally ended over thirty minutes later, and Luke escorted Miss Garrick back to her mother's side. Several minutes passed before he managed to escape.

"How was your dance?" asked Maggie, taking in his irritated expression.

"The dance was lovely. Conversing with Lady Garrick tends to take a toll on me, however."

She attempted to keep a straight face. "I don't understand what your problem is. The woman is *perfectly amicable.*"

Luke huffed. "She might be if she'd quit badgering me with hints of courting her daughter. Neither Miss Garrick nor myself are interested in the woman's notions."

"Does Miss Garrick have her sights on anyone in particular?" She couldn't help herself. Lord Branbury's deflated expression haunted her thoughts. The poor man. She believed his flirtatious demeanor was meant as a disguise. There was more to the earl than he let anyone see.

"Not to my knowledge," said Luke. "She and I have an understanding in regards to each other, but beyond that, I'm afraid I do not know her well. She's quite reserved, at least around her mother."

That had been made clear the day Miss Garrick and her mother visited Windgate. Miss Garrick was quiet, but from what Maggie could tell, exceptionally kind and bright. Perhaps her mother simply overshadowed the girl with her expectations. Maggie understood all too well what that felt like. As well-intentioned as her own mother's actions were to match her with someone who would compliment her family's lifestyle and reputation, they hindered and suffocated her. The sense of inadequacy and disappointment threatened to break her. An innate desire to please her family, one that she couldn't seem to rid herself of, held her back from finding her own potential—from truly finding herself.

Falling into a different century had loosened those chains. If she could help Miss Garrick find that same freedom, she would do so.

Luke glanced around them and then leaned close to her. "Miss Garrick is wearing a pearl necklace."

Her heart leaped. "She is?"

He nodded. "Perhaps you can get a look at it while we dance. Then you will know if it is yours. I hope it is. Approaching Miss

Garrick about the necklace will be much easier than speaking to Lady Garrick."

"Agreed."

The musicians began again, and Luke took her hand. "Are you ready, Miss McCarthy?"

"Not in the slightest, but I trust my charming partner."

Luke's smile eased the dread welling inside her. She'd probably embarrass herself with her lack of skill, maybe embarrass him as well, but somehow it didn't seem to matter. He wouldn't abandon her for not meeting Society's expectations. He'd embraced her for being different—for being *her*.

His hand wrapped around her waist, and Luke lifted her hand above her head. The musicians dove into a charismatic tune, and Luke pulled her closer. Eyes watched them as he glided around the room with her. She stumbled repeatedly, tripping over her own feet and his, each time making him chuckle and tighten his hold on her. Moving alongside him—allowing him to lead her through the unfamiliar footwork—both terrified and exhilarated her. She'd never felt so secure.

"I'm so sorry," she said after stepping on his foot for what had to be the hundredth time.

"Do not apologize. You warned me beforehand, and I regret nothing."

"It's not too late to back out of the next dance."

Luke pulled her a little closer. "I retract my initial request. May I have *all* of your dances?"

"Mrs. Bielle might kill you. She takes her role very seriously. Besides, I thought you had no wish to ruin my reputation?"

He continued to guide her through the steps with perfect timing. "No, not ruin your reputation but make a statement."

"What sort of statement?"

"The most vulnerable kind of declaration I can fathom."

Happiness threatened to envelop her, and the sensation muddled her footwork worse than before. "You and I need to have another conversation without a chaperone, it sounds like."

"A discussion for later, my dear. Right now, I merely wish to enjoy dancing with you. Shall we gracefully flutter toward Miss Garrick and her partner?"

"You are pretty good at stealth mode."

His eyes twinkled with the light of the candles overhead. Luke guided them closer to Miss Garrick and the gentlemen leading her. The couple flitted past them, and Maggie caught sight of the iridescent beads hanging around Katherine's neck.

She knew those pearls.

And she knew what they were capable of doing.

Suffolk, 1815

Maggie's heart pounded, and it had nothing to do with the dance. Her gaze flitted back to Luke. There was no sense in watching Miss Garrick right now. She needed to focus on her footwork...and not falling flat on her face.

Not that Luke would actually let her fall on her face.

When the music stopped, they were both out of breath. Luke leaned down to her ear, whispering. "Well, Miss McCarthy, would you trust your partner to lead you in another dance?"

"I would trust him to lead me anywhere."

That response made him grin. Everything in his eyes told her that had they not been in a room full of people, he would have showered her in kisses again.

"I am honored to be held in such high esteem." His gaze flicked to Miss Garrick. "Did you find what you were looking for during our dance?"

"Yes. They're mine."

He nodded. "Then we should go speak with Miss Garrick, and—
"

"No." She grabbed his arm, and he returned a perplexed expression. "Let me talk to her. I appreciate your help, but I also don't want to overwhelm her. If that doesn't work, then you can step in."

"You mean use my title to coax the Garricks into giving up their new treasure?"

She wrinkled her nose. "Actually, I was thinking your smile. It seems to work wonders on Lady Garrick."

Luke hummed. "I wonder if my smile works on anyone else?"

Maggie turned away. No way was she confessing to that even if her flushing cheeks gave it away.

"Very well," said Luke, not bothering to hide the amusement in his tone. "You speak with Miss Garrick once this set is finished. Until then, perhaps we might enjoy the refreshments."

"Deal."

Luke led her to the spread of decadent-looking treats, and Maggie helped herself to a berry-filled tart. Since the second dance of the set was another reel, they watched the dancers while sipping glasses of lemonade. Twenty minutes passed before the music came to an end, and Maggie zeroed in on Miss Garrick's small frame weaving through the crowd. She turned to Luke, and he gave her a nod of understanding without words.

She squeezed between the men and women conversing in the middle of the room until she reached the outskirts of the now skewed chalk designs on the floor. When she caught sight of Miss Garrick following a gentleman in a burnt orange tailcoat into the corridor, she darted after them and reached the hallway in time to see the hem of Miss Garrick's skirts disappear into another room.

Their muffled voices echoed through the open door as she approached, and she tucked herself behind a potted plant. She'd approach Miss Garrick once the gentleman left.

"I cannot keep doing this, Katherine."

"Why not?" Miss Garrick's voice came out as a squeak, barely above a whisper. "Are you afraid of my mother? She shan't find out."

"Everyone is afraid of your mother," the low voice responded. "I have no desire to incur her wrath. This is the last time."

Katherine sighed, and then deep disappointment resonated in her tone. "Very well. I thank you for bringing me this, Andrew."

Footsteps grew louder, and when the man in the burnt orange tailcoat swept through the doorway, Maggie held her breath. He walked right past her, his attention fixated on his feet as he marched to the empty hallway and back into the ballroom.

What had all that been about?

Maggie zipped out from behind the bushy shrub and into the room. Miss Garrick stood near the window, her nose stuck in the open book she held in her hands. Maggie closed the door softly, and the young woman took no notice of her approach until she was only a few feet away. Katherine squealed, her hands shooting to her mouth. The book fell to her feet, landing on its spine, and bounced toward Maggie. She picked it up, looking over the cover.

"*Letters of Euler to a German Princess on Different Subjects of Physics and Philosophy.*" Maggie glanced at Katherine with raised brows. It wasn't her cup of tea, but to each her own.

Katherine shifted her weight. "May I please have my book back, Miss McCarthy?"

"Of course." She shouldn't ask more. It wasn't her business, but... "Why did that gentleman give you this in secret? For a moment I thought the two of you—"

"Oh heavens, no! Lord Fitzley is a good friend of mine. He often brings me books, or at least, he did. My mother, as you may have guessed, is very particular. If she knew what I was reading, that I..." Katherine met her gaze with pleading eyes. "Please do not tell her. I know it is unusual for a lady to find numbers so appealing, but I—"

"You don't have to worry." Maggie handed the book to her. "I understand perfectly what it's like to feel odd. I'm sorry your mother doesn't understand. It's not fair that women should be excluded from learning about something simply because they are female."

"I wholeheartedly agree." She sighed, her brows bunching. "But it is the way of the things, I suppose."

It was in 1815. Things had changed much in two hundred years.

"Someday, women will be encouraged to receive formal education," said Maggie. "To own businesses and property. Even run for political offices."

"That sounds more like a dream. I wish I possessed your faith in the future."

"Trust me; it'll happen. I know because..."

Katherine tilted her head, curiosity burning in her eyes. It wasn't wise to trust a woman she'd just met with such a big secret, but Maggie was tired of the lies—of holding it all inside. She was bursting at the seams with the need to confess, the truth threatening to make her explode if she didn't release it.

She shifted on her feet. "Katherine, this will sound insane, but I swear to you it's the truth. I know that the world will change, that things will be different, because I'm from the future. When those highwaymen attacked me, they stole my family heirloom, the very pearls you're wearing. The very pearls that brought me here."

Katherine's hands lifted to the beads, and Maggie winced. Every time someone laid hands on those, there was a chance they might be swept away to a different era.

"That necklace brought me to the past," she hurried to say. "When I heard your father won it, I knew I had to get it back. The last thing I want is for you or anyone else to be taken from everything they've ever known."

She held her breath as Miss Garrick studied her for several long moments. "How can I believe such a thing? It is...well, it is impossible."

"I know it must seem that way. Even in my era mankind has not harnessed time. But it's the truth. I have no way of proving it to you. Some people could spew equations and laws of physics that back claims that time travel is possible, but I'm not one of them. All I can tell you is that I'm here."

Katherine looked unconvinced, and that made Maggie's heart pound. This had been a mistake, and she had no idea how to fix the situation. She could regurgitate an endless amount of facts about the future, but that was more likely to make things worse than better.

Perhaps she needed one fact specifically catered to Katherine's interests. Which apparently happened to be physics. She hadn't studied that particular subject during her four years at USC. Frustration gripped her. "What was the purpose of getting a college degree if I can't even think of one thing to say that might convince you? The point of all those required Gen Ed courses was to make me a well-rounded person, yet I've got nothing."

"College? You attended university?"

Maggie blinked. "Yeah. I have a degree in business. My mother owns a major textile company in my time, and she wants me to take over someday. You could say I'm a student of numbers, too, but I don't like them enough to read textbooks in my free time."

"And physics? Did you have the opportunity to study it?" There was a spark of eagerness in her tone. Perhaps physics was the key.

Maggie shook her head. "Opportunity, sure, but I didn't choose it as an elective. In college, I focused my attention on music and that sort of thing, but I did have physics in high school."

"High school?"

"Right. You don't have those. It's the schooling one receives before college. You would have had a governess for the same purpose."

Katherine nibbled her lip. Disbelief still riddled her features, but there was something more there. Something that looked like hope. "Physics has come far, then? In the future, I mean?"

" *Very* far. It isn't exactly a subject I know much about. The only equation I remember is $E=mc^2$. E is, like, energy and the m is mass. C is...something about light. Squared."

Einstein would be so proud of her.

Katherine cocked her head. "Energy and light are related? I am not certain I understand."

"Well, the theory of relativity won't be invented for another hundred years, so I'm guessing it doesn't make sense to you. I mean, it doesn't to me either, and I live like a hundred years *after* it was invented."

Katherine smiled. "Mama said she thought you odd, but I think you are intriguing. Are things truly so different in the future? For women?"

Did Katherine believe her? She hadn't thought the woman would accept the notion easily, but the hopefulness in Katherine's eyes...like somehow the promise that the future would be brighter had touched her soul.

"Yes, women have made great strides," said Maggie. "Being thrown into both the past and a country I've never been to before has been a difficult adjustment for me. I'm not used to so many rules...or at least not these ones specifically."

Katherine chuckled and shook her head, making the blonde ringlets bounce against her face. "You know, telling me how much better things are in the future does not convince me to hand these over to you, Miss McCarthy. The future sounds like an appealing place to live."

"Believe me, the future is better in some ways and worse in others. Besides, the pearls can be dangerous. They could send you to live with cavemen for all we know."

"Oh dear. I certainly do not want that." Katherine's hands moved to the back of her neck and fiddled with the clasp until it came free and the necklace lay loosely across her palm. "What do you plan to do now? Will you go back?"

"At first, I thought going home was what I wanted," Maggie answered. "But now..."

"You want to stay with the duke," Katherine finished with a knowing glint in her eyes.

Maggie's face warmed. "He is a pretty convincing reason to stay."

"Well, I'm happy that you are not leaving. Once you marry him, my mother can stop attempting to force us into a courtship." She wrinkled her nose and shook her head. "The duke is a kind man, but I am content with my studies at present. I'm glad he found you, Miss McCarthy. I do not believe I have ever seen him so happy. Just promise me one thing?"

"Of course."

"You will tell me more about the future. That we can be friends?"

"I would really like that."

Katherine handed her the pearls, and Maggie hesitated a moment before taking them. She would need to put them someplace safe—somewhere no one could accidentally touch them and be whisked through time.

"What in heaven's name is happening here?"

Lady Garrick stood at the door, her hand gripping the knob and fury etched into every inch of her expression. Her gaze dropped to the pearls in Maggie's hand, and she took several steps forward. "What are you doing with those, Miss McCarthy?"

"Mama, she needs them." Katherine darted over to her. "The man Papa won them from had stolen them. They belong to her."

Lady Garrick narrowed her eyes. "Is that so? How convenient, like so much of your *story.*"

"Maggie?" Luke's voice floated in from the doorway. The moment his gaze found her, he rushed to her side. "Are you well?"

"Things are certainly not well, Your Grace." Lady Garrick pointed at Maggie, sending her heart plummeting into her stomach. "We have all been deceived by that vile creature!"

"You are out of line, my lady," said Luke, his voice almost a growl.

Lady Garrick lifted her chin. "It pains me to inform you of this as you clearly have formed an attachment to Miss McCarthy—if that is even her name. I caught her coercing my daughter into giving her a set of valuable pearls just now."

Luke's gaze fell to the necklace in Maggie's hands. "The necklace is hers. She lost it the day she was attacked."

"Oh, I have no doubt she told you that. They may even be hers, but they were not stolen in the way she has led you to believe."

What was Lady Garrick talking about?

The woman continued when no one said a word. "When my husband won those pearls from Lord Doxly, he said the man ranted about how he cared not for losing them. Said he would soon be a wealthy man and would have no need for such a trinket."

Luke clenched his fist. "Your point?"

"We all know Lord Doxly to associate with the worst scoundrels, and with his family fortune all but gone...well, people do desperate things when they face financial ruin. Lord Doxly said he would have more money at his fingertips than he could count in a matter of weeks."

Luke massaged his forehead. "I do not follow your line of reasoning."

The woman puffed herself up to match the peacock feathers on her head. "How better to come into money than to have an accomplice tie themselves to a man of wealth and title? Lord Doxly pretends to attack her, and you, being the kind gentleman that you are, come to her rescue. The act granted her entry into your home...granted her access to *you*."

"What?" Maggie fixed Lady Garrick with an incredulous look. How had the woman even come up with such a far-fetched story? "You can't be serious. You think I made it all up just to marry him?"

Lady Garrick scoffed. "Desperate social climbers will do anything. How much did you agree to give Lord Doxly for his role in this scheme?"

"There was no scheme!"

Lady Garrick ignored her and fluttered forward to Luke's side. "Think on it, Your Grace. She claims her father is a wealthy gentleman, yet you, a man of vast connections, cannot find him or anyone who has even heard of him. Surely, you can see how she has manipulated you?"

"That's not true," said Maggie, her voice cracking.

She met Luke's eyes, and the doubt she found in them knotted her stomach. He searched her gaze, and his uncertainty seemed to deepen with every second that passed. "You told me you wanted to stay because you felt safe with me," he whispered.

"I did—I do. I have always felt safe with you."

"With your money, no doubt," said Lady Garrick, sneering. "People like her, a woman determined to climb the social ladder by any means necessary, will tell you what they believe you wish to hear. She only wants your wealth for herself, and she has put on an act to get it. Tell us how much you were planning to hand off to your co-conspirators after you said the marriage vows."

"Mama," said Katherine. "I do not believe—"

"Do not defend her. She does not deserve it."

"Stop. That is enough." Luke released a shaky breath. He turned to face Maggie. "Did you travel to England with your father?"

She shifted on her feet. She didn't want to keep lying to him, but she couldn't reveal her secrets in front of Lady Garrick, either. If only she'd told him before the ball. "Can we talk about this somewhere else? In private?"

"So you can continue withholding the truth from him?" Lady Garrick snapped.

Luke looked between them, the uncertainty in his eyes making her chest ache. He settled his attention on her, his expression pleading.

Maggie swallowed. "No, I did not come with my father."

Lady Garrick opened her mouth, but Luke silenced her with a lifted hand. "Are you struggling with your memories?"

"No, but—"

"Did you conspire with Lord Doxly to ensnare me?" His voice broke, and the pain in his expression hurt her heart. Luke had confided his fears to her about courting and marriage. He hadn't trusted himself to judge the character and motives of ladies, worried they would only seek his attention for title and wealth. Now he questioned her about the very thing he feared most.

"No," she said as firmly as her emotions would allow. "I would never do that to you."

"But you have lied to me?" He tilted his head, his glossy eyes still hopeful for a different response.

"I did, but not about this. Not about Doxly."

"Maggie, I do not understand. I need the truth."

"I want to tell you, but..." She didn't know how, nor did she know if she should with Lady Garrick in the room, listening to every word with a wicked, pleased grin. If she confessed to time travel, the woman would tell everyone of her insanity. She didn't care about her reputation, but Luke would suffer from it, too. Claims that he'd fallen in love with someone who was mad would make him a laughingstock. She couldn't do that to him.

Luke looked away, his hand over his mouth as he shook his head. She had lost his trust, and reality pressed down on her with the weight of an eighty-story skyscraper.

"Luke," she whispered, reaching for his hand.

He shifted out of her reach, avoiding her gaze. She couldn't breathe. It was as if someone had sucked all the air out of the room. She needed to speak to him alone, but even then, her words may not fix this.

"At least your egregious scheme has finally come to light," said Lady Garrick. With one quick lunge, the woman grabbed the pearl necklace. Maggie's instincts took over, curling her fingers around the beads, but it didn't stop Lady Garrick. She wrenched the piece, and the silk thread snapped, sending pearls bouncing across the hardwood floor like marbles in a pinball machine.

Maggie gasped, watching as they scattered under furniture and rattled against the walls. Her one chance of going home had just exploded. She had thought herself trapped before, but now she truly *was* stuck in 1815.

"Now look at what you have done!" shouted Lady Garrick. "I will call for the constable at once. I will not allow a thief and a liar to tarnish my family's possessions."

In a tidal wave of panic, Maggie's flight response took control. She took one last look at Luke's pained expression and bolted from the room, carrying the pieces of her shattered heart.

Chapter
20

Suffolk, 1815

Tiny, round beads lay scattered over the floor. Luke bent to pick one up and added it to those already in his hand. His body trembled, uncertainty gripping him. He had never felt so betrayed and confused and therefore hadn't the slightest idea how to face the chaos tearing through his thoughts.

He had opened his heart, let down his guard long enough for it to be broken. Maggie's confession had reaffirmed the validity of his fears.

"Your Grace?"

Luke glanced up. Miss Garrick stood over him, her outstretched hand holding a glass jar.

"Here," she said. "You can put the pearls in this."

"Thank you." The words came out choked.

She nodded and passed a quick glance over her shoulder to where her mother spoke frantically to several guests, likely spreading rumors about Maggie to as many people as possible. He had asked the viscountess not to call for the constable. At least not yet. He needed to sort everything out before they went to such extremes.

Maggie had professed to have lied to him, but not about Doxly. Luke still had no idea what she meant. Why else would she put on such a thorough act if not to trick him into marriage?

The thought stung. He had believed her to be different. Luke placed two more pearls in the jar. He needed to confront her.

"I know it is not my place," Miss Garrick began, dropping her voice to a low whisper, "but for what it is worth, I believe Miss McCarthy."

Luke rose, his brows furrowed. "What do you mean?"

"I mean, I do not believe she was consorting with Lord Doxly. She had other reasons for lying to you."

Irritation flared within him. "What sort of other reasons?"

Miss Garrick shook her head. "You should give her the chance to tell you herself."

"I did. She did not take the opportunity to explain."

She heaved an annoyed exhale, her gaze flickering to the ceiling. "Did it occur to you that perhaps she did not wish to tell everyone in this room? You know how my mother is. Secrets are not safe with her."

Maggie had hesitated when he asked for the entire truth. She'd even requested to speak to him in private. Could Miss Garrick be right in that Maggie had simply not wished to reveal everything with an audience? Perhaps he should have taken her somewhere to discuss things, but the entire situation had shocked him out of his wits.

"You care for her." Miss Garrick folded her arms as if the display would keep any argument away. "Even after all this, or you would not appear so sullen. I see no reason why you should not give Miss McCarthy a chance to explain. You will regret it if you do not; I am certain of it."

One might think Miss Garrick was a shy woman until they spent time in her company. In her mother's presence, she refrained from engaging in much conversation, but away from the matron's watchful eyes and intent ears, Miss Garrick became impertinent and sociable. Luke suspected the viscountess tried to hide her daughter's lack of social grace by ordering the young woman to remain silent among peers.

Either way, she was not wrong. His heart ached, and he desperately wished to understand. "I intend to speak with her, assuming I am able to find her."

"Then allow me to help you with these." She crouched to pick up several beads. "There are twenty to be found. How many have you already recovered?"

"Ten so far."

He joined her, and together they searched the room. Once they had finished, he stared down at the jar with renewed determination. He would demand an explanation from Maggie. She owed him that much, and he would not rest until he had one.

MAGGIE HELD UP HER SKIRTS AS SHE RAN DOWN THE DIRT road with nothing more than moonlight to guide her. Her eyes burned, blurring her vision, and her feet ached inside the thin fabric slippers. No matter how much she wanted to stop, to plop down and give in to the emotions raging inside her, she couldn't.

She'd acted like a complete fool.

Luke had given her his trust, and she'd repeatedly betrayed him with lies. But none of it mattered now. She had seen the hurt in his eyes as Lady Garrick laid everything before him to suit her own interests. The woman had wanted her out of the way, and she'd succeeded.

However, she couldn't blame the lady for her predicament. If she'd been honest from the beginning, maybe none of this would have happened. Luke may not have believed her, but at least she wouldn't have broken his heart. How would she ever forgive herself for that?

She wiped away her tears with the back of her hand. A steady throb fired through the arches in her feet with each step. She'd been running for what felt like ages and had little left to give.

Crickets chirped their melodious tunes, and more than once, something rustling in the dark shadows of the woods startled her. She pressed on until Windgate Estate appeared through the trees and, for a minute, stood at the end of the drive, staring down the lane of manicured shrubs as the night ticked on.

What was she supposed to do? Luke would never allow her to stay after what had happened. And her pearls...

Her pearls. She pushed the images of them strewing across the room to the back of her mind. She had decided to stay in 1815, to stay with Luke, but with that plan obliterated and her family heirloom ruined, she had nothing. She had no way of going home.

Her feet carried her without permission toward the estate. She followed the path around the circular drive and bounded up the stairs. This wasn't her home, but it was the closest thing she had to one, and right now she needed to feel the safety its walls provided. Would Luke call the constable to drag her off when he found her here? She wouldn't blame him if he did. He seemed to believe the things Lady Garrick had said even if they were only half based in truth.

Despite the prospect, she knocked on the door. After a few minutes, Mr. Tolley answered, exhaustion riddling his wrinkled face. It twisted to concern when he looked her over, but he didn't deny her entrance. Why would he? The butler had no reason to do so—not yet. The rest of the servants had all gone to bed at this late hour, not expecting the duke home until well into morning. She tiptoed up the stairs and into her room. One flickering candle sat on the desk, likely lit to await her return. She curled up on the bed, allowing her sobs to finally break over her cheeks without restraint.

The comfort she garnered was short-lived. Clopping and the grate of carriage wheels sounded outside her window. She jumped up and rushed to the glass. She watched the horses come to a stop. Luke exited first and waited just long enough to hand Mrs. Bielle down before running toward the front door.

Maggie wrapped her arms around her midsection, holding her breath while she listened for the click of his boots against the stairs. The sound froze her heart, each one growing louder until he appeared in the frame of her open door.

He stared at her for several long moments before crossing the threshold and coming to stand a few feet in front of her. Luke extended his arm and offered her a tall glass that looked like a vase. Over a dozen tiny beads rested inside it. His pained voice carried to her ears. "Your pearls."

She accepted them, useless as they now were. She supposed she could sell them if nothing else.

Luke looked as though he longed to say more, but he didn't, instead scanning her face, his mind clearly searching for a way to approach the impending conversation. He took several steps backwards as if needing to put distance between them.

"I was never interested in your money or your title," said Maggie. "I did lie to you, but not in the way Lady Garrick accused. Not in the way you think I did."

"Pray, tell. How did you lie to me then? And perhaps try the truth this time. I am quite tired of being beguiled."

Her grip tightened around the glass. She had no reason to fear explaining everything now. She'd already lost him, but dread still clawed its way to the surface. "These pearls have been in my family for generations. When those men attacked me, they took them. Then I woke up here." She glanced around, the memories of waking up in a strange room flashing through her mind. It seemed like so long ago. "I was scared. And desperate. When I realized where I was—*when* I was—"

"When you were? What do you mean?"

She met his gaze. Bewilderment had replaced his frustration, but he remained rigid, his defenses fortified against her. She sucked in a deep breath. "When I asked Mrs. Bielle the year, I realized I had...I had traveled through time. My pearls transported me here from the future, Luke. That is why you could not locate my father. That is why you find the way I speak, how I act, so strange."

Luke shook his head, a humorless laugh escaping his throat. "You must really think me a fool, and after so thoroughly deceiving me once, I suppose you have every reason to."

"No, I don't think you're a fool. You are intelligent and kind and—"

"I do not need your flattery. You have given me enough false sentiments, I should think. Now you expect me to believe that you are from the future? How many more lies do you intend to tell, Miss McCarthy? Is that even your name?"

Fresh tears streamed over her cheeks. She didn't blame him for his reaction, but that didn't make it hurt any less. "I could tell you a thousand things about the future: buildings a hundred stories tall, machines that can fly passengers from one side of the world to the other in a matter of hours, rockets that take people into outer space—in nineteen sixty nine we even land on the moon. But there would be no point in telling you those things because you would never believe me." Her voice dropped into a whisper. "I lied because I knew you wouldn't believe me, and I don't blame you for that."

"You're right—I do not believe any of it. You need help, Miss McCarthy, and I'm afraid I cannot give it to you any longer." His words broke into a breathless whisper, and he blinked back tears of his own.

Maggie nodded and picked a single pearl out of the vase. She'd never been certain they would return her to the future, but now that the necklace had broken, she wondered if the odds were even less likely. Fate seemed a cruel friend. Once she'd made the decision to remain in the past, it had taken away the reason for wanting to stay and simultaneously made it impossible to leave.

She rolled the pearl over her palm. "I never meant to hurt you. I never thought that I would..."

Tears pricked at her eyes. She'd never thought she would fall in love.

"What do you want me to say?" asked Luke. "I trusted you. I cannot pretend tonight never happened. I do not know which part of you is real and which is not, and even if I did, you sound as though you are on the brink of insanity."

"I know."

He ran his hands through his hair. "Then what do you want?"

He said it as an almost plea, as if gripping for some last hope of understanding. But there was nothing more she could give him. He knew everything, even if he didn't believe her.

Her voice cracked mid sentence. "I want to go home."

The room spun as a warm sensation crawled over her body. She gasped, and her hold on the vase faltered. The glass hit the floor and shattered, spilling the pearls and scattering them across the room. Her legs turned to gelatin and crumpled beneath her. She fell to the floor, and a shard of glass dug into her shoulder, sending a blast of pain radiating down her arm.

"Maggie!"

His face appeared above her as she fought the encroaching shadows. He swept the hair away from her face and cupped her cheek with a tenderness she didn't expect. Panic and concern flooded his features as he stared down at her, all signs of resentment gone. "What is it? Are you in pain?"

She pinched her eyes closed. Her thoughts reeled too much to respond.

"Maggie, look at me."

His voice coaxed her to obey. Blotches of gray still ate at her visibility, and blinking did nothing to clear them. Warm tears rolled over her skin, and her breathing came in ragged gasps. "I'm sorry," she rasped. "I'm so sorry."

His expression contorted, and he shushed her, his thumb caressing the skin next to her ear. "Do not worry about that right now." He looked over his shoulder at the door and shouted for Mrs. Bielle before returning his attention to her. Luke brushed his fingers through her hair, his eyes glazing with more unshed tears. How could he still care about her after everything she had done?

"I know none of this makes sense." Her breathless words struggled to escape, but she needed them out. "And I should have told you sooner."

"I want to believe you, but..." Luke shook his head, and she understood. He couldn't believe her, and she had never expected him to.

Maggie opened her mouth, but words were lost to her sharp breaths.

When the housekeeper didn't appear, Luke took her face between both of his hands. "Hold on, Maggie. I'm going to get help." He tenderly kissed her forehead, allowing his lips to linger for several moments as he whispered, "Please, hold on."

Luke bounded for the door, and the last thing she saw before darkness filled her view was his shadowed form fading into oblivion.

Chapter 21

Los Angeles, 2022

White walls surrounded Maggie, one covered in a row of oak cabinets with silver handles, and the room had that *recently disinfected to the extreme* smell that made her nose burn. She shifted, and the paper lining the examination table crackled. To her left, a blood pressure machine took up most of the corner, and across from her sat Dad, twiddling his fingers like they were engaged in a square dance. The closed door did little to hide the panic in Mom's voice while she spoke to the doctor on the other side.

Both her parents and the physician had asked her what happened—where she'd been for the last week and a half—and rather than make up a story with details that would require more memory to keep straight than she felt capable of, she'd told them the truth. Of course, Mom had descended into a state of frantic worry with the confession, the idea of time travel holding responsibility for her daughter's disappearance enough to bring on talk of mental illness.

Maggie glanced at her father. He'd been quiet since the moment he and Mom arrived at the hospital, and she wondered what he made of all this. If anyone would believe her, surely the man who had given her the cursed pearl necklace in the first place would.

And she needed him to believe her. She needed someone to tell her the whole thing hadn't happened inside her head, that she'd really time hopped to the past and...

Maggie shook her head. So far, she'd managed to keep the memories at bay, but one second of failed concentration would allow them to resurface. And those memories carried a lot of emotion she wasn't ready to face.

After waking up on the beach with strangers hovering over her, she'd kept her attention on the present. She took one moment at a time and restricted her thoughts to what was happening now—restricted them to calling her parents, to consoling Mom, and defending her sanity. Mom had insisted on going to the hospital, a demand to which Maggie resentfully conceded if for no reason but to put her mother at ease.

She'd stayed with Dad in the waiting room while Mom spoke to the receptionist, and her father had taken that opportunity to request the pearls back. She'd had no hesitation to give him the one bead she possessed; the farther away she was from the pearl, the better.

Her father had said nothing more after that, not even spoken up when she spilled the details of where she'd been.

"Dad," Maggie whispered. "The heirloom—"

"I know." He met her gaze, and Maggie noted the emotion filling his brown eyes. Dad heaved a sigh and pushed himself up from the chair. He came to her side and wrapped an arm around her shoulder. "I know, Mags. I believe every word you said."

"You do?"

He nodded. "But your mother doesn't. There was a reason I told you to keep the existence of the necklace to yourself." He rubbed a hand over his graying beard, his bushy brows knitting together. "I never should have given them to you. It was a mistake."

"No. It wasn't a mistake. Traveling through time may have been the scariest experience of my life, but I'm not sorry it happened." She stared at her dangling feet. She couldn't regret the journey the pearls had taken her on, because to do so would be like wishing none of it had ever happened.

"I met the most amazing people," said Maggie. "Witnessed an era that can only be seen through history books. You gave me that."

"I put you in danger." He sighed, and his shoulders lifted and fell along with it. "I should have been more clear—made sure you understood how serious the charge of watching over the heirloom was."

"Will you tell me more about the pearls? I want to understand them fully. How they were cursed. How you ended up with them."

The door knob jostled, and he glanced toward it, rushing his words. "I will. But not today."

Maggie swallowed her disappointment, but she couldn't blame Dad, either. Mom wouldn't take well to him encouraging her in this *nonsense* as the woman had put it.

The door opened, and when it wasn't her mother who entered, she gasped. Gerard's tall form stood in front of her, the man the same a picture of gorgeousness she remembered. Add the bouquet of flowers he held to his neatly parted hair and tailored business casual and most women wouldn't have stood a chance, but Maggie's heart didn't so much as flutter.

Gerard closed the door and took the few steps to put himself next to her. "How are you feeling?"

"I'm fine, but how did you know—"

"Your mom called me." Gerard glanced at the door and grimaced. "And she told me what you said happened."

"She told *you*?" Why would Mom do that?

Gerard rubbed the back of his neck. "Full confession? I begged her to tell me. I've been trying to contact you for several days—she gave me your number during the party." His expression turned sheepish. "But anyway, when I couldn't seem to reach you, I tried your Mom instead, only to find out you'd disappeared. LeAnn kept me in the loop about the investigation."

"And you don't think I'm crazy?" Maggie crossed her arms. No way Mr. Gorgeous would believe her. Mom didn't even believe her.

He studied her for a moment and then placed the bouquet next to her thigh. "I believe you, Maggie. The time travel—all of it."

She glanced at Dad, who merely shrugged. Why Gerard believed her so easily, she didn't understand, but right now her ability to care was nonexistent. Having another person who didn't judge her or suggest mental evaluation eased the tension building in her chest.

"Just don't tell your mom I believe you," said Gerard. "She wouldn't approve."

Maggie returned his smile. "I won't say anything. Thank you, Gerard."

The door swung open again, and Mom entered with the doctor in tow. Gerard and Dad moved to the back of the room and took a seat, which unfortunately left enough space for her mother to make use of. "Are you feeling any better?"

The unspoken question irked Maggie. Mom wanted to know if she'd given up her delusions of time travel. "You wanted the truth. It isn't going to change just because you don't like the answer."

Her mother glanced at the doctor, and the man shifted on his feet. "Often traumatic events can affect the mind in ways we don't understand. With time, and a bit of therapy, Magdalena will likely make a full recovery."

"I don't need a shrink," said Maggie with a growl.

Mom ignored her. "We would appreciate a recommendation. And I know that you will keep things discreet. Patient confidentiality and all that, yes?"

The doctor nodded. "Of course. I'll print off some recommendations for therapists. You may grab them from the front desk on your way out." His eyes bounced between her and her mother. "Take as much time as you need."

Maggie sighed with the close of the door, and her mom placed a tentative hand on her arm. The genuine concern in her mother's expression erupted the volcano of guilt in her stomach.

"I'm glad you're okay," whispered Mom. "Your Dad and I were really worried." She paused, the furrow in her brows suggesting she was giving her next words a lot of thought. "I know you've been through an ordeal, but this talk of time travel...I think it would be best if you didn't tell people you traveled through time."

"It's what happened. Would you rather I lied about it?"

Her lack of response was answer enough. Maggie shook her head, but Mom continued. "I don't want you to face ridicule because of this. And besides, as the future CEO—"

"No." Maggie glanced at Gerard. Having this conversation with him here wasn't ideal, but she needed to address the situation. She didn't want to inherit the company, and Mom's refusal to believe her did nothing but add fuel to fire.

She slid off the table, making the examination paper crinkle noisily. She was done doing what was expected of her. Relying on everyone else had only ever brought her misery and heartache.

"You don't need to worry about the company being affected," said Maggie. "I'm not taking over."

Her mother tilted her head, a different kind of concern growing in her expression. "I can push my retirement back by a few months. I don't expect you to take over until you've had time to recover."

"No, Mom. I mean I'm not taking over *ever*. I don't want to be CEO, and I never did. I'm sorry I didn't tell you sooner." Relief poured over her, instantly dousing the remainder of her frustration. Why had she not done this sooner? The hurt in Mom's eyes left an ache in her chest, but she felt lighter. Free.

Her mother's mouth opened and closed several times, but she seemed incapable of speech. Maggie felt the impulse to get out of the tiny, suffocating room before her mother remembered how to speak and turned to Gerard. "Would you mind giving me a ride home?"

"Sure. I can take you as soon as you're ready." He glanced at her mother with a look of uncertainty. Maggie had made this awkward for him, and for that she was sorry, but he seemed like he'd make a good getaway driver. Her parents weren't always on the best of terms, but Dad still had a way of consoling Mom, and the woman would likely need him after that confession.

"Now," said Maggie. "I'm ready now."

She headed for the door, Gerard on her heels. Mom must have made to follow because Dad's soft voice encouraged her to stay. A twinge of guilt twisted her gut, but she had no regret.

Perhaps one day you will discover the courage to find out which of the two is more valuable.

Luke's words rang through her mind, and she smiled. She'd found her courage. Her happiness was more valuable, and she couldn't help but think the duke would be proud of her.

THE KITCHEN TABLE VIBRATED WHEN MAGGIE'S CELL PHONE buzzed. For the third time, she punched the button to ignore the call and returned her attention to the rows of paper in front of her. She had collected quite the mound of research over the last few months, and though much of it remained over her head, she finally had a miniscule grasp on time travel.

Turns out, experiencing it firsthand helped little in regards to understanding the actual physics behind the phenomenon. Not that science gave her much to go on since there were no recorded incidences of traversing time.

A knock at the door interrupted her concentration. She leaped from the chair and tiptoed to the door. Pressing her nose against it, she peaked through the eyehole and relaxed.

She opened the door, and Gerard's lips lifted into a smile. "Hi."

"Hi." Maggie jutted her chin to the pizza box in his hands. "What's that? A bribe? I told you I didn't want to go out tonight."

His green eyes twinkled. "I'm smarter than that. Call it a 'concerned-about-whether-you've-eaten-today' visit."

Maggie sighed and gestured him inside before closing the door. "You know I can take care of myself despite what my mother would have you believe." She grabbed a plate from the cabinet and offered it to him. Gerard shook his head, which was not all that surprising since he only ate *healthy* food unless descending to her level for junk food binges, but even that was rare. The man had far too much self control.

He took a seat at the table, though, indicating his intention to keep her company. Or perhaps ensure she ate. He'd been a good friend that way, and she appreciated his concern even if she believed it misplaced.

"By all means." He folded his arms, his expression full of skepticism. "When did you last eat?"

Maggie shrugged. "I had Poptarts for breakfast."

The man's gaze dropped to the pile of papers scattered over the table. "And have you done anything today besides...this?" He gestured over the mess with raised brows.

"I had a piano student this morning." Maggie tapped a finger against the table. "Look, I get it. I sound like a nutcase. Mom's worried—"

"Maggie, *I'm* worried. Can't you see this has become an obsession?"

She rubbed her forehead, likely leaving behind a trail of pizza grease. Gerard wasn't necessarily wrong. She had spent countless hours researching in addition to the time sorting through online archives searching for evidence of Luke's existence. She'd found his name on a handful of things—one mentioning his birth and another indicating his application to take over the title of Duke of Avendesh, but beyond that there was nothing. Why she needed more, she didn't know. How many times had she told herself to stop, to leave the past alone and forget?

She bit into her pizza, and her stomach grumbled with delight. Maybe she hadn't eaten enough today.

"I'm not obsessed," she said after swallowing. "Can you blame me for wanting to understand?" She tapped one of her clean fingers on the paper in front of her. "Have you ever heard of a grandfather paradox? It happens when someone travels to the past and attempts to change events. If their actions would change the future enough that the person would no longer exist, then the universe prevents them from succeeding."

She glanced at Gerard, and he raised one of his brows. Ignoring his skeptical look, she continued. "That means that my trip back to 1815 had no effect on the future, otherwise I wouldn't have been permitted by the universe to time hop. I was always meant to do it."

"So, you were destined to go back in time...according to this theory."

"Exactly."

He didn't appear nearly as intrigued by the concept as she'd been, but since Gerard was one of two people who actually believed she'd traveled through time, she had no reason to complain.

"Your mother asked me to let you know they settled the Orvax deal," said Gerard. "She's holding a party in three days to celebrate."

"And she wants me to be there." Maggie finished the unspoken expectation and sighed. "I'm betting that's why she's called me a billion times."

"That, and she hopes you've changed your mind about becoming CEO."

"Yeah, that hasn't happened. And it's not going to."

Gerard nodded. "So don't go to the party. If your mom can't see how much her disbelief and disappointment hurts you, then I don't see any reason to talk to her."

She and her mother hadn't spoken since the hospital visit. Why should she give the woman any attention when all LeAnn McCarthy cared about was appearances? She didn't plan to shout about her journey through time on the rooftops, but Mom seemed to think otherwise. Truthfully, all she had wanted was her mother's support. Her understanding. But only Gerard and Dad had been there for her.

Even Diana had bombarded her with concern and skepticism. Having Mom not believe her was one thing, but Diana was supposed to be her confidant—at least in this century—and not having her support felt a lot like betrayal. It hurt, and she'd cut ties with her because of it.

But that didn't matter. She could handle things on her own. She didn't need to rely on anyone else or bow to the expectations that had always plagued her life.

Maggie took another bite of pizza and then downed the last bit with a sip of water. "There's no chance I'm going to Mom's party."

The phone buzzed, and Maggie rolled her eyes. Gerard watched the phone dance across the table with furrowed brows. "You know, eventually she's going to give up calling and drag you out of here herself."

He had a point. Mom wasn't going to give up, and she had no desire to confront the woman at present. She wanted to be as far away from the soiree as possible.

"I've got it!" Maggie grabbed her phone, and fingers moved like mad across the keyboard. "I'll book a flight and go see Dad. I can't go to a party if I'm not even in the state. She won't know I'm gone until it's too late." She glanced up, her eyes narrowed. "Unless you tell her."

"I'd rather be an accomplice. Would you like some company on your trip?"

Maggie hesitated. That felt a little too much like *bringing a guy home*, and she wasn't ready for a new relationship. How could she when she spent hours pining after the old one? Perhaps she deserved to live with a shattered heart after what she'd done to Luke.

Gerard rose and rounded the table to stand in front of her. "Hey, I know you're still sorting through things, but I don't want you to go alone. I'm only coming as a friend."

He pinned her with a look that said he'd guessed her thoughts, which was slightly embarrassing.

"Don't you have work?" she asked. "Your company—"

"Will manage fine without me for a few days. I can meet with them via Zoom, anyway." He took her hand and squeezed it. "Besides, your Dad's cool, and I'd like to get to know him better."

Her leg bounced beneath the table. "Just as a friend?"

"As a friend," he confirmed.

"Are you sure about this?"

"Completely." Gerard smiled, and her pulse calmed. Maybe this was a good idea. Gerard had been her constant support since she left the hospital. He checked in on her, spent time with her...brought her pizza. But more importantly, the man *believed* her.

"Okay," said Maggie. "Let's do this." After all, Dad still owed her answers about the pearl heirloom.

Suffolk, 1815

I f there was one thing Luke hated, it was being held hostage to the effects of alcohol. He had heavily partaken of the substance a few times during his days at Oxford, every one of which he'd regretted. Luke had sworn off complete intoxication, resigning himself to the occasional evening port with limited intake.

But now...

The notion to pass his troubles onto something else for a time sounded rather inviting. Relief, even the temporary kind, was a welcomed idea he might pay forfeit to.

He poured the dark amber liquid from the decanter and stared at the bubbles rising from the bottom. Unlike his internal turmoil, they were allowed to escape. The tiny pockets of air found freedom the moment they breached the surface.

But he couldn't give himself the same reprieve. Luke had always kept his emotions to himself. His father hadn't cared, and Luke had never wanted to burden Mrs. Bielle with more work than she had already taken on. The woman had raised him and his brother after their mother passed, a job no one expected of her but one she happily accepted, but even the housekeeper remained ignorant of the depths of his concerns and fears. He had never confided those things to anyone.

Until *she* came along.

Miss Magdalena McCarthy. Maggie.

Invisible ropes constricted around his throat, and it required effort to draw a breath. His heart wasn't in much better shape. Ever since the night Maggie disappeared, he had felt lost, and the four months that followed had led him through a battlefield of emotion. He buried himself into improving his tenant houses and political aspirations, but none of them had distracted him thoroughly enough.

Luke picked up the glass and swirled the brandy inside. Every day he poured himself a drink, though he had yet to take a single sip. His ability to resist wore thinner with each passing moment. He wanted to forget the memories that haunted him.

He had rushed into the hallway to look for Mrs. Bielle after Maggie collapsed. Maggie had needed a doctor—that much was clear by her ragged breath and pale skin. In those moments, all of his anger and doubt had flitted away, replaced by his concern for her health. But in his few seconds of absence, something had happened, and he'd returned to an empty room.

At first, he had determined the whole occurrence nothing more than an illusion created by heightened emotions. The pearls that dotted the floor, however, had served to ground him. He hadn't imagined the whole thing, though accepting the truth still proved difficult at times. Mrs. Bielle hadn't known what to make of his frantic shouts, and he had decided not to tell the housekeeper what actually occurred. He never told anyone.

For all England knew, Magdalena McCarthy had disappeared after her confrontation with Lady Garrick.

And she had.

Just not in a way anyone would believe.

The idea that she had traversed time to end up in his life wasn't the easiest notion to accept, but the more he thought on his time with her, the more plausible Maggie's declarations became. Her strange phrasings had been the thing that first ignited his intrigue, soon followed by her clear struggle with maintaining the rules of propriety. He had equivocated both to her being from the American continent, which he supposed may still hold some responsibility, but not all.

Two weeks following her disappearance, news of Bonaparte's surrender reached the whole of England. Maggie had been confident the Frenchman would eventually give himself over. Confidence, he imagined, came easily when one knew events before they happened.

Maggie lived in a world where things were very different from his own. She had mentioned flying machines and mankind traveling to the moon, both of which were beyond his comprehension. He realized now that he remained ignorant of what year she'd arrived from—what century she existed in. With so many lies, he questioned whether he'd truly known her at all.

At least, he had for a time.

But those moments spent discussing things as one another's confidants had felt too real—too raw—to be anything less than truth. Maggie understood him in a way no one else did. She had spoken to him as though he held no title. The vulnerability he'd experienced during that conversation on the grass had opened his heart to not only marriage but to her.

And she'd taken his heart with her back to the future.

A knock pulled him from his musings.

"Enter!" Luke pushed the still full glass a little farther away with his knuckles.

Mr. Tolley opened the door and dropped into a deep bow. "Lord Branbury is here, Your Grace. Shall I see him in?"

Luke heaved a sigh. "Yes, please do."

If there was one person who had relentlessly pestered him for details the last few months, it was Nicholas. His friend seemed to think there was more to Maggie vanishing than Luke let on. How right his assumptions were.

Nicholas entered the study with his typical wide grin. He marched across the room and plopped into the chair in front of Luke's desk before crossing his leg over his knee.

"Branbury," said Luke, sinking a little in his own chair as he leaned back and folded his arms. "To what do I owe another visit?"

"You say it as though I were here yesterday."

"Not yesterday, but the day before. I have work to do."

Nicholas snickered and jutted his chin toward the cup of brandy. "Yes, you appear very busy. Tell me, are you going to drink it this time or stare daggers into it?"

"I am not—why are you here? Is there a reason for this visit, or do you simply enjoy irritating me?"

"I certainly enjoy it, but no, that is not why I'm here." He scooted to the edge of the padded chair and propped his elbows on the desk. His amusement faltered, replaced by an expression of seriousness that Luke rarely saw on the man. "I am concerned about my friend."

Luke scoffed. "I have told you no short of a hundred times that there is no need for it."

"You sitting here in your study, day after day, staring at cups of brandy proves otherwise."

"Why does it matter what I do? Is there something more pressing I should concern myself with?"

Nicholas groaned and swiped the glass from the desk. He downed the contents in seconds and then slammed the cup down with a *clunk*. Luke swallowed his agitation. He would have to pour another once the irritant left.

"You were supposed to meet me yesterday for a few rounds of fencing, or have you forgotten?" asked Nicholas.

He had, in fact, forgotten, but nevermind that. "Is that what has you so bothered?"

Nicholas shook his head, the motion shifting strands of his sandy brown hair into his eyes. "Luke, I am *worried* about you. Ever since Miss McCarthy—"

"Do not say her name."

"—disappeared, you have been completely unreachable. You hole yourself in here, rarely leave the estate to even visit your tenants. You were boring before, but this is insufferable. It is not like you to ignore those under your ward, either."

Luke jumped up from his chair and dove into an aggressive pace across the room. The movement did little to dispel the excess energy or frustration. "What would you have me do? I cannot..." He stopped in front of the window and rubbed a hand over his face. His throat burned as emotions he had fought for months to restrain clawed their way to the surface. "I cannot stop thinking about her. Every moment of every day, she's all my mind can focus on."

He had expected Nicholas to respond to his plight with a snarky remark, but his friend only stared back at him with sympathy. Perhaps he understood more than Luke had anticipated.

"Then why are you here contemplating drunkenness when you could be out there searching for her?" asked Nicholas.

How did he even begin to explain? It wasn't as though he could order his carriage to take him to see her. And even if he could, would Maggie *want* to see him? Their last conversation had been the opposite of pleasant.

"It is not that simple," said Luke.

Nicholas stood, and with four long strides, made it to the door. "No, I suppose it is not. Life would be easier if we could simply speak our feelings and have them returned. If only we fell in love with those who shared our sentiments."

"You could still do so," said Luke. "Just because I am a lost cause does not mean you must be."

"I'm afraid I was a lost cause long before you, my friend." For a moment, his brows furrowed, a hidden pain breaking over his features. Nicholas shook his head. "Fencing. Will you join me for a few rounds? I am quickly falling out of practice without my dueling companion."

"Very well. I will come by on Monday."

His friend drummed his fingers over his thigh. "Miss McCarthy changed you, Luke. For the better. I have never seen you so open with someone—not even me or Edwin. She made you happy, and I think you should give searching for her some real thought."

"It does not pay to be vulnerable. If I have learned anything, it is that." Luke stared out the window at the cloudy gray sky. The weather had turned cold, and the dingy appearance of the outside world reflected his inner turmoil.

No matter how much his heart longed for Maggie's company, she had broken his trust. She had lied to him.

His stomach tossed like a tiny boat on the sea. Could he truly blame her for not telling him the truth?

"You are right," said Nicholas. "Vulnerability, love—I have only seen them bring people pain. Yet human nature compels us to seek them all the same. Why do you suppose that is?"

"Because we are all naught but fools, myself included."

"Either way, even fools should not wither away in their studies."

Luke gave him a curt nod. "I will see you in a few days."

Nicholas nodded and then disappeared into the hall. Perhaps his friend was right. Hiding in his study would do him no favors. It would not solve his problems or eliminate the pain. Only one thing— or one person, rather—had the potential to do that. But she was forever out of his reach.

Los Angeles, 2022

M aggie drew in a deep breath and exhaled slowly. People bustled down the narrow aisle, bags and suitcases in hand. Flights didn't normally make her nervous, but she'd felt uncomfortable in public spaces as of late. It was like everyone knew her secret and was silently judging her.

She glanced out the tiny window and watched the carts full of luggage rolling toward the plane. At least spending some time at Dad's would give her the chance to ask him more about the pearls. Perhaps this trip was as much about answers as it was about avoiding Mom. She needed closure, and until she understood more about the heirloom, she didn't think her mind or heart could let things go.

She tensed when Gerard made his way down the aisle gripping his cell phone with a grimace and sat down in the seat beside her. She angled herself toward him. "How much trouble am I in?"

"She isn't happy."

"I figured that much." But really, what could Mom do? Maggie wasn't a teenager. She could live her life how she wanted.

Her stomach churned. Somehow running away from the party didn't feel much like living how she wanted, but visiting the farm always brought her peace. Truthfully, she'd considered moving to Oklahoma indefinitely. It seemed the only place she'd ever been truly happy.

"She calmed down when I said I was going with you," said Gerard, "but I expect you'll have to face her fury when we get back."

Maggie slumped in her seat. That was a problem for later, one she would avoid as long as possible.

"This will be fun," said Gerard, his tone all reassurance. "I'm excited to see your dad."

She shifted closer to the window. "I think I'm going to take a nap. See you there?"

Gerard chuckled. "Alright. Pleasant dreams."

She leaned her head against the window. Perhaps they would be if she didn't dream about a man with dark hair and brown eyes, one who possessed a smile that made her legs wobble like Jell-O.

A pang shot through her chest, and she closed her eyes. That smile would haunt her forever.

Suffolk, 1815

LUKE GENERALLY ENJOYED SILENCE, BUT THE QUIET THAT rested between him and Edwin right now was far from pleasant. The air felt heavy, almost ominous, as he waited for his brother to react. He had recited the words he'd been planning for days, and although he'd decided to tell Edwin the truth no matter how impossible it sounded, he worried doing so had been a mistake.

Edwin wet his lips and opened his mouth to respond but closed it again. Luke shifted in the armchair. Should he say something more? How could he reassure his brother that he hadn't gone mad?

"Listen," he began. "I know this sounds—"

"Sounds? Luke, this is preposterous. Tell me you don't truly believe that young woman came from the future."

"I did not believe her at first, but as ridiculous as it seems, the notion makes sense. She even knew about Bonaparte's surrender, and you cannot deny the way she spoke...she was different, Edwin. My understanding of why did not come until she had already gone."

Edwin ran his fingers through his hair with a groan. Luke couldn't blame him for the skepticism, but he did need his brother to come to terms with it. After all, if Edwin was to take over the duchy, he deserved to know why Luke had disappeared.

He had tussled with his thoughts and feelings every night since Maggie left. He did not know if he could ever trust her completely again but needed to see her once more and apologize for not giving her the chance to explain. He needed to know if the moments they had shared were as real for her as they had been for him.

"Whatever rumors Lady Garrick has spread are untrue," said Luke. "I do not believe the entire situation was premeditated, as the viscountess claims." He leaned forward and rested his arms flat against his legs. "What happened when I confronted her was not an act, Edwin. She was in no shape to run anywhere. What other explanation can there be?"

"How do you know it was not another performance? I want you to be right about her. For your sake, I really do. But this notion of time travel...how can I accept that? By all means, find the lady. Your heart is clearly set on it, and you needn't my approval."

No, not his approval. What he needed was for his brother to understand. Finding Maggie—going after her—meant he would never see him again. It meant Edwin would become the new Duke of Avendesh.

"I intend to go after her, but as I will no longer live in 1815, the family title will pass to the next in line." Edwin shook his head, but Luke continued. "The estates will all belong to you. I trust you to do with the fortune and properties as you see fit. I only ask that you keep Mrs. Bielle on—ensure she lives the rest of her life in security."

Edwin rose and marched to the window, his posture stiff with agitation. "Of course I would never put Mrs. Bielle out! She is as close as family. But this entire discussion is pointless. I have no intention of taking over your role. I am not a duke, and if you haven't forgotten, I have no heir, either."

Luke winced. He knew that would always be a soft spot for his brother. Edwin had married young, and Juliana had come along soon after. Both he and his wife, Rachel, had been beyond ecstatic, but the pregnancy had taken a turn for the worse. Juliana had come early, and Rachel had died after the delivery.

"You have time to remarry," said Luke. "Older men than you do it on a regular basis."

"I have no desire to remarry." Edwin's tone was laced with his displeasure of the idea. "No one could ever replace Rachel."

His brother's face crumpled, and he turned toward the window. It pained Luke to think that Edwin refused to open his heart again, though he'd never been one to berate him about it. After all, he had been unwilling to do the same until recently.

Luke joined Edwin and placed a hand on his shoulder. "If nothing else, please consider giving someone a chance. You found love once; there is no reason to think you cannot convince a woman to love you again."

"Convince?" Edwin chuckled. "Since when do you get to give me advice, especially about that? You have been a bachelor forever."

"I am older. It is my duty to give you advice."

"By a single year, and at seven and twenty I believe myself capable of making my own decisions."

Luke shrugged and folded his arms. "Mrs. Bielle would argue with that. I am the perfect example, am I not? She's pestered me about settling down for years. Look how long it took her to change my mind."

"Hah! Do not pretend it was the housekeeper who changed your stubborn mind."

"Miss McCarthy may have had something to do with it."

"A little more than something." Edwin sighed and leaned against the wall. The fading sunlight reflected off the gold buttons of his finely-fitted dark green tailcoat. As far as appearances went, the man looked every bit the part of a duke. Although their father had paid

Edwin even less heed than him, he knew his brother was plenty capable of running the duchy. As a second son, Edwin had taken forging his own path earnestly. Working for the government provided him a handsome yearly income in addition to the property he'd inherited. He knew how to manage an estate, and he had a sharp mind for politics.

"You are quite serious about all of this?" asked Edwin. "You truly believe Miss McCarthy traveled through time?"

"I do, and I cannot pretend otherwise."

Edwin nodded, seeming to muse over their conversation for several minutes. "I fear I may never hold your same certainty, but I wish for nothing more than your happiness. Miss McCarthy has surely given you that, though she seems to have taken it with her when she left."

No words could hold more truth than that.

"How soon do you intend to...leave?" asked Edwin.

"Tonight, if I can determine how the pearls work. I have no assurances that I will find success in the endeavor, but I cannot live with not trying. I will leave a note with my steward and direct him to advise you the moment everything is in order. It will likely take a month or so for my absence to be marked as a death officially. With any luck, it will all go as smoothly as I plan."

Edwin laughed, and Luke relished in the sound. He may never hear it again.

"Smoothly," said Edwin, scratching his head. "Nothing about this suggests that. Dare I ask what exactly you plan to do?"

Luke had concocted a rather complicated plan. He would not leave any speculation about his disappearance. Rumors caught too easily, and he would not have his brother accused of murder. "It is better that you do not know. At least, not yet."

"Very well. I suppose this will be our goodbye, then? I am to never see you again?"

Luke clenched his jaw, emotion gnawing at his composure. Neither of them had ever been quick to expose their vulnerabilities, but in this moment—perhaps the last they would ever share—Luke wore his feelings as openly as he wore the tight cravat about his neck.

Edwin embraced him, his voice cracking with the same sorrow Luke felt. "Do be careful. I will miss you terribly."

"I will miss you as well," said Luke as they parted.

His brother heaved a sigh. "We should go find Juliana. You cannot leave without also telling her goodbye."

Mrs. Bielle had taken his niece for a walk through the gardens, and it took him and Edwin several minutes to find them. Luke watched as she chased the falling snow, his heart aching. He would miss them wholeheartedly, but he needed to see this through.

After his family's departure, he snuck out to the stables and saddled his finest stallion. Making certain no one saw him, he raced into the woods behind his estate. He would leave the charcoal horse by the river with a note tucked away in a pouch attached to the saddle. By the time anyone thought to look for him, Luke would be long gone.

At least he hoped.

With renewed determination, Luke returned to Windgate on foot and used the servants' stairs to ascend to the first floor. He halted halfway when a woman with gray hair and a tight bun appeared on the landing. Mrs. Bielle tilted her head, studying him in that careful way she often had when he was yet a child.

"Is everything well, Your Grace?"

Luke climbed the remaining stairs and smiled down at the woman who had become dear as family to him. "All is well."

Her brows furrowed.

He retrieved two envelopes from the pocket of his coat and held them out to her. "Would you mind posting these letters for me?"

"Of course."

She reached for the letters, but Luke pulled them away. "Not yet. I need you to wait a week. Will you do that for me?"

He had decided a week would give him proper time to gauge both his own feelings and Maggie's. Though he knew what his heart wanted, sorting through the lingering sting of betrayal was another thing. If he could not come to terms with what happened, or if his sentiments were unrequited, Luke would return to 1815. There would be no point to franking his letters then.

"One week." Mrs. Bielle nodded, and Luke had the strangest feeling that she understood far more than she let on.

Luke cleared his throat. "I want you to know that I...well, I offer my sincerest gratitude for everything you have done for me. If I am to never see you again, then you must know I have always thought of you as family."

Her lip quivered for a moment before she dove against him. Her small body trembled in his arms as she held him tighter than he would have thought possible for someone of her age. "Take care, dear. Know that I love you."

A tear fell over his cheek. What a watering pot he'd become today. He longed to repay her words in kind, but they stuck in his throat. Those three words hadn't graced his lips since his mother passed. Saying them would unleash vulnerability, and Luke wasn't ready to expose himself in that way. Though Maggie had opened his mind and heart, fear still remained beneath the surface, lurking like some dark creature that held no qualms about pulling him under.

She pulled away, her expression content. "Safe travels. I do hope it doesn't make you ill."

Luke tilted his head. What an odd thing for her to say. For all the housekeeper knew, he'd be taking the carriage. Carriages had never made him ill. "What do you mean?"

Mrs. Bielle took his hand, and her wrinkled fingers patted against it. "Nevermind that. Go on, and be sure to give Miss McCarthy my love, too."

"I shall."

She descended to the ground floor, leaving him alone in the dimly-lit stairwell.

Luke's feet carried him with a lightness that felt as though he walked on air. He closed the door to his study and heaved a sigh. The pearls rested in a glass jar on his desk, the final piece of his plan. It had taken him time to find them all, each one having rolled into hidden corners and crevices when Maggie collapsed.

He approached them, apprehension twisting his stomach. He allowed himself several moments of indecision before pulling two pearls from inside the vase and rolling them across his palm.

How did they work?

Maggie had held them when Miss Garrick gave them back to her, and Katherine and Lady Garrick would have touched them several times before that. Lord Doxly had handled the beads when he'd stolen them and likely countless times before they ended up in Lord Garrick's possession. None of *them* had vanished—traveled across time at the mere touch of the pearls.

He cleared his throat and squared his shoulders, as if that would somehow prepare him for the journey. "I wish...to travel through time."

Silence reigned around him, so thick he could hear his heart pounding in his ears. He shifted. He hadn't thought it would be that simple, but a man could hope.

"Please, take me to the future."

Nothing.

"Ridiculous. What am I doing?" He growled, tapping his empty fingers against his thigh. Deuced things. Perhaps he was mad to even attempt this.

He glared at the tiny beads, the shimmer of candlelight from the table reflecting off them. Nothing had happened that night when Maggie first removed one, either. What had she said? She wanted to go home? He hoped the pearls had followed her wishes. For all he knew, she could be lost somewhere in history. What if *he* became lost in time?

He swallowed, stamping down his fears, and clenched the two spheres. "I...I want to see Maggie again."

Heat flooded over him, making his skin burn, and muffled laughter rang in his ears. The shelves lining the west wall of his study tilted, throwing off his balance. He crumbled to the floor and rolled onto his back, the pearls digging into his palm. His hand clenched them so firmly, pain radiated into his fingers.

He struggled to catch his breath. Shadows filled his vision, dragging him down into a dark void like an anchor into the sea. His body felt weightless yet heavy at the same time. He fought unconsciousness, but exhaustion depleted his ability to combat it.

Giving in, he closed his eyes and repeated the words in his mind. *I want to see Maggie again.*

Chapter 24

Oklahoma, 2022

A light breeze tousled his hair, and the cold air tickled his skin. Luke's eyes fluttered open, and he squinted up at the gray clouds. The fluffy streaks covered every inch of sky as if to paint the perfect portrait of an impending storm. He shifted, and his muscles throbbed with the movement as though he'd spent the last few hours fencing with Nicholas.

A rustling to his left drew his attention. Golden stalks of grain shifted in the wind. Luke sat up and evaluated his surroundings with furrowed brows. Crop fields flanked both sides of the dirt road he'd been lying on, seeming to stretch as far as he could see.

Luke pushed himself from the ground and brushed the dirt from his pantaloons. Where was he?

His eyes caught the glimmer of two small objects on the ground near his boots. Luke stooped over and picked up the pearls. Had they worked? Something inside him insisted they had. He supposed he could have ended up in one of his tenant's fields, but even that seemed unlikely.

A rumbling in the distance pulled his focus from the tiny beads, and he tucked them into the pocket of his greatcoat. Some sort of odd carriage charged toward him.

Where were the horses? It was as though the coach propelled itself.

The white carriage approached much faster than he thought possible, and he stumbled toward the field to get out of its path. His heart pounded. How did it move without an animal to pull it? And that sound? Perhaps he was hallucinating.

The carriage slowed and then came to a complete stop, stirring up a cloud of dust. The resonating hum mumbled into silence with a croak. Luke swatted at the air, coughing as he took in the strange contraption. The white frame was clearly made of metal, the surface smooth, and the front housed a glass panel that stretched from one side to the other like a large window. With no seat on the outside, Luke suspected the driver took a place on the inside, thus the need for the glass. He'd never seen anything quite like it, and a thousand questions left his mind reeling.

A door opened on the side opposite him, and a man—likely twice his age—stepped out. The gentlemen propped his elbows on the front of the rig and pushed up on his hat, revealing a pair of dark brown eyes that swept over Luke. "You lost?"

Yes. He certainly felt lost. "I believe I might be. Would you tell me where I am?"

"You're a Brit? Figured as much."

"I beg your pardon?"

The man sauntered toward him. His straw hat wasn't so unusual for someone of working class, but his pantaloons were nothing like Luke had ever beheld. The blue fabric had holes ripped in several places, revealing his skin through strands of white thread. Pieces of hair, the same color as the hat but for the hints of gray, stuck out wildly from beneath the brim, which cast a slight shadow over the top half of his face.

The stranger offered his hand. "Name's West."

"West?" As in the direction? Luke attempted to keep the bewilderment out of his expression, but he found it unlikely that he succeeded.

West chuckled, his arm still outstretched. "That's what my friends call me. My enemies would have other names for me."

"Your enemies? Do you have many of those?"

"Fortunately not. Mostly just an ex-wife."

Luke was uncertain how to take the man who seemed entirely too amused with himself. He accepted the gesture...and then his heart stalled. What name should he give him in return? As a peer of the realm, his title demanded formality.

At least it did in 1815.

What about here—or *now*, rather?

"Luke Halford," he said, deciding to skip the titles altogether. After all, if everything went as he planned, he would no longer be a duke. "Pleasure to meet you."

West's eyes swept over him again, and he smirked. "So, were you on your way to a ball in that getup?"

Luke blinked. "No. Listen, if you could perhaps convey me into town, that would prove helpful. Then I might—"

"Oh, no. Town is the last place I'm taking you today. Best to start things slow. I learned that the hard way." He turned, gesturing toward the carriage. "Hop in, and I'll take you back to the house. Are you hungry?"

Luke's stomach grumbled, and he swallowed. He needed to go into town if he were to have any luck finding Maggie, but he also hadn't the slightest clue which direction that was. Perhaps having something to eat first would be best. But what did the man mean by taking things slowly?

He followed him to the white rig. The wheels were black and thick and made of some sort of strange substance, nothing like the wooden spokes of his carriages. Luke pressed a finger to one. It was...squishy yet hard, a combination that made little sense. The enclosed portion of the coach was tiny in comparison to the back, which looked more like an open cart meant for transporting *things* rather than people. He peeked through the window and counted two padded seats. They looked comfortable enough, but...

"Come on," the man's muffled voice called to him as he plopped inside and shut the door. After a few tries with the handle, Luke opened his side but hesitated to sit down. Was this thing safe? He still didn't know how it worked without horses.

"I'm not so bad a driver as that," said West. "We aren't going far, anyway. A few miles that way."

Luke glanced in the direction he pointed, only to see the road stretch on endlessly. Walking was certainly out of the question, and the man seemed amicable enough. He inched onto the soft seat and closed the door with a thud.

"Are you ready?" asked West.

Luke narrowed his eyes. "For what, precisely?"

West only responded with a laugh, which did nothing to calm his pounding heart. Maybe trusting this stranger had been a horrible mistake.

Something jingled, and Luke turned to face him. West inserted a key into a slot next to a wheel.

What the devil was a wheel doing *inside* the coach?

West twisted the key, and a rumble vibrated through the rig. With the yank of some sort of handle situated between them, the rig jolted forward. Luke tensed and grasped onto the seat like his life depended upon it.

"Don't worry," said West, not bothering to hide his amusement. "Just like a nice ride through Hyde Park."

Luke's knuckles turned white with his tightened grip when they sped over a bump, jarring him so hard his hair grazed the ceiling. "This is nothing like a ride through Hyde. How are you controlling this thing?"

"Well, this here works the steering." West turned the wheel with a few sharp jerks up and down, and the carriage responded in kind, throwing Luke into the door.

"That's quite enough!" On second thought, perhaps he didn't want to know how the deuced contraption worked.

Unfortunately, West seemed incapable of reading Luke's thoughts or his tone. Or he found him too entertaining to care.

"Down here at my feet," the man continued, "are some pedals. One for stopping and one for going."

Luke's body flew forward, and he braced himself with his palms against the interior before he could smack into the glass. West grinned as the carriage pulled forward again, and Luke slumped back into his seat, his hands fumbling for anything secure he could hold onto.

"That's why we have seat belts," said West, pointing to some sort of... Luke shook his head. There was no use in describing the things he saw. He couldn't understand any of it. If one thing was certain, this death trap had reaffirmed he'd traveled to the future.

"How much farther?" asked Luke, swallowing against the bile that rose into his throat. Much longer, and he might spill the contents of his stomach.

West shrugged. "Another minute or so."

Minute? Hadn't the man said they were several miles from his home? How fast did this thing go? He dare not ask. West might give him a proper demonstration, and that would certainly empty his belly.

West steered the carriage to the left, and after a few bumps, the wheels rolled onto a smooth road. Luke stared at the black path in awe. His stomach preferred this route to the dirt one they'd traversed the last few minutes.

The crop fields disappeared outside his window, replaced by estates and trees. Another sharp turn had Luke grabbing at the seat again, and then the carriage pulled to a stop in front of a house. West twisted his keys, and the rumbling ceased.

After struggling with the door handle for several seconds, Luke clambered outside and leaned against the side of the rig.

"You alright?" asked West, coming to his side.

"Yes, but I need a moment."

Perhaps a few.

"No shame in feeling sick the first time," said West. "I threw up."

How comforting.

"Would you like to see how the truck works?" asked West. "I know you have a thousand questions."

"Truck?" No, he should not be asking questions. Every time he did so, West responded with a mad demonstration.

"Yeah, truck," West said with a chuckle. He waved for Luke to follow him to the front, and when Luke remained in place, the man grinned. "We aren't getting back inside it right now. Come take a look."

Luke groaned and forced his feet to move. There was a *pop* and a *creak* as the man lifted part of the carriage, uncovering a well of metal the likes of which Luke had never seen. His eyes rounded. "Does all of this make the carriage—er—truck move?"

"Yup, this here is the engine. Simply put, fuel goes in, and energy comes out."

"What sort of fuel?" Luke clenched his jaw. He couldn't contain his curiosity.

"Petroleum, but that will require more of an explanation. Let's get you something to eat first."

Luke nodded as West put the carriage back together. He led him to the wooden veranda that wrapped around the house. West's home wasn't as large as Windgate Estate, but it was beautifully built and spoke of wealth. Curious how the house did not reflect the way the man spoke or dressed.

Then again, he hadn't the slightest idea how different social classes dressed in the future.

"Why don't you take a seat out here while I make us a sandwich," said West. "You still look a little pale. Could probably use the fresh air."

Luke sat down on a blue chair, one made of an odd, smooth material. He stared out at the crop fields in the distance. He'd eat something and then ask West to take him to town, although the idea of riding in the *truck* again held little appeal. But the second time would be better now that he had the experience, would it not?

Regardless, he'd deal with the nausea if it meant finding Maggie. He hoped the pearls had spat him out somewhere in her vicinity. The American continent was much larger than England. At least the first person he'd met in the future had been cordial.

Well, mostly cordial.

The man seemed far too amused by Luke's bewilderment.

Why *was* the man so entertained? Didn't he seem strange to him? Maggie certainly had to Luke, though he'd thought her intriguing. West had spoken to him almost as if he knew that—

"Here you are," said West, dropping into the chair next to him. He handed him a plate with a sandwich, and Luke's stomach gave another grumble. Time travel made one famished.

A smile pulled at his lips. *Hungry enough to eat a horse,* as Maggie had put it.

"I hope you'll forgive the light meal," said West. "I'm not much of a cook."

Luke swallowed a large bite. "This is much appreciated, I assure you. Far better than nothing."

"I suppose so, but dinner will be better. You'll want to stay, of course."

He said it as a statement rather than a question, making Luke pause from taking another bite. "I do not wish to burden your hospitality. If you will take me into—"

"You won't be a burden. This house is far bigger than I need. Several spare rooms. Besides, you won't want to miss out on dinner. Maggie is an excellent cook, at least compared to me."

Luke choked on a chunk of bread and meat. "Maggie?"

West turned toward him, mischief rampant in his eyes. "As I said, Luke, there's no need for you to go into town yet."

Chapter 25

Oklahoma, 2022

A few moments of stunned silence in which Luke's mouth hung open passed by before he managed to overcome his shock and speak. "You are Maggie's father? Weston?"

Only now did Luke make the connection. The realization made his heart pound harder. How much did the man know? Had Maggie told her father about him? If so, he likely hadn't made a good first impression.

The man's chuckle confirmed the question, but he nodded. "Yes, and I know who you are, *Your Grace.*"

That explained why he found nothing odd about Luke's confusion. "Maggie told you about me."

"She told me how you helped her—took care of her while she was in an unfamiliar place where she could have been severely hurt. The world is not generally forgiving, now or in eighteen fifteen. I owe you my gratitude."

"You give me far too much credit. I did help her, but Maggie is strong enough to take care of herself. She would have been fine without my assistance. Perhaps better off." Especially after he'd showered her with criticism and refused to listen. Luke glared at his sandwich.

"Even dukes aren't perfect," said West. "I know about your argument. But it may interest you to know that she doesn't blame you for reacting the way you did."

"Responding as I did to notions of time travel is one thing. Belittling her attempts to be honest with me—to confide in me—is another entirely. She broke my trust, and I responded in kind. I am not proud of that."

"Trust, like most things, can be lost and found. Breaking it is easy; earning it back is difficult but not impossible. The question is whether you have the desire to put forth the effort. I'm guessing that since you're here, you're inclined to rectify the situation?"

"I am. I believe we can work through what happened."

"Then you have wonderful timing. Maggie is on her way here as we speak. Should arrive in a few hours."

"She said you did not spend much time at your home in Philadelphia." Luke looked out over the fields. "That you preferred to live outside of town. How far away does she live?"

"Philadelphia? Is that what she told you? I suppose that makes sense. LA barely existed in your time."

"LA?"

"Los Angeles," said Weston. "You've landed yourself in the Midwest. LA is on the west coast—more than a thousand miles from here. Maggie is flying into Oklahoma City and then has a short drive. But, just so we're clear—I never visit Los Angeles. Her mother has no desire to see me, and I can't say the feeling isn't mutual."

Flying? His mind reeled again, and the man's words from earlier flooded his thoughts. "Ex-wife. You said she was your enemy. Do you mean to say you are divorced?"

"Precisely, Mr. Halford. You'll find that separation of man and wife is common in today's society. A sad fact but true, nonetheless. Maggie's mother and I ended our marriage ten years ago, after which I moved here, purchased this farm, and have lived happily. My only regret is missing out on so much time with my daughter."

Luke scratched the back of his head. "And neither of you have suffered from the social repercussions?"

West laughed and shook his head. "Things are different. We have not been cast out from society because of our divorce as we would have been in your era. Now, finish your food, and I'll give you a tour of the house. Probably best I show you some modern conveniences before Maggie arrives."

Weston's statement that things were different failed to adequately describe the future. The moment they entered the house, Luke felt overwhelmed. Glass candles hung in every room and lit with the flip of a switch. When West pointed an object at a black rectangle on the wall and images appeared, Luke's jaw dropped. West spent several minutes explaining how people managed to get inside the thin box, but Luke struggled to concentrate, too distracted by the moving picture that constantly changed before his eyes.

The water closet held just as much intrigue. Apparently the future had given way to *indoor plumbing*. He and West stood in front of what looked like a fancy chamber pot, an invention of his time but not one heavily adopted by society, including the most affluent. The sound it made when West toggled the handle startled him. Luke supposed flushing away unwanted contents made things better for the servants.

Where were the servants?

He stole a moment to ask West, only to discover that most households in the future had none. That concept perplexed him, but musing over it quickly became moot when West showed him the shower. Hot water rained from a metal head attached to the wall as if on command.

After a thorough tour, Luke joined West in an open drawing room—the same one that housed the strange box with the moving pictures. Luke slumped onto the settee, mentally drained.

"We'll take you into town tomorrow," said West. "You'll need some clothes. I don't believe I have anything that would fit you." His gaze flitted over him. Weston was right; he stood half a foot taller, and his shoulders were broader, but he disliked the idea of burdening the man in any way. Maggie had said her father was a wealthy businessman...but Maggie had said a great many things, and Luke had learned some of them were untrue.

"I do not wish you to incur debt on my behalf," said Luke. "I will manage with what I have."

West swatted the air. "Don't be ridiculous. You helped my Maggie when she needed it most, and you can't plan to wear that for days on end. Besides, I can handle the expense. I may be a farmer, but that isn't as bad as you might assume."

A farmer. He had suspected, but then the nice estate had left him confused. "Maggie said you were a businessman, which clearly was untrue, but she also mentioned she was an heiress."

Asking such personal questions defied propriety, but West obliged him with a smile. "A farm the size of mine does require business skills, but yes, Maggie would be considered an heiress in your terms. Her mother, LeAnn, inherited a highly successful company. She expects Maggie to take over." He heaved a heavy sigh. "Problem is Maggie is more like me—prefers a quieter life. Has no interest in being a socialite." His gaze grew distant as if he had lost himself to his memories. "At one time, her mother didn't want the company, either."

The topic seemed a sore spot, so Luke decided to lay that conversation to rest. He looked around the room, and his gaze landed on the side table next to him. A small portrait of Maggie rested in a wooden frame. Luke picked it up. It was not a painting but looked as though someone had captured a moment in time—a real moment. Regardless, the piece depicted with perfect accuracy the woman he had come to know, not simply in appearance but in the warmth that exuded from her eyes and smile.

"A photograph," said Weston. "We have the technology to take pictures as life happens. Then we simply print them onto paper. I took that one last time Maggie came to visit."

Luke positioned the portrait back on the table. "Does she visit often?"

"When LeAnn and I separated, Maggie would stay here during the summers. After she turned eighteen, she went to college. I saw her less then, but she always made time when she could. She stayed in LA once she'd finished school—began attending meetings and visiting the corporate office with her mother. None of it made her happy. I could see the strain it put on her, but LeAnn became so insistent that Maggie take over."

Weston's expression brightened. "But after Maggie returned, she completely walked away from the company. She found the courage to stand up to her mother and has been taking on students for piano lessons. Now *that* has brought her true joy."

"That evokes little surprise. Maggie is exceptionally talented with the instrument."

"Ah, she played for you? I'm curious what she chose to perform."

"Something about dragons," said Luke with a chuckle. The whole thing had been surprising and strange then, but now that he knew Maggie had come from the future, much of his time with her made sense. No wonder she had been so nervous around him. The fear that she might mistakenly paint herself as mad would have been stressful. Yet, her true self had often slipped through.

A low rumble outside drew Luke's attention to the window across the room. Light flickered through the curtains, and Weston rose from his chair to peek through the parted cloth.

"She's here." The man turned to face Luke and smirked. "Are you prepared for this?"

Luke's heart plunged into his stomach. Was he prepared? The way everything inside him writhed, he suspected not.

He followed Weston to the front door but waited inside the house as the man stalked out onto the veranda. A shiny dark blue carriage, different in shape than the one Weston had driven earlier, came to a stop in front of the house. Through the glass, he could see a form with long, dark hair. His pulse raced. What would Maggie say when she saw him? Would she be happy?

Maggie popped out of the coach, and his gaze stuck to her, incapable of pulling away. It had been four months, but his heart responded the same way it always had in her presence, and a familiar warmth spread through him from head to toe. She looked different, and not simply in that her brown curls hung loosely over her shoulders or that she wore pantaloons much like her father's. Those were peculiar, of course, but there was a contentedness in Maggie's expression that drew him in, one that spoke of her zeal for life. It stoked the flames inside him, fueling the desire to scoop her into his arms and share in the happiness she exuded.

Weston rushed forward and wrapped her in a tight embrace. "There's my girl!"

She pulled away, beaming. "Hey, Dad. It's good to see you."

"How was your flight?"

Maggie spouted a dramatic groan. "As good and horrible as always. If the airlines get any greedier, we'll need to purchase two tickets to keep from sitting on top of each other. But we had no delays, so I can be grateful for that."

They walked toward the stairs leading onto the veranda, and his heart stalled. She had yet to see him standing inside the open door, too busy speaking to Weston, and the impending moment closed in on him with suffocating intensity.

"I'm glad you made it safe and sound," said Weston. "By the way, we'll have an extra visitor during your stay."

Maggie halted, and Weston jutted his chin in Luke's direction. She turned, and her eyes rounded. She stared at him, gaping, for what felt like an eternity. He told himself to say something, but the words would not come.

"Luke?" Her voice was so soft, he barely heard it.

He swallowed and left the safety of the house, crossing the veranda until he stopped at the edge of the stairs. "Good evening, Maggie."

Before either of them could say more, a man approached carrying a trunk in each hand. "I don't know about you, but I could use a nap. I'm completely jet-lagged." He stopped next to her and dropped one bag to place a hand on her shoulder. His forehead furrowed when she didn't respond, and he followed her gaze. "Oh, who's this?"

That was a question Luke would have liked the man to answer. Maggie hadn't come alone, and the weight of what that might mean bore down on him until he couldn't breathe.

Oklahoma, 2022

All of the oxygen had definitely left the atmosphere, and Maggie knew she would suffocate. She had fallen off the deep end and now drowned in a hallucination specifically designed to torment her. What else could explain how a man who had lived two hundred years ago, a man whose heart she'd broken, stood on Dad's porch?

"Maggie?" Gerard's concerned voice pulled her from her trance. She turned to face him, and his brow lifted. "Who's this?"

"He's a friend. Or was. Is?" Fudge. She didn't know what to call him.

Luke winced, her answer seeming to stab at him as much as it did her. Gerard dropped one of the bags and bounded up the steps, his hand outstretched. "It's always good to meet one of Maggie's friends. I'm Gerard Burke."

Luke accepted the gesture. "Luke Halford."

"Nice to—oh! You're him, aren't you?" Gerard released his hand and motioned over Luke's form. "Clearly you are, what with the old-fashioned clothes."

The way Luke's brows rose suggested he took offense to the comment, and her heart jolted. This was a nightmare, one that had no chance of ending given that Gerard continued.

"Luke The Duke, isn't that right, Maggie? She's told me all about you and her trip to the past. Very fascinating. Say, do you think I could ask you some questions? What does time travel feel like? Maggie says she can't remember, but I thought maybe you could."

Nope. This went beyond a nightmare.

"You know what," said Maggie, grabbing the bag Gerard had left behind. "I think I'm going to go unpack and then make dinner." She pushed past both of them. Her body felt like it would explode if she didn't get out of there. Gerard had too many questions for Luke, and Luke had too many questions for her. She could see them in his eyes.

And she wasn't ready to answer them.

Maggie crossed the threshold but paused a few feet into the house to glance at Luke. She should at least say *something* to the man, shouldn't she?

"I...it's nice to see you." There. That's all he was getting right now.

She spun around and darted up the stairs, her suitcase thudding against each one like a drum as she dragged it behind her. She needed solitude to sort out her thoughts. This trip was supposed to be an escape, yet somehow she'd walked into...what, exactly? Seeing Luke made her heart leap in ways it shouldn't. She'd hurt the man and didn't deserve to have him in life nor had she believed he would *want* to ever see her again.

But he was here. In the future. On Dad's porch.

Maggie closed her bedroom door and shuffled to the window. She leaned her head against the glass and focused on breathing. It didn't help.

She yanked her phone out of her back pocket, intent on scrolling through social media or something to distract herself, but a text notification popped up on the screen before she could.

DIANA: Your mom said you went to your dad's. Just text me when you land safe, OK? Please.

Maggie drew a deep breath. She hadn't spoken to Diana in almost two months. Her friend's disbelief had hurt her, and although Diana meant well, she couldn't seem to forget. Perhaps it was petty, but she had a strong desire to prove her friend wrong.

MAGGIE: Landed. Luke is here.

There was a long pause filled with three dots.

DIANA: Like, the dude from your hallucination?

MAGGIE: It wasn't a hallucination.

She tempered her irritation with a slow exhale. What she needed was physical proof.

Shifting to the edge of the window, she could see the front lawn. Luke had joined Gerard and Dad on the grass. She snapped a quick picture and sent it to Diana, and then watched the men while she waited for a response. Gerard moved his hands animatedly, and she wondered what impertinent questions he was asking.

DIANA: He has nice hair.

Maggie groaned.

MAGGIE: How observant of you.

DIANA: Chica, I'm sure the rest of him is nice, too. Can't really tell when he's so tiny. Why don't you go ask him for a better picture so I can evaluate properly.

She smiled. Diana still didn't believe her, yet the short interaction had calmed the monster of irritation living inside her. She missed her friend, perhaps more than she'd realized.

MAGGIE: I can't. I don't know what to say.

DIANA: 'My best friend wants to see a picture of you' will probably work.

MAGGIE: No way!

DIANA: Pleeease!

Maggie tossed the phone onto her bed. Nope, not happening.

The phone dinged several times, but Maggie did her best to ignore it. She plopped her suitcase on the bed and tugged at the zipper. She could handle this. All she needed was a few minutes to calm down. Let the situation soak.

A knock at the door froze her fingers. "Who is it?"

"Gerard."

A mixture of relief and disappointment swirled inside her. She rushed to the door, and after checking the hallway, pulled Gerard inside.

"You look frantic, Maggie." Gerard placed a hand on her shoulder. "Do you need to sit down?"

Yes. She needed to go to bed and sleep for a few days until she woke up from this crazy dream. "No, I'm fine. Just...shocked."

"For good reason."

"Yeah." She grabbed two pairs of pants and crossed the room to the dresser. Perhaps she was frantic and even had good reason to be, but confessing that did nothing to solve the problem.

"Are you happy to see him?" asked Gerard.

Maggie shut the dresser drawer with a loud thud. "What?"

Gerard moved to her side, his expression sympathetic. "Pardon the pun, but you two have a history. Do you still have feelings for the duke?"

"I don't know what I feel right now beyond mentally and physically exhausted."

"I would understand if you did. That wasn't so long ago. You do realize why he's here, don't you?"

She marched back to the bed, and Gerard followed. He watched as she fumbled through the suitcase, pulling everything out and placing it in a chaotic pile on the bed. When she had emptied the contents, Gerard closed the bag. "Maggie, he wants—"

"Can we not talk about this right now? Please."

Gerard held his hands up in surrender, and Maggie brushed past him to hang her shirts in the closet. Several minutes passed in silence, and she wished he would leave her to have some peace.

"Do you think he brought the pearls with him?" asked Gerard. "Maybe he'll give them back to you."

"I assume so. How else would he be here?"

"You said the necklace broke. Do you think he brought them all with—"

"Gerard." She flipped around, doing her best not to glare. "I don't know. You seemed to have no problem interrogating him a few minutes ago, so why don't you go ask?"

He averted his gaze, the muscles in his jaw tightening. Honestly, why was the man so concerned about it? But then, he had been the one person she leaned on the last few months. He cared, simple as that.

Maggie sighed. "I'm sorry. This whole thing has me stressed. I need a few minutes to just"—she lifted her hands into the air and allowed gravity to bring them crashing down against her thighs—"take it all in."

"I understand. I'll go unpack. Let me know when you head downstairs or if you need me."

She nodded, and Gerard turned and left the room. Her hands trembled at the thought of going back downstairs...at facing Luke. She still cared for him; there was no denying that. But she'd also betrayed his trust, and the guilt would haunt her for the rest of her life.

LUKE CROSSED HIS ARMS AND GAVE WESTON A HARD GLARE. Neither of them spoke until Gerard had entered the house and the door closed with a thud. Reuniting with Maggie had not gone how he planned in the slightest, and besides the disappointment, he felt a great deal of irritation.

"You might have warned me," said Luke. "Are they...?" He swallowed, the last half of his question rotting on his tongue like a piece of old fruit.

"Dating—or courting, as you would call it." Weston rubbed the back of his neck. "I don't know if I'd call it that, but Gerard has spent a lot of time with her since she came back. I do think he likes her. Just hasn't made a move."

Luke ran his hand through his hair. "Why the devil did you not say something!"

West folded his arms. "First, I've known you for less than four hours. I wasn't entirely sure of your intentions when you showed up; however, your reaction has made them quite clear. Second, I didn't want to tell you because I was afraid you'd give up and go back to 1815."

"Perhaps I should?"

The man tilted his head and lifted a brow. Luke groaned. Neither of them believed him capable of abandoning hope that quickly, it seemed. "Fine, I have no desire to go back, but I at least deserve to know the details of the situation. How long have they been...been..."

He could not even bring himself to say the deuced word.

"From what Maggie has told me, Gerard checks in on her almost every day. Has done so since she left the hospital."

"Hospital?"

"She was fine," Weston added hastily. "Her mother demanded a checkup. Maggie agreed to calm the hysterics, but regardless,

Gerard seems pretty interested. You'd better make a move quickly if we're to stop this from going any further."

Luke scoffed. " *We?* Do you have something against the man?"

West shrugged and shoved his hands into the pockets of his pantaloons. "He seems like a nice enough fellow, I suppose. Problem is, I'm not sure he makes Maggie happy. She *wants* to be happy, but I'm not convinced he's the one. Something about him...he just isn't her person. Doesn't fit the bill."

"And you believe I, the man you have known not more than a few hours, fits the... *bill?*" Whatever that meant.

West had that mischievous look in his eyes again. He stepped closer and planted a firm hold on Luke's shoulder. "If you'd seen the way Maggie lit up when she spoke of you, confidence wouldn't be a problem. I know my daughter, Luke. Now, quit wasting time and get in there."

Warmth constricted his chest. Maggie had spoken highly of him, and that fueled his desire to speak with her. He needed to find out whether they could move past everything that had happened. He wanted Maggie in his life—he always had—but after so many lies, he was uncertain she felt the same.

There was nothing for it but to find out.

He and Weston parted ways inside the foyer, and Luke darted up the stairs. He crept through a long hallway, listening intently for any indication of where Maggie might be. He peered inside an open doorway, and his heart sputtered. She sat on the edge of a bed, her eyes glistening in the last of the sunlight entering through the window.

Her expression reminded him of the night they'd met. Those fear-stricken eyes had pierced his soul then, but now they stabbed daggers into his heart. His presence had caused her pain, and he wondered if his journey to the future had been a mistake. Losing her once had broken him. How would he survive it a second time?

Luke cleared his throat, and Maggie's attention turned to him sharply. Her mouth parted in a gasp, and she jumped up from the bed. "Luke."

The whispered word sent chills down his arms. "Maggie, I know this must be overwhelming, but I need to speak with you." He hesitated to move. The last thing he wanted to do was corner her, and this discussion warranted privacy, but to enter a lady's bedchamber...

"You can come in," she said, seeming to sense his internal dilemma.

He entered, and she came to his side and closed the door.

Luke swallowed, his heart taking on a pace much too fast for someone standing still.

"You don't have to worry," she whispered. "Reputations aren't nearly as fragile in the future. And I promise not to ensnare you." She dropped her gaze, and his fingers twitched with the urge to pull her against him.

"I know you would never do that, regardless of the era." Even as he said the words, doubt and fear laced his thoughts. He wanted to believe she was the lady he thought her to be, but how could he know for sure when so much of their time together had been threaded with mistruths?

She glanced up at him as if she had read his thoughts again. "You don't mean that. I know I lost your trust."

Her tears escaped, and he pulled her into his arms. She sobbed against his chest, and as he held her close, the ache that had been his constant companion for months dulled.

"I'm so sorry," she said between shuddering breaths. "I wanted to tell you before the ball, but I was scared, and..." She choked on the words, and more tears rolled down her cheeks.

He tightened his hold and rested his cheek against her head. "I understand. You had every right to fear telling me the truth. I cannot pretend the information would have been received well no matter when you told me."

"But waiting hurt you."

Luke closed his eyes. He would not deny the claim. The lies, even after learning the entirety of the situation, had pierced him deeply. He had allowed her closer than anyone, and though she had good reason to betray his trust, it did not alleviate the pain.

He allowed her to weep until her breathing evened. Holding her in his arms felt right, but he could not afford to let his heart lead, not until he better understood where they stood.

Maggie backed away from him, and his hands slid down her shoulders until she had moved completely out of his grasp. She wiped her eyes, now swollen and red, with the back of her hand. "So, what made you risk time traveling to the future?"

"A few things," said Luke. "I wanted to ensure you were well. I also wanted to apologize."

"For what? You have nothing to be sorry for."

He clasped his hands behind his back. "Your confession did hurt me. I cannot pretend otherwise, but I also reacted poorly when you tried to explain. I did not give you the benefit of an open mind, and for that I am sorry."

"How can I be mad at you for thinking I was crazy?" She shook her head. "Before I ended up in your era, I wouldn't have believed me, either."

"I confess you handled the situation well, all things considered. You knew enough about the past to convince me you were a genteel lady, albeit a bit odd at times."

Her face brightened with a smile, and he warmed at the response. He had needed to see her smile.

She tilted her head with a look of mock annoyance. "Odd? Surely not. I daresay my turn of phrase was completely proper and my gait one of perfect elegance. My curtsy, too."

Luke chuckled, images of her wobbly balance filling his mind. "Much of the time, but those occasions when your act faltered were more enjoyable."

Her cheeks tinted, and she turned away. But his own words distracted his thoughts too thoroughly to focus on teasing her. Those moments, the ones where Maggie had been herself, had drawn him in. Those moments where she forwent the expectations of Society and surprised him were the ones that coaxed him into vulnerability. They were the interactions where she stole his heart.

For so long, he had worried that he knew nothing about the woman his heart yearned to see again, that the lies made her little more than a stranger, but perhaps he had it backwards. Luke had not fallen for the façade, but for the person she had tried to hide. He did not love the woman she'd pretended to be, but the one she'd kept hidden.

The realization calmed his soul in a way he hadn't expected. Perhaps he could extinguish the feelings of betrayal knowing Maggie had been her true self around him. It eased the hurt buried in his heart, but fear lingered. She may have acted like herself, but that did not mean she felt for him as he did her. Each touch, each kiss—what if that was only to persuade him to help her?

Luke shook his head. He could not allow his mind to conjure what ifs. This was, after all, the purpose of his voyage through time. He could sort through the questions and finally have answers.

"Luke?"

Her voice had sunk into a soft whisper, but his name on her lips still sent chills down his spine. He met her gaze and found uncertainty in her eyes. What did she feel when she looked at him? Did her heart beat as erratically as his own?

Maggie tucked a strand of hair behind her ear. "I guess you plan to return to eighteen fifteen now? You said you came to check on me and apologize. You've done that."

"I suppose I could go back," he said, watching her expression. Asking her outright if she cared for him was too impertinent and would not give him complete clarity. He needed to see it. *Feel* it.

She hugged her stomach and wouldn't quite meet his eyes. "Time travel is exhausting business. You should consider staying for dinner and spending the night at least."

Luke suppressed a grin. That sounded an awful lot like she wanted him to stay. "If you insist. Your father did say your cooking was better than his. I admit that statement has me curious."

Her brows lifted. "Don't get your hopes too high. Nearly anyone could cook better than him."

Luke rubbed his chin, taking note of his stubble for the first time. He hadn't given much thought about how long he'd laid on the road, and now he wondered given the amount of hair. Perhaps Weston would let him borrow some things to take care of the matter. "I'm anxious to learn about your skills for myself. I shall leave you to unpack so as to not prolong my curiosity further."

"I'll see you at dinner, then?"

The hopefulness in her voice elated him. She truly wanted him to stay.

"At dinner," he confirmed.

The way her expression brightened constricted his chest. He bowed and entered the hallway filled with a sense of peace. He had no intention of making another journey through time until he knew whether she reciprocated his feelings, nor did he plan to make a brash decision, but for the first time since Maggie told him the truth, hope outweighed his concern and the future seemed bright, indeed.

Chapter 27

Oklahoma, 2022

Weston had been correct in his statement of Maggie's skill. Dinner the night before had been delicious, and although not the elaborate display from his cook at Windgate, his stomach had found nothing to complain about. Naturally, that meant he should stay for breakfast today.

Luke watched Maggie dart around the kitchen from the archway, his stomach grumbling in response to the smell of biscuits, bacon, and eggs that wafted his way. It had taken a lengthy conversation for him to understand why a young lady in her position would know how to prepare a meal at all. The notion that few households in the future employed a cook baffled him.

Maggie brushed a stray piece of hair from her face with the back of her hand. She'd pulled the rest up with some sort of circular band. Did women still use pins in the future?

Just one more question for him to tuck away. He had so many; he could scarcely keep track of them all.

She moved to the other side of the room and scraped the cooked eggs onto a plate. She had dressed differently today—a long-sleeved shift that draped over a pair of tight, black pantaloons that clung to her curves—

Luke shook his head. He should *not* be observing her body so closely. It was difficult not to notice, however, when he found the attire of the future so appealing—*intriguing.*

He found it intriguing.

Carrying the steaming eggs, Maggie started toward him. When she finally noticed he stood at the door, surprise graced her features, and she smiled. "Good morning. I wasn't sure if you'd be joining us for breakfast or not."

Ah, yes. He hadn't told her of his intention to stay and would keep things that way until he determined her feelings for himself.

"With how delightful the food was last evening, I could hardly turn down the opportunity. I may see what all the future has to offer before I return, so long as I'm not a burden to anyone."

"Of course you're not. We're happy to have you."

"Does the *we* include you? After your reaction yesterday—"

"You surprised me, but it was a good surprise...at least in hindsight. A bit overwhelming at first, but I've missed you and..."

She turned away, a hint of embarrassment touching her cheeks. Why did every blush or smile feel like a victory?

"I missed you, too, Maggie." His fingers brushed against hers when he took the plate of food from her grasp. "Allow me."

"Thank you."

"My pleasure. I shall be back in a moment to help."

She narrowed her eyes. "Okay."

Luke took the plate into the dining room where Gerard and Weston both sat at the table. Weston's nose was buried in a newspaper, while Gerard had his attention focused on a...well, Luke didn't know what that *thing* was, but it seemed to be causing the man a great deal of frustration. His brows pinched so close together they almost connected.

Positioning the eggs beside a tray of bacon, Luke fought a grin. The man's perturbed expression amused him, and he desperately wished to know the cause of it.

"Sticking around?" asked Gerard when his gaze lifted long enough to notice him.

Luke shrugged, and the man's resulting scowl nearly stole his composure. "I do not recall ever saying I planned to leave."

"Of course you don't." Gerard's attention returned to the object in his hand, and he groaned. "West, is there anywhere in town with free Wi-Fi? A coffee shop or something? Last night the internet worked perfectly, but today I can't even open Safari. I have two Zoom meetings. I can't miss them."

With his focus on the *thing*, Gerard missed the twinkle of mischief in West's eyes. "There are several places in town."

Luke spun around and returned to the kitchen. Trying to understand everything Gerard said made his head hurt, and he refused to request an explanation. He'd figure out the future without asking him for help. Gerard had bombarded him with a great many impertinent questions, but perhaps he had no reason to dislike the man beyond the fact that he had traveled with Maggie. Alone.

Reminding himself that this century was not like his own did little to help. Until he could deduce precisely what the man's relationship with her entailed, Gerard was a potential threat.

Maggie poured some batter into a large pan as Luke approached. He gingerly touched her shoulder. "What can I do to assist you?"

She tilted her head, her eyes wandering over his face. "You were serious?"

Luke scoffed. "That surprises you? I feel I should be offended."

Her attention returned to the bubbling cake. She used a flat utensil to flip it over, and a distinct sizzle filled the room. "I'm not surprised you offered to help, just that you offered to help with *cooking* specifically. Have you ever prepared a meal in your life?"

Luke hummed for a moment. "Does slicing bread, cheese, and meat count? I have done that."

Maggie laughed. Another victory.

She jutted her chin to the cupboard behind them. "You could grab me a plate."

He did as she asked and returned to her side. "What are you making?"

"Pancakes." Maggie scooped up the round cake and placed it onto the plate before adding more batter to the pan. For the next several minutes, he stood next to her as she cooked and stacked pancakes. She could have asked him to place the plate on the counter. It wasn't as though his holding it actually helped in any way, but if doing so gave him an excuse to be with her, then he'd perform the task. He preferred to think Maggie enjoyed his company.

Luke took the pancakes into the dining room followed by Maggie's quiet steps. She sat down in the chair next to Gerard, and Luke claimed the empty chair beside her.

"This smells wonderful, Mags," said West, lowering his newspaper. "Thank you."

Maggie grabbed several slices of bacon. "I had wonderful help."

She glanced at Luke, and West lifted a brow. "Is that so?"

"Yes, my skill of holding a plate is quite impressive," said Luke. "It seems I may need to stay for a few days. My talents are clearly needed."

"Clearly," Maggie teased. "How did we ever manage without you?"

Gerard turned to face her, seemingly oblivious to their playful conversation with his stoic expression. "I need to go into town. West says there's a café I can use for my meetings. I've had no luck with the Internet here. Would you mind taking me?"

Maggie nodded and swallowed a mouthful of food before answering. "Of course I can take you. I need to run a few errands, anyway."

"Take Luke with you, too," said West. "He'll need clothes if he's going to stay."

The man reached into his pocket and pulled out a leather pouch. He removed a stack of notes, and Maggie shook her head when he tossed them to her from the other side of the table. "I have enough savings to take care of it, Dad. I still owe him a debt. He did the same for me."

She sent Luke a smile, one filled with unspoken gratitude, and his heart stuttered. He wanted to tell her that she owed him nothing, but he couldn't bring himself to say anything that might erase the look she was currently giving him.

"Thank you," he finally managed. Though the idea of Maggie purchasing things on his behalf did not sit well with him. As someone of wealth and title, he had never relied on anyone in such a way.

"Luke The Duke needs something less old-fashioned or he'll be the talk of the town," said Gerard. "We wouldn't want to draw attention to his unique circumstance. Imagine if the wrong people found out. He'd become a government guinea pig in no time."

Luke did not know exactly what *that* meant, but judging by the look on Gerard's smug face, he didn't want to be a guinea pig.

"That's not funny, Gerard." Maggie heaved a sigh. "He isn't wrong, though. Even today people would think you're crazy for stating you've traveled through time. Best we keep the information to ourselves."

Gerard scoffed. "Might be difficult to hide. An accent in a small town is bound to attract some ears...and eyes." His brows furrowed. "I never understood why so many women find a *British* accent appealing."

She shrugged, swallowing another mouthful of food. "Accents are sexy."

Sexy? What in heaven's name did that mean? He could guess, but perhaps he would ask Maggie later.

Gerard rolled his eyes and stood. "Whatever you say. Let's get going. My meeting starts in less than an hour."

Maggie gave West a kiss on the cheek and darted upstairs after informing them she needed to grab her *purse.* She met them at the door a few minutes later with a large reticule featuring straps that went over her shoulder. Luke assumed that was the purse she'd spoken of. Gerard had his hands full with his own purse, though it was bigger and flatter than Maggie's. He mentioned something about a *laptop,* but Luke had given up trying to make sense of anything the man said.

They left the house, and Luke followed them to the—

He halted at the head of the carriage Maggie had arrived in the day before. Did he really wish to get in one of those again? No, not particularly.

"Come on!" Gerard waved at him to keep moving as he ducked inside. "My meeting starts soon."

The man had the patience of a famished wolf. What was so important about this meeting, anyway?

Maggie appeared at his side, her face contorted with concern. "Dad said you took a ride in his truck after he found you. Do vehicles make you nervous?"

"Nauseous would be a better descriptive."

Understanding dawned on her features. "You get motion sickness."

"I never have before, but these contraptions are not exactly the same as a coach."

She grabbed his hand, and it felt like a bolt of lightning surged up his arm. She led him to Gerard's side, where the man fiddled with the same object he had earlier that morning, the door still open.

"Gerard, would you please sit in the back? Luke isn't used to riding in a car. The front will be gentler on his stomach."

"Sure." Gerard slid off the seat and stood. His gaze flicked to where Maggie still clasped his hand. Irritation etched into the man's expression, but he said nothing as he opened the door and plopped onto the backseat.

Luke sat down, and Maggie rounded to the other side.

"Seat belt," she said, pointing to something over his shoulder. He followed her lead, wrapping the strange belt across his chest and shoving it into some sort of latch at his side. He watched her every movement—how she inserted the key and shifted the lever. It was rather fascinating, and she seemed to go through the motions with little thought.

"I'll try not to jostle you too much," she said. "But if you do feel sick, let me know. I'd rather you didn't throw up in the car. It's a rental."

"I would rather I did not do so, either. And thank you. I think experiencing your father's driving was far more strenuous than traveling through time."

"Maybe he was testing your stamina."

"Do you suppose I passed? Likely not. I did nearly retch after we arrived."

Gerard groaned. "Can we stop talking about vomit and *go*?"

Amusement reached Maggie's brown eyes, and she passed Luke a subtle grin.

Another victory.

Chapter 28

Oklahoma, 2022

Maggie tried to focus on the road, but Luke's reaction as they rolled into town made that difficult. He looked completely awestruck with his mouth agape and his nose nearly pressed to the window like a kid peering into a candy store.

She pulled into the parking lot of Molly's Cafe, and Luke looked over his shoulder when Gerard shifted on the back seat. Gerard scooted to the edge and leaned forward, poking his head between them. "It'll be about two hours, maybe three. Should I text you once I've finished?"

"Yeah, text me," Maggie answered.

"Thank you." Gerard kissed her cheek, and she stiffened. Why had he done that? He'd never kissed her before, and to say it left her utterly perplexed and uncomfortable was an understatement. The only man who seemed to notice, however, was Luke. He stared at her with a contemplative look that only made her wish to squirm.

Gerard grabbed his laptop bag and opened the back door. "We'll go to lunch after. That little country diner you're always telling me about?"

"Okay." She turned her attention away from Luke's considering eyes and onto the man who'd just kissed her cheek. It took effort to keep her voice even. "That sounds good."

Gerard entered the building, and an awkward silence settled between her and Luke. He'd allowed her to apologize last night, and a weight had lifted from her shoulders, but one apology didn't erase the damage she'd done. Maybe nothing ever would.

Maggie shifted gears, and taking notice of Luke's study of her movements, put the vehicle back in park and turned off the engine.

"Would you like to know how to make this thing work?" He nodded, and she proceeded to explain each step of getting the car into motion from start to finish. The information seemed to appease his curiosity and distract him from the questions that still lingered between them.

At least it did until he spoke again. "So..."

"Is there a question there?" She placed the car in drive and pulled onto the practically vacant street, a benefit to living in a community so small. Traffic was something she wouldn't miss if she chose to stay in Oklahoma.

Luke rubbed the back of his neck. "You and Gerard...is there an understanding between the two of you? A serious one?"

Heat filled her cheeks, but she kept her eyes focused on the road. She was not ready for this conversation, but what could she do about it? Running wasn't exactly an option at the moment.

She tapped the wheel. "After I came back, I was in an awful state. Everyone wanted to know what had happened, but no one would believe me when I told them—not even my mother. Most of them wrote it off as trauma. But not my father...and not Gerard."

She couldn't begin to explain the hurt lingering in her heart. She hadn't expected Mom to believe her, just as she hadn't expected Luke to, but that didn't make the pain go away.

The car entered the parking lot of Target, and Maggie chose a space near a cart return. Tears pooled in her eyes, and everything inside her screamed to bolt for the building, to let this conversation drop. But Luke deserved answers, and she couldn't avoid the inevitable forever.

"Maggie, I am sorry." He lifted his hand as though to take hers but must have decided against the idea, settling it back into his lap instead. Disappointment flooded over her, quickly followed by guilt. She had no right to expect him to comfort her.

He shifted on the leather seat. "Upsetting you was not my intention. I only—"

"You have a right to know." She drew a deep breath and clenched the steering wheel. "I met Gerard at one of my mother's parties the night I time hopped, and since I returned, he's been there for me. He's been understanding and patient through this whole thing, a wonderful friend, but..."

But she didn't love him, and until recently, she hadn't felt Gerard wanted more than friendship. Had she read him wrong? He'd never made a move to suggest it...until a few minutes ago. What was she to do with that gesture? Even if he cared for her in that way, she wasn't sure she could ever return the sentiment. She didn't feel the need to be near Gerard or miss him when he left. Her thoughts still revolved around one person, and although she'd hoped to eventually move on, she wasn't sure she could.

Having Luke nearby only made it seem more impossible. She cared about him, more than she had ever cared about any man, but she couldn't allow herself to think about the possibilities or analyze his reasons for being there. She didn't trust herself not to hurt him again and refused to be responsible for shattering his heart a second time.

"What do you say we find you some modern clothes?" she asked.

Luke tilted his head at the change in topic. He still had questions—she could see it in his dark eyes—but he didn't push her. He leaned forward and peered up at the store's giant sign. "Here?"

"Here," she confirmed. "Come on."

Luke kept close to her as they walked toward the building, his eyes darting from one thing to another like he was following a Golden Snitch in a game of Quidditch. He halted so quickly at the automated doors that he nearly fell over.

"They have little sensors that detect movement," said Maggie.

"Are you certain they are not simply bewitched?"

"Positive."

She gestured for him to follow. His mouth dropped the moment they passed through the second set of doors. He did a slow scan of the first aisle, completely awestruck. She withdrew her phone from her pocket. She hadn't intended to give in to Diana's request, but part of her still wanted to prove her sanity. Not only that, but Luke wouldn't stay here forever, and the thought of having something to remember him by prompted her to capture the moment.

She took a quick picture and sent it to Diana before returning the phone to her back pocket. She grabbed one of the dark red carts and stepped up beside him. "You must have a thousand questions."

"Yes. Perhaps more than a thousand."

Maggie pushed the cart forward, and Luke kept pace beside her.

"Well, if you have questions, I'm always happy to answer them," she said. "Anything in particular you'd like to know?"

He turned to face her, and for a moment she worried he might bring up her relationship with Gerard again.

"Gerard mentioned a *laptop* before we left. Said he needed it for his meeting. Perhaps we could start there."

"Of course you would pick something complicated. A laptop is a machine. It can do a lot of things—more than I even know how to explain. Some people use it for playing games, others for creating presentations and documents. You can read on it, keep track of expenses, access the Internet—"

"The Internet. What is that? Gerard mentioned it as well."

"How on earth do I explain..." She thought for a moment. "Think of it like a giant library."

"A library?"

She nodded. "You can find almost anything there. Say you wanted to know how to cook pancakes, for instance. You simply type—or write—your query on the machine, and it gives you the answer. You can watch tutorials on how to do something or search through records, purchase nearly anything you could think of—the Internet is like a collection of everything humanity has learned. But it can also be trained to function on its own. We've programmed computers to do amazing things, and the Internet is like the road that allows us to travel through centuries of knowledge."

His brows furrowed. "I am not certain I understand."

Maggie stopped to pull her phone from her pocket.

"Gerard has one of those," said Luke. "He seemed rather annoyed with it this morning."

"I believe he was frustrated because he couldn't connect to the Internet. Nearly everyone has a cell phone nowadays. It's like having the world at your fingertips."

His confused expression made her smile. She shifted closer to him and held the phone out in front of them. "This is a cell phone. With it, I can call, or speak, to anyone else in the world who also has one. I could call my mother in LA or—"

"Diana?" Luke grinned when she looked at him with surprise. "You said you called her when you needed to vent your concerns. Is this what you meant?"

"Exactly. But this device can also access the Internet." Maggie tapped on the Safari icon. "What's something that interests you—or something you've always wanted to know more about?"

The way he looked at her, with an intensity she was sure could see straight into her soul, washed her in warmth. She had questioned whether he could still feel something for her—questioned whether her lies had snapped every thread of trust they had weaved. The way he'd held her in her room was one thing, but this—the tender expression he displayed—shattered all doubt.

But he hadn't come to the future to stay, and that alone demolished any romantic notions her mind created. Completely destroyed them.

Luke stepped closer, peering at the phone screen, and her heart pulled a Grinch and grew several sizes. Apparently, it hadn't gotten the demolition memo.

Maggie shifted, and a mischievous glint sparkled in Luke's eyes. "What about that word you used this morning? Sexy—what does that mean?"

Heat spread over every inch of her face. Why had she said that about accents? It was true, of course, but she'd basically confessed she found Luke's manner of speaking sexy. In hindsight, that hadn't been wise.

She pressed the button on the side of her phone, shutting off the screen, and tucked it back into her pocket. "Searching for the word *sexy* on the Internet is a bad idea."

"Why? You said it could tell you any—"

"Oh, you'd find plenty. Far more than you want."

Luke smirked, which only made her embarrassment worse. She had only herself to blame, having given him leave to ask anything. Surely he didn't intend to use the allowance as a means to tease her?

Judging by the way his lips rose even higher, teasing was definitely his intention.

LUKE FOLDED HIS ARMS, BARELY RESTRAINING THE amusement bubbling inside him. Maggie had offered to answer anything he wished to know, and after their discussion about Gerard had flopped without giving him any clarity, he needed to ease the tension between them.

"Very well," he said. "*You* tell me what it means. Though I could make some deductions."

She glanced around them as if checking to make sure no one was listening. "It means attractive—appealing in the way of...certain desires."

He cocked a brow. He'd assumed as much but had no interest in passing on the opportunity to tease her. "Certain *desires?*"

Maggie shushed him and grabbed his arm. She pulled him from the walkway into the throng of long dresses and floral print shirts, leaving their empty basket behind. Apparently the subject was as socially forbidden today as it was in 1815—that, or the topic merely embarrassed her. Maggie's restless feet suggested it was more the latter.

How unfortunate for her.

"So, you find the way I speak sexy," said Luke. "Is that the only reason you kissed me before the ball?"

She scowled. "No! That isn't the only thing about you that I—"

Maggie snapped her mouth closed. He had never seen a lady's face turn so red. She was making this far too easy for him, and he had no intention of relenting, either.

"Pray, tell me what else you find appealing."

She spun around and began searching aimlessly through the rack of clothing. "We did not come here to talk about your...qualities. We need to find you something to wear."

Luke hummed. "I do not believe dresses suit me so well."

Her fingers stilled, likely realizing the particular display she had been fumbling through only contained articles catered to women. Laughter leaped out of him, and she glared over her shoulder with a wrinkled nose.

He extended the skirt on one particularly vibrant gown with a pattern of small dogs in rainbow vests. "This one would look lovely on you, however."

Mirth broke over her expression, but it quickly faded to something akin to panic.

"Is something amiss?" he asked.

Maggie peeked around the circular dress display and gasped. Before he could question her again, she parted the dresses and yanked him into the center behind her. They crouched, the space forcing them so close he pressed against her.

"What—"

She covered his mouth, shushing him again, and his lips curled beneath her palm. Voices sounded from beyond the clothes—two elderly ladies as best he could tell.

"I swear I've never seen anything like it," said one of them. "He was dressed so oddly, like someone from five hundred years ago."

Five hundred? Just how far into the future had he gone?

"You sure? I don't see anyone."

Someone scoffed. "I know what I saw. There's a cart here. How do you explain that?"

Their continued conversation became lost as Maggie leaned closer to whisper in his ear. "Serena Thatcher. She's the biggest gossip in town. Knows everything about everyone."

Ah. So that's why they were hiding. Luke pried her hand from his mouth. "Are you embarrassed to be seen with someone who is five hundred years old?" he asked, keeping his voice low.

"I'm not embarrassed to be seen with you...and you're not five hundred years old."

"Do tell me how old I am, then."

Her brows furrowed into that endearing expression he enjoyed. "I don't know how old you are. That's something you should keep up with yourself, *Your Grace*."

"Then tell me the year that I might deduce the number out on my own."

"Two thousand twenty two."

Over two hundred years? That was only slightly better than five hundred. "Two hundred thirty-five. Well, I have certainly aged well, if I might say so."

"Do I detect an ego?"

He shrugged and shifted a little closer to her. "You are the one who called me sexy."

Maggie's hand darted to her mouth to cover a very unladylike snort but not fast enough.

"Did you hear that?" said one of the women.

Maggie pressed both hands to her mouth, her face red, while he struggled to hold in his own amusement.

"Now you're hearing things," said the other woman. "Let's go. I have better things to do than chase down your hallucinations."

"Like what? Clean your dentures?"

Their voices drifted farther away. Luke turned to Maggie, and when their eyes met, they both laughed. The familiarity of the situation only reaffirmed his conclusion that this woman was precisely who he'd always thought her to be. Whatever walls he had reconstructed crumbled into a heap of dust.

Maggie slapped his shoulder. "What were you thinking? Do you want to be the talk of the town?"

"Your snorting was no fault of mine. Learn to maintain your composure. And do not think I have forgotten that you have yet to answer my question. I wish to know what other qualities of mine you find appealing."

"I'm not answering that, especially after you nearly got us caught."

"Fine, but I believe I already know the answer."

She gave him a skeptical look, a challenge that only fueled him. He leaned closer, crossing his arm over her and placing his hand on the floor at her side. Inches from her nose, he could see every spec of color in her eyes. "What you find most appealing about me is my ability to make you snort at the most inconvenient of times."

Maggie sucked in her lower lip. He nearly had her.

"Also," he continued, "you enjoy my flattery. Therefore, I must tell you that you look beautiful even if you are wearing pantaloons."

Just as he had hoped, a snort grated from her nose.

"Stop," she said, her voice too full of chuckles to be taken seriously. "What if they come back?"

"Then I would be permitted to stay here with you a little longer, and I cannot say the notion displeases me."

Her expression softened into something gentle, a tender look in her eyes that made his heart race. It would only take the smallest movement for his lips to reach hers. His gaze fell to them with the thought, and the desire to eliminate the remainder of the space between them ignited in his chest.

Chapter 29

Oklahoma, 2022

Maggie's pulse pounded in her ears. Every one of Luke's warm exhales teased strands of her hair. Hiding inside the clothing rack had seemed like a good idea a minute ago, but the forced proximity made her heartbeat erratic. Him staring at her lips didn't help, either.

Luke glanced up, the question clear in his eyes. Heaven knew she wanted the man to kiss her. She'd wanted more since the first time he'd taken her by surprise before the ball. But the memory only reminded her of the events that followed. The damage she'd done. The hurt she'd caused.

Vibration in her back pocket startled her, and Luke pulled away as she retrieved her phone.

DIANA: WHAT?! That guy is your hallucination personified? You'd better not come home until you've thoroughly kissed that.

She groaned. Not helping.

"Is something the matter?" asked Luke.

"No. It's just Diana being...Diana." She parted the clothes and peeked out. "I believe we've managed to evade them. Should we go find you some clothes before you catch more attention?"

"That is likely a good idea. We cannot have people thinking I am five hundred years old."

Maggie chuckled. "New clothes will definitely fix that."

Luke followed her to the men's section, and they began sorting through shirts and pants. Every time he held something up and stared at it with furrowed brows, she had to tuck away her amusement. His reaction to things was entertaining, but she also enjoyed the pure wonder that overtook his expression as they weaved through the store.

"What about this?" She held up an olive-colored cotton tee. "It goes well with your eyes."

Luke held the piece against him and batted his eyelashes. "Does it? I shall take your word for it. Fashion has never been my *forte*." He placed the jeans that were hanging over his arm into the cart. It had taken them fifteen minutes to figure out his size, but Luke seemed happy with them. Had even declared them to be quite comfortable.

Once they had collected enough clothes for a five-day wardrobe, Maggie led Luke to the other side of the store for some basic toiletries. The shaving essentials and toothpaste were easy enough since Luke figured out those on his own, but the antiperspirant aisle left him dumbfounded.

"Here." She removed the cap from a stick of Old Spice and offered it to him. "Smell this. You always wear something cinnamon-y. I think you'll like it."

He cocked his head with a lopsided grin. "You paid attention to how I smelled?"

"No. I mean, I noticed when you held me—like when we danced and..." Her face warmed. Fudge.

"And kissed," Luke supplied, all too entertained by her embarrassment.

"Yeah, that too." She held the deodorant closer to him and nodded at it, willing her cheeks to take an ice bath. "Go on. Give it a sniff."

He obeyed, but his expression spoke nothing to his thoughts on the scent as he inhaled. Luke seemed to consider it for a moment. "Do you like it?"

She shrugged. She wasn't about to confess that the scent was completely intoxicating. "It's nice enough."

He stepped closer to her than necessary and placed the antiperspirant into the shopping cart. "If you approve, then it suits me fine."

The hairs on her arms rose when he lingered in her bubble. The man was making it difficult not to have a make out session in the middle of the store. Despite Diana's encouragement, she had no intention of kissing Luke. She would not hurt him again.

She backed away and grabbed the front of the cart. "Well, I think we have everything then."

She paid for the items, and Luke changed out of his old clothes in the dressing room before they headed to the car. He plopped onto the seat with a sigh, and she turned toward him, inserting the keys into the ignition. "Everything alright?"

"Allowing you to pay for my things hurts my pride."

"I told you that I owed—"

He shook his head, and before she could finish, he reached across the center console and curled his fingers around her hand. "You have never owed me anything. Never." Luke brought her hand to his lips and left a soft kiss on her knuckles. Her whole body caught fire at the gentle touch. How was she ever going to survive his visit? What if he decided to stay in the future?

Her heart gave a happy lurch, but her stomach knotted like a thousand pieces of intertwined string.

Luke released her hand and averted his gaze. Did he sense the same dread she felt? The ease that always existed between them had returned, and if they weren't careful, they would both end up hurt again. Perhaps he realized it as well.

Her phone buzzed, and she pulled it out of her pocket. "It seems we have good timing; Gerard is finished."

She twisted the keys, and the car hummed. They made the drive back to the cafe in silence. Luke had said he wanted to see what the future had to offer, and only now did she wonder if his words were directed more at her than experiencing a new era. But he was a duke; he would never consider giving up his title and wealth.

She parked the car, her heart pounding at an alarming rate. She needed to know how long he planned to stay, to understand his intentions, but Luke spoke before she could work up the courage to ask. "Maggie, before you left—before Lady Garrick made her accusations—were you planning to stay in 1815?"

Her grasp on the steering wheel tightened. She'd worked tirelessly to forget, to bury her emotions, and they all worked their way to the surface now with a vengeance. But the moment she'd seen Luke on Dad's porch, she'd sworn not to lie to him again, and she wouldn't do so now, even if the admission shattered her.

"Yes," she whispered. "I had decided to stay."

"Even if you discovered the pearls were yours? Even if we retrieved them?"

She nodded, her voice choking as she blinked back tears. "I wanted to stay with you."

She had wanted to, but in hindsight the decision was made in error. Staying would have required her to maintain the façade even if she'd confessed the truth to Luke. Society never would have accepted her, either, and how could she live a life like that? How could she put Luke through it? No, returning to 2022 had been for the best. She only regretted the pain it had brought them both.

When Luke didn't respond, she caved and turned to face him. He stared at her with a mixture of emotion, but his expression remained soft. She wanted to tell him everything—to confess how far she'd fallen and how much of her heart belonged to him—but guilt prodded at her, unrelenting.

She could trust Luke with her heart, but his wasn't safe with her. She had already proven that and would not give herself the chance to break it again.

LUKE SWALLOWED AGAINST THE LUMP IN HIS THROAT. *I wanted to stay with you.* Those words dug under his skin and left him undone. He had feared his feelings for Maggie were not reciprocated, that the time they had spent together was nothing more than part of her act. But if he had discovered anything in the last twenty-four hours, it was that he had an effect on her and she genuinely cared about him.

The back door swung open, and Gerard slid onto the seat. He poked his head between them. "Well now, it looks like you found His Dukeness some clothes."

Luke pushed down his agitation. He would not give the man the satisfaction of a response.

"How were your meetings?" asked Maggie.

"They went well," Gerard answered, slumping back into his seat. "My company has accepted offers for two more buildings, and I've been asked to head the projects, of course."

Maggie had noted his confusion and took it upon herself to explain as she pulled onto the street. "Gerard is an engineer. He designs skyscrapers."

"Sky...*scrapers?*" Would his confusion never end?

Gerard's voice rang with smugness. "Imagine a structure over a hundred stories tall and *voilà*...a skyscraper. Thousands of windows. Stairs. Elevators. Some of them even have gardens inside them or on top. Designing them takes great skill, and the pay isn't so bad, either."

If the buildings were anywhere near as massive as the man's ego, Luke imagined they did require a great deal of skill. Jealousy pricked at him. In his time, he had been the one with wealth and title, but here, Gerard had the upper hand. He had nothing, and that did not bode well for reclaiming Maggie's heart.

Maggie pulled off the street and parked in front of Perry's Diner. Luke combed over the signs posted in the windows as they exited the carriage. *Quarter pounder and chocolate malt...* The future might very well make his mind explode.

Gerard rushed past him as though he were being chased by a rabid animal. The man held the door of the establishment open for Maggie, and she smiled.

Well played.

He needed to focus, but too many oddities distracted him. This time they had cost him a victory.

The moment Luke entered the building, a variety of scents assaulted his nose. It certainly smelled like someone had their hands busy in the kitchen, though what exactly was being prepared he could only guess. Maggie sat down on a bench not big enough for more than two people, and Gerard rushed past Luke to steal the position next to her. Shoving away his frustration, Luke claimed the seat across from them. At least from here he had a better view of her handsome face.

A woman with short curly hair approached and placed a menu in front of him. "Hello, my name is Lela, and I'll be your server today. Can I get you a drink while you decide?"

"Water for me," said Gerard.

"Coke," Maggie answered.

Luke cocked a brow. "Coke?"

Maggie chuckled, turning toward the woman. "He'll have a Coke, too."

Her eyes flicked to him, a mischievous glint in them and an almost dare for him to overturn her statement. She was up to something, and though he ought to be leery, he did not argue against the beverage. "Coke sounds lovely, thank you."

The woman nodded, and her eyes swept over him with the rise of her lips. "I'll be back in a few minutes."

"You know drinking that stuff is terrible for you," said Gerard, looking over his menu.

Maggie shrugged. "So is eating raw cookie dough, but I'm not about to quit doing that, either."

Gerard shook his head. "I think I'll just have a—"

"Salad," Maggie finished. "How adventurous. You know, your healthy eating is commendable but it makes me look like a junk food addict."

Junk food addict? Luke attempted to piece together the phrase's meaning, but it was no use.

"With the heavy dinners you make, I prefer to keep lunch on the lighter side," said Gerard. "I can be adventurous later."

Adventurous. He was adventurous, was he not? After all, he had not turned down the Coke. And he had traveled through time.

"Luke, what would you like?" asked Maggie.

"I have not decided." Which was not a lie. He had yet to figure out what most of the items on the menu even were, let alone pick one.

Maggie shifted on the bench. "Would you like help?"

A smug smile crossed Gerard's lips, and Luke suppressed a growl. "No, thank you. I believe I am capable."

He stared at the menu, hoping to spot at least one thing he recognized. No, he would choose something he'd never eaten before, not that it would be difficult considering the options may as well have been written in German.

"Luke The Duke looks confused," said Gerard.

Luke tapped his finger against the table. He was growing rather tired of that name. Ignoring the irritant proved difficult when the man rankled him by merely existing.

"Have we decided?" Lela had returned and placed each of their drinks in front of them. Luke's and Maggie's were dark with bubbles and froth settling just below the rim of the glass. Luke scooted it closer, eyeing it suspiciously. Their server removed a pencil and small pad of paper from a pocket on her apron.

Gerard ordered his salad first followed by Maggie. "The quarter pounder with the works."

Perhaps Maggie spoke German, also, because none of that made any sense.

The woman turned to him, and Luke shifted under her intense, expectant gaze. "I will have...the same as her."

"Alright. It will be right out." She winked and walked away.

She winked? He had certainly imagined it.

Maggie lifted her cup to her mouth and drank deeply, her eyes fixed on him. Was that a challenge? Luke pursed his lips, picking up the glass. Well, if Maggie intended to throw him through the adventure gauntlet, then he would rise to the occasion.

He downed a heavy gulp and instantaneously knew he'd made a mistake. A strange sensation tickled his mouth and throat. His nose burned, and he fell into a fit of coughs. Muffled laughter rang from across the table where Maggie had buried her face into her arm.

"What on earth did you order me to drink?" he asked, still feeling the effects at the bridge of his nose. He pinched the area, but it did little to help. He'd consumed soda water before, but this had still managed to take him by surprise.

"Coca-Cola," Maggie answered.

"It is terribly sweet. Not at all what I expected." Luke pushed the glass away, uncertain he wanted to continue on *that* particular adventure.

"Water is always the safer choice," said Gerard, certainly not as amused.

When their food arrived, Luke was relieved to see that a quarter pounder was nothing more than a thick sandwich. He could handle that. Although, the salted potatoes that came with it were unusual, as was eating them with his fingers. It took several attempts, but Maggie finally convinced him to try one with a red sauce. *Catch-up*, she called it. He wondered why anyone would name food such a thing, but at least it did not make his nose feel as though it were on fire.

When they had finished eating, Gerard pulled some notes out of a leather wallet and placed a few on the table. He then handed Maggie some sort of card. "Will you take care of this? I want to make one last call before we leave."

"You don't have to pay. I can—"

"I insist." Gerard stood and straightened his coat.

"Thank you," she whispered before he walked away.

Between the man kissing her cheek and paying for his food, Luke thought he might be sick. Lela returned again, her expression cheerful. "Can I get you anything else?"

"No," said Maggie. "But thank you."

The woman leaned forward and set a slip of paper in front of him. This time he was sure she winked at him before spinning around and walking away. Luke picked up the piece. A string of numbers had been scribbled across it.

"What is this for?" he asked, turning it around to show Maggie.

"She gave you her number." Maggie covered her mouth, her shoulders shaking.

Luke ran a hand through his hair. "Do you intend to tell me why that is so amusing? What am I to do with this?"

"Lela is hoping you'll call her."

"Call her?" His brows furrowed as realization dawned on him. "As in, she wants me to court her?"

Well, that seemed rather bold.

"Something like that, yes." Maggie patted his hand, sending shivers up his arm. "It's likely the accent"—her gaze wandered over his face—"among other things."

Heat rushed up his neck and into his ears. He supposed he deserved it after teasing her so relentlessly at Target.

Maggie grabbed the card Gerard had left behind and stood. "I'll meet you at the car."

Luke nodded, and Maggie joined a line of people next to the counter. When he was certain Lela wasn't looking, he placed her note under his plate. He had no need for it, and having her *number* nearby made him uncomfortable. There was only one lady he had any desire to call upon.

He made his way outside, expecting to see Gerard near the car, but the carriage was empty. The man hadn't gone far, though. Luke could hear his voice echoing from around the corner of the building. He edged closer and pressed against the bricks, focusing on the conversation happening in the alley.

"Delays happen," said Gerard, his tone laced with irritation. "I wasn't expecting the opportunity to acquire more."

Several moments of silence followed, and Luke assumed the person on the other end of this strange form of communication was speaking. Hoping to better eavesdrop, he peeked around the corner.

"Tomorrow night," said Gerard. "I need time to plan everything. I'll call you as soon as it's done."

What was Gerard doing tomorrow night?

Gerard shoved the phone into his pocket, and Luke scrambled back to the car. Leaning against the front of the rig, he waited for the man to appear. Gerard stepped around the corner, a smug grin automatically filling his expression. smugly grinned "Did you enjoy your meal? You're welcome."

Luke clenched his fists. He was not thanking that man for anything. "Big plans for tomorrow night?"

The question halted Gerard in his tracks. For a moment, the man merely glared. Then he stomped forward and poked a finger into Luke's chest. "You stay out of my business. It's none of your concern."

"I suggest you take your hand off of me. It was nothing more than a friendly question as a mutual guest in Weston's home. Unless, of course, your plans do not involve Maggie or West at all?"

Gerard sneered, dropping his hand. "As a matter of fact, they do. If you really must know, I intend to propose tomorrow night."

Luke's blood ran cold. "I beg your pardon?"

"I intend to propose to Maggie."

No. Maggie would never accept. He'd seen the way she reacted to the man's attention. She would turn him down...would she not?

His silence only increased the haughtiness lining Gerard's expression. "Better luck next time, Your Dukeness." Gerard brushed past him and opened the rear door. "Shame really. You do seem to care about her. But don't worry; your trip to the future wasn't in vain."

The door slammed closed.

Luke braced himself against the car. He remained uncertain of where he and Maggie stood, but his heart and mind had finally aligned. He wanted her in his life. He wanted her to be the one to break down the walls he'd reconstructed.

But Gerard threatened to steal her away, and although Maggie did not appear to possess the same fondness for the man, he feared she might agree to the man's proposal. The thought of losing her again ripped through him like a knife.

He needed to tell her the truth—that he loved her—and he was running out of time.

MAGGIE CLEARED THE DINNER TABLE AND HAULED A STACK of plates to the sink. Warmth filled her chest when she entered the kitchen to find Luke already scrubbing away at the silverware. She never thought she'd witness the duke washing dishes but had to admit there was something all too appealing about watching him use a scrubber with his long sleeve shirt rolled up to his elbows.

He looked pretty good in denim jeans, too.

She crossed the room and set the plates down on the counter. He turned to catch her eye, pausing from his work, and smiled.

"Thank you," she said. "You don't have to do this."

Luke shrugged and continued his scrubbing. "There is little else I can do to help, and I wish to ease your burdens after you spent so much time preparing the meal."

She could have kissed him, and if he'd known how much she wanted to he might have put the scrubber and fork down. Fortunately, he couldn't read her mind, because keeping her resolve firm was getting harder by the second.

Luke rinsed a cup and placed it in the dish strainer. "Maggie, there is something I wish to discuss with you."

"Oh. Okay."

He shook his head. "Not here. Perhaps after—"

"Maggie?" Gerard poked his head through the open archway leading into the dining room. "Could I steal you for a few minutes?"

She nodded, but before leaving she offered Luke an apologetic look. His dark brows furrowed, not with hints of jealousy like she'd seen there that afternoon, but with deep worry. About what, she didn't know, but her fingers itched to smooth away the wrinkles in his forehead. "I'll come back and help you with this."

He nodded, but she could see the frustration in his eyes. He wanted to tell her something, and she suspected what the topic would be. Was she ready to have a frank discussion with him?

No. Because she felt torn between what her heart wanted and protecting his.

She followed Gerard into the dining room. He took her hand, and she fought the urge to yank it away. Gerard had claimed to come here as a friend, but today his actions told a different story. She was still trying to process the change, but the situation needed to be dealt with. Perhaps this chat would give her the chance to clear the air.

"I know it's cold, but I'd like to go outside if that's alright?" he asked.

She hesitated. "Umm, okay...sure."

He guided her out the front door and onto the veranda. Moonlight illuminated the white wraparound porch, and moving toward the railing, she could see the bright stars twinkling in the darkened sky. Gerard turned her to face him fully, and the moonbeams caught his green eyes. She still thought him a handsome man, but neither her heart nor her mind could manage anything deeper.

"I wanted to thank you for allowing me to come," said Gerard. "It's been nice to spend time with you and your Dad."

"Oh. Yeah, it was nice to have some company on the plane."

What more should she say? Gerard was a nice guy, and she didn't want to break his heart, but things had become increasingly uncomfortable. Not once had even ever hinted at something serious between them. Was it simply because of Luke's arrival? She could certainly sense the tension between the two men.

"I'm happy to give you whatever support you need." Gerard tucked a strand of her hair behind her ear, and Maggie stiffened. "You're a beautiful girl, Maggie. I know things haven't been easy for you lately, but you've handled it all so well."

"Thank you."

Gerard glanced at the window and then stepped closer to her. Maggie backed up, and her back pressed against the railing. He took her hand, gently, and her heart rate sped out of control.

"If it's not obvious, I care a great deal for you, Maggie. I wanted you to know that I'd like our relationship to be more."

All the words she should have spoken stayed stuck in her throat. Her cheeks heated, and Gerard smiled. He leaned forward before she could make sense of what was happening and placed a kiss on her lips.

Whatever chains had bound her tongue loosened. Maggie shoved against his chest. "Please don't do that again."

His brows furrowed, and irritation twisted his features. "Why not?"

"You said you wanted to come as a friend." She swallowed. This had to stop. When had things gotten so out of control? "I'm sorry if I made you think this was more than friendship. It wasn't my intention to lead you on."

"Because of him, right?" Gerard rubbed a hand over his face. "You're hung up on the duke. You've made doe-eyes at him since we got here."

Maggie wanted to deny his claims, but truthfully, he wasn't wrong. "It doesn't matter what my relationship is with Luke. I've never felt anything more between *us*. I've appreciated your support the last few months. Truly, I have. But I won't let you have false hope that it will ever grow into something more. I'm sorry."

A humorless chuckle escaped him, but he nodded. "Goodnight, Maggie." Gerard gave one last look to the window and then entered the house.

She stood in stunned silence. Gerard had wanted more? She should have seen it. Why would the man spend so much time with her if he didn't. Somehow her distracted mental state had chosen to overlook it, and now she'd broken his heart, too.

That seemed to be a talent of hers.

After several minutes, Maggie went back inside. She entered the kitchen, and her heart sank when she found Luke no longer there.

"He's gone to bed."

Maggie whirled around. Dad leaned against the archway into the kitchen, his arms folded. "Seemed pretty upset after he looked out the window, almost like he saw something he didn't like."

Her gut writhed. Was that why Gerard kept looking at the window? He wanted to make sure Luke saw the kiss? Irritation pricked at her. She understood both of them cared for her, but that seemed childish.

"Mags." Dad's soft voice brought her gaze to him. "I know you've had a rough time lately, but if you're not careful—"

"I'll hurt Luke again." Maggie knew that, yet no matter how much she tried to avoid allowing the duke near, each minute spent with him brought her closer to failing.

"It's not just him I worry about."

"You worry about Gerard, too?" she asked in a teasing tone.

Dad passed her an incredulous look, and Maggie winced. Dad may have returned home after she was released from the hospital, but he called every day. He'd always had an affinity for sensing her mood even over a phone call, and she knew how concerned he'd been.

"I'll figure it out, Dad. You don't have to worry."

He nodded, but Maggie suspected he would worry, and in reality, he had every reason to.

Chapter 30

Oklahoma, 2022

Maggie paced her room, the early morning sunbeams illuminating the space with a warm glow that she wished her soul mirrored. What was she going to do? Gerard had kissed her last night, crossing a line she didn't want, and she'd practically *dumped* the man.

Could one call it dumping when they weren't actually in a relationship? She didn't think so, but his reaction suggested he had taken it that way. His eyes had held frustration, but she imagined there was hurt beneath it. A wounded pride if not a broken heart.

Fudge. Why did she struggle so much with dating? Or not dating. She *wasn't* dating Gerard, or at least she didn't think so.

Looking back on things now, perhaps her grief and haste to depend on the man had come across that way.

And Luke had seen the one kiss she'd ever shared with Gerard, terrible as it had been.

Her stomach twisted. She'd likely hurt him again, even if it wasn't entirely her fault.

The situation might make her explode.

Her phone buzzed, but she ignored it. Mom had called several times the last few days, but she hadn't felt ready to receive the scolding she knew would come from answering. She had enough to worry about and needed to focus on solving the problems here first.

Like reigning in her desire to kiss Luke.

She swallowed as memories of their time together in the clothing rack resurfaced. Attraction was one thing, but her feelings for the duke were all-consuming. He made her laugh and smile, and the comfort she felt when near him was hard to ignore. Things had been shaky between them, and for good reason, but after she confessed to having planned to remain in 1815, something had changed.

Each glance Luke had passed her at dinner, each touch—they all spoke of a sure confidence he hadn't possessed two days ago. What quiet decision had he made that would spark such determination in his eyes? Had he forgiven her?

Her heart leaped at the idea. Meanwhile, her stomach flopped like a fish—one taking its last breaths.

The phone buzzed again and vibrated itself off the nightstand and onto the floor. Maggie stooped over to pick it up, expecting to see Mom's name across the top but finding Diana's instead.

"Hello?" said Maggie.

"Chica, what are you doing! You can't ignore me like that. Do you know how worried I am?"

The words sounded slightly slurred, and Maggie planted a hand on her hip. "Are you eating?"

"Coco Puffs. Why?"

Maggie rolled her eyes. Yes, her friend was terribly concerned. "I didn't mean to ignore you—well, I did, but only because you were making me more stressed. Mom won't stop calling. She's furious I left before her soiree. And now I'm dealing with Luke and Gerard." She rubbed her forehead, wincing. "I can't handle anything else."

"You know, you could solve one of those problems by picking the guy you like most and kissing him senseless."

"You make it sound so easy." Maggie plopped down on the bed and fell backwards. The soft blankets brushed against her exposed skin, the sensation comforting in a strange way. "I know which one I *like most*, but I don't want to hurt him more than I already have."

"Pretty sure kissing him isn't going to hurt, unless you're like a vampire or something."

Maggie grinned. "You watch too many movies. But you're right, kissing him isn't the problem. He's going to go back to 1815, and I...I can't go with him." That much she had decided upon seeing Luke again. She didn't belong in the nineteenth century, and while she had decided to stay there before, the decision had been made in haste and with a mind muddled in love. She cared for Luke, but the idea of becoming a duchess was...overwhelming. She wanted to be a woman of title as much as she wanted to be CEO. It simply wasn't the life she wished to live.

"Trust me," said Maggie. "I belong in 2022, and Luke has too many obligations to stay here."

"Oh yeah, he's *from the past*." Diana's voice turned monotone. She'd probably given the words air quotes.

"I know you think I'm crazy, but it's true."

"Whatever, that doesn't matter. Have you kissed him yet?"

Heat filled Maggie's cheeks. "Not in this century."

"Sooo...what are you waiting for?"

Maggie heaved an exasperated sigh. "I can't. Weren't you listening?"

"Can't or won't?"

"Both."

Diana remained quiet for a few seconds, and when she finally spoke again, her tone had changed from annoying friend to woman of wisdom. "Mags, it's okay to be selfish once in a while. What's the point of living if you never do anything for yourself? You're standing in the way of your own happiness."

Maggie's chest constricted. Diana's words struck her deeply, but was her happiness worth someone else losing theirs? Luke would be risking his heart, and it would break the moment he realized she had no intention of time hopping again..

"I don't know if this Luke dude is playing along with your hallucination, but have you considered asking *him* what he wants? Maybe he isn't planning to go back to...wherever. Or maybe he'd reconsider if he knew how you felt."

Maggie stilled. She hadn't allowed herself to consider that option. Luke had duties. He had a family in 1815. She could never ask him to leave it all behind for her. He would come to resent her for making him stay here—for making him give up everything.

"Do me a favor," said Diana. "At least think about it."

"Sure, I'll think about it." Unfortunately, she was *already* thinking about it.

"Good. I have to go to work. Call me later?"

They said their goodbyes, and Maggie stared up at the ceiling. What if she let herself make the choices that would allow her to be happy? What if things didn't turn out as bad as she thought they would? She buried her face in her hands and sucked in a deep breath. Regardless of what she wanted, her problems would not resolve themselves, and the longer it took her to make a decision, the harder it would be.

THE SMELL OF PANCAKES DREW HIM DOWNSTAIRS. LUKE expected to find Maggie at work in the kitchen, but instead, West stood by the stove, flipping the flakey circle while he hummed.

"Good morning," said Luke, hoping he had kept the disappointment out of his tone.

"Ah, good morning. Did my superior cooking skills wake you?"

Luke leaned against the counter and folded his arms. "I confess it was not you I had hoped to find in here."

West scooped a pancake onto his utensil and gave it a flip. "I can guess as to whom you would have preferred. Have you made headway on that subject?"

He had planned to speak to Maggie yesterday, but Gerard made the task impossible. Anytime he gained her attention, the man stole it away and never bothered to hide his smirk when he did so, either.

"I wish I could say I brimmed with confidence, but lying is not a virtue," said Luke.

West scratched the back of his head. "Have you tried kissing her?"

"I—you *want* me to kiss your daughter?" Societal rules had clearly changed much since 1815.

West added the pancake to the towering stack on the plate and lifted his brow. "What I want is for my daughter to be happy. You may not have confidence, but I'm a thousand percent certain that you kissing her would achieve that."

A thousand percent did sound rather sure...

Luke ran a hand through his hair. How could he consider such a thing when he had witnessed Gerard doing just that the night before? The man had wanted him to witness the act as well, as evident by his checking the window, and the only solace for Luke's soul rested in Maggie's reaction. She had pushed Gerard away with a less than pleased look. Luke had abandoned his position at the window then with a bit of satisfaction.

Still, Maggie might react to *him* kissing her the same way. "Things are not that simple. I cannot—"

"Don't misunderstand, Luke. I appreciate that you care enough for my daughter to give her space and time, but if you do nothing..." He gave him a look before he grabbed the plate of pancakes and marched into the dining room. Luke followed, and West continued, "I'm only saying it may be too late if you wait. The man could propose tomorrow for all we know."

Or tonight.

"Do you truly think she would accept?" asked Luke. "She does not appear to welcome his attention." And he did not believe that merely because he wanted Maggie for himself. Every time Gerard kissed her cheek or held her hand, Maggie looked uncomfortable, and it required a great deal of energy for Luke not to rush to her aid.

"Right now? No, I don't think she would, but my Maggie also has a difficult time saying no to people. Gerard doesn't seem the type to give up, either."

They sat down at the table and began filling their plates. "May I ask you something?" said West. Luke nodded, and he continued, "Why did you come to the future?"

Luke stared at him with furrowed brows. Surely the man knew? "I would think that quite obvious. I care for your daughter."

"Yeah, that's obvious, but is that the only reason?"

"What other reason should I have?"

West shrugged and began pouring syrup over his stack of pancakes in a circular motion. "Look, I'm happy you were willing to come after her. You're dedicated, I'll give you that, but you can't make everything about Maggie. A marriage never works if you only focus on making the other person happy."

"Maggie makes me happy," said Luke slowly. "Is that not enough?"

The man took a bite of his food, and a string of syrup caught on his graying beard. He wiped it away with a paper napkin before answering. "No, I would say it isn't. Being happy with one another is a fine thing, but a strong foundation needs more than that. I don't know what you intend to do, but I have my doubts that Maggie will jump at the idea of returning to your time. So, that might mean you must stay here. Are you prepared to do that?"

"I am. In fact, I ensured everything was taken care of in that regard before I left."

West hummed. "But are *you* prepared? A life here would be very different from what you're accustomed to. Your title means basically nothing. Your wealth is...well, you are as broke as a doorknob, to be frank, so you'll have to earn a living somehow. Those things may not be easy for a duke. You must consider whether the sacrifice will lead to resentment unless you believe you can find happiness in this new lifestyle. Not just with Maggie."

The man made valid points which Luke had never before considered. What would he do in the future? But as he thought on the last few days and the quiet life of Weston's farm, he found his answer. Luke had always enjoyed working with his tenants, and not simply in ensuring they had what they needed. He'd always possessed the desire to help, though his title restricted him to supervision at most. The notion of engaging in hard labor would disgust most men of the peerage, but Luke found the idea appealing. His experience was lacking, and perhaps he might change his mind in the thick of that life, but the desire to try rested within him, just as it had since he was a young boy.

A farmer need not worry about the motivations of those around him. A farmer need not attend balls or wrestle with deciphering political agendas. Luke would be, in a sense, free. Farming would be hard work, undoubtedly, but he clung to the picture forming in his mind—the pride he would take in his work, the happiness he would feel free of the burden his title demanded. And by his side stood Maggie, his confidant and friend. A life with her could only add to the contentment he would find. He knew it with a surety that dashed all doubt. He need only discover whether she would share in his vision of the future.

"Good morning." Maggie entered the dining room and gave her father a kiss on the cheek. "You beat me to breakfast, Dad. Why didn't you wait?"

"I was up early. Besides, I need to go into town this morning."

"You're going into town?" Gerard's voice sounded from the arched entryway, and Luke drummed his fingers on the table. Shame the man never slept in. "Would you mind if I tagged along? The Internet appears to be down *again,* and I need to...take care of some things."

He passed a rather sour glance at Maggie, which intrigued Luke, but not quite as much as West's smirk.

"Of course you're welcome to come with me," said West, a hint of mischief in his tone. "Sit down and eat. I'm leaving in fifteen minutes."

Gerard grimaced. "Perfect."

A warm hand fell on Luke's shoulder, and he looked up to find Maggie staring at him with concern. His heart stammered, and he fought the urge to steal her hand into his own. He could pull her away right now, but Gerard would never allow him privacy.

"Are you okay?" Maggie asked. "You seem a bit tense this morning."

"I am well, but thank you for asking." He was nervous, perhaps, but having found clarity offered him a great deal of relief. All that remained was to speak with Maggie directly. Gerard's trip to town would provide the perfect opportunity.

"Good," she said. "I know the future must be overwhelming for you."

Maggie sat down in the chair next to him, and his chest constricted. "I cannot deny the future is overwhelming, but I have enjoyed coming here as well."

Silence settled around the room. Little conversation passed between them as they finished their morning meal. Maggie disappeared the moment she'd finished, and Luke determined to find her once Gerard and West had left.

"Ready?" asked West, tapping the table in front of Gerard to get his attention.

"Yeah. Let me grab my coat."

When Gerard had disappeared into the hallway, West leaned close to Luke, his voice low. "Maggie likes to read in the barn. I'm betting that's where she'll go." He tilted his head and gave Luke an expectant look.

"I shall take a walk to the barn," said Luke, suppressing his amusement. At least he had her father's approval.

West gripped his shoulder. "Good man. I'll see you in an hour or so. Don't dilly-dally. I can only hold him off for so long."

A few minutes later, West's truck hummed to life, and they were gone. The cool fall air sent chills across Luke's skin the moment he stepped outside, but he ignored them, making a quick dash around the back of the house to the barn. The building had once been painted red, but the outer walls appeared due for a fresh coat. Perhaps if he remained in the future, he could help West apply a new layer. Luke had never painted before, but surely he could manage.

The smell of horses bombarded him when he entered the barn. A beam of light percolated from the loft, illuminating the dirt path between the stalls. Maggie lay on her stomach near the back of the barn, her feet crossed and her nose in a book. Straw littered the floor around her, and he wondered what made her enjoy this activity in such an odd place.

Whatever she was reading had captured her attention so thoroughly that his approach went unnoticed. He plopped down next to her, and she started with a gasp.

"You scared me!" She whacked his arm, giving him the chiding glare he'd come to miss.

"I gathered that. What are you reading?"

Maggie turned the book toward him, allowing him a clear view of the front.

"*Framing the Viscount?*" he asked with a chuckle. "That sounds intriguing."

"It's very entertaining. How did you know where I was?"

"Your father told me you often came out here to read," Luke confessed.

She sat up. Straw clung to her long-sleeved shirt and pantaloons. Today she wore blue ones like those she had purchased for him. How strange that women and men wore similar clothes.

Maggie brushed the dry pieces away. "So you decided to interrupt my peace and quiet by startling me."

"I like to think I am far more entertaining than your book. My purpose in seeking you out was to test that theory though I am quite certain in my assumptions."

"Your arrogance is showing again."

"A faux presentation, I assure you. A particular young woman has stolen any actual confidence I might have possessed. The least she could do is humor me and perhaps allow me to rebuild it."

Her brows lifted with her smile. "That's quite the burden you've placed on me. A man's confidence can be a fragile thing, and I'm no expert at building anything. I also didn't know I wielded the power to steal it."

"You have more power than you know. So, are you up to the challenge?"

"Maybe I prefer to keep you humble."

Luke grabbed a handful of straw from the floor and tossed it at her. Maggie turned, and the pieces caught in her hair. When she looked at him again, her mouth hung open. Luke scooped up more straw and continued his assault. She shielded her face with her arm, giggles sounding from beneath a curtain of curls. Maggie flung handfuls back at him, and soon they had both descended into a fit of laughter.

He raked up an armful and lunged forward. Maggie squealed and fell onto her back, crossing her arms over her face as straw rained down on her.

"Do you surrender?" asked Luke.

Maggie put on an expression of mock contemplation, and Luke gathered more straw into his hands. "No, don't!" she shouted. "I surrender!"

Luke hovered over her. Maggie breathed heavily, and the warmth and mirth in her brown eyes only increased his desire to scoop her into his arms. To hold her. To kiss her.

"I must look quite the mess for you to stare at me like that," she whispered.

"You are beautiful," he muttered. "Surely you must know that."

Her lips parted, drawing his attention to them. West had told him to kiss her, but did he dare? Such action could push her away, but there was no time to take things slowly. Gerard certainly had no intention of doing so.

Luke lifted his hand to her hair and pulled a piece of straw from between the soft strands. She closed her eyes, her body shuddering under his touch. He brushed his fingertips over her cheek, tracing his thumb across the freckles there, and her eyes flew open. Conflict warred in her features, and when his gaze dropped to her lips again she sat up and scooted away from him.

Maggie rose to her feet, and Luke scrambled to his knees in time to catch her by the wrist before she could take enough steps to be out of reach. "Maggie, wait."

"I can't do this." Her eyes pleaded with him, stabbing at his heart, but she did not tug her hand away.

Luke shifted to his feet, keeping a gentle hold on her. "Please, stay. I promise I will not try to kiss you." He paused, thinking better of making such a promise. "Unless you ask me to do so."

He loosened his grip and slid his fingers down to hers. "I have a confession to make. I did not come to the future simply to apologize. I came to court you." When he took a step closer, her hand tightened around his. He drew a breath, hoping to calm the erratic beat of his heart. "I know I waited too long. It took me time to understand—to realize what I had lost. You have become so much more than my confidant, but say the word—tell me that I have no need to hope and that I have lost you forever—and I will return to 1815. But if there is even the *smallest* chance that you see a future with me, you need only say so."

She turned away. "Why? How can you trust me after what I did? I don't even trust me. What if I hurt you again?"

Luke cradled her face with both hands, bringing her attention to him, and used his thumbs to brush away the little droplets trickling over her cheeks. "Oh, Maggie. Of course you shall hurt me again, just as I am likely to hurt you. We are two imperfect people, but that does not mean we should sacrifice what we have found together. My life is decidedly better with you in it, and I am willing to work through whatever troubles may come our way if you are willing to do the same."

"I can't go back. I thought making a life in 1815 with you was what I wanted, but I don't belong there, Luke. How could someone like me be a duchess? And even if I managed to figure it out, I don't think I would be happy. The expectations, the rules, the constant social excursions—those are not things I want." She shook her head. "You would have to stay, and I won't ask that of you. It wouldn't be fair. You have a life, and I can't keep you from your obligations, from your family."

"You do not have to ask. I would wait a hundred years—traverse time and give up everything I own. I have already done so."

Her brows furrowed, and the flutter of her lashes cleared away the tears lingering there. "What do you mean?"

He released her face and scooped up both of her hands. "My title now belongs to Edwin, as does everything I ever owned. I never wanted to go back, Maggie. You and I are not so different in wishing for a quiet life, and I hope we are also not so different in our affections, for I love you dearly and wish to remain in the future with you—to start a life *here* with you."

Chapter 31

Oklahoma, 2022

The Duke of Avendesh had many ways of stealing her breath, but him firmly declaring his love for her had to be at the top of the list. Maggie tightened her hold around his hand to make sure the moment was real. The four months since returning had dragged her through heartache and regret, but the last three days felt more like a whirlwind. She'd been full of pent-up, anxious energy since she saw Luke on the porch, terrified of opening up to him and feeding the love-sick flames glowing in her heart. Terrified of hurting one of the people she cared about most.

As though he could read her thoughts, Luke released one of her hands and weaved it through her hair. "You needn't worry so much after my heart. The risks are infinitely worthwhile, but if it assists your decision at all, I will be completely shattered if you do not want me."

She gave him an incredulous look. "How is that supposed to help? It makes this harder."

He chuckled, playing with a strand of hair in a way that made her sigh with contentment. "Someone once told me that people cannot see your full potential until they truly know you. I have never wished to lay all of my secrets before another person, to offer such vulnerability as I do with you. I want you to always be my confidant, Maggie. You are the only one I wish to confide in, the only person whom I desperately want to see all that I can be."

Her entire body warmed. How had her words, spoken without much thought after Luke gave her a tour of his house, had such a profound effect on him? He wanted her to be his confidant, and not simply as his friend. She wanted the same. What if Diana was right? Living with everyone else's happiness at the forefront of her mind had done nothing for her own. Maybe it wasn't so wrong to be a little selfish. Maybe the risks were worth the possibilities.

Maggie placed her hands on his chest and looked up at him, shoving down what remained of her fear. "Kiss me."

A grin stretched across his face, reaching all the way to his eyes. His arm wrapped around her waist and brought her flush against him. The other hand buried into the hair at the nape of her neck, and his lips descended on hers. Each kiss solidified the words he'd already spoken. Luke loved her; she felt it more with every touch.

Maggie slid her hands over his shoulders and pulled down on his neck. Their kisses deepened, and her body wanted to melt, but the desire to continue kept her upright. He tasted delectably of pancake syrup, and he'd started using his Old Spice, much to her delight. Why had she fought so hard against this?

She pulled away enough to bring their make-out session to a stop. Luke's brows furrowed. "Do not tell me you have changed your mind. I will kiss you until you change it back again."

She smiled and cupped her hand to his cheek, rubbing her thumb over his freshly shaven skin. "I'm okay with that, but...are you sure about this? What if I—"

"I am sure. I confess the lies hurt, and I did not know whether I could give you my full trust again. The idea of having fallen for a woman who had pretended to be someone they were not while in my company terrified me. My greatest fear had become a reality, and it has taken a great deal of reflection to come to terms with it all. But it was not the perfect lady of society that I fell in love with. You, the woman from the future, are who I love. Not the person you pretended to be."

Luke swept an arm behind her knees, lifting her off her feet, and she squealed in surprise. He carried her to the back of the barn and plopped her onto a stack of bales before wedging himself between her knees. The extra height left her face even with his, the perfect position for another round of kisses.

And she certainly kissed him.

Luke trailed his lips along her jaw, and she sighed when he touched the tip of his nose to hers.

"Thank you, Maggie."

"For what? Kissing you? It wasn't a selfless act."

Luke chuckled, the sound rumbling from deep in his chest. "That is good to know, but I meant for helping me. For showing me how to open my heart. How to confide in someone."

"I need to thank you, too. When I told my mother I didn't want to be CEO, it was you I thought of. I admired the way you commanded a room so easily, the way you stood firm in the things you wanted." Maggie brushed her fingers over his cheek. "Ever since I saw you standing on the veranda, I was afraid to let you get close. I had already hurt you once and couldn't stand the thought of doing it again. But I realize now that what scares me more than anything is losing you a second time. Diana told me I needed to be more selfish...and kiss you thoroughly." Her friend would be proud.

"I like Diana very much already and must remember to thank her."

"She'll definitely want to meet you."

His smile lingered a few moments before his expression melted into something serious. Luke rested his forehead against hers and softly, with a dulcet tone that sent shivers down her spine, whispered. "Marry me. I have crossed a sea of time to beach upon your shore. I am a castaway in an era not my own—stranded, and yet I have no desire for rescue. Allow me to always stay by your side. End my torment and say you will have me."

She clasped her hands behind his neck, holding him to her. "As my confidant, there's something I need to tell you first."

"You could not possibly have any worse secret than that you traveled through time. I can handle whatever this one may be."

Her gaze wandered to his hair, and she plucked out a few pieces of straw. Luke shifted on his feet. "What is this secret of yours?"

"I love you, Luke," she said gently. "I loved you then, and I love you now. And yes, I will marry you."

Relief swept over his expression, and he tightened his hold around her. Safe in his arms, happier than she'd ever been, the burden of her fear lifted. Diana had been right. This was worth the risk—it was worth a little selfishness. She would strive every day to protect Luke's heart, and although she would probably fail a time or two, they would get through things together.

And if their celebratory kisses were any indication of how a life with Luke would be, she couldn't ask for a better one.

"I should probably go inside." Maggie pulled a piece of straw from her hair and glared at it. "I'm a mess because of you. In more ways than one."

Luke shrugged. "You could always stay here and allow me to pull out the pieces. I could at least manage that mess. What other one have I caused?"

"An emotional one. I feel like I may explode with happiness."

"I daresay I like that sort. You needn't do anything about that mess in particular." He tilted his head and feigned contemplation. "You have no need to worry about your hair, either. Straw suits you."

"Straw suits me? Time travel has made you delirious, Your Grace."

"I am uncertain my travels are to blame, but regardless, you are lovely no matter what you wear, even well-placed pieces of dried grain."

"Well-placed? Is that what you call throwing it on me?" She shook her head. "Anyway, I'm hardly in the right state of mind or appearance to face Gerard. He'll probably leave since I sort of dumped him."

"Dumped?"

She winced. "We were never dating, but based on his actions last night, he may have been under a different impression. I told him there was nothing between us but friendship. He didn't take it so well." She pressed a finger to his grinning lips. "You don't need to look so pleased about it."

"I cannot help it." Luke pulled her hand away. "All will be well, Maggie. Would you like me to be there when he returns?"

"No. It might be best if you aren't even in the house when I confess my new engagement. He deserves to know and have some closure."

He nodded and backed up a step so she could hop down from the bale.

"I shall wait here." Luke glanced around the barn, and the light from the loft window caught his eyes. "Perhaps take a nap or read a book. Would you lend me *Framing The Viscount?*"

"Only if you don't make fun of me for reading it."

"I fear I can promise no such thing. Teasing you is a pleasant pastime."

Maggie wrinkled her nose. "I'll see you later. I'd best go get a shower before Dad and Gerard get home."

"Come find me right after," said Luke. "And then we can tell your father the *good* news together."

"Okay."

Luke pulled her back to him for one final kiss, and then she left him standing in the barn.

As she walked to the house, elation and excitement swirled within her, tossing and turning like ocean waves in a storm, but they were quickly doused by a realization. She had to cut ties with Gerard. She'd never meant to lead the man on, and she hadn't expressed herself the most gracefully the night before. How would he respond to a second conversation?

Likely not well, but she wouldn't run away from this. She owed it to both men to be honest, and that's what she intended to do.

MAGGIE HAD JUST FINISHED BLOW-DRYING HER HAIR WHEN the rumble of Dad's truck drew her to the window. He and Gerard exited, and her heart skittered with the thud of the doors. She gripped the window sill and took in several deep breaths. Nothing would calm her nerves, and part of her wanted to slide under the bed and stay there. Gerard would have to go back to work eventually, wouldn't he?

She shook her head. No, it was time to face this. If she could survive time travel, then this should be as easy as eating fudge.

After ten minutes of bolstering her courage, Maggie descended the stairs, her heart pounding. Gerard's muffled voice echoed from the living room. When she entered, Dad was sitting on the floor with wide eyes and his hand pressed to the back of his head. He turned towards her and shouted. "Maggie, run!"

Gerard, who stood a few feet from Dad, spun around and pointed a gun at her. "Don't move."

"Gerard, what's going on?"

He stalked toward her brandishing his pistol. "Where is he?"

Her stomach flopped. He meant Luke. Had the man gone mad with jealousy? Surely he couldn't care for her *that* much. "I don't know."

Gerard shook his head. "Nice try. Perhaps it's better this way, though. I'll have the advantage if he comes to me."

"The advantage for what?"

"Don't you worry about that." He withdrew a set of handcuffs from his coat pocket and tossed them at her. "Put those on."

"Why?"

Gerard shifted, aiming the gun at her father. "Because I'll shoot him if you don't."

"Mags, don't!" Dad pleaded. "Gerard, I'll get it. Just let her go."

Get it? Get what?

"Why would I settle for one when I can have more?" Gerard turned his attention back to her and lifted his brows. "Well? Are you going to put them on, or do I need to blow a hole in his leg first?"

Allowing Gerard to take her anywhere was a bad idea, but what choice did she have? She clicked the cuffs around her wrists. She wouldn't risk her father's life.

Once the metal restraints were in place, Gerard grabbed her by the upper arm, directing his next order at her father.

"Tell Luke to bring the pearls to the old dairy. All of them"—he yanked Maggie closer—"and come alone, or she's dead."

Gerard wanted the pearls? Her mind swam back to the night they'd met. Pointing them out had been one of the first things he'd done. But he hadn't known what they could do then. Had he?

Gerard tugged her rigid body to the front door and onto the veranda. She shivered without her coat as the cold air brushed over her skin. Her heart raced. Should she scream? Luke would hear her, no doubt, but drawing his attention would put him in the crosshairs.

"Why do you want the pearls?" she asked, stumbling to keep up with his hasty pace to the car.

"Gee, I don't know. What could I possibly want to do with a set of pearls that possess the ability to time hop?" Gerard holstered his gun and ripped open the back door. He jutted his chin toward the seat. "Get in."

Red hot anger boiled in her stomach. "Were you after them this whole time? Is that the only reason you stuck around?"

The man smirked. "You've given me no other reason. My superiors weren't happy when you came back with only one, by the way. I suspect they'll have some questions for you once we've dealt with your ancient boyfriend."

Her heart sank into the pit of her stomach. Gerard had no intention of letting her go, which meant he likely had no intention of letting Luke live, either. Well, she wasn't about to be an idle victim.

Maggie gripped Gerard's coat and thrust her knee into his groin. Those self defense classes were really coming in handy this year.

She stumbled backwards into the car when Gerard fell forward. His knees bent, and he landed in the gravel with a groan. Maggie bolted toward the barn. Gerard still had a gun, and she probably hadn't made the wisest decision, but going with him seemed a sure way to end up dead..

The sound of foot falls hitting gravel sounded behind her. Arms wrapped around her waist and jerked her back, sending a wave of pain through her ribs. She screamed as Gerard dragged her back to the car and threw her onto the backseat. She sat up as Gerard positioned himself behind the wheel. He engaged the locks before she could pull on the door handle.

The car kicked up a cloud of dust, the wheels spinning against the gravel. Luke's muffled shout caught her ear, and she peered out the rear window to see him running after them. The vehicle quickly left him behind in a puff of dust along with her last hope of getting out of this alive.

Chapter 32

Oklahoma, 2022

L uke panted, coming to a stop with clenched fists. The car disappeared behind a thick cloud, the hum dissipating the farther it went. Gerard had clearly not taken his rejection well.

He turned, scanning the area and pushing down his panic. Right now, he needed a way to go after them. His mind flew to the horses in the pasture first, but even they couldn't keep up with Gerard's hasty escape. His eyes fell on West's truck, and a plan took hold.

A horrible plan.

Luke scrambled toward the house, his feet entangling as he clambered up the stairs. In his haste, he nearly toppled over onto the veranda. He called for West when he entered the house, and a pained response echoed from the drawing room. He found the man sprawled out on the floor, clutching his head. Splotches of crimson coated his fingers.

"You're injured." Luke crouched beside him.

"Maggie...he took her."

"I know." Luke helped him into a sitting position and checked over his wound. It wasn't deep, only a thin gash. "I am going after her. Where are the keys to your carriage?"

West's brows furrowed. He likely thought the plan horrible, too, but Luke had no time to argue. "The keys," he demanded, gripping Weston's shoulders.

With a nod toward a shelf by the door, the man said, "Over there."

Luke started to rise, but West grabbed him by the arm. "Wait! He left me with a message. You're to take the pearls."

"The pearls?"

"When we returned home, Gerard demanded the pearl Maggie used to come home. I refused, and he threw one blow to my stomach. Knocked the wind out of me, and I dropped to my knees. Then he hit my head, likely with his gun." He winced, his fingers fumbling over the wound. "I was too dizzy to even stand."

The man's eyes glazed, and he turned away, guilt riddling his features. "Gerard was so anxious. Then Maggie came downstairs, and he grabbed her. He looked so desperate, Luke. Something in his eyes... He said to tell you to come to the old dairy. Alone. And he wants all the pearls." West turned his eyes back on him, his expression hard. "Tell me you still have the others. That man won't hesitate to hurt her."

Luke's hand dropped to his back pocket. He'd kept them close since he arrived in the future, and although he could feel the two pearls pressing against him, he needed the confirmation they were still there. Those tiny beads were now more important than ever. "I have them. I will get her back; you have my word."

West nodded. "Help me onto the couch."

He moaned when Luke lifted him, and his body slumped into the cushions. "Gerard will be waiting at Ashgrove. It's an abandoned dairy about a mile from here. Follow the main road until you see a silo and then make a right. You can't miss it. The place looks like something out of a horror movie."

Horror, Luke understood, but movie...

He hadn't the time to puzzle it out right now.

"Shall I call for a doctor?" asked Luke. "Your injury—"

West swatted the air. "I'll be fine. It's you who needs assistance."

"You cannot possibly think of coming?"

"No." West winced as he reached into his pocket and pulled out a phone. "But I can call for back-up. I trust you, but I won't put all my eggs in one basket. Not when my daughter's life is at risk. You go, and I'll have the police there in fifteen—twenty minutes, tops."

Luke gave him a curt nod. "Where is Maggie's pearl?"

"Upstairs in my bedroom. It's inside the closet in a safe." He clenched his jaw. "There's a revolver in there, too. Think you can manage to make use of it?"

"I believe myself capable, yes."

With a set of numbers and instructions, Luke darted up the stairs. Within minutes, a third pearl rested alongside the others. He clutched the keys, standing beside the contraption that had terrified him upon his arrival. Riding with West had made him sick; driving might kill him.

Luke placed the gun onto the seat next to him and exhaled a long, shuddering breath. Maggie's step by step explanation rang through his mind. He inserted the key into the slot and turned, just as he had watched her do several times. The truck hummed to life, sending his heart into a frenzy.

Two pedals—one for stopping and one for going—West had told him.

He tucked his chin, glancing at the floor, and searched for them with his foot. He found the first and gave it a gentle push. The truck grumbled, and he surmised that was the *going* pedal. His gaze drifted to the lever between the seats. Both Maggie and West had shifted it before moving. He looked over the letters. Which one had Maggie told him would put the coach into motion?

Currently, a light was illuminated beside the letter *P*, whatever that meant. There was also an *R*, *N*, *D*, and *B*.

What did all of those even mean?

Luke groaned and ran a hand through his hair. He would simply have to try them all.

He placed his left foot on the stop pedal and pressed. If he was going to do this then he would make sure the machine stayed put until he was ready. He shifted the lever to the *R* position and slowly released the pressure on the pedal.

Nothing happened. Perhaps he needed to give it a bit of the *go* pedal.

In his haste, he applied more pressure than he should have, and the carriage jerked backwards. The movement took him so thoroughly by surprise that he failed to push the stop pedal quickly enough, and the back end of the truck crashed into something, jostling him in the seat. A screech echoed from the underside of the carriage, pulling him out of his daze. He released one pedal to slam down on the other, and his body smacked against the wheel with the abrupt halt of the truck.

Luke swore, peeking over the front of the carriage with a scowl. A metal box attached to a thick post lay on the ground. Part of it hung open, and the visible side was dented in multiple locations. A little red flag had bent in half.

He added it to the list of things he would help West fix.

Keeping his foot firmly in place, Luke shifted the lever to the *N*. That did nothing, but at least he hadn't crashed into something else. He moved the handle into position next to the *D* and sighed with relief when the carriage lurched forward.

Now if he could get to Maggie without dying.

Luke guided the carriage onto the smooth road. Fortunately, he had paid attention during his trip to town and knew to stick to the right side of the lines. He didn't pass another coach, but he could only imagine what would happen should two of them collide.

The road stretched on for an eternity until the silo came into view. Luke released one pedal and tapped lightly on the other, jerking his body each time until the truck slowed to a near stop. He rotated the wheel, and the carriage moved onto a dirt road. As he increased his speed, his thoughts turned to Maggie. Her scream still rang in his ears. He should have trusted his gut and never let her confront Gerard alone. Something about him had always seemed sinister.

All Gerard wanted was the pearls.

And the man would get them.

Gerard likely had ill plans for the time travel beads, but regardless of whatever dark purposes he intended to use them for, Luke would never trade Maggie's life to stop him.

Luke passed a large painted sign and approached a forlorn-looking building. He grated the truck to a stop and shifted the lever back to the initial *P*, which seemed to be the correct decision since the wheels stayed put. With the turn of the keys, the hum subsided.

He grabbed West's gun and exited the coach. The place appeared completely deserted but for the dark blue carriage that sat in front the run-down building. Light reflected off the rig's metallic surface from where the sun rested behind him, and beyond Gerard's carriage a door made of rotting boards stood ajar.

Luke pulled the pearls from his back pocket and clenched them in his hand. He gathered his composure, forcing the rage building inside him into some far corner of his soul. Allowing his emotions to lead would do neither him nor Maggie any favors.

Luke stepped into the building, each movement hesitant. Though West had claimed the dairy abandoned, it still housed the smell of animals. What little light streamed through the dusty windows cast a faint glow into the center of the room, shimmering off of the broken glass that littered the floor, while the surrounding walls held tight to their secret shadows. What lurked in the darkness—or who—set Luke on edge.

Something clanked against the floor beyond the illuminated space, and Luke stared at the dark outlines of objects he could only guess the purpose of. Nothing else moved, but he sensed he was being watched, or perhaps hunted. If Gerard were anything, a predator would fit. The man had lured Maggie into his clutches with false kindness and fake sentiments. He had tricked them all into believing he cared for her.

Across the room, something jingled like the rattle of a chain, and Luke's hair stood on end. "Gerard! I have what you want. Stop hiding!"

A deep, low chuckle sent chills down his spine. Luke searched for the source, but Gerard remained hidden. The coward.

"Come out! What have you done with Maggie?"

"You look frustrated, Your Grace."

Luke turned to face the menacing tone as Gerard's form emerged from the shadows, his lips curled and Maggie squirming at his side. His nose wrinkled with his sneer. "You were a fool to come."

Chapter 33

Oklahoma, 2022

L uke's gaze dropped from Maggie's face to the cuffs on her hands. Fury overtook his expression, and that only made her more anxious. She wanted to shout for him to leave, but with a gun pointed at her head, she decided that may not be the best idea.

"I see you came armed." Gerard's tone sounded amused. "Put the weapon on the ground."

"Not until you let her go."

Gerard shoved the barrel of the gun against her temple, and she flinched. She'd spent the last half hour wondering how she hadn't seen this side of him. How had she been so oblivious? The mistake would cost her. It might cost Luke, too.

Gerard's grip on her arm tightened. "Don't push my patience, Luke. Put down the gun."

Luke's jaw clenched, but he did as Gerard demanded and placed his gun on the floor. He backed away from it, and Gerard dragged her forward to sweep the gun into the shadows with his boot.

"I have the pearls, and I'll give them to you without a fight. Just let her go." Luke held out his hand, open-palmed, revealing the beads.

Gerard stiffened. "Only three? Where are the rest?"

"In 1815."

The madman swore, and her breath hitched when metal dug deeper into her skin.

"It seems I do still need you," Gerard whispered in her ear. "Or one of you. Perhaps Luke The Duke will retrieve the rest in exchange for your life, Maggie. What do you think?"

"Leaving her here with you is the last thing I shall do." Luke spoke the words through gritted teeth, but they were firm, nonetheless. "If you want the remainder of the pearls, then release her. I will fetch them for you but not unless I know she's safe."

Gerard scoffed. "And trust you'll bring them to me? I don't think so. Then again, I don't really need either of your help. I can get them myself." Gerard jutted his chin toward a table a few feet away from them. "Put the pearls over there and don't try anything. One misstep, and I'll shoot you both."

Luke took slow, hesitant steps to the table. He set the pearls down, and the sliver of light slipping through the dirty windows behind them gave their surface an iridescent glow.

"Very good." Gerard shoved her to the ground, and she glared up at him. There was a glint in his eyes that spoke of madness, but she also didn't miss the hint of desperation. A dangerous combination.

"Why do you want the pearls?" asked Luke. "What do you intend to do with them?"

"The same thing you and Maggie did with them. They say that money controls the world, but that isn't true. Time does. It controls everything—determines the course of our lives in ways money can't. Whoever possesses those pearls holds the key to the universe. Think of how much a person could do if they knew what events would occur beforehand. Think of the wealth one could acquire...the influence. He who wields time holds the power to shape the world."

Chills rushed over her. She had never given much thought to how dangerous the pearls could be in the wrong hands. Gerard sought far more than a relaxing vacation. Could his travels change everything?

Luke took a step away from the table. "So it is your intention to destroy the future, change it to suit your needs? What exactly do you have planned?"

"I intend to reap the benefits, but the plan is not my own. There's much more at work here than you know."

Maggie propped herself into a sitting position. "You can't change the past. It's impossible even with pearls that allow you to time travel. Your plan will never work."

Gerard laughed. "Ah, yes. I'd forgotten how much effort you've put into studying the subject the last few months. Rest assured, we've considered and analyzed everything. We know what we're doing."

The mounting betrayal irked her. Gerard had watched her study for weeks. He had probably thought her ridiculous, and there he'd been with more answers than she'd ever find on her own. Each moment he'd spent with her had never been out of concern but in an effort to get his hands on the pearls. Every question he'd asked about them surfaced in her mind, fueling her anger into a burning rage.

"And who exactly is *we?*" asked Luke.

The question drew Gerard's attention, and Maggie turned to face Luke. Her gaze lingered on him for a few moments before flicking to where sunlight glinted off the shattered glass scattered over the ground. Luke tensed as if he sensed her plan.

"Simpleton," answered Gerard. "If you think I'd give you that information, then you're more the fool than I thought."

Maggie shifted closer to the glass and curled her fingers around a jagged piece. It dug into her palm, but she ignored the pain.

"You intend to change the past to suit your goals," said Luke. "Is that it?"

"One can't change the past," said Gerard. "It's already written. To disrupt events that have already occurred is impossible. The universe would find ways to stop any attempts. There are some things humanity will never control."

"Gerard, see reason. These people you work for...they are using you. You cannot tell me you feel nothing for Maggie—that you would take her life. You intended to propose."

What? Gerard had planned to propose? Ludicrous.

Gerard laughed, seeming to also think the idea was ridiculous. "I told you that for a bit of fun. I never actually planned to profess my love. Toying with you was nothing more than entertainment, but I hoped to ensure you stuck around. Couldn't have you taking off with the pearls."

Maggie shifted closer to Gerard with as much subtlety as she could, which proved difficult given her cuffed hands and new sense of rage. It did invoke more determination, however. Gerard had used her—pretended since the moment they met, all to get his power-hungry hands on her heirloom. But she would thwart his plan and get herself and Luke out of this mess. Luke must have suspected her intentions because he continued to ask questions, providing the perfect distraction. Gerard took each piece of bait the duke offered like someone on a diet deprived of dessert for months.

Which probably wasn't inaccurate.

"If you do not intend to change the past, then what is your plan?" asked Luke.

"As I said, the past is written, but the future is not. With the pearls, we will have foresight into events before they take place. We can change things in the present to produce the future we want."

Luke shook his head. "Again with the *we*. Not capable of pulling this off by yourself? You are a puppet."

Gerard's eyes darkened, and his finger caressed the trigger of his gun. Her breath caught, but the man kept his attention on Luke, unaware of how close she drew to him. "You have no idea the undertaking this has required. We've searched for the pearls for a long time. They evaded us once. I won't let them slip away this time."

Luke shifted with obvious discomfort, and the madman seemed to find amusement in the reaction, his smug grin growing to fill his face. Maggie looked at Luke and lifted her hands, positioning the piece of glass next to Gerard's leg. Luke's brows furrowed and gave his head a subtle shake. Perhaps this wasn't the best plan, but it was all they had, and she wouldn't let him die for her.

"Enough talk," said Gerard. "You're going to tell me where those pearls are in the past or I'll pull the trigger."

This was it. They were out of time. She mouthed 'I love you,' and before Luke could attempt to dissuade her, she plunged the glass shard into Gerard's calf.

A SCREAM AND A *BANG* BLASTED THE ROOM WITH A dissonance that sent Luke's hands over his ears. He shot forward and rammed his shoulder into Gerard. The impact knocked the man to the floor, and the gun skidded into the shadows. Gerard shouted what Luke assumed were rather colorful modern curse words, and blood seeped between the man's fingers as he clutched his leg.

Luke spun around to search for Maggie. She'd scooted away from them, her hands still tightly curled around the glass. He rushed to her side. Red tinted her fingers, but he saw no other signs of injury. Thank the heavens; the bullet had missed.

"How badly are you hurt?" he asked, looking her over again.

She shook her head. "I'm fine."

He gently slid the glass out of her grip and placed it on the floor. He could do nothing about the handcuffs without a key.

Taking her hands, he lifted her from the floor, but before he could pull her against him, an arm wrapped around his neck from behind and yanked him backwards. He tried to take a breath, but Gerard's chokehold constricted his airway.

"Your time in the future is up," said Gerard with a growl as he squeezed tighter. "You were destined to bring these pearls to me. Now that you've fulfilled your purpose, I'll end you both."

Luke pried at his arm and writhed in his hold until black dots filled his vision and the room spun.

Another scream shattered the silence, and Luke fell to the floor when Gerard's grip loosened. The madman grabbed Maggie by the wrist as she attempted to plunge the glass shard into him. His sleeve was already damp with blood below the shoulder. She'd stabbed him again.

Maggie ripped away, and Gerard smacked her across the face. She tumbled backwards and crashed to the floor. Gerard held up the bloodied glass he had snatched from her hand, and his lips curled into a snarl as he towered over her.

Pure rage ignited within Luke, and he scrambled to his feet, drew his fist, and slammed it into Gerard's jaw. The man stumbled sideways but caught himself before careening forward. He swung, and Luke ducked beneath his arm before spinning around with a right hook. Gerard evaded and landed a blow to Luke's face. Pain erupted through his jaw, and the world blurred.

The madman reared his fist, but Luke grabbed it and pounded an elbow into the man's nose. Gerard collapsed with a bellow but immediately pushed himself up. A *click* echoed from across the room, halting the skirmish completely. Maggie stood with both hands holding a gun, the barrel aimed at Gerard.

"Move, and I'll shoot," she declared.

Gerard sneered. "You don't have it in you, sweetheart."

Had the fool forgotten she had stabbed him twice? Apparently so because he shifted as if preparing to stand. The piercing sound of the gunshot made Luke jump. Gerard screamed, gripping his knee and writhing on the floor.

"You shot me in the leg!" he said through clenched teeth.

Maggie took three steps forward, the gun still pointed at him. "Then you should count yourself lucky, because I was aiming a tad higher and missed."

"I suggest you keep still," said Luke. "I would wager she will not miss a second time." He went to Maggie's side and placed a hand over her shaky ones. Gently, he took the gun from her, and she sagged into his arms when he pulled her tight against him. Her sobs brought out his own tears, and he kissed the top of her head. "He's not going anywhere. You were so brave."

"I was terrified."

He tightened his hold around her. "You needn't be anymore."

Blue lights danced across the dirty windows, filling the room with their strange glow, and loud sirens sounded from outside. Gerard tried to stand, but collapsed back to the ground with a wail. Luke released Maggie to retrieve the pearls. She followed and tucked herself back against him once he'd traded the gun for the tiny beads and placed them into his pocket.

"The police," Maggie whispered against his chest. "Dad must have...Dad! Is he okay?" She pulled away, her expression stricken with worry.

He brushed the hair from her damp cheeks. "He's fine."

Her expression softened, and she reached for his face with her cuffed hands. Her fingers traced beneath his eye, which was fairly swollen judging by his reduced visibility. "I am fine, also."

A half smile lifted her lips. "You are, but I believe there's a better word than that."

"'Tis this dangerous look. I pull it off well, do I not?"

"Very well." She rested her cheek against his chest and her arms slid inside his coat and wrapped around his waist. "But let's promise to never get into trouble like this again."

"I shan't make that promise as the woman I love has a tendency to find trouble, and what sort of gentleman would I be if I did not venture to her rescue?"

Her only response was to squeeze him tighter. The old doors swung open, and shouts filled the room as people in black vests stormed inside. The ordeal had ended. Maggie was safe in his arms, and he had no intention of ever letting her go.

Chapter 34

Oklahoma, 2022

L uke yawned and rubbed a hand over his face. Pinks and oranges had replaced the blues in the sky now that the sun hovered over the horizon. Beyond the driveway, the winter wheat danced in the light breeze. He had barely left the settee today, and for good reason. Yesterday had been the most emotional day of his life. From the high of kissing Maggie—asking her to marry him—to nearly losing her at the hands of a madman, he had been completely drained.

A contented sigh escaped the woman nestled at his side, and Luke smiled. The two of them had been inseparable since the moment the police hauled Gerard off on a flat board moaning in agony. After over an hour of questioning and a thorough medical examination for both them and West, they were released to come home. He and West had begged Maggie to go to bed, to get some rest, but she insisted on staying with him.

And he couldn't refuse her after everything they'd gone through. Truthfully, he had been completely relieved to keep her at his side. So, they had curled up on the settee, and Maggie had fallen asleep resting against him. When morning came, West convinced her to eat a pancake, but after that, they'd returned to the cushions. By late afternoon, she had drifted to sleep again.

West checked on them frequently, each time displaying a knowing grin that made Luke squirm. They had yet to tell him about their engagement, and he held no doubt the man would take great satisfaction in the announcement, but it hardly made things any less uncomfortable.

His stomach grumbled, and the sound pulled Maggie back to consciousness. She sat up, blinking furiously. "How late is it?"

"Late enough for sunset."

"Sunset?" She winced as if the words brought her pain. "I'm sorry. All I've done is sleep on you all day."

He shrugged. "I see no reason for you to apologize for it. I certainly was not going to complain."

She rested her chin on his shoulder and looked up at him from beneath her dark lashes. "Your eye has turned purple."

"It is a good thing I still have a sexy accent; otherwise, I might not manage to keep you."

"I didn't accept your proposal because of your accent, but it might have been a contributing factor."

"Proposal?" West stood across the room, a mischievous glint in his eyes. "You proposed? I suspected you'd taken my advice, but this is a surprise."

He had taken it. Repeatedly, in fact. Luke rubbed the back of his neck, hoping to dispel the heat there.

"What advice?" asked Maggie.

"Nothing to concern yourself over," said Luke.

West's smirk widened, unrelenting. "I told him to kiss you."

Maggie gaped. "You *what*? Were you conspiring against Gerard the entire time?"

"Not the entire time," said West. "Just since the duke showed up. I may have unplugged the Internet a few times to irritate him. Besides, the way you looked at Luke gave me every confidence it was the right decision. You're clearly attracted to him."

Her cheeks turned a bright red, and she growled. "*Dad!*"

"Actually, she has a better word to describe me," said Luke, hoping it would bring a blush to her face again. He wasn't disappointed.

Maggie whacked his arm. "What am I going to do with the two of you?"

"I'm sure you'll think of something." West folded his arms and lifted a brow. "But that isn't what I came in here to discuss with you. *Someone* ran over my mailbox."

It was Luke's turn to blush. "Mailbox? Is that what it was?"

"You ran over the mailbox?" asked Maggie between chuckles. "Uh, oh. He's really fond of that thing. She even has a name—Agatha."

Why would anyone name a box? "My apologies. I have never driven one of those contraptions and was in a bit of a hurry. The love of my life happened to be in dire danger."

"And that's the only reason I'll forgive you," said West with a huff. "Otherwise, you'd be in big trouble. A friend gave Agatha to me."

"I shall help you fix it," promised Luke.

West swatted the air. "I can manage, but if you intend to stick around, don't think I won't put you to work."

"I welcome the prospect. Hoped for it, even."

"Speaking of which," said Maggie, turning to face him. "We'll need to figure out how to create an identity for you."

An identity? What did that mean?

"The government likes to keep track of people," she continued, noting his confusion. "Birth certificates, social security numbers—you'll need a paper trail so they don't wonder why you appeared out of nowhere."

"Don't worry yourself over that," said West. "I know a guy."

Maggie's brows shot to her hairline. "You *know* a guy? Why would you know someone who could take care of...something of that nature?"

"That's a discussion for another time. Right now, we have company." West gestured toward the window. A yellow car the color of a buttercup pulled up the drive. Maggie gasped when a woman with long blonde hair stepped out.

"Fudge. Mom's here?"

"Of course, she's here. How did you think she would react to me telling her our daughter was abducted? She hopped on a plane right after I called."

"I don't know. You could have simply *not* told her. She'll never stop worrying now."

"She might if you tell her you'll soon have a husband to look after you. Heaven knows you need supervision."

Maggie scowled, but Luke couldn't help feeling a bit giddy about the new title he would acquire nor could he stop himself from laughing. "Your father has a point. You do tend to get into trouble."

She narrowed her eyes. "You realize every time I get into trouble, it involves you."

Touché. And quite honestly, he did not care to have it any other way.

THE DOOR BURST OPEN, AND MOM SCURRIED INSIDE. MAGGIE stood, and the moment her mother caught sight of her, she ran, her high heels clicking against the wooden floor. She squeezed Maggie in a tight hug, sobbing.

"I'm okay, Mom." She pushed out the words with dying breath, and her mother loosened her hold.

"Oh, sweetheart! I'm so sorry. This is all my fault. I was the one who introduced you to that despicable man."

"This isn't your fault. You couldn't have known Gerard was such a monster."

Mom pulled away completely and wiped the tears from her cheeks, careful not to scratch herself with her long fingernails. "I can't imagine how scared you must have been. Twice now, I've almost lost you. But don't you fret; you can move back in, and I'll surround you with bubble wrap if I have to."

Maggie's stomach flopped, but Diana's words rang through her thoughts. If she had come to realize anything the last few days, it was that her own happiness mattered. "No, I won't be moving back in with you."

Mom's perfectly trimmed brows drew together. "You don't want the company—you've made that perfectly clear—but you've failed to tell me what it is you *do* want. I'm your mother; I can't help worrying about your future."

"I want to stay here with Dad. Help out with the farm, maybe even take on piano students in town." Maggie looked over her shoulder and found Luke's warm gaze watching her. "I want to stay here with Luke."

The duke beamed with what looked a lot like pride.

"Luke?" Mom leaned sideways to glance around her.

Luke stepped forward and bowed. "Luke Halford. It is a pleasure to make your acquaintance, Mrs. McCarthy."

Mom turned her attention back to her daughter, brows furrowed, creating a deep line across her forehead. "In your story, Luke was the name of that handsome duke you went on and on about."

Maggie groaned, her cheeks burning hotter than the sun. Luke grabbed her hand and smirked. "Apparently, she finds me quite attractive. I'm compiling a list of words she's used to describe me."

"Don't forget to add arrogant," muttered Maggie, wrinkling her nose. "Old and well-traveled—"

Luke scooped her into his arms, making her squeal. Mom's eyes darted between them, twinkling as if she had realized something. It disappeared when Luke set Maggie down again.

"Wait, if your name is Luke, and the way you talk...then the story was..." Mom staggered, and Luke released Maggie to stabilize her.

Dad rushed to their side and gripped Mom's shoulders. "Easy, LeAnn. The story is true. Maggie really did travel to the past."

"This is all too much."

She placed a hand to her forehead, and Dad chuckled. "Come on. You should rest for a bit. You've had a long flight and probably worried the whole time."

"Yes...yes, you're right. I should rest." She allowed him to guide her a few feet before she halted and turned to face them again, her sight firmly set on Luke. "Do you intend to stay? Or will you go back to your time?"

"He can't marry Maggie if he goes back," said Dad. "Well, unless he takes Maggie with him."

Luke shook his head. "I intend to stay here."

"Marry...?" Mom's eyes rounded. She wrenched free of Dad's hold and scrambled toward them. Luke stiffened when she wrapped him in a tight embrace, and Maggie lost herself to laughter. The poor man looked super uncomfortable. Dukes didn't get hugs very often.

"Alright, LeAnn," said Dad, not bothering to hide his amusement. "You don't want to chase him off."

Relief flooded over Luke's expression when Mom released him. "Oh! Your wedding will be the talk of the century. Leave it to me to plan *everything*! Now, I have so much to do. I should start making a list. Spring would be the perfect time for a wedding, or perhaps you'd prefer Winter? I'll need to make a guest list...at least a thousand people..."

"No," said Maggie firmly. "Small, Mom. A *small* wedding."

"Oh, fine. But at least let me go all out on the decor?"

She waited, bouncing on her feet like a kid who'd eaten too much candy. Maggie didn't feel she needed elaborate decor, but Mom had asked for permission, and she couldn't help the way it warmed her. Her mother hadn't made a fuss about her decision to turn down the CEO position when she arrived, either. They'd finally reached some level of understanding.

"Okay. You can do whatever you like with the decor," said Maggie. "But I want to be involved in everything else, deal?"

"Deal!" Mom's sudden gasp made Luke jump. "I must call my florist immediately. This time of year, the flowers may need to be imported..." Her voice trailed off into muttered, indecipherable words as she scampered out of the room, and Maggie heaved a sigh.

"She seems a little excited," said Luke.

"I wouldn't laugh if I were you. Wait until she starts fussing over your tux."

"My what?"

She grinned, and Luke narrowed his eyes.

"Need I procure a license, or are those moot in the future?" he asked. "And what of the banns being read?"

Maggie pinched her lips. The duke had a lot to learn about the twenty-first century, and she was excited to teach him. He seemed to sense her thoughts and wrapped his arms around her waist, pulling her against him. "You will have to be patient with me. You may also be subjected to thousands of questions a day."

"I think I'll find your questions entertaining."

"At least your life will never be boring."

No, it certainly wouldn't.

"There'll be paperwork," said Dad, rubbing his chin, unabashed by their display. "A license, among other things. But let me worry about that. We need to get your ID taken care of first, anyway."

Maggie slid out of Luke's hold and planted her hands on her hips. "Yes, back to that. How do you know someone who can make fake IDs? Have you been involved in something I should know about?"

Dad shrugged. "I needed a fake ID, once upon a time."

"For what? Sneaking into a nightclub?"

"For the same reason Luke needs one."

"What do you mean?"

Her father sauntered over to an armchair and slumped onto the cushion with the most nonchalant of movements. She folded her arms and pinned him with a pointed look. "*Dad.*"

"I mean, I needed to create a new identity. People might look at me strangely if my driver's license said I was born in 1864."

She blinked. "Were you born in 1864?"

"Yes, sweetheart." He drew a deep breath, the mirth fading from his eyes. "In 1892, the pearls brought me to the future—brought me to 1992. They had been in my family for five generations at that point, always passed to the eldest child, and my uncle was extremely jealous when my father inherited them. He offered to buy the pearls, even attempted to steal them, but my father never gave in, fearing his brother's intentions. The pearls became an obsession, and soon my uncle had an entire following determined to have them.

"One night the man became particularly adamant. My father and I escaped to the fields behind our house, but we were followed. My father gave me the necklace and told me to hide. I did as he asked and hid in the crop. His scream was the last thing I heard before..."

She rushed to her father's side and crouched, taking his hand and giving it a squeeze. "Oh, Dad. I'm so sorry. Why didn't you ever tell me? Does Mom know?"

His brows furrowed. "No, and you're not to tell her. Give her time to grasp all of this." He gestured to Luke. "Time travel is not an easy notion to swallow."

Wasn't that the truth.

Dad leaned back in his chair and stretched out his legs. "I learned how to live in a world I wasn't accustomed to, and so will Luke, with time."

"What about Gerard?" asked Maggie. "How did he know about the pearls?"

"My uncle's followers were as determined as him, and I suspect they knew I had time jumped. After your mother inherited the company, her frequent parties invited the worst sort of people into our lives. The wealth and status put us on display. I did my best to keep my past hidden, but somehow they found me—or found the person I'd passed the pearls to, rather."

"Me," said Maggie.

Dad nodded. "I had hoped that the pearls and the curse they carry would be forgotten—fade, even. I stayed in the future believing that I could keep them out of the wrong hands. But I failed, Maggie. I put you in danger. I should have told you all of this, but I truly thought my uncle's cult had disbanded. When Gerard demanded them last night, I discovered just how wrong I'd been."

"You think he's part of the same cult your uncle created?"

"Precisely. They've been searching this entire time."

"Gerard said the plan was not his own," said Luke. "He was working for someone, which means there are still people out there who both know about the pearls and desire them. Do you have any idea of the size of your uncle's following?"

"By now, it could be dozens. Could be hundreds. Either way, I don't think we've seen the last of them. We have to keep those beads out of their hands. My safe upstairs can only do so much, but I've yet to come up with a better solution."

"They're just pearls," said Maggie. "Couldn't we...I don't know, destroy them?"

"My father tried when his brother began to grow desperate. He never had any luck. I suppose we have more options today, but magic is a powerful force. I'm not sure anything could destroy them." Dad rose, and taking Maggie's hands, pulled her up. "Don't worry, sweetheart. We'll figure something out. I have a few ideas, but for now, I should go check on your mother."

He gave her a smile, but it didn't hide the concern that lingered in his features. He was right to worry. If there were more people after the pearls, they could all still be in danger.

Luke moved to her side and wrapped his arm around her shoulder. She looked up at him, and noted the fear pouring from his brown eyes. "You only brought two of the pearls with you. The rest are still in 1815."

He nodded. "Edwin and Juliana. Do you think we should retrieve the pearls? If something happened to my family..."

She considered the dilemma a moment. "They might be safer in the past. It would be difficult for this organization to find them, anyway."

"Yes, and Edwin knows about the pearls and what they are capable of. He will put them where no one else will fall victim to their curse."

"Is that what you are?" she teased. "A victim?"

Luke grinned and pulled her into his arms. "Pearls aside, we are all victims to time. Everyone is born and dies, but some of us are fortunate enough to spend the moments between in the company of those we love. I shall be forever grateful that a few tiny beads granted me such luck."

"So will I," she whispered. "Whatever the future holds, I'm happy I won't face it alone."

"Never." Luke tilted his head, bringing their faces a little closer. "I am in need of my confidant. There is something I wish to confess."

"And what might that be?"

Luke leaned forward, barely hiding a smirk as he whispered into her ear. "I would prefer a winter wedding. I am far too impatient to wait until spring."

And she made sure he knew she agreed.

M aggie bit her lip, although why she bothered trying to hide her amusement, Luke would never know. The light in her eyes always betrayed her if her expression did not. He exhaled, hoping it would calm his racing pulse, but fear and anxiety fought their way to the surface again. He should not be so hard on himself. After all, this hadn't gone well the last time.

"Take your time," said Maggie. "Right pedal is the gas; the left pedal is the brake."

"Gas?"

"Yes, gas. Just a reference to gasoline—the fuel that powers the engine."

"Very well, but I figured that much out last time."

She leaned toward him, and his heart responded to her proximity in its usual way as she peered down at his feet. "Only use one foot. Switch between the pedals."

"Why?"

"I—well, because that's what you're supposed to do."

That reasoning did not seem very sound to him, but Maggie had been driving... How long had she been driving? He pushed the question to the back of his mind. Every night, he bombarded her with a multitude of them through dinner. Most of the time he went to sleep completely overwhelmed. West had said he would become accustomed to the future with time but failed to mention how long that would take. Two weeks certainly had not been enough.

"Okay," said Maggie. "Press on the brake and shift it into drive."

"Drive? Oh, I presume that is what the *D* means?"

"Park, Reverse, Neutral, and Drive." She pointed at each letter as she spoke.

"What about the *B*?"

"It's like a brake."

"I thought the pedal was the brake?"

She scratched her head. "Yes, the pedal is the brake, but this is more for coasting downhill. There aren't really any steep downgrades around here, so you can ignore it for now."

He nodded and started to shift the lever into the *Drive* position. A peck on the window startled him before he could do so, and Luke turned to see Weston propped against the truck and peering inside at them.

"Roll the window down," said Maggie.

"Roll?" How the devil did one *roll* a window?

She chuckled and leaned across him, practically throwing herself into his lap. His heart lurched.

Maggie pressed a button, and like magic, the window disappeared into the door. He gaped.

"Going for a drive I see," said West.

Maggie moved back to her side of the carriage. "Just around the field. I thought we'd start slowly."

"That's a good idea. Don't let him run over my crops like he did my mailbox."

She snickered, and Luke shot her a glare. Would they ever let him forget?

Likely not.

"Alright," said West. "Be careful."

Her father patted the truck and sauntered toward the barn. Maggie pointed to the button, and Luke toggled it until the glass reappeared. Then he fought the urge to play with it some more. Sometimes he felt like an overly curious child. Everything about the future fascinated him.

Luke drew a breath and eased his foot off the break. He guided the carriage onto the road and followed Maggie's directions. They made a lap around the field, and she insisted on a second for *practice*. Admittedly, he enjoyed driving now that he knew what he was doing. West had promised to teach him to operate the larger machines and allow him to help with the farm work once he became confident behind the wheel.

"Pull over here," said Maggie, pointing to a spot beside the field.

Luke obeyed her instructions. He shifted the lever into park and turned the keys as Maggie hopped out. He followed suit, and she took his hand and pulled him into the field. Together, they entered into the strands of grain, still green and only reaching to their knees. They walked for several minutes before coming to a stop, and she turned to face him. She said a word, but her gaze seemed to penetrate his soul as though she were looking for something.

"What are we doing out here?" he asked.

She shifted closer, and Luke's arms raised without prompting to encompass her. She rested her forehead against his chest. "I have always wanted a simple life, one not full of expectations or parties. I never cared about wealth or being a socialite. But you were born into that life, too. I just...I don't want you to be unhappy, Luke. Life on a farm will be far different than the one you're used to. Are you sure—"

Taking her face between his hands, he cut her off with a kiss and used the next several minutes to reassure her of how certain he was about the situation.

"Maggie, I may not be accustomed to this sort of living, but I shan't miss the life I left behind. A quiet existence with my confidant sounds perfect in every way."

"As much as I like the sound of that, I can't promise *quiet*. My mom wants us to come to LA for Christmas, and trust me, that city is anything but quiet."

"I cannot deny my curiosity. Visiting Los Angeles will be different from visiting London, will it not?"

She grimaced. "Very different from *your* London. This trip will definitely be an adventure."

Luke nudged her chin with his knuckle, bringing her warm gaze to his. "Be they in the past or future, adventures with you, my dear, are all I have ever wanted."

THE END

So, what does Luke think of peanut butter fudge? Find out in the FREE Extended epilogue.

T he entire house smelled of spices and pine, the latter the result of the seven foot tree standing in the drawing room. Luke had already tucked a hundred questions away to ask Maggie over dinner later that night, most of them revolving around the strange traditions surrounding Christmastide. He could not quite make sense of most of them despite Weston's attempts to educate him, but perhaps he would gain a firm understanding over the next three weeks.

Presents were to be left under the tree, supposedly by a rather round elf named Santa Claus who possessed a long white beard and rosy cheeks. Weston had shown him several miniature representations of the jolly man, and Luke had wondered how such a figure came to be associated with the season. In addition to the tree, stockings large enough to hold a small feline had been hung over the fireplace—one who's flames erupted at the turn of a dial. He had spent the better part of an hour playing with the fireplace last week, watching the flames burst from seemingly nowhere until Weston tugged him away from it and scolded him for making the room smell of gas.

Continue here:
https://dl.bookfunnel.com/84epd1iw6j

Thank you for joining Luke and Maggie on their adventure. If you enjoyed this story, please consider leaving a review on your preferred retailer's website. Reviews help authors develop their craft and gain promotional marketing, and we love hearing from you!

MY BOOKS

Historical Romance:

THE TIME PEARLS
In Time With The Duke
The Future With The Marquess
Courting A Modern Lady

Fantasy Romance:

CHRONICLES OF VIRGÁM
The Matchmaker Prince
The Prisoner of Magic
The Witch of Selvenor
The Warlock of Dunivear
Origins of Virgám
The Seer of Verascene
Shadows of Aknar
Path to Irrilám
The Sorcerer of Kantinar

CHILDREN OF MAGIC
Blood & Magic
Love & Magic
Revenge & Magic
War & Magic

AUTHOR NOTES

Writing a historical novel comes with a very unique set of challenges. I strived to paint an accurate picture of life during the early nineteenth century as often as the story would allow. While not everything presented in this novel is perfect for the period, I hope it provided a realistic enough setting to transport you through time.

I can't begin to describe how much I learned while writing this book. As my first historical, there was much knowledge to acquire for accuracy, which included studying titles and address of the English peerage, societal rules, and a TON of word etymology. As Maggie stated, we take so many words for granted, and learning the origins of phrases was really fun.

One of my favorites, of course, was the word *fudge*. Before I even introduced Luke, I'd made it one of Maggie's favorites (likely because I, myself, say it often), and it wasn't until I looked up the origin that I discovered it had once meant a lie or exaggeration. Naturally this provided a fun moment for Maggie and Luke that I had to take advantage of.

I look forward to learning more as I continue this series, and if you found yourself enjoying Luke's and Maggie's journey, I hope you'll join me as Katherine and Nicholas take their own trip through time in *The Future with the Marquess.*

ACKNOWLEDGEMENTS

This book has been one of the most difficult and gratifying novels I've completed. It has taken the help of so many to get it right (or close to right!), and I appreciate all those who have supported me the entire way.

To my husband who is the best muse for a romance novel and always pushes me to keep going. To my critique partner and dear friend, Justena White, who has gotten me through more episodes of imposter syndrome than I can count.

To my writing group pals, Christina Allen and Alexis Hanson, for helping with the first chapter and blurb and just overall writing craft. I continue to get better because of you.

To my alpha and beta readers (don't hold your breath; there are many!) who helped shape this book in so many ways: Mindy Porter, Kaybree Cowley, Melissa Bolton, Rosie Wylor-Owen, Beba Andric, Leigh Walker, Brittany Reeves, Whitney Hurst, Bev Kunz, Mariah Martinez, Melanie Mason, Kerri Jensen, Terry Deighton, Melanie Atkinson, Susan Allred, Mitzy Roberts, and Kasey Stockton.

To Jacque Stevens who helped me nail down the themes and sort out so many issues. I will be forever grateful for your guidance.

To my readers who continue to follow and support me on the author journey, I thank you from the bottom of my heart.

ABOUT THE AUTHOR

Brooke Losee lives with her husband and three children in central Utah where she enjoys fishing, exploring, and gathering as many rocks as her pockets can hold. Brooke obtained a BS in Geology at Southern Utah University but has always had a passion for all things books.

Brooke began her journey to authorhood in 2020 with the notion of publishing one novel. That book turned into a series of seven, and the Pandora's box of ideas was unleashed. Her works range from fantasy to historical, all featuring a sweet and clean romance.

To follow her writing journey and keep informed about upcoming stories visit http://www.brookejlosee.com.

Made in United States
North Haven, CT
18 September 2023

41680905R00224